# A TRAITOR TO MEMORY

One fateful night at Wigmore Hall, twenty-eight year old virtuoso violinist Gideon Davies lifted his violin to play in a Beethoven trio . . . and everything in his mind related to music was gone. Gideon suffers from a form of amnesia, the cure for which is an examination of what he can remember. And what he can remember is little enough until his mind is triggered by the weeping of a woman and a single name: Sonia. One rainy evening, a woman called Eugenie travels to London for a mysterious appointment. But before she is able to reach her destination, a car swoops out of nowhere and kills her in the street. In pursuing the killer of Eugenie, Thomas Lynley, Barbara Havers and Winston Nkata come to know a group of people whose lives are inextricably connected by a long-ago death, a trial, and a prison sentence handed down as retribution for a crime no one has spoken of for twenty years.

# A TRAITOR
# TO MEMORY
## VOL 2

## Elizabeth George

## CHIVERS PRESS
### BATH

First published 2001
by
Hodder and Stoughton
This Large Print edition published by
Chivers Press
by arrangement with
Hodder & Stoughton
2002

ISBN 0 7540 1794 X

British Library Cataloguing in Publication Data available

Printed and bound in Great Britain by
BOOKCRAFT, Midsomer Norton, Somerset

For the other Jones girl,
wherever she might be

'O my son Absalom,
My son, my son, Absalom!
Would God I had died for thee.'

Samuel II, *XIX*, 4

# CHAPTER FOURTEEN

Jill Foster could see that Richard wasn't pleased at having to entertain another visit from the police. He was even less pleased to learn that the detective had just come from seeing Gideon. He took in this information politely enough as he motioned DI Lynley to a chair, but the manner in which his mouth tightened as the detective imparted his facts told Jill that he wasn't happy.

DI Lynley was watching Richard closely as if gauging his most minute reaction. This gave Jill a sense of disquiet. She knew about the police from years of having read newspaper accounts of famously botched cases and even more famous miscarriages of justice, so she was fairly well versed in the extremes they would go to in order to pin a crime on a suspect. When it came to murder, the police were more interested in building a strong case against someone—against *anyone*—than they were in getting to the bottom of what happened because building a case against someone meant putting an investigation to rest, which meant getting home to their wives and their families at a reasonable hour for once. That desire underlay every move they made in a murder inquiry, and anyone being questioned by them would do well to be wise to that fact.

The police are not our friends, Richard, she told her fiancé silently. Don't say a word that they can twist round and use against you later.

And surely that's what the detective was doing. He fastened his dark eyes—brown they were, not blue as one would have expected in a blond—on Richard and waited patiently for a reply to his statement, a neat notebook open in his large, handsome hand. 'When we met yesterday, you didn't mention you'd been advocating a meeting between Gideon and his mother, Mr Davies. I'm wondering why.'

Richard sat on a straight-backed chair that he'd swung round from the table on which he and Jill took their meals. He'd made no offer of tea this time. That suggested welcome, which the detective definitely was not. Richard had said upon his arrival and prior to DI Lynley's mentioning the call he'd made on Gideon, 'I do want to be helpful, Inspector, but I must ask you to be reasonable with your visits. Jill needs her rest and if we can reserve our interactions for daylight hours, I'd be very grateful.'

The detective's lips had moved in what the naïve might have concluded was a smile. But his gaze took in Richard in such a way as to suggest he wasn't the sort of man used to being told what was expected of him, and he didn't apologise for his appearance in South Kensington or make routine noises about not taking up too much of their time.

'Mr Davies?' Lynley repeated.

'I didn't mention that I was attempting to arrange a meeting between Gideon and his mother because you didn't ask me,' Richard said. He looked to where Jill was sitting at one end of the table, her laptop open and her fifth attempt at Act III, Scene I of her television adaptation of *The Beautiful and Damned* taking up space on her screen. He said, 'You'll probably want to continue working, Jill. There's the desk in the study . . . ?'

Jill wasn't about to be condemned to a sentence in that mausoleum-cum-memorial to his father that posed as Richard's study. She said, 'I've gone about as far as I can with this just now,' and she went through the exercise of saving and then backing up what she'd written. If Eugenie was going to be discussed, she intended to be present.

'Had she asked to see Gideon?' the detective asked Richard.

'No, she hadn't.'

'Are you sure?'

'Of course I'm sure. She didn't want to see either of us. That's the choice she made years ago when she left without bothering to mention where she was going.'

'What about why?' DI Lynley asked.

'Why what?'

'Why she was going, Mr Davies. Did your wife mention that?'

Richard bristled. Jill held her breath, trying to ignore the stab she felt in her breast at those words: *your wife*. How she felt about hearing anyone other than herself referred to with that term could not be allowed to matter at the moment because the detective's question got right to the crux of the topic that was of interest to her. She longed to know not only why Richard's wife had left him but also how he'd felt about her leaving him, how he'd felt then and, much more importantly, how he felt now.

'Inspector,' Richard said evenly, 'have you ever lost a child? Lost a child to violence? Lost a child at the hands of someone who's living right inside your own home? No? You haven't? Well, then, I suggest you think about what a loss like that can do to a marriage. I didn't need Eugenie to give me chapter and verse on why she was leaving. Some marriages survive a trauma. Others do not.'

'You didn't try to find her once she was gone?'

'I didn't see the point. I didn't want to keep Eugenie where she didn't want to be. There was Gideon to consider, and I'm not of the school who believe that two parents for a child are better than one no matter the condition of their marriage. If the marriage goes bad, it has to end. Children survive that better than living in a house that's little more than an armed encampment.'

'Your break-up was hostile?'

'You're inferring.'

'It's part of the job.'

'It's taking you in the wrong direction. I'm sorry to disappoint you, but there was no bad blood between Eugenie and me.'

Richard was irritated. Jill could hear it in his tone, and she was fairly sure that the detective could hear it also. This worried her, and she stirred on her seat and tried to get her lover's attention, to throw him a warning look that he would interpret and act upon, altering if not the substance of his replies then at least their timbre. She well understood the source of his irritation: Gideon, Gideon, always Gideon, what Gideon did and did not do, what Gideon said and did not say. Richard was upset because Gideon hadn't phoned and reported the detective's visit. But the detective wouldn't see it that way. He'd be far more likely to note it as Richard's reaction to being questioned too closely about Eugenie.

She said, 'Richard, I'm sorry. If you could help me for a moment . . .?' And to the detective, with

4

an exasperated smile, 'I'm running to the loo every fifteen minutes these days. Oh, thank you, darling. Heavens, I'm not quite right on my feet.' She held on to Richard's arm, acting the part of a woman lightheaded, waiting for Richard to say that he'd help her along to the loo, which would thus buy him some time to regroup. But to her frustration, he just fastened his arm round her waist for a moment to steady her and said, 'Do take care,' but made no move to assist her from the room.

She tried to telegraph her intentions to him. *Come with me.* But he either ignored or didn't get the message because once she was apparently solid in her stance, he let go of her and gave his attention back to the detective.

There was nothing for it but to go to the loo, which Jill did with as much dispatch as she could muster, considering her size. She needed to pee anyway—she always needed to pee now—and she squatted over the toilet while trying to hear what was going on in the room she'd just left.

Richard was speaking when she returned. Jill was gratified to see that he'd managed to wrest his quick temper under control. He was saying calmly, 'My son is suffering from stage fright, Inspector, as I've already told you. He's completely lost his nerve. If you've seen him, you've no doubt also seen that something's badly wrong with the boy. Now, if Eugenie could have helped with that problem in any way, I was willing to try it. I was willing to try anything. I love my son. The last thing I want to see is his life's destruction brought about by an irrational fear.'

'So you asked her to meet him?'

'Yes.'

'Why so long after the event?'

'The event?'

'The concert at Wigmore Hall.'

Richard flushed. He hated, Jill knew, any mention of the venue. She had little doubt that, should Gideon ever regain his music, his father would never again allow him so much as to pass over its threshold. It was the scene of his public humiliation, after all. Better to burn it to the ground.

Richard said, 'We'd tried everything else, Inspector. Aromatherapy, anti-anxiety treatments, pep talks, psychiatry, everything under the sun save having an astrologer do a reading of the stars. We'd been going those routes for several months, and Eugenie was simply the last resort.' He watched Lynley writing in his notebook and he added, 'I'd very much appreciate it if this information is kept confidential, by the way.'

Lynley looked up. 'What?'

Richard said, 'I'm no fool, Inspector. I know how you lot work. The pay's not good so you supplement it by passing along what you can without crossing the line. Fine. I understand. You've got mouths to feed. But the last thing Gideon needs right now is to see his problem splashed all over the tabloids.'

'I don't generally work with the newspapers,' Lynley replied. And after a pause during which he made a note in his book, 'Unless I'm forced to, of course, Mr Davies.'

Richard heard the implied threat because he said hotly, 'You listen here. I'm cooperating with you and you can damn well—'

'Richard.' Jill couldn't stop herself. There was

6

too much at risk to let him continue when continuing only promised to alienate the detective in ways that were unproductive.

Richard clamped his jaws shut and cast a look at her. With her eyes, she appealed to his better judgement. *Tell him what he needs to know and he'll leave us.* This time, it seemed, he got the message.

He said, 'All right.' And then, 'Sorry,' to the detective. 'This has put me on edge. First Gideon, then Eugenie. After all these years and when we needed her most . . . I tend to fly off the handle.'

Lynley said, 'Had you arranged a meeting between them?'

'No. I'd phoned and left a message on her machine. She'd not got back to me.'

'When had you phoned?'

'Earlier in the week. I don't remember which day. Tuesday, perhaps.'

'Was it like her not to return your call?'

'I didn't think anything of it. The message I left didn't say I was phoning her because of Gideon. I just asked her to ring me when she had the chance.'

'And she never asked you to arrange a meeting with Gideon for reasons of her own?'

'No. Why would she? She phoned me when Gideon had his . . . that difficulty he had at the performance. In July. But I believe I told you that yesterday.'

'And when she phoned you, it was only about your son's condition?'

'It isn't a condition,' Richard said. 'It's stage fright, Inspector. Nerves. It happens. Like writer's block. Like a sculptor making a mess of a few lumps of clay. Like a painter losing his vision for a week.'

7

He sounded, Jill thought, very much like a man who was desperately attempting to convince himself, and she knew that the inspector had to hear this as well. She said to Lynley, attempting to sound unlike a woman making excuses for the man she loved, 'Richard's given his life to Gideon's music. He's done it the way any parent of a prodigy must do it: with no thought of himself. And when one gives one's life to something, it's painful watching the project fall to pieces.'

'If a person is a project,' DI Lynley said.

She flushed and bit back a retort. All right, she thought. Let him have his moment. She wouldn't allow it to vex her.

Lynley said to Richard, 'Did your ex-wife ever mention her brother to you in all these phone calls?'

'Who? Doug?'

'The other brother. Ian Staines.'

'Ian?' Richard shook his head. 'Never. As far as I know, Eugenie hadn't seen him in years.'

'He tells me she was going to speak to Gideon about borrowing money. He's in a bad way—'

'When the hell is Ian not in a bad way?' Richard interrupted. 'Obviously, Doug's dried up as a source of funds if Ian turned to Eugenie. But she wouldn't help him in the past—this was when we were married and Doug was short of money—so I've little doubt she would have refused him now.' He knotted his eyebrows as he realised where the detective was heading. He said, 'Why're you asking about Ian?'

'He was seen with her the night she was killed.'

'How awful,' Jill murmured.

'He has a temper,' Richard said. 'He came by it

8

honestly. Their dad was a rager. No one was safe from his temper. He excused it by saying he never lifted a hand against any of them, but his was a special form of torture. And the bastard was a *priest*, if you can credit that.'

'What happened to their father?' Lynley asked.

'What're you getting at?'

'Whatever it was that Eugenie wished to confess to Major Wiley.'

Richard said nothing. Jill saw the pulse beat a rapid tattoo in the vein on his temple. He said, 'I hadn't seen my wife in nearly twenty years, Inspector. She might have wanted to tell her lover anything.'

*My wife.* Jill heard the words like a slim lance piercing her just beneath her heart. She reached blindly for the lid of her laptop. She lowered it and fastened it with more precision than was required.

The inspector was saying, 'Did she mention this man—ex-Army, Major Wiley—in any of your conversations, Mr Davies?'

'We spoke only of Gideon.'

'So you know nothing that might have been on her mind?' the detective pressed on.

'For God's sake, I didn't even know she *had* a man in Henley, Inspector,' Richard said testily. 'So how the hell could I possibly have known what she intended to speak to him about?'

Jill tried to locate the feelings beneath his words. She laid his reaction—and whatever emotion underscored it—next to his earlier reference to Eugenie as his wife, and she excavated in the dust round both to see what fossilised emotions might remain there. She'd managed to put her hands on the *Daily Mail* that morning, and she'd flipped

9

through it hungrily to find a picture of Eugenie. So she now knew that her rival had been attractive as Jill herself could never be attractive. And she wanted to ask the man she loved if that loveliness haunted him and, if so, what that haunting meant. She wouldn't share Richard with a ghost. Their marriage was going to be all or nothing and if it was meant to be nothing, then she wanted to know that so at least she could adjust her plans accordingly.

But how to ask? How to bring the subject up?

DI Lynley said, 'She may not have identified it directly as something she wished to talk to Major Wiley about.'

'Then I wouldn't have known what it was, Inspector. I'm not a mind read—' Richard stopped abruptly. He stood and for a moment Jill thought that, pushed to the extreme in having to talk about his former wife—*my wife*, he'd called her—he intended to ask the policeman to leave. But instead, he said, 'What about the Wolff woman? Eugenie might have been worried about her. She must have got that letter telling her about the release. She might have been frightened. Eugenie gave evidence against her at the trial, and she might have fancied that she—Wolff—would come looking for her. D'you think that's possible?'

'She never told you that, though?'

'No. But him. This Wiley. He was there in Henley. If Eugenie wanted protection—or just a sense of security, of someone looking after her— he'd have been the one to give it to her. I wouldn't. And if that's what she wanted, she'd've had to explain why she wanted it in the first place.'

Lynley nodded and looked thoughtful, saying, 'That's possible. Major Wiley wasn't in England

10

when your daughter was murdered. He did tell us that.'

'So do you know where she is?' Richard asked. 'Wolff?'

'Yes. We've tracked her down.' Lynley flipped his notebook closed and stood. He thanked them for their time.

Richard said quickly as if he suddenly didn't want the detective to leave them alone with what *alone* implied, 'She might've been intent on settling the score, Inspector.'

Lynley stowed his notebook in his pocket. He said, 'Did you give evidence against her as well, Mr Davies?'

'Yes. Most of us did.'

'Then watch yourself till we get this cleared up.'

Jill saw Richard swallow. He said, 'Of course. I will.'

With a nod to both of them, Lynley left.

Jill was suddenly frightened. She said, 'Richard! You don't think . . . What if that woman killed her? If she tracked down Eugenie, there's every chance that she . . . You could be in danger as well.'

'Jill. It's all right.'

'How can you *say* that with Eugenie dead?'

Richard came to her. He said, 'Please don't worry. It'll be all right. I'll be all right.'

'But you've got to be careful. You must watch . . . Promise me.'

'Yes. All right. I do promise that.' He touched her cheek. 'Good God. You've gone white as a ghost. You're not worried, are you?'

'Of course I'm worried. He as good as said—'

'Don't. We've had enough of this. I'm taking you home. No arguments, all right?' He helped her to

11

her feet saying, 'You told him an untruth, Jill. At least a partial untruth. I let it go when you said it, but I'd like to correct it now.'

Jill slid her laptop into its carrying case and looked up as she closed its zip. She said, 'Correct what?'

'What you said: that I've given my life to Gideon.'

'Oh. That.'

'Yes, that. It was true enough once; a year ago even, it was true. But not now. Oh, he'll always be important to me. How can he be otherwise? He's my son. But while he was the centre of my world for more than two decades, there's more to my life now, because of you.'

He held out her coat. She slid her arms into it and turned to him. She said, 'You are happy, aren't you? About us, the baby?'

'Happy?' He placed one hand on the mountain of her stomach. 'If I could climb inside you and reside with our little Cara, I would. That's the only way that the three of us could be any closer than we already are.'

'Thank you,' Jill said, and she kissed him, raising her mouth for the familiar joining to his, parting her lips, feeling his tongue, and experiencing the answering heat of desire.

Catherine, she thought. Her name is Catherine. But she kissed him with both longing and hunger, and she felt embarrassed: to be so hugely pregnant and still to want him sexually. But she suddenly possessed such a longing for him that the heat within her turned into an ache.

'Make love to me,' she said against his mouth.

'Here?' he murmured. 'In my lumpy bed?'

12

'No. At home. In Shepherd's Bush. Let's go. Make love to me, darling.'

'Hmm.' His fingers found her nipples. He squeezed them gently. She sighed. He squeezed harder, and she felt her body shoot fire to her genitals in reply.

'Please,' she murmured. 'Richard. God.'

He chuckled. 'Are you certain that's what you want?'

'I'm dying for you.'

'Well, we can't have that.' He released her, held his hands on her shoulders, and examined her face. 'But you do look completely done in.'

Jill felt her spirits plummet. 'Richard—'

He cut in. 'So you must swear to me that you'll go to sleep and not open an eye for at least ten hours afterwards. Is that a deal?'

Love—or something she took for love—flooded her. She smiled. 'Then take me home this instant, and have your way with me. If you don't do both, I won't answer for the consequences to your lumpy bed.'

*    *    *

There were times when you had to operate on instinct. DC Winston Nkata had seen that often enough while working an investigation in the company of one DI or another, and he recognised that inclination in himself.

He'd had that uneasy feeling for the entire afternoon once he'd visited Yasmin Edwards in her shop. It informed him that she wasn't telling him everything. So he stationed himself on Kennington Park Road and settled back with a lamb samosa in one hand and a carton of takeaway dal as a dipping sauce in the other. His mum would keep his dinner warm, but it might be hours before he could put his lips round the jerk chicken she'd promised him for that night's meal. In the meantime he needed something to settle the growling in his stomach.

He munched and kept his attention on the steamed-up windows of Crushley's Laundry just across the street and down three doors from where he'd parked. He'd sauntered by and taken a glimpse inside when the door swung open, and he'd seen her big as life in the back, labouring over an ironing board with steam rising round her like a sauna.

'She in today?' he'd asked her employer earlier over the phone not long after leaving Yasmin's shop. 'Just a routine check, this is. No need to tell her I'm on the blower.'

'Yeah,' Betty Crushley had said, sounding like a woman talking round a cigar. 'Got her mug where it ought to be for once.'

'Good to hear that.'

'If good's enough.'

So he was waiting for Katja Wolff to leave her place of employment for the evening. If she walked the short distance to Doddington Grove Estate, his instinct would require adjustment. If she went somewhere else, he'd know his feeling about her was right.

Nkata was dipping the last bite of his samosa into the dal when the German woman finally came out of the laundry, carrying a jacket over her arm. He crammed the pastry into his mouth, ready for action, but Katja Wolff merely stood on the pavement for a minute, just outside the laundry's front door. It was cold, with a sharp wind blowing the smells of diesel fuel against the pedestrians' cheeks, but the temperature didn't appear to bother her.

She took a moment to don her jacket and pulled from its pocket a blue beret into which she tucked her short blonde hair. Then she turned up the collar of her coat and set off along Kennington Park Road in the direction of home.

Nkata was about to curse his instincts for wasting his time when Katja did the unexpected. Instead of turning into Braganza Street, which led to the Doddington Grove Estate, she crossed and continued down Kennington Park Road without so much as a regretful glance in the direction in which she should have been heading. She passed a pub, the takeaway where he'd bought his snack, a hairdresser, and a stationery shop, coming to rest at a bus stop where she lit a cigarette and waited among a small crowd of other potential passengers. She rejected the first two buses that stopped, finally climbing onto the third one after she tossed her cigarette into the street. As the bus lumbered into the traffic, Nkata set off after it, glad that he wasn't in a panda car and grateful for the dusk.

He didn't make himself popular with his fellow drivers as he tailed the bus, pulling to the kerb when it did, keeping an eye peeled at its every stop to make sure he didn't lose Katja Wolff in the growing gloom. More than one driver gave him two fingers as he wove in and out of the traffic, and he nearly hit a cyclist in a gas mask when a request stop loomed up faster than he was prepared for it.

In this fashion, he lurched across South London. Katja Wolff had taken a window seat on the street side of the bus, so Nkata could get a glimpse of her blue beret when the street curved ahead of him. He was fairly confident that he'd be able to pick her out when she disembarked, and that proved to be the case when, after suffering through the worst of the rush hour traffic, the bus pulled up at Clapham Common.

He thought she meant to get a train there, and he wondered how conspicuous he'd be if he had to get on the same carriage as she. Very, he decided. But there was no help for it and no time to consider any other option. He looked desperately for a place to park.

He kept one eye on her as she worked her way through the crowd outside the station. Instead of moving inside as he'd expected her to do, however, she went to a second bus stop where, after a five minute wait, she embarked on another ride through South London.

She had no window seat this time, so Nkata was forced to keep an eye peeled each time passengers disembarked. It was anxiety producing—not to mention maddening to other drivers—but he ignored the rest of the traffic and kept his attention where it belonged.

At Putney station, he was rewarded. Katja Wolff hopped off and, without a glance right or left, she set off along the Upper Richmond Road.

There was no way Nkata could tail her in a car and not stick out like an ostrich in Alaska or become the victim of a commuter's road rage, so he drove past her and, some fifty yards farther along, he found a section of double yellow lines just beyond a bus stop across the street. He veered over and parked there. Then he waited, his eyes on the rear view mirror, adjusting it to take in the pavement opposite.

In due course, Katja Wolff came into view. She had her head down and her collar up against the wind, so she didn't notice him. An illegally parked car in London was no anomaly. Even if she glimpsed him, in the fading light he would be just a bloke waiting to fetch someone from the bus stop.

When she'd gained some twenty yards past him, Nkata eased his car door open and took up after her. He shrugged his large frame into his overcoat as he trailed her, tucking a scarf round his neck and thanking his stars that his mum had insisted upon his wearing it that morning. He faded into the shadows created by the trunk of an aged sycamore as up ahead of him Katja Wolff paused, turned her back to the wind, and lit a cigarette. Then she strode to the kerb, waited for a break in the traffic, and dashed across to the opposite side.

At this point, the road opened into a commercial area comprising an assortment of businesses that were fashioned with residences off-set above them. Here were the sort of enterprises local residents would patronise: video shops, newsagents, restaurants, florists, and the like.

Katja Wolff chose to take her custom to Frère Jacques Bar and Brasserie, where both the Union Jack and the French national flag snapped in the wind. It was a cheerful yellow building fronted by multi-paned transom windows, brightly lit from the interior. As she ducked inside, Nkata waited for a chance to cross over. By the time he got there, she'd removed her coat and handed it over to a waiter who was gesturing her beyond the rows of small tables to a bar that ran along one wall. There

17

were as yet no other patrons in the brasserie, apart from a well-dressed woman in a tailored black suit who sat on a bar stool nursing a drink.

She looked like money, Nkata thought. It spoke from her haircut, which was fashioned so that her short hair fell round her face like a polished helmet; it spoke from her attire, which was tasteful and timeless as only significant money can buy. Nkata had spent enough time leafing through *GQ* in the years in which he'd reinvented himself to know how people looked when they did most of their clothes buying in places like Knightsbridge, where twenty quid might get you a handkerchief but nothing else.

Katja Wolff approached this woman, who slid off her bar stool with a smile and came to greet her. They reached for each other's hands and pressed their cheeks together, air kissing in the batty way Europeans had of greeting each other. The woman gestured Katja Wolff to join her.

For his part, Nkata hunkered down into his overcoat and watched them from a place he made for himself in the shadows just beyond the bank of the brasserie windows and at the side of an Oddbins. Should they turn his way, he could give his attention to the sale announcements painted in front of him on the window—Spanish wine was going for a real treat, he noted. And in the meantime he could watch them and attempt to suss out what they were to each other, although he already had developed a fair set of suspicions in that direction. He'd seen the familiarity in their greeting, after all. And the woman in black had money, which Katja Wolff would probably like just fine. So the pieces were starting to fall into place,

18

aligning themselves with the German's lie about where she'd been on the night that Eugenie Davies had died.

Nkata wished there was a way he could have overheard their conversation, however. The manner in which they hovered over their drinks shoulder to shoulder suggested a confidential chat that he would have given much to hear. And when Wolff raised a hand to her eyes and the other put her arm round her shoulders and said something into her ear, he even considered sauntering in and introducing himself, just to see how Katja Wolff reacted to being caught out.

Yes. There was something definitely going on here, he thought. This was probably what Yasmin Edwards knew but did not want to speak of. Because one could always tell when one's lover started stepping outside for more than a breath of air or a packet of fags in the evening. And the toughest bit about coping with that knowledge was coming to accept it in the first place. People walked miles to avoid having to look at, talk about, or actually confront something that might cause them pain. Short sighted as it was to wear blinkers in relationships, it was still amazing to see how many people did exactly that.

Nkata stamped his feet in the cold and buried his hands in his coat pockets. He watched for another quarter of an hour and was considering his options when the two women began to gather up their belongings.

He ducked into Oddbins as they came out of the brasserie door. Half-hidden behind a display of Chianti Classico, he picked up a bottle as if to study its label while the shop assistant eyed him the way all shop assistants eyed a black man who wasn't quick enough to buy what he was touching. Nkata ignored him, his head bent but his gaze fastened on the shop's front windows. When he saw Wolff and her companion pass by, he set the bottle back onto the display, stifled what he wanted to say to the young man behind the till—when would he outgrow the need to shout 'I'm a copper, all right?' as he grabbed them by the necks of their shirts?— and slipped out of Oddbins in the women's wake.

Katja's companion had her by the arm, and she was continuing to talk to her as they strolled along. Over her right shoulder dangled a leather bag the size of a briefcase, and she held this firmly tucked under her arm like a woman who was wisely wary to what life on the streets could offer the unaware. In this fashion, the two of them walked not to the station but along the Upper Richmond Road in the direction of Wandsworth.

Perhaps a quarter of a mile along, they turned left. This would take them into a heavily populated neighbourhood of terraced and semi-detached houses. If they went into a residence there, Nkata knew he would need more than luck to find them. He increased his pace and broke into a jog.

He was still in luck, he saw, as he turned the corner. Although several streets turned off this road and bored into the crowded neighbourhood, the two women hadn't taken any of them yet. Rather they were continuing ahead of him, still in conversation but with the German woman talking this time, gesturing with her hands while the other listened.

They chose Galveston Road to turn into, a short thoroughfare of terraced houses, some converted into flats and some still standing as single homes. It was a middle class neighbourhood of lace curtains, fresh paint, tended gardens, and window boxes where pansies were planted in anticipation of the coming winter. Wolff and her companion walked along to the midway point, where they turned in through a wrought iron gate and approached a red door. The brass number fifty-five was posted on it, between two narrow translucent windows.

The garden here was overgrown, unlike the other small gardens in the street. On either side of the front door, shrubbery had been allowed to flourish, and tentacles from a star jasmine bush at one side and a Spanish broom on the other hungered outward towards the front door as if for an anchoring spot. From across the street, Nkata watched as Katja sidled through the shrubbery and mounted the two steps onto the front porch. She didn't ring the bell. Rather, she opened the door and let herself in. Her companion followed.

The door shut behind them and a light went on right inside the entrance. This was followed some five seconds later by a dimmer light, which began to glow behind the curtains at the front bay window. The curtains were such that only silhouettes were visible. But nothing more than silhouettes was necessary to understand what was going on when the two women melded into one figure and into each other's arms.

'Right,' Nkata breathed. So at last he saw what he had come to see: a concrete illustration of Katja Wolff's infidelity.

Laying this information in front of the unsuspecting Yasmin Edwards should suffice to get her to start telling what was what with regard to her

21

companion. And if he left this instant and jogged back to his car, he'd be able to make the drive to the Doddington Grove Estate far in advance of Katja herself, who thus wouldn't be able to prepare Yasmin to hear something which Katja could later label a lie.

But as the two figures in the Galveston Road sitting room moved apart to set about doing whatever it was that they intended to do for each other's pleasure, Nkata found himself hesitating. He found himself wondering how he could broach the subject of Katja's infidelity in such a way as to avoid making Yasmin Edwards want to kill the messenger instead of absorbing the message.

Then, he wondered why he was wondering that at all. The woman was a charlie. She was also a lag. She'd knifed her own husband and done five years and no doubt learned a few more tricks of the trade while she was inside. She was dangerous and he— Winston Nkata, who himself had escaped a life that could have sent him along a path similar to hers— would do well to remember that.

There was no need to rush over to the Doddington Grove Estate, he decided. From the looks of things here in Galveston Road, Katja Wolff wasn't going anywhere soon.

\*       \*       \*

Lynley was surprised to find his wife still at the St James house when he arrived. It was nearly time for dinner, long past the hour at which she usually departed. But when Joseph Cotter—St James's father-in-law and the man who had held the Cheyne Row household together for more than a

22

decade—admitted Lynley into the house, the first thing he said was, 'They're up in the lab, the whole flamin' lot of 'em. No surprise, that. His nibs's got them marching today. Deb's up there 's well, though I don't s'pose she's cooperating like Lady Helen's been doing. Even went without lunch. "Can't stop now," 'e said. "We're almost done."'

'Done with what?' Lynley asked, thanking Cotter when the other man set down a dinner plate he'd been carrying and took his coat.

'God knows. Drink? Cuppa? I made fresh scones—' this with a nod at the plate—' 'f you c'n be bothered to take 'em up with you. I did 'em for tea, but no one came down.'

'I'll investigate the situation.' Lynley took the tray from where Cotter had balanced it precariously on an umbrella stand. He said, 'Any message for them?'

Cotter said, 'Tell 'em dinner's at half eight. Beef in port wine sauce. New potatoes. Courgettes and carrots.'

'That should certainly tempt them.'

Cotter snorted. 'Should do, yes. But will do? Not likely. But mind you tell 'em there's no skipping this one 'f they want to keep me cooking. Peach is up there as well, by the way. Don't give her one of them scones, no matter what she does. She's on a diet.'

'Right.' Dutifully, Lynley mounted the stairs.

He found everyone where Cotter had promised they would be: Helen and Simon were poring over a set of graphs spread out on a worktable while Deborah was examining a string of negatives just inside her darkroom. Peach was snuffling round the floor. She was the first to spy Lynley, and the sight

23

of the plate he was carrying caused her to prance over to him happily, tail wagging and eyes alight.

'If I were naïve, I'd think you were welcoming me,' Lynley said to the animal. 'I've strict orders to refrain from feeding you, I'm afraid.'

At this, St James looked up and Helen said, 'Tommy!' and glanced at the window with a frown, adding, 'Good Lord. What time is it?'

'Our results aren't making sense,' St James said to Lynley without other explanation. 'A gram as the minimum fatal dose? I'll be laughed out of the hearing.'

'And when is the hearing?'

'Tomorrow.'

'It looks like a late night, then.'

'Or ritual suicide.'

Deborah came to join them, saying, 'Tommy, hello. What have you brought us?' Her face lit up. 'Ah. *Brilliant.* Scones.'

'Your father's sending a message about dinner.'

'Eat or die?'

'Something along those lines.' Lynley looked at his wife. 'I thought you'd be long gone by now.'

'No tea with the scones?' Deborah asked, relieving Lynley of the plate as Helen said, 'We seem to have lost track of time.'

'That's not like you,' Deborah said to Helen as she set the scones next to a large book that lay open at a grisly illustration of a man apparently dead of something that had caused a glaucous coloured vomit to discharge from his mouth and his nose. Either oblivious of this unappetising sight or completely used to it, Deborah scooped up a scone for herself. 'If we can't depend on you to remind us of mealtimes, Helen, what *can* we

24

depend upon?' She broke her scone in half and took a bite. She said, 'Lovely. I hadn't realised I was famished. I can't eat one of these without something to drink, though. I'm fetching the sherry. Anyone else?'

'That sounds good.' St James took up a scone himself as his wife left the lab and headed for the stairs. He called out, 'Glasses for all, my love.'

'Will do,' Deborah called back and added, 'Peach, come. Time for your dinner.' The dog obediently followed, her eyes glued to the scone in Deborah's hand.

Lynley said to Helen, 'Tired?' She had very little colour in her face.

'A bit,' she said, looping a lock of hair behind one ear. 'He's been rather a slave driver today.'

'When is he not?'

'I've a reputation for general beastliness to maintain,' St James said. 'But I'm a decent sort underneath the foul exterior. I'll prove it to you. Have a look at this, Tommy.'

He went to his computer table where Lynley saw that he'd set up the terminal that he and Havers had taken from Eugenie Davies' office. A laser printer stood next to it, and from its tray, St James took a sheaf of documents.

Lynley said, 'You've tracked her internet use? Well done, Simon. I'm impressed and grateful.'

'Save impressed. You could have done it yourself if you knew the first thing about technology.'

'Be gentle with him, Simon.' Helen smiled fondly at her husband. 'He's only recently been strong-armed into accepting e-mail into his life at work. Don't rush him too madly into the future.'

'It might result in whiplash,' Lynley agreed. He

pulled his spectacles from his jacket pocket. 'What've we got?'

'Her internet use first.' St James explained that Eugenie Davies' computer—not to mention computers in general—always kept a record of the sites that a user visited, and he handed over a list of what Lynley was pleased to see were recognisable even to him as web addresses. 'It's straightforward stuff,' St James told him. 'If you're looking for something untoward in what she was doing on the net, I don't think you're going to find it there.'

Lynley glanced through what St James identified as the URLs he'd picked up by examining Eugenie Davies' travel history: These were the addresses she would have typed into the location bar, he said, in order to access individual web sites. If one merely chose the dropdown arrow next to the location bar and left clicked on it, one had easy access to the trail an internet user left when he or she logged on. Vaguely listening to St James's explanation about the source of the information he'd handed over, Lynley made noises of comprehension and ran his gaze over Eugenie Davies' chosen sites. He saw that the other man had assessed the dead woman's usage of the internet with his usual accuracy. Every site—at least by name—appeared to relate to her job as director of the Sixty Plus Club: She'd accessed everything from a site dedicated to the NHS to a location for pensioners' coach trips round the UK. She appeared to have done some newspaper browsing as well, mostly in the *Daily Mail* and the *Independent*. And those sites she'd visited with regularity, particularly in the last four months. This was possible support for Richard Davies' contention that she'd been trying to assess Gideon's condition from the newspapers.

'Not much help here,' Lynley agreed.

'No. But there's some hope with this.' St James handed over the rest of the papers he'd been holding. 'Her e-mail.'

'How much of it?'

'That's the lot. From the day she started corresponding on line.'

'She'd saved it?'

'Not intentionally.'

'Meaning?'

'Meaning that people try to protect themselves on the net, but it doesn't always work. They choose passwords that turn out to be obvious to anyone who knows them—'

'As she did when she chose *Sonia*.'

'Yes. Exactly. That's their first mistake. Their second is failing to note whether their computer is set up to save all the e-mail that comes into it. They think they've got privacy, but the reality is that their world is an open book to anyone who knows which icons turn which pages. In Mrs Davies' case, her computer dumped all the messages it received into its Recycle Bin whenever she deleted them, but till she emptied the bin itself—which she appears not to have done, ever—the messages were just stored inside it. It happens all the time. People hit the delete button and assume they've got rid of something when all the computer has actually done is to move it to another location.'

'This is everything, then?' Lynley gestured with the stack of papers.

'Every message she received. Helen's to thank for printing them out. She's also gone through them and marked the ones that look like business messages to save you some time. The rest you'll want to have a more thorough look at.'

Lynley said, 'Thank you, darling,' to his wife, who had taken a scone from the tray and was nibbling its edges. He went through the stack of papers, setting aside the ones that Helen had marked as business correspondence. He read the rest of them in chronological order. He was looking for anything even moderately suspicious, something from someone with the potential to do Eugenie Davies harm. And although he admitted this only to himself, he was also looking for anything from Webberly, anything recent, anything embarrassing to the superintendent.

Although some of the senders used not their own names but rather monikers apparently related to their line of work or their special interests, Lynley was relieved to see that there were none among them that he could easily associate with his superior at New Scotland Yard. There was also no Scotland Yard address listed, which was even better.

Lynley breathed easier and kept on reading to find that there was also nothing among the messages from anyone identifying himself as TongueMan, Pitchley, or Pitchford. And upon a second examination of the first document St James had handed him, none of the URLs for the websites Eugenie Davies had visited looked as if they might be a clever cover for a chat room where sexual encounters were set up. Which might or might not, he concluded, move TongueMan-Pitchley-Pitchford off their list.

He went back to the stack of e-mail as St James

28

and Helen returned to their perusal of the graphs they'd been working with upon his arrival, Helen saying, 'The last e-mail she received was on the morning of the day she was killed, Tommy. It's at the bottom of the pile, but you might want to have a look at it now. It caught my eye.'

Lynley saw why when he pulled it out. The message comprised three sentences, and he felt a corresponding chill when he read them: *I must see you again, Eugenie. I'm begging. Don't ignore me after all this time.*

'Damn,' he whispered. *After all this time.*

'What do you think?' Helen asked although the tone of her voice indicated that she'd already reached her own conclusion in the matter.

'I don't know.' There was no closing to the message, and the sender was among the group who used a handle rather than a Christian name. *Jete* was the word that preceded the provider's identification. The provider itself was Claranet, with no business name associated with it.

This indicated that a home computer had probably been used to communicate with Eugenie Davies, which brought Lynley at least some measure of reassurance. Because as far as he knew, Webberly had no personal computer at his home.

He said, 'Simon, is there a way to trace the real name of an e-mail user if he's adopted a nickname?'

'Through the provider,' St James replied, 'although I expect you'd have to strong-arm them into giving it to you. They're not obliged to.'

'But in a murder investigation . . . ?' Helen said.

'That might be sufficient coercion,' St James admitted.

Deborah returned, carrying four glasses and a decanter. 'Here we are,' she announced. 'Scones and sherry.' She proceeded to pour.

Helen said quickly 'Nothing for me, Deborah. Thanks,' and helped herself to a dab of butter that she dotted on a scrap of the scone she'd taken.

'You've got to have something,' Deborah said. 'We've been working like slaves. We deserve a reward. Would you rather a gin and tonic, Helen?' She wrinkled her nose. 'What on earth am I thinking? Gin and tonic and scones? Now *that* sounds appetising.' She handed a glass to her husband and another to Lynley. 'This is quite a red-letter day. I don't think I've ever heard you turn down a sherry, Helen, especially after being run ragged by Simon. Are you all right?'

'I'm perfectly fine,' Helen said. And she glanced at Lynley.

Now was the moment, of course, Lynley thought. It was the perfect time for him to tell them. With the four of them congenially together in St James's lab, what was to stop him from saying off-handedly, 'We've an announcement, by the way, although you're probably moments away from guessing it. *Have* you guessed?' He could put his arm round Helen's shoulders as he spoke. He could carry on and kiss the side of her head. 'Parenthood looms,' he could saying jokingly. 'Goodbye to late nights and Sunday morning lie-ins. Hello to nappies and baby bottles.'

But he didn't say any of that. Instead, he held his glass up to St James and declared, 'Many thanks for the efforts with the computer, Simon. I'm in your debt once again,' and he threw back a mouthful of the sherry.

Deborah looked from Lynley to Helen curiously. For her part, Helen quietly gathered up the graphs as St James drank to Lynley's toast. A tight little silence fell among them, during which Peach scooted back up the stairs, her dinner behind her. She trotted into the lab expectantly, deposited herself beneath the worktable where the scones still sat, and gave one sharp bark as her plume of a tail dusted the floor.

'Yes. Well,' Deborah said. And then brightly as the dog barked again, 'No, Peach. You're not to have any scone. Simon, look at her. She's completely incorrigible.'

Focusing on the little dog got them through the moment, at the end of which Helen began gathering her belongings. She said to St James, 'Simon, dearest, while I'd love to stay and help you labour through the night on this problem . . .'

His reply was, 'You've been a brick to stay this long. I shall muddle onward heroically alone.'

'He's worse than the dog,' Deborah remarked. 'Shamelessly manipulative. You'd better be off before he traps you.'

Helen took the advice. Lynley followed her. St James and Deborah remained in the lab.

Lynley and his wife didn't speak until they were standing on the Cheyne Row pavement with the wind whipping up the street from the river. Then Helen said only, 'Well.' She spoke the word to herself, not to him. She looked a mixture of sad and tired. Lynley couldn't tell which was predominant, but he had a good idea.

Helen said, 'Did it happen too soon?'

He didn't pretend to misunderstand. 'No. *No.* Of course not.'

'Then what?'

He searched for an explanation he could give her, one that both of them could live with, which would not come back to haunt him sometime in the future. He said, 'I don't want to hurt them. I picture how they'll look, creating expressions of pleasure on their faces while inside they're screaming at the inequity of it all.'

'Life's filled with inequities. You of all people know that. You can't make the playing field level for everyone, just as you can't know the future. What's in store for them. What's in store for us.'

'I know that.'

'Then . . .'

'It's just not as simple as knowing, Helen. Knowing doesn't take their feelings into account.'

'What about my feelings?'

'They mean everything to me. You mean everything to me.' He reached for her and fastened the top button of her coat, adjusting the scarf round her neck. 'Let's get you out of the cold. Did you drive? Where's your car?'

'I want to talk about this. You've been acting as if . . .' She let her voice die. The only way to say it was to say it directly. No metaphor existed to describe what she feared, and he knew that.

He wanted to reassure her, but he couldn't. He'd expected joy, he'd expected excitement; he'd expected the bond of joint anticipation. What he hadn't expected was guilt and dread: the knowledge that he was obliged to bury his dead before he could wholeheartedly welcome his living.

He said, 'Let's go home. It's been a long day, and you need your rest.'

She said, 'More than rest, Tommy,' and she

turned from him.

He watched as she walked to the end of the street where, next to the King's Head and Eight Bells, she'd left her car.

\*    \*    \*

Malcolm Webberly replaced the telephone receiver in its cradle. Quarter to twelve and he shouldn't have rung them, but he couldn't stop himself. Even when his mind had said that it was late, that they would be asleep, that even if Tommy was still working at this hour, Helen would already be in bed and unlikely to be happy with a late night phone call, he hadn't listened. Because throughout the day, he'd waited for word and when it hadn't come, he'd realised that he wouldn't sleep that night until he spoke to Lynley.

He could have phoned Eric Leach. He could have asked for an update on the investigation, and Eric would have given him everything he had. But involving Eric would have brought everything back to Webberly with more piercing clarity than he could afford. For Eric had been too close to it all: there in the house in Kensington Square where it had all begun, there at nearly every interview he'd conducted, there to give evidence at the trial. He'd even been there—standing right beside Webberly—when they'd had their first look at the dead baby's body, an unmarried man then who had no idea what it was even to have to consider the loss of a child.

He'd not been able to stop himself thinking of his own Miranda when he'd seen the lifeless body of Sonia Davies lying on the postmortem table.

33

And as the first cut into her flesh was made, that telltale Y-incision that could never be disguised as anything other than the brutal but necessary mutilation it was, he'd flinched and held back a cry of protest that such a cruelty had to be practised where such a cruelty had gone before.

There was cruelty not only in the manner of Sonia Davies' death, though. There was cruelty in her life as well, even if it was only a natural cruelty, a minuscule blip on the genetic screen that had resulted in her condition.

He'd seen the doctors' reports. He'd marvelled at the succession of operations and illnesses that such a tiny child had managed to endure in her first two years of life. He'd blessed his own luck in having produced with his wife a miracle of health and vitality in his daughter Miranda, and he wondered how individuals actually coped when what they were given demanded of them more than they'd ever thought they'd be asked to produce.

Eric Leach had wondered the same himself, saying, 'Okay, I see why they had a nanny. It was too much to handle, with Granddad half a loon and the son another Mozart or whatever he is. But why'd they not get someone *qualified* to look after her? They needed a nurse, not a refugee.'

'It was a bad decision,' Webberly had agreed. 'And they're going to take a beating for it. But no beating they take in court or in the press will match the beating they'll be giving themselves.'

'Unless . . .' Leach hadn't completed his remark. He'd looked down at his feet and shuffled them, instead.

'Unless what, Sergeant?'

'Unless the choice was deliberate, sir. Unless

34

they didn't really want proper care for the baby. For reasons of their own.'

Webberly had allowed his face to reveal the disgust he felt. 'You don't know what you're talking about. Wait till you have a kid and then see how it feels. No. Don't wait. I'll tell you myself. It feels like killing anyone who'd even *look* at her sideways.'

And as more information came in over the next few weeks, that's how he'd felt—like killing—because he'd not been able to get away from seeing his own Miranda in the death of this child who was so unlike her. She was toddling round the house at that point, always with her tattered Eeyore clutched under her arm, and he started seeing danger to her everywhere. In every corner there was something that could claim her, ripping out his heart and gnawing at his entrails. So he'd begun to want to avenge the death of Sonia Davies as a way to insure his own child's safety. If I bring her killer to an unquestioned justice, he told himself, I will buy God's protection for Randie with the studied coin of my righteousness.

Of course, he hadn't known there was a killer at all, at first. Like everyone else, he'd thought a moment of negligence had resulted in a tragedy that would haunt the lives of everyone concerned. But when the post-mortem uncovered the old fractures on her skeleton and when a closer examination of the body revealed the contusions along her shoulders and her neck that spoke of her being held down and deliberately drowned, he'd felt the blossoming of vengeance within him. It was vengeance for the death of this child, imperfect though she had been born. But it was also

35

vengeance for the mother who had given birth to her.

There were no eye witnesses and little enough evidence, which troubled Leach but did not worry Webberly. For the crime scene told its own tale, and he knew that he could use that tale to support a theory that was quick in coming. There was the bath itself with its tray so placidly undisturbed, disavowing the claim that a terrified nursemaid had come upon her charge slipped under the water and frantically called for help as she pulled her out of the tub and attempted to save her. There were the medicines—a cabinet of them—and afterwards the extensive medical records and the story both told about the burden of caring for a child in Sonia's condition. There were the arguments between the nanny and the parents, sworn to by more than one member of the household. And there were the statements given by the parents, the elder child, the grandparents, the teacher, the friend who was supposed to have phoned the nanny on the night in question, and the lodger who was the only person who tried to avoid any discussion of the German girl at all. And then there was Katja Wolff herself, her preliminary statement, and after that her unbelievable and enduring silence.

Because she wouldn't speak, he had to rely on others who lived with her. *I didn't actually see anything that night, I'm afraid . . . Of course, there were moments of tension when she was dealing with the baby . . . She wasn't always as patient as she might have been but the circumstances were terribly difficult, weren't they . . . She seemed eager enough to please at first . . . It was an argument among the three of them because she'd overslept again . . . We'd*

*decided to sack her . . . She didn't think it was fair . . .*
*We weren't willing to give her a reference because we*
*didn't think she was suited to childcare.* From the
others if not from Katja Wolff herself, a pattern of
behaviour emerged. With the pattern had come the
story, a stitched-together fabric of what had been
seen, what had been heard, and what could be
concluded from both.

'It's still a weak case,' Leach had said
respectfully during a pause in the proceedings at
the magistrate's court.

'It's a case all the same,' Webberly had replied.
'As long as she keeps her lips locked up, she's doing
half our job for us and hanging herself for good
measure. I can't think her brief hasn't told her
that.'

'She's getting crucified in the press, sir. They're
reporting the hearing verbatim, and every time
you're talking about interviewing her when you say
"she refused to answer the question", it's making
her look—'

'Eric, what's your bloody point?' Webberly had
asked the other officer. 'I can't help what the press
are printing. That's not our problem. If she's
worried how silence might look to potential jurors,
then she might consider breaking it for us, mightn't
she?'

Their concern, he told Leach, and their job was
to bring justice into an ugly equation, to lay out
facts so the magistrate's court could decide to hold
her over for trial. And that's what he had done.
That was *all* he had done. He had made justice
possible for Sonia Davies' family. He could not
have brought them peace or an end to their
nightmares. But he could have brought—and did

37

bring—them that.

Now, in the kitchen of his home in Stamford Brook, Webberly sat at the table with a cup of Horlicks fast cooling in front of him, and he thought about what he'd learned in his late-night phone call to Tommy Lynley. Central to his thoughts was one item: that Eugenie Davies had found a man. He was glad of it. For the fact of Eugenie's finding a man might go some distance towards alleviating the remorse he'd never ceased to feel for the cowardly manner in which he'd ended the love between them.

He'd had the best of intentions towards her, right up until the day he knew their relationship could not continue. He'd begun as a dispassionate professional entering into her life to bring justice to her family, and when that rôle had begun to alter upon their chance encounter at Paddington Station, it had at first altered merely to the rôle of friend, and he'd convinced himself that he could maintain it, ignoring that part of him that soon wanted more. She's vulnerable, he'd told himself in a vain effort to hold his feelings in check. She's lost a child and she's lost a marriage, and you must never tread on ground that's so soft and insubstantial.

Had she not been the one to speak what should have remained unspoken, he wouldn't have ventured further. Or at least that was what he told himself during the long period of their affair. She wants this, he claimed, as much as I do, and there are instances when the shackles of social convention must be thrown off in order to embrace that which is obviously a higher good.

The only way for him to justify an affair such as

theirs had been to see it in spiritual terms. She completes me, he told himself. What I share with her happens on the level of the *soul*, not just on the level of the body. And how is a man to live a full life if he has no nurture on the level of the soul?

He didn't have that with his wife. Their relationship, he decided, was the stuff of the temporal, ordinary world. It was a social contract founded on the largely outdated idea of sharing property, having traceable bloodlines for potential offspring, and possessing a mutual interest in cohabitation. Under the agreements of the contract, a man and a woman were to live together, to reproduce if possible, and to provide each other with a lifestyle mutually satisfactory to them both. But nowhere was it written or implied that they were to give succour to each other's imprisoned and earthbound spirit, and that, he told himself, was the problem with marriage. It effected in its participants a sense of complacency. That complacency effected a form of oblivion in which the man and the woman so joined together lost sight of themselves and each other as sentient individuals.

So it had happened in his own marriage. So, he determined, it would *not* happen within the amorphously described marriage of spirits that he had with Eugenie Davies.

He went further down the path of self-delusion as time passed and he continued to see her. He told himself that his chosen career was tailor-made to support the infidelity that he began to label his God-given right. His job had always called for late and unstructured hours, for entire weekends given to cases under investigation, for sudden absences

39

resulting from phone calls in the night. Why had fate or God or coincidence brought him to such a line of work if he was not intended to use it to further his growth and development as a human being? Thus he persuaded himself to continue, acting the part of his own Mephistopheles, launching a thousand ships of faithlessness onto the sea of his life. The fact that he could maintain a virtual double existence by assigning responsibility for his absences to the Met began to convince him that such a double existence was his due.

But mankind's fatal failing was the desire for more of everything. And that desire had ultimately come to haunt what had begun as a celestial love, rendering it as temporal as everything else but simultaneously making it no less compelling. She'd ended her marriage, after all. He could end his. It would be a matter of a few uncomfortable conversations with his wife, and he would be free.

But he'd never managed to have those conversations with Frances. Her phobias had conversed with him instead, and he'd discovered that he, his love, and all the rightness he could muster to defend that love were no match for the affliction that possessed his wife and that ultimately came to possess them both.

He'd never told Eugenie. He'd written one final letter, asking her to wait, and he'd never written to her again. He'd never phoned her. He'd never seen her. Instead, he'd placed his life on hold, telling himself that he owed it to Frances to gauge each step of her recovery, anticipating the moment when she'd be well enough for him to tell her that he wanted to leave.

By the time he'd understood that his wife's

condition would not be something that was easily vanquished, too many months had passed and he could not bear the thought of seeing Eugenie again, only to have to tear himself from her permanently. Cowardice stilled the hand that might have held the pen or dialled the phone number. Better to tell himself that they'd really had nothing—just a few years of passionate interludes that wore the guise of loving unity—than to face her, to have to release her, and to recognise that the rest of his life would be without the meaning he longed to give it. So he just let things go, let them drift away, and he allowed her to think of him what she would.

She hadn't phoned him or sought him out, and he'd used those facts to assure himself that she'd not been as deeply affected as he by either the relationship itself or by the ending that had been thrust upon it. And having thus assured himself, he'd set about obliterating the image of her in his mind, as well as the memory of their afternoons, evenings, and nights together. In doing so, he'd been as unfaithful to her as he'd been to his wife. And he'd paid the price.

But she'd found a man, a widower, he'd learned, someone free to love her and to be to her all that she deserved. 'A chap called Wiley,' Lynley had said over the phone. 'He's told us she wanted to speak to him about something. Something, apparently, that had been keeping them from carrying on in a relationship together.'

'You think she might have been murdered to prevent her from speaking to Wiley?' Webberly asked.

'That's only one of half a dozen possibilities,'

Lynley had said.

He'd gone on to catalogue the rest of them, taking the care of the gentleman that he was—rather than employing the heartless determination of the investigator he should have been—not to mention whether he'd unearthed anything that pointed to Webberly's own ties to the murdered woman. Instead, he spoke at length of the brother, of Major Ted Wiley, of Gideon Davies, of J.W. Pitchley who was also James Pitchford, and of Eugenie's former husband.

'Wolff is out of prison,' Lynley said. 'She's been on parole for just twelve weeks. Davies hasn't seen her, but that's not to say she hasn't seen him. And Eugenie gave evidence against her at the trial.'

'As did nearly everyone else associated with that time. Eugenie's evidence was no more damning than anyone else's, Tommy.'

'Yes. Well. I think everyone connected with that case would be wise to take care till we've got things sorted out.'

'Are you considering this a stalking?'

'That can't be dismissed.'

'But you can't think Wolff's stalking everyone.'

'As I said, I'm thinking everyone should take a bit of care, sir. Winston phoned, by the way. He followed her earlier tonight to a house in Wandsworth. It looked like a rendezvous. She's more than she seems.'

Webberly had waited for Lynley to segue from Katja Wolff's rendezvous—from the message of infidelity it implied—to his own infidelity. But the connection wasn't made. Instead, the DI said, 'We're going through her e-mail and her internet usage as well. There's a message been left her—the morning of her death, and she read it because it was in the Recycle Bin—from someone called *Jete* asking to see her. Begging her, incidentally. After all this time. Those were the words.'

'On e-mail you say?'

'Yes.' Lynley paused on his end of the line before going on. 'Technology's fast outpacing my ability to understand it, sir. Simon did the delving into her computer. He's given us all her e-mail and all her internet usage as well.'

'Simon? What's her computer doing with St James? Bugger it, Tommy. You should have taken it straight—'

'Yes. Yes, I know. But I wanted to see . . .' He hesitated again, then finally took the plunge. 'There's no easy way to ask this, sir. Do you have a computer at home?'

'Randie's got a laptop.'

'Do you have access?'

'When it's here. But she keeps it in Cambridge. Why?'

'I think you probably know why.'

'You suspect that I'm *Jete*?'

'"After all this time." It's more a matter of crossing *Jete* off the list if it's you. You can't have killed her—'

'For God's *sake*.'

'Sorry. I'm sorry. But it's got to be said. You can't have killed her because you were at home with two dozen witnesses celebrating your anniversary. So if you are *Jete*, sir, I'd like to know so that I don't waste time trying to track him down.'

'Or her, Tommy. "After all this time." It could be Wolff.'

'It could be Wolff. But it's not you?'

'No.'

'Thanks. That's all I need to know, sir.'

'You got to us quickly. To me and Eugenie.'

'I didn't get to you. Havers did.'

'Havers? How the hell . . . ?'

'Eugenie kept your letters. They were all together in a drawer in her bedroom. Barbara found them.'

'Where are they now? Have you given them to Leach?'

'I didn't think they were germane to the case. Are they, sir? Because common sense tells me I shouldn't dismiss the possibility that Eugenie Davies wanted to talk to Ted Wiley about you.'

'If she wanted to talk to Wiley about me, it would have been only to confess past transgressions before getting on with her life.'

'Would that have been like her, Superintendent?'

'Oh yes,' Webberly sighed. 'Just like.'

She hadn't been brought up so, but she'd lived as a Catholic, with the Catholic's profound sense of guilt and remorse. That had coloured the way she'd lived in Henley, and that would have coloured the manner in which she faced the future. He was certain.

At his elbow, Webberly became aware of a gentle pressure. Alf, he saw, had lumbered up from his raggedy nighttime cushion by the stove and had come to join him, pressing the top of his head against his master's arm, perhaps sensing that canine solace was needed. The dog's presence reminded Webberly that he was late in taking the Alsatian for his regular nightly stroll.

He went upstairs first to check on Frances,

compelled by the twinge of guilt he felt at having spent the last forty-eight hours dwelling in mind and in spirit, if not in body, with another woman. He found his wife in their double bed, snoring gently, and he stood looking down at her. Sleep wiped the lines of anxiety from her face. While it did not render her youthful again, it served to provide her with an air of defencelessness that he'd never been able to ignore. How many times over the years had he done just this—stood looking down at his sleeping wife—and wondered how they'd come to this pass? how they'd gone so long just getting through days that turned into weeks that swiftly became months yet never once venturing each to understand what inner yearnings caused them to sing in their chains—faces held to the sky—when they were alone? But he had the answer to that question, at least on his own part, when he glanced at the window with its curtains shut tight, knowing that behind them the glass was locked and a wooden dowel lay on the floor for use as further security on the nights he wasn't at home.

They'd both been afraid from the start. It was just that Fran's fears had taken a form more readily apparent to the casual observer. Her fears had claimed him, making a plea for his constancy that was as eloquent as it was unspoken, and his own fears had bound him to her, terrified that he might have to become more than he'd lived as already.

A low whining from the foot of the stairs roused Webberly. He pulled the blankets over his wife's exposed right shoulder, whispered, 'Sleep well, Frances,' and left the room.

Below, Alfie had moved to the front door where he sat on his haunches expectantly. He got to his feet as Webberly went back to the kitchen for his jacket and the dog's lead. He was circling round in anticipation when Webberly returned to him and clipped the lead on his collar.

Webberly's intention was to take the Alsatian on a shorter walk tonight: just a circuit of the rectangle described by walking to the end of Palgrave Road, up to Stamford Brook Road, and back to Palgrave via Hartswood Road. He was tired, and he didn't much feel like trailing Alfie across the green that was Prebend Gardens. He realised that this wasn't giving the Alsatian his due. The dog was nothing if not patience, tolerance, and fidelity incarnate, and all he asked in return for his devotion was food, water, and the chance to run with happy abandon round, through, and across Prebend Gardens twice each day. It was small enough consideration for him, but tonight Webberly didn't feel up to it.

'I'll give you twice the time tomorrow, Alf,' he promised.

At the corner of Stamford Brook Road, traffic trundled by, lighter now than at another hour but still coughing with the occasional noise of buses and cars. Alf sat obediently as he'd been trained to do. But when Webberly would have turned to the left instead of crossing over to the gardens, Alfie didn't move. He looked from his master to the gloomy expanse of trees, shrubs, and lawn across the street, wagging his tail urgently against the pavement.

'Tomorrow, Alf,' Webberly told him. 'Twice as much time. I promise. Tomorrow. Come, boy.' He gave a tug on the lead.

The dog rose. But he looked over his shoulder at

46

the garden in such a way that Webberly felt he could not commit yet another act of betrayal by pretending to ignore what the animal so patently wanted to do. He sighed. 'All right. But just a few minutes. We've left Mum alone and she won't like it if she wakes up and finds neither one of us there.'

They waited for the traffic lights to change, the dog's tail flapping and Webberly finding his own spirits lifting at the animal's pleasure. He thought what ease there was in doghood: So little in life equated with a dog's contentment.

They crossed over and entered the garden, its iron gate creaking with autumn rust. With the gate closed behind them, Webberly released Alfie from the lead and in the dim light provided from Stamford Brook Road on one side and South Side on the other, he watched the dog lope happily across the lawn.

He'd not thought to bring a ball, but the Alsatian didn't seem to mind. There were plenty of nighttime smells to entice him, and he partook of them in his romp.

They spent a quarter of an hour like this, Webberly slowly pacing the distance from the west to the east side of the garden. The wind had come up earlier in the day, and he drove his hands into his pockets, regretting the fact that he'd come out without either gloves or scarf.

He shivered and crunched along the cinder path that bordered the lawn. Beyond the iron fence and the shrubbery, traffic whizzed by in Stamford Brook Road. Aside from the wind creaking the bare limbs of the trees, that was the only sound in the night.

At the far end of the garden, Webberly took the

lead from his pocket and called to the dog, who'd run once again to the opposite end of the green like a gambolling lamb. He whistled and waited as the Alsatian galloped the length of the lawn a final time, arriving in a happy heaving mass of damp fur hung with sodden leaves. Webberly chuckled at the sight of the animal. The night was far from over for them both. Alf would need brushing when they got home.

He clipped the lead back on. Outside the garden gate, they headed up the avenue towards Stamford Brook Road where a zebra crossing marked a safe passage to Hartswood. They had the right of way here, although Alfie did again what he'd been trained to do: He sat and waited for the command that indicated it was safe to cross.

He waited for a break in the traffic which, because of the hour, wasn't long in coming. After a bus trundled past, he and the dog stepped off the pavement. It was less than thirty yards across the street.

Webberly was a careful pedestrian, but for a moment his attention drifted to the pillar box that stood on the opposite side of the street. It had been there since the reign of Queen Victoria, and it was there that he'd dropped his letters to Eugenie over the years, including the final one that had ended things without ending things between them. His eyes fixed on it and he saw himself there as he'd been on a hundred different mornings, hurriedly stuffing a letter through the opening, casting a look over his shoulder in the unlikely event that Frances had come walking in his wake. Seeing himself as he'd been long ago, engaged by love and desire to act the apostate from vows that were asking the impossible of him, he was unprepared. He was unprepared just for a second, but a second was actually all it took.

To his right, Webberly heard the howl of an engine. At that same moment, Alfie began to bark. Then Webberly felt the impact. As the dog's lead flew up into the night, Webberly hurtled towards the pillar box that had been the receptacle of his countless outpourings of unending love.

A blow crushed his chest.

A flash of light pierced his eyes like a beacon.

And then it was dark.


*Gideon*

<u>*23 OCTOBER 1:00 A.M.*</u>
*I dreamed again. I woke, remembering it. I sit up in bed now, notebook on my knees, in order to scribble a summary.*

*I'm in the house in Kensington Square. I'm in the drawing room. I'm watching children playing outside in the central garden, and they see me watching them. They wave and gesture for me to join them and I can see they're being entertained by a magician in a black cape and a top hat. He keeps drawing live doves from the ears of the children, tossing the birds high into the air. I want to be there, I want the magician to draw a bird from my ear, but when I go to the drawing room door, I find there is no handle, just a keyhole through which I can peer in order to see the reception hall and the staircase.*

*But when I peer through that keyhole, which turns out to be much more like a porthole than a keyhole, I*

49

*see not what I expect to see but my sister's nursery on the other side. And although the light is bright in the drawing room, it's quite dim in the nursery, as if the curtains have been closed for naptime.*

*I hear crying on the other side of the door. I know the crying is Sonia's, but I can't see her. And then the door is suddenly not a door any longer but a heavy curtain through which I push, finding myself not in the house any longer but in the garden behind it.*

*The garden is much larger than it actually was in reality. There are enormous trees, huge ferns, and a waterfall that drops into a distant pool. In the middle of the pool is the garden shed, the same shed against which I saw Katja and the man on that night I've recalled.*

*Outside in the garden, I still hear Sonia crying, but she's wailing now, nearly screaming, and I know that I'm meant to find her. I'm surrounded by undergrowth that seems to grow by the moment, and I fight my way through it, beating down fronds and lilies to locate the crying. Just when I think I'm close to it, it seems to come from a different area entirely, and I'm forced to begin again.*

*I call for help: my mother, Dad, Gran, or Granddad. But no one comes. And then I reach the edge of the pool and I see that there are two people leaning against the shed, a man and woman. He's bent to her, he's sucking from her neck, and still Sonia is crying and crying.*

*I can tell by her hair that the woman is Libby, and I'm frozen there, watching, as the man I can't yet identify sucks upon her. I call to them; I ask them to help me find my little sister. The man raises his head when I call out, and I see he's my father.*

*I feel rage, betrayal. I am immobilised. Sonia still*

*cries.*

*Then Mother is with me, or someone like Mother, someone of her height and her shape with hair the same colour. She takes my hand and I'm aware I must help her because Sonia needs us to calm her crying, which is angry now, high-pitched with rage like a tantrum being thrown.*

*'It's all right,' the MotherPerson tells me. 'She's just hungry, darling.'*

*And we find her lying beneath a fern, covered completely by fronds. MotherPerson picks her up and holds her to her breast. She says, 'Let her suck me. She'll calm, then.'*

*But Sonia doesn't calm down because she can't feed. MotherPerson doesn't free her breasts for Sonia and even if she did, nothing would be accomplished. For when I look at my sister, I see she's wearing a mask that covers her face. I try to remove it, but I can't; my fingers keep slipping off. MotherPerson doesn't notice that there's anything wrong, and I can't make her look down at my sister. And I can't and I can't remove the mask that she's wearing. But I feel frantic to do so.*

*I ask the MotherPerson to help me, but that's no good because she doesn't even look down at Sonia. I hurry and fight my way back to the pool to find help there, and when I reach the edge, I slip and fall in, and I'm turning and turning beneath the water, unable to breathe.*

*That's when I wake up.*

*My heart was slamming. I could actually feel the way the adrenaline had shot into my blood stream. Writing all of it down has calmed my heartbeat, but I don't expect sleep to return to me tonight.*

*Libby isn't with you? you want to know.*

51

*No. She didn't return from wherever she jetted off
to when we got back from Cresswell-White's office
and found my father waiting at the house.*

*Are you worried about her?*

*Should I be worried?*

*There is no should to anything, Gideon.*

*But there is to me, Dr Rose. I should be able to
remember more. I should be able to play my
instrument. I should be able to take a woman into my
life without fearing that somehow I'll lose it all.*

*Lose what?*

*What's holding me together in the first place.*

*Do you need to be held together, Gideon?*

*That's how it feels.*


<u>*23 OCTOBER*</u>

*Raphael did his daily duty by me today but instead of
sitting in the music room and waiting for a miracle to
happen, we walked down to Regent's Park and
strolled through the zoo. One of the elephants was
being hosed off by a keeper, and we paused by the
enclosure and watched as sheets of water cascaded
down the side of the enormous creature. Sprouts of
hair along the elephant's backbone bristled like wires
as the water hit them, and the animal shifted its
weight as if trying to gain its footing.*

*'Odd, aren't they?' Raphael said. 'One wonders
about the design philosophy behind the elephant.
When I see a biological oddity like this, I'm always
sorry that I don't know more about evolution. How,
for example, did something like an elephant develop
out of the primordial muck?'*

*'He's probably thinking the same of us.' I'd noticed
upon Raphael's arrival that he was decidedly good*

*humoured. And he'd been the one to suggest we get out of the house and into the questionable air of the city and into the even more questionable fragrance of the zoo, where the atmosphere was redolent with the smells of urine and hay. This prompted me to wonder what was going on. I saw my father's hand in it. 'Get him out of that house,' he would have commanded.*

*And when Father commanded, Raphael obeyed.*

*That was the key to his longevity as my instructor: He held the reins to my musical training; Dad held the reins to the rest of my life. And Raphael had always accepted this division of their responsibilities towards me.*

*As an adult, of course, I could have chosen to replace Raphael with someone else to accompany me on my concert tours—apart from Dad, naturally— and to be a partner to my daily sessions of practice on the violin. But at this point with more than two decades of instruction, cooperation, and partnership between us, we knew each other's styles of living and working so well that to bring in someone else had never been a consideration. Besides, when I could play, I liked playing with Raphael Robson. He was— and is—a brilliant technician. There's a spark missing in him, an additional passion that would have long ago forced him to overcome his nerves and to play publicly, knowing that playing is forging a link with an audience, which makes the quadrinomial defined by composer-music-listener-performer complete. But aside from that spark, the artistry and the love are there, as is a remarkable ability to distil technique into a series of critiques, commands, adjustments, assignments, and instructions that are understandable to the neophyte artist and invaluable to the established violinist who seeks to improve*

53

himself on his instrument. So I never considered replacing Raphael, despite his obedience to—and loathing of—my father.

I must have always sensed the antipathy between them, even if I never saw it openly. They coped despite their dislike of each other, and it was only now when they'd begun to seem at such pains to hide their mutual loathing that I felt compelled to question why it had existed in the first place.

The natural answer was my mother: because of how Raphael may have felt about my mother. But that seemed to explain only why Raphael disliked my father so much, Dad being in possession of what Raphael might have wanted for himself. It didn't explain my father's aversion to Raphael. There had to be something more.

Perhaps it came from what Raphael could give you? you offer me as potential answer.

And it's true that my father played no instrument, but I think their dislike came from something more basic and atavistic than that.

I said to Raphael as we moved from the elephants to seek out the koalas, 'You were told to get me out of the house today.'

He didn't deny it. 'He thinks you're dwelling too much on the past and avoiding the present.'

'What do you think?'

'I trust Dr Rose. At least I trust Dr Rose the father. As to Dr Rose the daughter, I assume she's discussing the case with him.' He glanced at me anxiously as he said the word case, which reduced me to a phenomenon that would doubtless appear in a psychiatric journal at a later date, my name scrupulously withheld but everything else forming neon arrows that all pointed to me as the patient.

54

'He's had decades of experience with the sort of thing you're going through and that's going to count for something with her.'

'What sort of thing do you think I'm going through?'

'I know what she's called it. The amnesia bit.'

'Dad told you?'

'He would do, wouldn't he? I'm as much involved with your career as anyone.'

'But you don't believe in the amnesia, do you?'

'Gideon, it's not my place to believe or disbelieve anything.'

He led me into the koala enclosure where simulated eucalyptus trees were formed by crisscrossing branches that rose out of the floor, and the forest in which the bears would have lived in the wild was expressed by a mural painted on a tall pink wall. A single diminutive bear slept in the V of two of the branches, nearby him hanging a bucket that contained the leaves upon which he was supposed to feed. The forest floor beneath the bear was concrete, and there were no bushes, no diversions, and no toys for him. He had no companions to break his solitude either, only the visitors to his enclosure, who whistled and called out to him, frustrated that a creature nocturnal by nature would not accommodate himself to their timetable.

I looked at all this and felt a heaviness settle onto my shoulders. 'God. Why do people come to zoos?'

'To remind them of their freedom.'

'To exult in their superiority.'

'I suppose that's true as well. After all, as humans we hold the keys, don't we?'

'Ah,' I said. 'I did think there was a greater purpose behind this sojourn to Regent's Park than just getting

55

*some air. I've never seen you as interested either in exercise or in animals. So what did Dad say? "Show him he ought to count his blessings. Show him how bad life really can be?"'*

*'There are worse places than a zoo if that was his intention, Gideon.'*

*'Then what? And don't tell me you thought up the zoo on your own.'*

*'You're brooding. It's not healthy. He knows it.'*

*I laughed without humour. 'As if what's happened already is healthy?'*

*'We don't know what's happened. We can only guess. And that's what this amnesia business is. It's a qualified guess.'*

*'So he's brought you on board. I wouldn't have thought that possible, your past relationship with him considered.'*

*Raphael kept his gaze on the pathetic koala. 'My relationship with your father isn't your concern,' he said steadily, but the pinpoints of perspiration—always his Nemesis—began to sprout on his forehead. Another two minutes and his face would be dripping and he'd be using his handkerchief to mop up the sweat.*

*'You were in the house the night Sonia drowned,' I said. 'Dad told me that. So you've always known everything, haven't you? Everything that happened, what led up to her death, and what followed it.'*

*'Let's get some tea,' Raphael said.*

*We went to the restaurant in Barclays Court although a simple kiosk selling hot and cold drinks would have done as well. He wouldn't say anything until he'd meticulously looked over the mundane menu of grilled everything and ordered a pot of Darjeeling and a toasted tea cake from a middle-aged*

56

*waitress wearing retro spectacles.*

*She said, 'Got it, luv,' and waited for my order, tapping her pencil against her pad. I ordered the same although I wasn't hungry. She took herself off to fetch it.*

*It wasn't a mealtime, so there were few people in the restaurant and no one at all near our table. We were next to a window, though, and Raphael directed his attention outside, where a man was struggling to unhook a blanket from the wheels of a push chair while a woman with a toddler in her arms gesticulated and gave him instructions.*

*I said, 'It feels like night in my memory, when Sonia drowned. But if that's the case, what were you doing at the house? Dad told me you were there.'*

*'It was late afternoon when she drowned, half past five, nearly six. I'd stayed to make some phone calls.'*

*'Dad said you were probably contacting Juilliard that day.'*

*'I wanted you to be able to attend once they'd made you the offer, so I was lining up support for the idea. It was inconceivable to me that anyone would think of turning down Juilliard—'*

*'How had they heard of me? I'd done those few concerts, but I don't remember actually applying to go there. I just remember being invited to attend.'*

*'I'd written to them. I'd sent them tapes. Reviews. A piece that* Radio Times *did on you. They were interested and invited the application, which I filled out.'*

*'Did Dad know about this?'*

*Again, the perspiration speckled his forehead, and this time he used one of the napkins on the table to mop it up. He said, 'I wanted to present the invitation as a* fait accompli *because I thought that if I had the*

57

*invitation in hand, your father would agree to your attending.'*

*'But there wasn't the money, was there?' I concluded grimly. And just for a moment, oddly enough, I felt it again, that searing disappointment bordering on fury to know as an eight-year-old that Juilliard was not and would never be available to me because of money, because in our lives there* never *was nearly enough money to live.*

*Raphael's next words surprised me, then. 'Money was never the issue. We would have come up with it eventually. I was always certain of that. And they'd offered a scholarship for your tuition. But your father wouldn't hear of your going. He didn't want to separate the family. I assumed his main concern was leaving his parents, and I offered to take you to New York on my own, allowing everyone else to remain here in London, but he wouldn't accept that solution either.'*

*'So it wasn't financial? Because I'd thought—'*

*'No. Ultimately, it wasn't financial.'*

*I must have looked either confused or betrayed by this information because Raphael continued, saying quickly, 'Your father believed you didn't need Juilliard, Gideon. It's a compliment to us both, I suppose. He thought you could get the instruction you needed right here in London and he believed you'd succeed without a move to New York. And time proved him right. Look where you are today.'*

*'Yes. Just look,' I said ironically, as Raphael fell into the same trap that I'd fallen into myself, Dr Rose.*

*Look where I am today, huddled into the window seat in my music room where the last thing made in the room is music. I'm scribbling random thoughts in an effort that I don't quite believe in, trying to recall*

58

*life details that my subconscious has judged as better forgotten. And now I'm discovering that even some of the details that I do dredge up out of my memory— like the invitation to Juilliard and what prevented me from accepting it—are not accurate. If that's the case, what can I rely on, Dr Rose?*

*You'll know, you answer quietly.*

*But I ask how you can be so sure. The facts of my past seem more and more like moving targets to me, and they're scurrying past a background of faces that I haven't seen in years. So are they actual facts, Dr Rose, or are they merely what I wish the facts to be?*

*I said to Raphael, 'Tell me what happened when Sonia drowned. That night. That afternoon. What happened? Getting Dad to talk about it . . .' I shook my head. The waitress returned with our tea and tea cakes spread across a plastic tray that, in keeping with the overall theme of the zoo, was painted to look like something else, in this case wood. She arranged cups, saucers, plates, and pots to her liking, and I waited till she had gone before I went on. 'Dad won't say much. If I want to talk about music, the violin, that's fine. That looks like progress. If I want to go in another direction . . . He'll go, but it's hell for him. I can see that much.'*

*'It was hell for everyone.'*

*'Katja Wolff included?'*

*'Her hell came afterwards, I dare say. She couldn't have been anticipating the judge recommending she serve twenty years.'*

*'Is that why at the trial . . . I read that she jumped up and tried to make a statement once he'd passed sentence.'*

*'Did she?' he asked. 'I didn't know. I wasn't there on the day of the verdict. I'd had enough at that*

point.'

'You went with her to the police station, though. In the beginning. There was that picture of the two of you coming out.'

'I expect that was coincidence. The police had everyone down for questioning at one time or another. Most of us more than once.'

'Sarah-Jane Beckett as well?'

'I expect so. Why?'

'I need to see her.'

Raphael had buttered his tea cake and raised it to his mouth, but he didn't take a bite. Instead, he watched me over the top of it. 'What's that going to accomplish, Gideon?'

'It's just the direction I think I should go. And that's what Dr Rose suggested, following my instincts, looking for connections, trying to find anything that will jar loose memories.'

'Your father's not going to be pleased.'

'So take your telephone off the hook.'

Raphael took a substantial bite of the tea cake, no doubt covering his chagrin at having been found out. But what else would he expect me to assume other than that he and Dad are having daily conversations about my progress or lack thereof? They are, after all, the two people most involved with what has happened to me, and aside from Libby and you, Dr Rose, they are the only two who know the extent of my troubles.

'What do you expect to gain from seeing Sarah-Jane Beckett, assuming you can even find her?'

'She's in Cheltenham,' I told him. 'She's been there for years. I get a card from her on my birthday and at Christmas. Don't you?'

'All right. She's in Cheltenham,' he said, ignoring my question. 'How can she help?'

60

'I don't know. Maybe she can tell me why Katja Wolff wouldn't talk about what happened.'

'She had a right to silence, Gideon.' He placed his tea cake on his plate and took up his cup, which he held in both hands as if warming them.

'In court, right. With the police, right. She didn't have to talk. But with her solicitor? With her barrister? Why not talk to them?'

'She wasn't fluent in English. Someone might have explained her right to silence and she could have misunderstood.'

'And that brings up something else I don't understand,' I told him. 'If she was foreign, why did she serve her time in England? Why wasn't she sent back to Germany?'

'She fought repatriation through the courts, and she won.'

'How do you know?'

'How could I help knowing? It was in all the newspapers at the time. She was like Myra Hindley: Every legal move she made from behind bars was scrutinised by the media. It was a nasty case, Gideon. It was a brutal case. It destroyed your parents, it killed both your grandparents within three years, and it damn well might have ruined you had not every effort in the world been made to keep you out of it. So to dig it all up now . . . all these years afterwards . . .' He set down his cup and added more tea to it. He said, 'You aren't touching your food.'

'I'm not hungry.'

'When did you last have a meal? You look like hell. Eat the tea cake. Or at least drink the tea.'

'Raphael, what if Katja Wolff didn't drown Sonia?'

He put the teapot back on the table. He took the sugar and added a packet to his cup, following this

61

with the milk. It came to me then that he did it all in reverse of the usual order.

He said once the pouring and sugaring was done, 'It hardly makes sense that she'd keep quiet if she hadn't killed Sonia, Gideon.'

'Perhaps she suspected that the police would twist her words. Or the Crown prosecutors, should she have stood in the witness box.'

'They might have done, all of them, yes. Indeed. But her solicitor and her barrister would have been unlikely to twist her words should she have seen fit to give them any.'

'Did my father make her pregnant?'

He'd lifted his cup, but he set it back on its saucer. He looked out of the window where the couple with the push chair had now unloaded it of a bag, two baby bottles, and a pack of disposable nappies. They'd turned the chair on its side and the man was attacking the wheel with the heel of his shoe. Raphael said quietly, 'That has nothing to do with the problem,' and I knew he was not speaking about the blanket that continued to make the push chair impossible to roll forward.

'How can you say that? How can you know? Did he make her pregnant? And is that what destroyed my parents' marriage?'

'Only the people within a marriage can say what destroyed it.'

'All right. Accepted. And as to the rest? Did he make Katja pregnant?'

'What does he say? Have you asked him?'

'He says no. But he would do, wouldn't he?'

'So you've had your answer.'

'Then who?'

'Perhaps the lodger. James Pitchford was in love

with her. The day she walked into your parents' house, James fell hard and he never recovered.'

'But I thought James and Sarah-Jane . . . I remember them together, James the Lodger and Sarah-Jane. From the window, I saw them heading out in the evening. And whispering together in the kitchen, like intimates.'

'That would have been before Katja, I expect.'

'Why?'

'Because after Katja arrived, James spent most of his free hours with her.'

'So Katja displaced Sarah-Jane in more than one way.'

'You could say that, yes, and I see where you're heading. But she was with James Pitchford when Sonia drowned. And James confirmed that. He had no reason to lie for her. If he was going to lie for anyone back then, he would have lied for the woman he loved. In fact, had Sarah-Jane not been with James when Sonia was murdered, I expect James would have gladly given Katja an alibi that would have made her seem merely derelict in her duties and consequently responsible for a tragic death, but not a malevolent one.'

'And as it was, it was murder,' I said reflectively.

'When all the facts were presented, yes.'

## Gideon

<u>25 OCTOBER</u>

When all the facts were presented, Raphael Robson said. And that's what I'm looking for, isn't it, an accurate presentation of the facts.

*You don't reply. Instead, you keep your face expressionless as you no doubt were instructed to do as a psychiatric intern or whatever it was that you were as a student, and you wait for me to offer an explanation for why I have veered so decidedly into this area. Seeing this, I flounder for words and I begin to question myself. I examine the motive for what might prompt me to engage in displacement—as you would call it—and I admit to every one of my fears.*

*What are they? you ask.*

*You already know what they are, Dr Rose.*

*I suspect, you say, I consider, I speculate, and I wonder, but I do not know. You're the only one who knows, Gideon.*

*All right. I accept that. And to show you how wholeheartedly I accept that, I'll name them for you: fear of crowds, fear of being trapped in the underground, fear of excessive speed, complete terror of snakes.*

*All fairly common fears, you note.*

*As are fear of failure, fear of my father's disapproval, fear of enclosed spaces—*

*You raise an eyebrow at that, a momentary lapse in your lack of expression.*

*Yes, I'm afraid to be enclosed and I see how that relates to relationships, Dr Rose. I'm afraid of being suffocated by someone, which fear in and of itself indicates a larger fear of being intimate with a woman. With anyone, for that matter. But this is hardly news to me. I've had years to consider how and why and at what point my affair with Beth fell completely apart and believe me I've had plenty of opportunities to dwell on my lack of response to Libby. So if I know and admit my fears and take them out into the sunlight and shake them like dusters, how can you or Dad or anyone else accuse me of displacing them onto an unhealthy interest in my sister's death and its consequences?*

*I'm not accusing you of anything, Gideon, you say, clasping your hands in your lap. Are you, however, accusing yourself?*

*Of what?*

*Perhaps you can tell me.*

*Oh, I see that game. And I know where you want me to head. It's where everyone wants me to head, everyone save Libby, that is. You want me to head to the music, Dr Rose, to talk about the music, to delve into the music.*

*Only if that's where you want to go, you say.*

*And if I don't want to go there?*

*We might talk about why.*

*You see? You're trying to trick me. If you can get me to admit . . .*

*What? you ask when I hesitate, and your voice is as soft as goose down. Stay within the fear, you tell me. Fear is only a feeling; it is not a fact.*

*But the* fact *is that I cannot play. And the fear is of the music.*

*All music?*

*Oh, you know the answer to that, Dr Rose. You know it's fear of one piece in particular. You know how* The Archduke *haunts my life. And you know that once Beth suggested it as our performance piece, I could not refuse. Because it was Beth who made the suggestion, not Sherrill. Had it been Sherrill, I could have tossed out a 'Choose something else', without a thought because even though Sherrill has no jinx himself and consequently might have questioned my rejection of* The Archduke, *the fact is that Sherrill's talent is such that for him to make the shift from one*

65

*piece to another is so simple that to question it would have taken more energy than he'd have wished to expend on the matter. But Beth is not like Sherrill, Dr Rose, either in talent or in* laissez-faire. *Beth had already prepared* The Archduke, *so Beth would have questioned. And questioning, she may have connected my failure to play* The Archduke *with that other more significant failure of mine with which she was once all too familiar. So I didn't ask for a different choice of music. I decided to confront the jinx head-on. And put to the test of that confrontation, I failed.*

*Before that? you ask.*

*Before what?*

*Before the performance at Wigmore Hall. You must have rehearsed.*

*We did. Of course.*

*And you played it then?*

*We would hardly have mounted a public concert of three instruments had one of them—*

*And you played it without difficulty then? During rehearsal?*

*I've* never *played it without difficulty, Dr Rose. Either in private or in rehearsal, I've never played it without a bout of nerves, of burning in the gut, of pounding in the head, of sickness that makes me cling to the toilet for an hour first, and all* that *and I'm not even performing it publicly.*

*So what about the Wigmore night? you ask me. Did you have that same reaction to* The Archduke *before Wigmore Hall?*

*And I hesitate.*

*I see how your eyes spark with interest at my hesitation: evaluating, deciding, choosing whether to press forward now or to wait and let my realisations*

66

*and admissions come when they will.*

*Because I did not suffer before that performance.*
*And I haven't registered that until now.*

## 26 OCTOBER

*I've been to Cheltenham. Sarah-Jane Beckett is Sarah-Jane Hamilton now and has been Hamilton for the last twelve years. She's not much changed physically since she was my teacher: She's put on a bit of weight but she's still not developed breasts, and her hair is as red as it was when we lived in the same household. It's a different style—she wears it held off her face with a hair band—but it's straight as a poker as it always was.*

*The first thing I noticed that's different about her now was her manner of dress. She's apparently moved away from the sorts of clothes she wore as my teacher—which were heavily given to floppy collars and lace, as I recall—and she's advanced to skirts, twinsets, and pearls. The second thing I noticed that's different was her fingernails, which are no longer bitten to the quick with chewed up cuticles but are instead long and bright with polish, the better to show off a sapphire and diamond ring that's the size of a small African nation. I noticed her fingernails because whilst we were together, she made a great job of waving her hands when she spoke, as if she wanted me to see how far she'd advanced in good fortune.*

*The means to her good fortune wasn't at home when I arrived in Cheltenham. Sarah-Jane was in the front garden of their house—which is in a very smart neighbourhood where Mercedes-Benzes and Range Rovers appear to be the vehicles of choice—and she was filling an enormous bird feeder with seed,* standing on a three-step ladder and pouring from a weighty bag. I didn't want to startle her, so I said nothing till she was off the steps and rearranging her twinset as well as patting her chest to make sure the pearls were still in place. That was when I called her name, and after she greeted me with surprise and pleasure, she told me that Perry—husband and provider of largesse—was on business in Manchester and would be disappointed to discover upon his return that he'd missed my visit.

'He's heard enough about you over the years,' she said. 'But I expect he's never believed that I actually know you.' And here she trilled a little laugh that made me distinctly uncomfortable although I could not tell you why except to say that laughs like that never sound genuine to me. She said, 'Come in. Come in. Will you have coffee? Tea? A drink?'

She led the way into the house where everything was so tasteful that only an interior decorator could have managed it: just the right furniture, just the right colours, just the right objets d'art, subtle lighting designed to flatter, and a touch of homeliness in the careful selection of family photographs. She snatched up one on her way to make our coffee and she thrust it at me. 'Perry,' she said. 'His girls and ours. They're with their mother most of the time. We have them every other weekend. Alternate holidays and half terms. The modern British family, you know.' Again that laugh and she disappeared behind a swinging door through which, I assumed, the kitchen lay.

Alone, I found myself looking at the family in a studio portrait. The absent but seated Perry was surrounded by five women: his wife sitting next to him, two older daughters behind him with one hand each upon his shoulders, one smaller girl leaning into

Sarah-Jane and the last—smaller still—upon Perry's knee. He had that look of satisfaction that I can only assume comes when a man successfully creates offspring. The older girls looked bored to tears, the younger girls looked winsome, and Sarah-Jane looked excessively pleased.

She popped back out of the kitchen as I was replacing the picture on the table from which she'd fetched it. She said, 'Step-mothering is rather like teaching: It's a case of constantly encouraging without ever being actually free to say what one really thinks. And always there are the parents to contend with, in this case their mother. She drinks, I'm afraid.'

'Is that how it was with me?'

'Good heavens, your mother didn't drink.'

'I meant the rest: not being able to say what you think.'

'One learns diplomacy,' she said. 'This is my Angelique.' She indicated the child on Perry's knee. 'And this is Anastasia. She has something of a talent for music herself.'

I waited for her to identify the older girls. When she did not, I asked the obligatory question about Anastasia's choice of instrument. Harp, I was told. Suitable, I thought. Sarah-Jane had always possessed an air of the Regency about her, as if she'd somehow been a displaced person from a Jane Austen novel, more fitted for a life of writing letters, doing lacework, and creating inoffensive water colours than for the scramble and dash of existence enjoyed by women today. I couldn't envisage Sarah-Jane Beckett Hamilton jogging through Regent's Park with a mobile phone pressed to her ear any more than I could see her fighting fires, mining coal, or crewing a yacht in the Fastnet Race. So steering her eldest

69

*natural daughter towards the harp rather than something like the electric guitar was a logical act of parental guidance on her part, and I had no doubt she'd employed it deftly once the girl had decided she wanted to play an instrument.*

*'Of course, she's not in your league,' Sarah-Jane said, presenting me with another photograph, this one of Anastasia at her harp, arms raised gracefully so that her hands—stubby, unfortunately, like her mother's—could pluck the strings. 'But she does well enough. I hope you'll hear her sometime. When you* have *the time, naturally.' And she trilled her gay little laugh again. 'I do so wish Perry were here to meet you, Gideon. Are you in town for a concert?'*

*I told her that I wasn't there for a concert but I didn't add the rest. She'd obviously not seen any accounts of the incident in Wigmore Hall, and the less that I had to delve into that with Sarah-Jane, the better I would feel about it. Instead, I told her that I was hoping to talk to her about my sister's death and the trial that followed.*

*She said, 'Ah. Yes. I see.' And she sat on a plump sofa the colour of newly cut grass and motioned me over to an armchair whose fabric featured a muted autumn hunting scene with dogs and deer.*

*I waited for the logical questions to come.* Why? Why now? Why dig up all that is past, Gideon? *But they did not come, which I found curious. Instead, Sarah-Jane composed herself, her legs crossed at the ankles, her hands lying one on top of the other—with the sapphired one on top—and her expression perfectly attentive and not the least guarded, as I'd come to expect.*

*'What is it you'd like to know?' she asked.*

*'Anything you can tell me. About Katja Wolff,*

70

*mainly. About what she was like, what living in the same house with her was like.'*

*'Yes. Of course.' Sarah-Jane sat quietly, gathering her thoughts. Finally, she began by saying, 'Well, it was obvious from the first that she didn't belong in the position as your sister's nanny. It was a mistake for your parents to employ her, but they didn't see that before it was too late.'*

*'I've been told she was fond of Sonia.'*

*'Oh* fond *of her, yes. It was very easy to be fond of Sonia. She was a fragile little thing and she was fractious—well, what child wouldn't be, in that condition?—but she was terribly sweet and quite precious as any infant after all, and who finds it impossible to be fond of a baby? But she had other things on her mind, did Katja, and they got in the way of her devotion to Sonia. And devotion is what's required with children, Gideon. Fondness won't get you through the first bout of wilfulness or tears.'*

*'What sort of things?'*

*'She wasn't serious about childcare. It was a means to an end for her. She wanted to be a fashion designer—although God only knows why, considering the bizarre ensembles she put together for herself— and she intended to stay in your parents' employ only as long as it took her to save the money she needed for . . . for wherever it was that she intended to be trained. So there was that.'*

*'What else?'*

*'Celebrity.'*

*'She wanted fame?'*

*'She had fame already: The Girl Who Made it Over the Berlin Wall As Her Lover Died in Her Arms.'*

*'Died in her arms?'*

71

'Hmm. Yes. That's how she told the tale. She had a scrap book, mind you, of all the interviews she'd done with newspapers and magazines from round the world after that escape, and to hear her tell the story was to be asked to believe that she'd designed and inflated the balloon on her own, which I seriously doubt was the case. I always said it was a lucky turn of events that made her the only survivor of that escape. Had the boy lived—and what was his name? Georg? Klaus?—I've little doubt he would have told an entirely different tale about whose idea it was and who did the work. So she came to England with her head swollen, and it got larger during the year she spent at the Convent of the Immaculate Conception. More interviews, lunch with the Lord Mayor, a private audience at Buckingham Palace. She was ill-prepared psychologically to fade into the woodwork as your sister's nanny. And as for being physically and mentally prepared for what she was going to have to face—not to mention temperamentally suited . . . She wasn't. Not in the least.'

'So she was destined to fail,' I remarked quietly, and I must have sounded contemplative because Sarah-Jane appeared to reach a conclusion about what I was thinking, and she hastened to make an adjustment.

'I don't mean to imply that your parents hired her because she was ill-prepared, Gideon. That wouldn't be an accurate assessment of the situation at all. And it might even go so far as to suggest that . . . Well, never mind. No.'

'Yet it was obvious right off that she couldn't handle the responsibility?'

'Only if you were looking was it obvious,' she replied. 'And certainly, you and I were thrown together

72

with Katja and the baby more than anyone else, so we could see and hear . . . And we were in the house—the four of us—far more than your parents, both of whom worked. So we saw more. Or at least I did.'

'What about my grandparents? Where were they?'

'It's true that your granddad hung about a lot. He rather fancied Katja, so he kept her under his eye. But he wasn't actually altogether there, was he, if you understand my meaning? So he could hardly be prepared to report on anything irregular that he saw.'

'Irregular?'

'Sonia's crying going unattended to. Katja's absences from the house when the baby was having a nap in the middle of the day. Telephone conversations during your sister's mealtimes. A general impatience with the baby when she was difficult. Those sorts of things that are questionable and disturbing while not being out-and-out grossly negligent.'

'Did you tell anyone?'

'Indeed. I told your mother.'

'What about Dad?'

Sarah-Jane gave a little bounce on the sofa. She said, 'The coffee! I'd quite forgotten . . .' And she excused herself and hurried from the room.

What about Dad? The room was so quiet, and the neighbourhood outside was so quiet, that my question seemed to bounce off the walls like an echo in a canyon. What about Dad?

I got up from my chair and went to one of the two display cabinets that stood on either side of the fireplace. I examined its contents: four shelves filled with antique dolls of all shapes and sizes, representing everything from infants to adults, all of them dressed in period clothes, perhaps from the period during

73

*which the dolls themselves had been manufactured. I know nothing of dolls, so I had no idea what I was looking at, but I could tell that the collection was impressive: by the numbers, the quality of the dress, and the condition of the toys themselves, which was pristine. Some of them looked as if they'd never actually been handled by a child, and I wondered if Sarah-Jane's own daughters or step-daughters bad ever stood before this case or the other, gazing wistfully at what they could never themselves possess.*

*Sarah-Jane re-entered bearing a large tray on which she'd assembled an ornate silver coffee pot with a matching sugar bowl and cream jug. She'd accompanied this with porcelain coffee cups, small coffee spoons, and a plate of ginger biscuits that were, she confided, 'Home made, just this morning.' Unaccountably, I found myself wondering how Libby would react to all this: to the dolls, to the coffee presentation, to Sarah-Jane Beckett Hamilton herself, and most of all to what she had said so far and what she had avoided saying.*

*On a coffee table, she set down the tray and did the pouring. She said, 'I was less than charitable about Katja's manner of dress just now. I do that sometimes. You must forgive me. I spend so much time alone—Perry travels, as I've said, and the girls are at school, of course—that I forget to monitor my tongue on the odd occasion when someone comes to call. What I should have said was that she had no experience with fashion or colour or design, having grown up in East Germany. And what would one actually expect from someone from an eastern bloc country, haute couture? So it was admirable, really, that she even had the ambition to go to college and learn fashion design. It was just unfortunate—it was tragic, really—that she brought both her dreams and her inexperience with children into your parents' home. That was a deadly combination. Sugar? Milk?'*

*I took the cup from her. I was not about to be sidetracked into a discussion of Katja Wolff's clothes. I said, 'Did Dad know that she was derelict in her duties towards Sonia?'*

*Sarah-Jane took up her own cup and stirred the coffee although she'd put nothing in it to require stirring. 'Your mother would have told him, naturally.'*

*'But you didn't.'*

*'Having reported to one parent, I didn't think it would be necessary to report it to the other. And your mother was more often in the house, Gideon. Your father was rarely about as he had more than one job, as you may recall. Have a ginger biscuit. Do you still have a fondness for sweets? How funny. I've just recalled that Katja had a real passion for them. For chocolates, especially. Well, I suppose that comes of growing up in an eastern bloc country as well. Deprivation.'*

*'Had she any other passions?'*

*'Any other . . . ?' Sarah-Jane looked perplexed.*

*'I know she was pregnant, and I've remembered seeing her in the garden with a man. I couldn't see him clearly, but I could tell what they were doing. Raphael says it was James Pitchford, the lodger.'*

*'I hardly think so!' Sarah-Jane protested. 'James and Katja? Heavens!' Then she laughed. 'James Pitchford wasn't involved with Katja. What would make you think that? He helped her with her English, it's true, but apart from that . . . Well, James always had something of an air of indifference towards women, Gideon. One was forced to wonder about his . . . if I might say it . . . his sexual orientation at the*

75

end of the day. No, no. Katja wouldn't have been involved with James Pitchford.' She took up another ginger biscuit. 'One naturally tends to think that when a group of adults live under one roof and when one of the female adults becomes pregnant, another of the cohabitants must be the father. I suppose it's logical, but in this case . . . ? It wasn't James. It couldn't have been your grandfather. And who else is there? Well, Raphael, of course. He could have been the pot calling the kettle black when he named James Pitchford.'

'What about my father?'

She looked disconcerted. 'You can't possibly think your father and Katja . . . Certainly you would have recognised your own father had he been the man you saw with her, Gideon. And even if you hadn't recognised him for some reason, he was completely devoted to your mother.'

'But the fact that they separated within two years after Sonia died . . .'

'That had to do with the death itself, with your mother's inability to cope afterwards. She went into a very black period after your sister was murdered—well, what mother wouldn't?—and she never pulled herself out of it. No. You mustn't think ill of your father on any account. I won't hear of that.'

'But when she wouldn't name the father of her child . . . when she wouldn't talk at all about anything to do with my sister—'

'Gideon, listen to me.' Sarah-Jane set down her coffee, placing the remainder of her biscuit on the saucer's edge. 'Your father might have admired Katja Wolff's physical beauty as all men did. He might have spent the odd hour now and again alone with her. He might have chuckled fondly at her mistakes in

English, and he might have bought her a gift at Christmas and two on her birthday . . . But none of that means he was her lover. You must drive that idea straight from your mind.'

'Yet not to talk to anyone . . . I know Katja Wolff never said a word about anything, and that doesn't make sense.'

'To us, no. It doesn't,' Sarah-Jane agreed. 'But you must remember that Katja was headstrong. I've little doubt that she'd got it into her mind that she could say nothing and all would be well. To her way of thinking—and coming from a communist country where criminal science isn't what it is in England how could she think otherwise?—what evidence had they that couldn't be argued away? She could claim to have been called to the telephone briefly—although why she would claim something that could be so easily disproved is far beyond me—with a tragic accident being the result. How was she to know what else would become public that, taken in conjunction with Sonia's death, would serve to prove her guilt?'

'What else did become public? Beyond the pregnancy and the lie about the phone call and the row she'd had with my parents. What else?'

'Aside from the other, healed injuries to your sister? Well, there was her character, for one thing. Her callous disregard for her own family in East Germany. What happened to them as a result of her escape. Someone did some digging round in Germany after her arrest. It was in the papers. Don't you recall?' She took up her cup again and poured herself more coffee. She didn't notice that I had not yet touched mine. 'But no. You wouldn't have done, would you? Every effort was made never to talk about the case in front of you, and I doubt you saw the

77

papers, so how would you remember—or even know in the first place—that her family had been tracked down—God knows how although the East Germans were probably happy to offer the information as a caveat for anyone who might think of escaping . . .'

'What happened to them?' I pressed.

'Her parents lost their jobs, and her siblings their university places. And had Katja shed a single tear about any of her family while she was in Kensington Square? Had she tried to contact them or help them? No. She never even mentioned them. They might not have existed for her.'

'Did she have friends, then?'

'Hmmm. There was that fat girl who always had her mind in the gutter. I remember her last name— Waddington—because it reminded me of waddle which is how she walked.'

'Was that a girl called Katie?'

'Yes. Yes, that was it. Katie Waddington. Katja knew her from the convent and when she moved in with your parents, this Waddington—Katie—hung about quite regularly. Usually eating something—well, just consider her size—and always going on about Freud. And sex. She was obsessed with sex. With Freud and sex. With sex and Freud. The significance of orgasm, the resolution of the Oedipal drama, the gratification of childhood's unfulfilled and forbidden wishes, the rôle of sex as a catalyst for change, the sexual enslavement of women by men and men by women . . .' Sarah-Jane leaned forward and took up the coffee pot, smiling at me and saying, 'Another? Oh, but you haven't touched a drop yet, have you? Here, then. Let me pour you a fresh one.'

And before I could reply, she snatched up my coffee cup and disappeared into the kitchen, leaving

78

*me with my thoughts: about celebrity and the abrupt loss of it, about the destruction of immediate family, about the possession of dreams and the crucial ability to delay the immediate fulfilment of those dreams, about physical beauty and the lack thereof, about lying out of malice and telling the truth for the very same reason.*

*When Sarah-Jane came into the room, I had my question ready. 'What happened the night my sister died? I remember this: I remember the emergency people arriving, the paramedics or whoever they were. I remember us—you and me—in my bedroom while they were working on Sonia. I remember people crying. I think I remember Katja's voice. But that's all. What actually happened?'*

*'Surely your father can give you a far better answer to that than I. You've asked him, I take it?'*

*'It's difficult for him to talk about that time.'*

*'Naturally, it would be . . . But as for me . . .' She fingered her pearls. 'Sugar? Milk? You must try my coffee.' And when I obliged her by raising the bitter brew to my mouth, she said, 'I can't add much, I'm afraid. I was in my room when it happened. I'd been preparing your lessons for the following day and I'd just popped into James's room to ask him to help me devise a scheme that would get you interested in weights and measures. Since he was a man—well, is a man, assuming he's still alive and there's certainly no reason to assume otherwise, is there?—I thought he'd be able to suggest some activity that would intrigue a little boy who was—' And here she winked at me—'not always cooperative when it came to learning something he thought was unrelated to his music. So James and I were going over some ideas when we heard the commotion downstairs: shouting and*

pounding feet and doors slamming We went running down and saw everyone in the corridor—'

'Everyone?'

'Yes. Everyone. Your mother, your father, Katja, Raphael Robson, your grandmother . . .'

'What about Granddad?'

'I don't . . . Well, he must have been there. Unless, of course, he was . . . well, out in the country for one of his rests? No, no, he must have been there, Gideon. Because there was such shouting going on, and I remember your grandfather as something of a shouter. At any rate, I was told to take you into your bedroom and stay with you there, so that's what I did. When the emergency services arrived, they told everyone else to get out of the way. Only your parents stayed. And we could still hear them from your room, you and I.'

'I don't remember any of it,' I said. Just the part in my room.'

'That's just as well, Gideon. You were a little boy. Seven? Eight?'

'Eight.'

'Well, how many of us have explicit, full memories even of good times from when we were children? And this was a terrible, shocking time. I dare say forgetting it was a blessing, dear.'

'You said you wouldn't leave. I remember that.'

'Of course I wouldn't have left you alone in the middle of what was going on!'

'No. I mean, you said that you wouldn't be leaving as my teacher. Dad told me he'd sacked you.'

She coloured at that, a deep crimson that was the child of her red hair, hair that was dyed to its original hue now that she was approaching fifty. 'There was a shortage of money, Gideon.' Her voice was fainter

80

*than it had been.*

*'Right. Sorry. I know. I didn't mean to imply . . .
Obviously, he wouldn't have kept you on till I was
sixteen if you'd been anything less than extraordinary
as my teacher.'*

*'Thank you.' Her reply was formal in the extreme.
Either she had been wounded by my words or she
wanted me to think so. And believe me, Dr Rose, I
could see how my believing I'd wounded her could
serve to direct the course of the conversation. But I
chose to eschew that direction, saying, 'What were
you doing before you asked James for his advice on
the weights and measures activity?'*

*'That evening? As I said, I was planning your
lessons for the following day.'*

*She didn't add the rest but her face told me she
knew I'd appended the information myself. She had
been alone in her room before she asked James to
help her.*

## CHAPTER FIFTEEN

The ringing forced Lynley to swim upwards, out of
a deep sleep. He opened his eyes into the darkness
of the bedroom and flailed out for the alarm clock,
cursing when he knocked it to the floor without
managing to silence it. Next to him, Helen didn't
stir. Even when he switched on the light, she
continued to sleep. That had long been her gift and
it remained so, even in pregnancy: She always slept
like an effigy in a Gothic cathedral.

He blinked, became semi-conscious, and
realised it was the phone and not the alarm. He

saw the time—three-forty in the morning—and knew that the news wasn't good.

Assistant Commissioner Sir David Hillier was on the line. He barked, 'Charing Cross Hospital. Malcolm's been hit by a car.'

Lynley said, 'What? Malcolm? What?'

Hillier said, 'Wake up, Inspector. Rub ice cubes over your face if necessary. Malcolm's in the operating theatre. Get down here. I want you on this. Now.'

'When? What's happened?'

'God damn bastard didn't even stop,' Hillier said, and his voice—uncharacteristically torn and sounding completely unlike the urbane and measured political tones that the AC usually employed at New Scotland Yard—illustrated the level of his concern.

*Hit by a car. Bastard didn't stop.* Lynley was instantly fully awake, as if a mixture of caffeine and adrenaline had been shot into his heart. He said, 'Where? When?'

'Charing Cross Hospital. Get down here, Lynley.' And Hillier rang off.

Lynley bolted from the bed and grabbed the first items of clothing that came to hand. He scrawled a note to his wife in lieu of waking her, giving her the bare details. He added the time and left the note on his pillow. Thrusting one arm into his overcoat, he went out into the night.

The earlier wind had died altogether, but the cold was unremitting and it had begun to rain. Lynley turned his coat collar up and jogged round the corner to the mews where he kept the Bentley in a locked garage.

He tried not to think about Hillier's terse

82

message or the tone with which it had been given. He didn't want to make an interpretation of the facts till he had the facts, but he couldn't stop himself from making the leap anyway. One hit and run. And now another.

Despite its narrowness and its daytime congestion, he assumed there would be little traffic on the King's Road at this time of night, so he headed directly for Sloane Square, coursed half way round the leaf-clogged fountain in its centre, and shot past Peter Jones where—in a bow to the growing commercialism of their society— Christmas decorations had long since been twinkling from its windows. He flew past the trendy shops of Chelsea, past the silent streets of dignified terraces. He saw a uniformed constable squatting to talk to a blanket-shrouded figure in the doorway of the town hall—the disenfranchised homeless yet another sign of their disparate times—but that was the only life he encountered beyond the few cars he passed on his flight towards Hammersmith.

Just short of King's College, he made a turn to the right, and he began to cut across and upwards to reach Lillie Road, which would take him closest to Charing Cross Hospital. When he zoomed into the car park and set off to casualty at a sprint, he finally allowed himself a look at his watch. It had been less than twenty minutes since he'd taken Hillier's call.

The AC—as unshaven and dishevelled as Lynley himself—was in the waiting area of the casualty ward, speaking tersely to a uniformed constable while three others clustered uneasily nearby. He caught sight of Lynley and flicked a finger at the uniform to dismiss him. As the constable rejoined his colleagues, Hillier strode to meet Lynley in the middle of the room.

Despite the hour, rain made casualty a busy place. Someone called out, 'Another ambulance coming from Earl's Court,' which suggested what the next five minutes were going to be like in the immediate vicinity, and Hillier took Lynley by the arm, leading him beyond casualty, down several corridors, and up several flights of stairs. He said nothing till they were in a private waiting area that served the families of those undergoing surgery in the operating theatre. No one else was there.

Lynley said, 'Where's Frances? She's not—'

'Randie phoned us,' Hillier cut in. 'Round one-fifteen.'

'Miranda? What happened?'

'Frances phoned her in Cambridge. Malcolm wasn't home. Frances'd gone to bed and she woke up with the dog barking outside in a frenzy. She found him in the front garden with the lead on his collar, but Malcolm not with him. She panicked, phoned Randie. Randie phoned us. By the time we got to Frances, the hospital had him in casualty and had rung her. Frances thought he'd had a heart attack while walking the dog. She still doesn't know . . .' Hillier blew out a breath. 'We couldn't get her out of the house. We got her to the door, even had it open, Laura on one arm and myself on the other. But the night air hit her and that was it. She got hysterical. The bloody dog went mad.' Hillier took out a handkerchief and passed it over his face. Lynley realised that this moment constituted the first time he'd seen the assistant commissioner even slightly undone.

He said, 'How bad is it?'

84

'They've gone into his brain to clear out a clot from beneath the skull fracture. There's swelling, so they're dealing with that as well. They're doing something with a monitor . . . I don't remember what. It's about the pressure. They do something with a monitor to keep note of the pressure. Do they put it in his brain? I don't know.' He shoved his handkerchief away, clearing his throat roughly. 'God,' he said and stared in front of him.

Lynley said, 'Sir . . . Can I get you a coffee?' and felt all the awkwardness of the offer as he spoke it. There were gallons of bad blood between himself and the assistant commissioner. Hillier had never made an effort to hide his antipathy for Lynley, and Lynley himself had never seen fit to disguise the disdain he felt for Hillier's rapacious pursuit of promotion. Seeing him like this, however, in an instance of vulnerability as Hillier confronted what had happened to his brother-in-law and friend of more than twenty-five years, painted Hillier in a different shade than previously. But Lynley wasn't sure what to do with the picture.

'They've said they're probably going to have to take out most of his spleen,' Hillier said. 'They think they can save the liver, perhaps half of it. But they don't know yet.'

'Is he still—'

'Uncle David!' Miranda Webberly's arrival broke into Lynley's question. She flew through the door to the waiting area, wearing a baggy track suit with her curly hair pulled back and held in place with a knotted scarf. She was bare of foot and white in the face. She had a set of car keys clutched in her hand. She made a beeline for her uncle's arms.

'You got someone to drive you?' he asked her.

'I borrowed a car from one of the girls. I drove myself.'

'Randie, I told you—'

'Uncle David.' And to Lynley, 'Have you seen him, Inspector?' And then back to her uncle without waiting for an answer, 'How is he? Where's Mum? She's not . . . ? Oh God. She wouldn't come, would she?' Miranda's eyes were bright liquid as she went on bitterly, saying, 'Of course not, of *course* not,' in a broken voice.

'Your aunt Laura's with her,' Hillier said. 'Come over here, Randie. Sit down. Where're your shoes?'

Miranda looked down at her feet blankly. 'God, I've come without them, Uncle David. How *is* he?'

Hillier told her what he'd told Lynley, everything except the fact that the accident was a hit and run. He was just reaching the part about attempting to save the superintendent's liver when a doctor in surgical garb pushed through the doorway, saying 'Webberly?' He surveyed all three of them with the bloodshot eyes of a man who wasn't bearing good news.

Hillier identified himself, introduced Randie and Lynley, put his arm round his niece, and said, 'What's happened?'

The surgeon said Webberly was in recovery and he'd go from there straight to intensive care where he would be kept in a chemically induced coma to rest the brain. Steroids would be used to ease the swelling there, barbiturates to render him unconscious. He'd be paralysed with muscle anaesthetics to keep him immobile until his brain recovered.

Randie seized upon the final word. 'So he'll be all right? Dad'll be all right?'

They didn't know, the surgeon told her. His condition was critical. With cerebral oedema, it was always touch and go. One had to be vigilant with the swelling, to keep the brain from pushing down on its stem.

'What about the liver and the spleen?' Hillier asked.

'We've saved what we could. There're several fractures as well, but those are secondary in comparison to the rest.'

'May I see him?' Randie asked.

'You're . . . ?'

'His daughter. He's my dad. May I see him?'

'No other next of kin?' This the doctor asked Hillier.

'She's ill,' Hillier said.

'Rotten luck,' was the reply. The surgeon nodded at Randie, saying, 'We'll let you know when he's out of recovery. It won't be for several hours, though. You'd be wise to get some rest.'

When he left, Randie turned to her uncle and Lynley, saying anxiously, 'He won't die. That means he won't die. That's what it means.'

'He's alive right now, and that's what counts,' her uncle told her, but he didn't say what Lynley knew he was thinking: Webberly might not die but he also might not recover, at least not to a degree that made him fit for something more than life as an invalid.

Without wanting it to happen, Lynley found himself thrust back in time to another head injury, and another bout of pressure on the brain. That had left his own friend Simon St James much in the state he was in today and the years that had passed since the man's long convalescence had not returned to him what Lynley's negligence had taken.

Hillier settled Randie on a PVC sofa where a discarded hospital blanket marked another anxious relative's vigil. He said, 'I'm going to fetch you some tea,' and he indicated to Lynley that he was to follow. Out in the corridor, Hillier paused. He said, 'You're acting superintendent till further notice. Put together a team to scour the city for the bastard that hit him.'

'I've been working on a case that—'

'Is there something wrong with your hearing?' Hillier cut in. 'Drop that case. I want you on this one. Use whatever resources you need. Report to me every morning. Clear? The uniforms below will put you in the picture of what we've got so far, which is sod bloody all in a basket. A driver going the opposite direction got a glimpse of the car, but it didn't register beyond something large like a limo or a taxi cab. He thought the roof might be grey, but you can discount that. The reflection of street lights would have made it look grey and when was the last time you saw a two-tone car?'

'Limo or taxi. Black vehicle, then,' Lynley said.

'I'm glad to see you haven't lost your remarkable powers of deduction.'

The jibe gave credence to how little Hillier actually wanted him involved in the case at hand. Hearing it, Lynley felt the old quick heat, felt his fingers draw inward to form a fist. But when he said, 'Why me?' he did his best to make the question sound polite.

'Because Malcolm would choose you if he were able to speak,' Hillier told him. 'And I intend to honour his wishes.'

'Then you think he won't make it.'

'I don't think anything.' But the tremor in Hillier's voice gave the lie to his words. 'So just get onto it. Drop what you're doing and get onto it now. Find this son of a bitch. Drag him in. There're houses along the road where he was hit. Someone out there has got to have seen something.'

'This may be related to what I'm working on already,' Lynley said.

'How the hell—'

'Hear me out, if you will.'

Hillier listened as Lynley sketched in the details of the hit and run two nights earlier. It was another black car, he explained, and there was a connection between Detective Superintendent Malcolm Webberly and the victim. Lynley didn't spell out the exact nature of their connection. He merely let it suffice that an investigation from two decades in the past might well be what lay behind the two hit and runs.

Hillier hadn't reached his level of command without his fair share of brains, however. He said incredulously, 'The mother of the child and the chief investigating officer? If this is connected, who the *hell* would wait two decades to go after them?'

'Someone who didn't know where they were till recently, I expect.'

'And you've someone likely among the group you're interviewing?'

'Yes,' Lynley said, after a moment's reflection. 'I believe we may have.'

\*       \*       \*

Yasmin Edwards sat on the edge of her son's bed

89

and curved her hand round his small perfect shoulder. 'C'me on, Danny. Time to get up.' She gave him a shake. 'Dan, di'n't you hear your alarm?'

Daniel scowled and burrowed further beneath the covers so that his bottom made an appealing hillock in the bed that caught at Yasmin's heart. He said, 'Jus' a more minute, Mum. Please. C'me on. Jus' a more minute.'

'No more minutes. They're adding up too fast. You'll be late for school. Or have to go without breakfast.'

'Tha's okay.'

'Not,' she told him. She smacked his bum, then blew in his ear. 'You don't get up, the kiss bugs're gonna go after you, lad.'

His lips curved in a smile although his eyes stayed closed. 'Won't,' he said. 'Got m' bug killer on.'

'Bug killer? I think not. You can't kill a kiss bug. Just you watch and see.'

She descended on him and planted kisses on his cheek, his ear, and his neck. She began to tickle him as she kissed him, until he finally came fully awake. He giggled, kicked, and fought her off half-heartedly, crying, 'Yech! No! Get them bugs off me, Mum!'

'Can't,' she said breathlessly. 'Oh m'God, there's *more*, Dan. There's bugs crawling everywhere. I don't know what to *do*.' She whipped back the covers and went for his stomach, crying, 'Kiss, kiss, kiss,' and revelling in what always seemed like the newness of her son's laughter despite the years that she'd been free. She'd had to teach him the kiss bug game all over again when she'd come out, and

90

they had a lot of kisses to recapture. For being the victim of kiss bugs wasn't the sort of hardship a child in care ever had to endure.

She lifted Daniel to a sitting position and rested him back against his *Star Trek* pillows. He caught his breath and ended his giggles, gazing at her with brown-eyed contentment. She felt her insides swelling and glowing when he looked at her like that. She said, 'So what's for Christmas hols, Dan? 'D you think about it like I told you?'

'Disney World!' he crowed. 'Orlando, Florida. We c'n go to the Magic Kingdom first and then the Epcot Center and after that Universal Studios. *Then* we can go to Miami Beach, Mum, and you c'n lay on the sand and I c'n surf in the sea.'

She smiled at him. 'Disney World, is it? Where'd we get the dosh for that? You planning to rob a bank?'

'I got money saved.'

'Do you? How much?'

'I got twenty-five pounds.'

'Not a bad start, but not quite enough.'

'Mum . . .' He gave that two syllable expression of a child's disappointment.

Yasmin hated to deny him anything after what the early years of his life had been like. She felt tugged in the direction of her son's desires. But she knew there was no sense in getting his hopes up— or her own for that matter—because there was more to consider than his will or hers when it came to how they were going to spend Daniel's Christmas holiday.

'What about Katja? She wouldn't be able to go with us, Dan. She'd have to stay behind and work.'

'So? Why can't you 'n me go, Mum? Just you 'n

91

me? Like before.'

'Because Katja's part of our family now. You know that.'

He scowled and turned away.

'She's out there making your breakfast, she is,' Yasmin said. 'She's doing those little Dutch pancakes you fancy.'

'She c'n do what she wants,' Daniel said.

'Hey, luv.' Yasmin bent over him. It was important to her that he understand. 'Katja belongs here. She's my partner. You know what that means.'

'Means we can't do *nothing* without her round, stupid cow.'

'Hey!' She tapped his cheek lightly. 'Don't talk nasty. Even if it was just you and me, Dan, we still couldn't go to Disney World. So don't you make Katja feel your disappointment, boy. I'm the one who's too short of money.'

'Why'd you ask me, then?' he demanded with the manipulative shrewdness of the eleven-year-old. ' 'F you knew we couldn't go in the first place, why'd you ask me where I want to go?'

'I asked you what you'd fancy *doing,* Dan. You changed it to where you'd fancy going.'

She'd caught him out and he knew it, and the miracle of her son was that somehow he'd escaped learning and liking to argue the way so many children his age argued. But still he was just a boy, without a full arsenal of weapons to fight off disappointment. So his face grew cloudy, he crossed his arms, and he settled into the bed for a sulk.

She touched his chin to lift his head. He resisted. She sighed and said, 'Someday we'll have more than we got right now. But you got to be patient. I love you. So does Katja.' She rose from his bed and went to the door. 'Up now, Dan. I want to hear you in that bathroom in twenty-two seconds.'

'I wan' to go t' Disney World,' he said stubbornly.

'Not half as much as I want to take you there.'

She gave the door jamb a thoughtful pat and went back to the room she shared with Katja. There, she sat on the edge of the bed and listened to the sounds in the flat: Daniel rising and toddling to the bathroom, Katja making those tiny Dutch pancakes in the kitchen, the sizzle of the batter as she plopped a small portion into the shell-shaped crevasse where the hot butter waited, the snip of cupboard doors opening and closing as she fetched the plates and the sugar, the click of the electric kettle switching off, and then her voice calling out, 'Daniel? There are pancakes this morning. Your favourite breakfast I've made.'

Why? Yasmin wondered. And she wanted to ask but to ask meant to question much more than the simple actions of blending the flour and milk, adding the yeast, and stirring the batter.

She brushed her hand along the bed, still unmade, that bore the impressions of their two bodies. The pillows still held the indentations of their heads, and the tangle of blankets and sheets together reflected the manner in which they slept: Katja's arms round her, Katja's warm hands cupping her breasts.

She'd pretended sleep when her partner had slid into bed. The room was dark—no light from a prison corridor *ever* cutting again through the black of a nighttime room in which Yasmin Edwards

93

lay—so she knew that Katja couldn't tell if her eyes were open or closed. She'd breathed, 'Yas?' but Yasmin hadn't answered. And when the covers shifted as she lifted them, as she slipped into the bed like a sailing boat docking so sleek and sure where it always docked, Yasmin made the sleep sounds of a woman only half roused from her dreams by the interruption, and she noted that Katja froze for an instant as if waiting to see how far into consciousness Yasmin would be able to come.

That moment of immobility had said something to Yasmin, but its full meaning was not entirely clear. So Yasmin turned to Katja as she drew the covers up to her shoulders. She said, 'Hey, baby,' in a sleepy murmur and eased her leg over Katja's hip. 'Where you been?'

'In the morning,' Katja whispered. 'There's too much to tell.'

'Too much? Why?'

'Sshh, now. Sleep.'

'Been wanting you here,' Yasmin murmured, and she tested Katja in spite of herself, knowing that she was testing her, but not knowing what she'd do with the results. She lifted her mouth for her lover's kiss. She slid her fingers to graze the soft hair of her bush. Katja returned the kiss as always and after a moment gently pushed Yasmin onto her back. She whispered deep in her throat, 'Crazy lipstick girl,' to which Yasmin replied, 'Crazy for you,' and heard Katja's breathy laugh.

What was to tell from making love in the darkness? What was to tell from mouths and fingers and lingering contact with sweet soft flesh? What could anyone learn from riding the current

94

till it flowed so fast that it no longer made a difference who was guiding the ship to the port just so long as it reached its destination? What the hell was there ever to be gained in the field of knowledge from that?

I should've switched on the light, Yasmin thought. I could tell for certain if I'd seen her face.

She told herself simultaneously that she had no doubts and that doubts were natural. She told herself that there was in life no single sure thing. But still she felt the hard knot of not knowing tighten inside her like a screw being turned by an unseen hand. Although she wanted to ignore it, she couldn't ignore it any more than she could have ignored a tumour that was threatening her life.

But she shook off these thoughts. The day ahead intruded. She rose from the edge of the bed and began to make it, telling herself that if the worst was true, there would be other opportunities to know it.

She joined Katja in the kitchen, where the air was sweet with the smell of the little Dutch pancakes that Daniel loved. Katja had made enough for all three of them, and they were mounded like snow-dashed cobblestones in a metal baking dish that stood keeping warm on the hob. She was adding to their breakfast something decidedly English: Several rashers of bacon were sizzling on the grill.

'Ah, here you are,' Katja said with a smile. 'Coffee's ready. Tea for Daniel. And where is our boy? Does he shower? This is new, yes? Is there a girl in his life?'

'Don't know,' Yasmin said. 'If there is, he hasn't said.'

'That will happen soon, Daniel and girls. Sooner than you think. Children now grow up so very fast. Have you talked to him yet? Life talk. You know.'

Yasmin poured herself a mug of coffee. 'Facts of life?' she asked. 'Daniel? You talking 'bout how babies get made?'

'It would be useful information if he yet knows nothing of the matter. Or would he have been told already? In the past, I mean.'

Carefully, Katja didn't say 'when he was in care', and Yasmin knew she would avoid voicing those words and invoking the memories attached to them. Katja's way had always been to move forward, making no reference to the past. 'How do you think I abide inside these walls?' she'd once said to Yasmin. 'By making plans. I consider the future and not the past.' And Yasmin, she'd gone on, would be wise if she followed that example. 'Know what you're going to do when you're out of here,' she'd insisted. 'Know exactly who you will be. Then make it happen. You can do that. But start making that person now, in here, while you have the chance to concentrate on her.'

And you? Yasmin thought in the kitchen as she watched her lover begin to scoop the pancakes onto their plates. What of you, Katja? What were your plans when you were inside and who was the person you wanted to be?

Katja had never said exactly, Yasmin realised now, just, 'There will be time when I am free.'

Time for who? Yasmin wondered. Time for what?

She'd never considered before what safety there was in imprisonment. The answers were simple when you were inside, and so were the questions.

96

In freedom, there were too many of both.

Katja turned from the cooker, one plate in her hand. 'Where *is* that boy? His pancakes will be like leather if he doesn't hurry.'

'He wants to go to Disney World for his Christmas hols,' Yasmin told her.

'Does he?' Katja smiled. 'Well, perhaps we can make that happen for him.'

'How?'

'There are ways and there are ways,' Katja said. 'He is a good boy, our Daniel. He should have what he wants. So should you.'

Here was the opening, so Yasmin took it at once, saying, 'And if I want you? If that's all I want?'

Katja laughed, placed Daniel's plate on the table, and came back to Yasmin. 'See how easy it is?' she said. 'You speak your wish, and it is granted at once.' She kissed her and went back to the cooker, calling out, 'Daniel! Your pancakes are ready for you now! You must come. Come!'

The doorbell buzzed and Yasmin glanced at the small chipped clock that stood on the cooker. Half past seven. Who the hell . . . ? She frowned.

Katja said, 'This is very early for a neighbour to call,' as Yasmin loosed and retied the obi on the scarlet kimono she wore as a dressing gown. 'I hope there is no trouble, Yas. Daniel has not played the truant, has he?'

'Better not have,' Yasmin said. She strode to the door and looked through its spy hole. She drew in a sharp breath when she saw who stood there, waiting patiently for someone to answer, or perhaps not so patiently because he reached out and pushed the bell once again. Katja had come to the kitchen door, pan in one hand and spatula in

97

the other. Yasmin said to her in a terse whisper, 'It's that damn bloody *copper*.'

'The black man from yesterday? Ah. Well. Let him in, Yas.'

'I don't want—'

He rang the bell again and as he did so, Daniel popped his head out of the bathroom, shouting, 'Mum! There's the door! You gonna get it or wha'?' without noticing her standing in front of it like a disobedient child avoiding castigation. When he saw her, he looked from his mother to Katja.

Katja said, 'Yas. Open the door.' And to Daniel, 'You've got pancakes waiting. Two dozen I've made you, just as you like them. Mum says you want Christmas at Disney World. Put your clothes on and tell me about it.'

'We're not going,' he said sullenly as the bell rang yet again.

'Ah. You know the future that well? Get dressed. We need to talk about this.'

'Why?'

'Because talking makes dreams more real. And when dreams are more real, they have a better chance of coming true. Yasmin, *mein Gott*, will you answer that door? He's heard us, that man. He plans to stay till you open.'

Yasmin did so. She jerked on the door so hard it nearly flew from her hand as behind her Daniel ducked into his bedroom and Katja returned to the kitchen. She said without preamble to the black constable, 'How'd you get up here, then? I don't recollect buzzing you into the lift.'

'Lift door was ajar,' DC Nkata said. 'I helped myself.'

'Why? What more you want with us, man?'

'A few words. 'S your . . .' He hesitated and looked beyond her, into the flat where the kitchen light made an oblong of yellow on the carpet squares in the sitting room where no other lights were yet lit. 'Katja Wolff here as well?'

'Half past seven in the morning, where'd you expect her to be?' Yasmin demanded, but she didn't like the expression on his face as she asked the question, so she hurried on. 'We told you everything there is to tell when you 'as here before. Another time through everything i'n't going to make no difference to what we already said.'

'This's something new,' he told her evenly. 'This's something else.'

'Mum,' Dan called out from his bedroom, 'where's m' school jumper? Is it on the telly 'cause I can't find it with the rest—' His words trailed off as he left his bedroom in search of the piece of clothing. He was wearing his white shirt, his underpants and socks, and his hair still glistened with the water from his shower.

'Morning, Daniel,' the copper said to him with a nod and a smile. 'Getting ready for school?'

'Never you mind what he's gettin' ready for,' Yasmin snapped before Daniel could answer. And then to her son as she snatched his jumper from one of the hooks next to the door, 'Dan, mind you see to that breakfast. Those pancakes're dead trouble to make. See you eat them all.'

' 'lo,' Daniel said shyly to the cop, and he looked so pleased that Yasmin's insides quaked. 'You 'membered my name.'

'Did,' Nkata said agreeably. 'Mine's Winston, it is. You like school, Daniel?'

'Dan!' Yasmin spoke so sharply that her son

jumped. She tossed him his sweater. 'You heard me, right? Get dressed and get yourself into that breakfast!'

Daniel nodded. But he didn't take his eyes from the cop. Instead he *drank* him in, with such unabashed interest and eagerness to know and be known that Yasmin wanted to step between them, to shove her son in one direction and the copper in another. Daniel backed into his bedroom, gaze still on Nkata, saying, 'You like pancakes? They're little ones. They're special. I 'xpect we got enough to—'

'Daniel!'

'Right. Sorry, Mum.' And he flashed that smile—thirty thousand watts, it was—and disappeared into his room.

Yasmin turned to Nkata. She was suddenly aware of how cold the air was coming in the door, how it swept insidiously round her bare legs and bare feet, how it tickled her knees and caressed her thighs, how it hardened her nipples. The very *fact* of their hardness was an irritant to her, making her vulnerable to her own body. She shivered in the chill, undecided about slamming the door upon the detective or allowing him in.

Katja made the decision for her. She said quietly, 'Let him in, Yas,' from the kitchen doorway where she stood with the pan of pancakes in her hand.

Yasmin stepped back as the constable gave a nod of thanks to Katja. She shoved the door shut and reached for her coat, taking it from its hook and cinching it so tightly round her waist that it might have been a corset and she a Victorian lady with an hour glass figure on her mind. For his part, Nkata unbuttoned his own overcoat and loosened his scarf like a guest come to dinner.

'We are having our breakfast,' Katja said to him. 'And Daniel must not be late for school.'

'What d'you want, then?' Yasmin demanded of the detective.

'Want to see if you'd like to change anything you told me 'bout the other night.' He spoke to Katja.

'I have no change to make,' Katja said.

'Tha's something you might want to think over,' he told her.

Yasmin flared, her anger and fear triumphing over her better judgement. She cried, 'This is harassment, this is. This is *harassment*. This is *bloody* harassment and you *bloody* well know it.'

'Yas,' Katja said. She slid the pancake pan onto the hob just inside the kitchen door. She remained where she was, in its frame, and the light from the kitchen behind her cast her face into shadow, which was where she kept it. 'Let him have his say.'

'We heard his say once.'

'I expect there's more, don't you?'

'No.'

'Yas—'

'No! I bloody well don't intend to let some sodding nig-nog with a warrant card—'

'*Mummy!*' Daniel had come back into the room, dressed for school now, and on his face such an expression of horror that Yasmin wanted to pull the slur out of the air where it hung among them like a laughing bully, slapping her own face with far more power than it managed to slap the detective's.

She said abruptly, 'Eat your breakfast,' to her son. And to the copper, 'Have your say and get out.' For an awful moment, Daniel didn't move, as if waiting for direction from the detective, such as the black man's permission to do what his mother had just told him to do. Seeing this, Yasmin wanted to strike someone, but instead she breathed and tried to still her heart's vicious pounding. She said, 'Dan,' and her son moved to the kitchen, pushing past Katja who told him, 'There's juice in the fridge, Daniel,' as she stepped to one side.

None of them said anything till muted sounds from the kitchen told them Daniel was at least making an attempt to eat his breakfast despite what was going on. All three of them maintained the positions they'd taken when the policeman had first come into the flat, forming a triangle described by the front door, the kitchen, and the television set. Yasmin wanted to leave her spot and join her lover, but just when she made her first move to do so, the detective spoke and his words were what stopped her.

'Things don't look nice when a story gets changed too far down the line, Miss Wolff. You sure you were watching telly th' other night? That boy goin' t'say the same 'f I ask him?'

'You leave Daniel alone!' Yasmin cried. 'You don't talk to my boy!'

'Yas,' Katja said, her voice quiet but insistent. 'Have your breakfast, all right? It seems the detective wishes to speak to me.'

'I won't leave you talking to this bloke alone. You *know* what cops do. You know how they are. You can't trust them with anything but—'

'The facts,' Nkata broke into her words. 'And you c'n trust us with the facts just fine. So 'bout the other night . . . ?'

'I have nothing to add.'

'Right. Then what about last night, Miss Wolff?'

Yasmin saw Katja's face alter at this question, just round the eyes which narrowed perceptibly. 'What about last night?'

'You watching telly like before?'

'Why d'you want to know?' Yasmin asked. 'Katja, you don't tell him *anything* till he says why he's asking you. He's not going to trick us. He's going to tell us why he's asking what he's asking or he's going to get his big black bum and his cut up mug right *out* of my flat. That clear to you, mister?'

'We got us another hit and run,' Nkata said to Katja. 'You want to tell me where you were last night?'

Bells and alarms went off in Yasmin's head, so she very nearly didn't hear Katja say, 'Here.'

'Round half past eleven?'

'Here,' she repeated.

'Got it,' he said and then he added what Yasmin realised he'd been meaning to say from the moment she opened the door to him, 'So you didn't spend the whole night with her, then. You just met her, shagged her, and went on your way. That how it happened?'

There was a horrible silence, broken by nothing but the voice inside Yasmin's head shouting, 'No!' She willed her partner to answer in some way, not to use silence and not to walk off.

Katja looked at Yasmin when she said to the copper, 'I don't know what you're talking about.'

'I'm talking 'bout a trip 'cross South London by bus last evening after work,' the detective said. 'I'm talking 'bout ending up in Putney at Frère Jacques Bar. 'Bout walking down to Wandsworth to Number Fifty-five Galveston Road. I'm talking 'bout what went on inside and who it went on with.

103

This sounding familiar to you? Or were you still watching the telly last night? 'Cause if what I saw's any indication, if the telly was on, you two had your eyes glued elsewhere.'

'You followed me,' Katja said carefully.

'You and the lady in black. That's right. White lady in black,' he added for good measure and he cast a quick look at Yasmin as he said it. 'Keep the lights off next time you do something interesting in front of the windows, Miss Wolff.'

Yasmin felt wild birds fluttering in front of her face. She wanted to wave her arms to frighten them off but her arms wouldn't move. *White lady in black* was all she heard. *Keep the lights off next time.*

Katja said, 'I see. You've done your work well. You followed me—high marks for that. Then you followed us together—higher marks still. But had you lingered, which you obviously did not, you would have seen us leave within a quarter of an hour. And while this is no doubt the time you yourself would devote to doing something interesting—as you call it, Constable—Yasmin will confirm that I am a woman who takes rather longer when it comes to giving pleasure.'

Nkata looked nonplussed, and Yasmin revelled in that look, as much as she revelled in Katja's seizing upon the advantage that she'd just gained by saying, 'Had you done your homework more thoroughly, you would have discovered that the woman I met at Frère Jacques was my solicitor, Constable Nkata. She's called Harriet Lewis and if you require her phone number to confirm my story, I shall give it to you.'

'And Number Fifty-five Galveston Road?' he said.

'What about it?'

'Who lives there that you and—' His hesitation and the emphasis he placed on the word told them he'd be checking her story—'your *solicitor* went calling on last night, Miss Wolff?'

'Her partner. And if you ask what I was consulting them about, I shall have to tell you it's a privileged matter, which is what Harriet Lewis will tell you herself when you phone her to confirm my story.' Katja strode across the small sitting room to the sofa where her shoulder bag lay against a faded tapestry pillow. She switched on a light and dispelled the morning gloom. She took out a packet of fags and lit one as she rooted in her bag for something else. This turned out to be a business card, which she brought over to Nkata and extended to him. She was the personification of calm, drawing in on the fag and sending a plume of smoke towards the ceiling as she said, 'Phone her. And if there is nothing else you wish to learn from us this morning, we have our own breakfast to eat.'

Nkata took the card and, his eyes on Katja as if they'd pin her to the spot she stood on, he put it in the breast pocket of his coat, saying, 'You best hope she matches you A to Z. 'Cause if she doesn't—'

Yasmin cut in. 'That all you want, then? 'Cause if it is, time for you to fuck off.'

Nkata moved his glance to her. 'You know where to find me,' he said.

'Like I'd want to?' Yasmin laughed. She jerked the door open and didn't look at him as he left. She slammed the door behind him as Daniel called out, 'Mummy?' from the kitchen.

She called back, 'Be there in a moment, luv. You

keep on with the pancakes.'

'Don't forget that bacon as well,' Katja said.

But as they spoke to Daniel, they looked at each other. They looked long and unwavering as each waited for the other to say what needed to be said.

'You didn't tell me you'd be meeting Harriet Lewis,' Yasmin said.

Katja lifted her cigarette to her mouth and took her time about inhaling. She finally said, 'There are matters to be dealt with. There are twenty years of matters to be dealt with. This will take time for us to work through.'

'What d'you mean? What kind of matters? Katja, you in trouble or something?'

'There is trouble, yes. But it is not mine. Just something that needs to be resolved.'

'What? What needs—'

'Yas. It is late.' Katja rose and ground out her cigarette in an ashtray on the coffee table. 'We must work. I cannot explain everything right now. The situation is far too complex.'

Yasmin wanted to say, 'And that's why it took so long to discuss it? Last night, Katja? Because the situation—whatever it is—is too complex?' but she didn't say it. She placed the question in the mental file that held all the other questions she'd not yet asked. Like the questions about Katja's absences from work, the questions about her absences from home, the questions about where she took the car when she borrowed it and why she needed to borrow it in the first place. If she and Katja were to establish something lasting—a connection to each other outside prison walls that was not defined by the need to maintain a bulwark against loneliness, despair, and depression—then they were going to

106

have to start dispelling doubt. All her questions grew from doubt, and doubt was the virulent disease that could destroy them.

To drive it from her mind, she thought of her first days in Holloway on remand, of the medical unit where she was watched for signs that her despondency would lead to derangement, of the humiliation of the initial strip search 'Let's have a look up the grumble and grunt, Missy'—and of every strip search that followed it, of stuffing envelopes endlessly mindlessly in what went for rehabilitation in prison, of anger so deep and so profound that she thought it might eat its way into her bones. And she thought of Katja as Katja had been in those first few days and all through her trial, watching her from a distance but never speaking till Yasmin demanded what she wanted one day over tea in the dining room where Katja sat alone as she always sat, a baby killer, the worst sort of monster: one who did not repent.

'Don't mess with Geraldine,' she had been told. 'That kraut bitch's just *waiting* for a good sorting out.'

But she'd asked anyway. She'd sat at the German's table, slamming down her tea tray and saying, 'What you *want* with me, bitch? You been watching me like I'm next week's dinner ever since I walked in here, and I'm dead sick of it. You got that straight?' She'd tried to sound tough. She knew without ever having been told that the key to survival behind walls and locked doors was never to show a sign of weakness.

'There are ways to cope,' Katja had told her in answer. 'But you will not manage if you do not submit.'

'Sub*mit* to these fuckers?' Yasmin had shoved her own cup away so hard that tea sloshed out and soaked the paper napkin with milky brown blood. 'I don't *belong* in here. I 'as defending my life.'

'And that is what you do when you submit. You defend your life. Not the life inside here but the life to come.'

'What sort 'f life *that's* going to be? I get out of here, my baby won't know me. You know how that feels?'

And Katja had known, though she never spoke of the child she herself had given up on the day he was born. The miracle of Katja as Yasmin came to know her was that she knew how *everything* felt: from the loss of freedom to the loss of a child, from being tricked into trusting the wrong people to learning that only the self would stand steadfast. It was on the foundation of Katja's understanding that they'd put the first tentative stones of their association with each other. And during the time they spent together, Katja Wolff—who had been in prison ten years when Yasmin encountered her—and Yasmin developed a plan for their lives when they were finally released.

Revenge hadn't been part of the plan for either of them. Indeed, the word vengeance hadn't crossed their lips. But now Yasmin wondered what Katja had meant all those years ago when she'd said, 'I am owed', while imprisoned, without ever giving an explanation of what the debt was or who was to pay it.

She couldn't bring herself to ask where her lover had gone last night when she left that house in Galveston Road in the company of her solicitor, Harriet Lewis. The thought of the Katja who had counselled her, who had listened to and loved her throughout her sentence was what kept Yasmin's every doubt in check.

But still, she couldn't shake off the memory of that moment when Katja had frozen in the act of getting into bed. She couldn't dismiss what that abrupt stillness in her lover meant. So she said, 'I di'n't know Harriet Lewis had a partner.'

Katja looked away from her at the window where the curtains were closed upon the growing daylight. She said, 'Funny enough, Yas. Neither did I.'

'Think she'll be able to help you, then? Help with what you're trying to sort out?'

'Yes. Yes, I hope she will help me. That would be good, wouldn't it: to put an end to the struggle.'

And then Katja stood there, waiting for more, waiting to hear the scores of questions that Yasmin Edwards could not bear to ask her.

When Yasmin said nothing, Katja finally nodded as if she herself had asked something and received a reply. 'Things are being taken care of,' she said. 'I'll be home straight after work tonight.'

## CHAPTER SIXTEEN

Barbara Havers got word of Webberly's condition at seven forty-five that morning when the superintendent's secretary phoned her as she was towelling herself dry from her wake-up shower. Upon instruction from DI Lynley who'd been given the rank of acting superintendent, Barbara was told, Dorothea Harriman was ringing every detective under Webberly's command. She had little time to chat, so she was sparing with the details: Webberly was in Charing Cross Hospital, his condition was critical, he was in a coma, he'd been hit by a car late last night while walking his dog.

'Bloody hell, Dee,' Barbara cried. 'Hit by a *car*? How? Where? Will he . . . ? Is he going to . . . ?'

Harriman's voice grew tight, which told Barbara all she needed to know about the effort that Webberly's secretary was making to sound professional in the midst of her own concern for the man she'd worked for for nearly a decade. 'That's all I know, Detective Constable. The Hammersmith police are investigating.'

Barbara said, 'Dee, what the hell happened?'

'A hit and run.'

Barbara grew dizzy. At the same time, she felt the hand that held the telephone receiver turn numb, as if it were no longer part of her body. She rang off in a deadened state, and she dressed herself with even less regard than she normally gave to her appearance. Indeed, it wouldn't be until much later in the day that she'd glance in the mirror while making a visit to the ladies' toilet and discover that she'd donned pink socks, green stirrup trousers with sagging knees, and a faded purple T-shirt on which were printed the words 'The truth ISN'T out there, it's under here' rendered in ornate Gothic script. She crammed a Pop Tart into the toaster, and while it was heating, she dried her hair and smeared two blobs of fuchsia tinted lipstick on her cheeks to give some colour to her face. Pop Tart in hand, she gathered her belongings, grabbed her car keys, and dashed

110

outside to set off into the morning . . . without coat, scarf, or the least idea of where she was supposed to be going.

The cold air brought her abruptly to her senses six steps from her own front door. She said, 'Hang on, Barb,' and scurried back to her bungalow where she forced herself to sit at the table which she used for dining, ironing, working, and preparing most of what went for her daily dinners. She fired up a fag and told herself that she had to calm down if she was going to be any use to anyone. If Webberly's misfortune and the murder of Eugenie Davies were connected, she wasn't going to be able to assist in the inquiry if she continued to run round like a clockwork mouse.

And there *was* a connection between the two events. She was willing to bet her career on that.

She had achieved very little joy from her second trip to the Valley of Kings and the Comfort Inn on the previous evening, learning only that J.W. Pitchley was a regular at both establishments, but so much a regular that neither the waiters at the restaurant nor the night clerk at the hotel had been able to say with certainty that he'd been there on the night Eugenie Davies had been murdered.

'Oh my yes, this gentleman has a way with the ladies,' the night clerk had commented as he examined Pitchley's photograph over the sound of Major James Bellamy and his wife having a set-to in an ancient episode of *Upstairs, Downstairs* that was playing nearby on a VCR. The night clerk had paused, had watched the unfolding drama for a moment, had shaken his head and sighed, 'It will never last, that marriage,' before turning to Barbara, handing back the photograph she'd snagged in West Hampstead, and going on. 'He brings them here often, these ladies of his. He always pays cash and the lady waits over there, out of sight in the lounge. This is so I will neither see her nor suspect that they intend to use the room for a few hours only, for sexual congress. He has been here many many times, this man.'

And it was much the same at the Valley of Kings. J.W. Pitchley had eaten his way through the entire menu at the restaurant and the waiters could account for everything he'd ordered in the last five months. But as to his companions . . . ? They were blonde, brunette, red headed, and grey haired. And all of them were English, naturally. What else would one expect of such a decadent culture?

Flashing the photo of Eugenie Davies in the company of the photo of J.W. Pitchley had got Barbara exactly nowhere. Ah yes, she was another Englishwoman, wasn't she? both the waiters and the night clerk had asked. Yes, she might have been with him one night. But she might not. It was the gentleman, you see, who interested everyone: How did such an ordinary man have such an extraordinary way with ladies?

'Any port in a storm,' Barbara had muttered in reply, 'if you know what I mean.'

They hadn't known and she hadn't explained. She'd just gone home, deciding to bide her time till St Catherine's opened in the morning.

*That* was what she was supposed to be doing, Barbara realised as she sat at her little dining table, smoked, and hoped that the nicotine would rattle her brain into operation. There was something not right about J.W. Pitchley, and if his address in the possession of the dead woman hadn't told her that

112

much, then the thugs leaping out of his kitchen window and the cheque he'd been writing—to one of them, surely—did.

She could do nothing to improve the condition of Superintendent Webberly. But she could pursue her intended course, looking for whatever it was that J.W. Pitchley was trying to hide. What that was might well be what tied him to murder and tied him to the attack on Webberly. And if that was the case, she wanted to be the person who brought the bugger down. She owed that much to the superintendent because she owed Malcolm Webberly more than she could ever repay.

With more calm this time, she rustled her donkey jacket from the wardrobe, along with a tartan scarf that she wound round her neck. More appropriately garbed for the November chill, she set out again into the cold, damp morning.

She had a wait before St. Catherine's opened, and she used the time to tuck into a hot bacon and mushroom sandwich in the sort of fine, fried-bread-serving old caff that was fast disappearing from the metropolis. After that, she phoned Charing Cross Hospital, where she got word that Webberly's condition remained unchanged. She phoned Inspector Lynley next, getting him on his mobile on his way to the Yard. He'd been at the hospital till six, he told her, at which time it had become clear that hanging round in the intensive care waiting room was only going to rub his nerves raw while doing nothing to improve the superintendent's condition.

'Hillier's there,' Lynley said abruptly, and those two words served as adequate explanation. AC Hillier wasn't a pleasant man to be around at the

113

best of times. At the worst of times, he'd likely be impossible.

'What about the rest of the family?' Barbara asked.

'Miranda's come down from Cambridge.'

'And Frances?'

'Laura Hillier's with her. At home.'

'At home?' Barbara frowned, going on to say, 'That's a bit odd, isn't it, sir?' to which Lynley said, 'Helen's taken some clothes over to the hospital. Some food as well. Randie came tearing up in such a hurry that she wasn't even wearing shoes, so Helen's taken her a pair of trainers. She'll phone me if there's any sudden change. Helen, that is.'

'Sir . . .' Barbara wondered at his reticence. There was ground to till here, and she meant to grab the hoe. She was a cop to her core, so—her suspicions about J.W. Pitchley aside for a moment—she couldn't help wondering whether Frances Webberly's absence from the scene might mean something that went beyond shock. Indeed, she couldn't help wondering if it meant something that indicated Frances's knowledge of her husband's past infidelity. She said, 'Sir, as to Frances herself, have you thought—'

'What are you on to this morning, Havers?'

'Sir . . .'

'What did you come up with on Pitchley?'

Lynley was making it more than clear that Frances Webberly was a subject he wasn't about to discuss with her, so Barbara filed her irritation—if only for the moment—and instead recounted what she'd discovered about Pitchley on the previous day: his suspicious behaviour, the presence in his home of two yobbos who'd climbed out of a kitchen

114

window rather than be confronted by her, the cheque he'd been writing, the confirmation of the night clerk and the waiters that Pitchley was indeed an habitué of the Comfort Inn and the Valley of Kings.

'So what I reckon is this: If he changed his name once because of a crime, what's to say he didn't change it before because of another?'

Lynley said that he thought it unlikely, but he gave Barbara the go-ahead. They would meet later at the Yard.

It didn't take too long for Barbara to troll through two decades of legal records in St Catherine's, since she knew what she was looking for. And what she finally found sent her to New Scotland Yard post haste, where she got on the blower to the station that served Tower Hamlets and spent an hour tracking down and talking to the only detective who'd spent his entire career there. His memory for detail and his possession of enough notes to write his memoirs several times over provided Barbara with the vein of gold she'd been seeking.

'Oh, right,' he drawled. 'That's not a name I'm likely to forget. The whole flaming lot of them've been giving us aggro's long as they've been walking the earth.'

'But as to the one . . .' Barbara said.

'I can spin a tale or two about *him*.'

She took notes from the detective's recitation and when she rang off, she went in search of Lynley.

She found him in his office, standing near the window, looking grave. He'd apparently been home between his early morning visit to the hospital and

115

coming to the Yard, because he looked as he always looked: perfectly groomed, well-shaven, and suitably dressed. The only sign that things were not normal was in his posture. He'd always stood like a man with a fence pole for a spine, but now he seemed slumped, as if carrying sacks of grain on his shoulders.

'The only thing Dee told me was a coma,' Barbara said by way of hello.

Lynley recounted for her the extent of the superintendent's injuries. He concluded with, 'The only blessing is that the car didn't actually run over him. The force he was hit with threw him into a pillar box, which was bad enough. But it could have been worse.'

'Were there any witnesses?'

'Just someone who saw a black vehicle tearing down Stamford Brook Road.'

'Like the car that hit Eugenie?'

'It was large,' Lynley said. 'According to the witness, it could have been a taxi. He thought it was painted in two tones, black with a grey roof. Hillier claims the grey would be the street lights' reflection on black.'

'Bugger Hillier for a lark,' Barbara scoffed. 'Taxis are painted all sorts of ways these days. Two tones, three tones, red and yellow, or covered tyres-to-top with advertisements. I say we should listen to what the witness says. And as we're talking about a black car once again, I expect we've got a connection, don't you?'

'With Eugenie Davies?' Lynley didn't wait for a reply. 'Yes. I'd say we've got a connection.' He gestured with a notebook he'd taken up from his desk and he put on his spectacles as he walked round to sit, nodding for Barbara to do likewise. 'But we've still got virtually nothing to go on, Havers. I've been reading through my notes trying to find *something,* and I'm not getting far. All I can come up with is a conflict among what Richard Davies, his son, and Ian Staines are saying about Eugenie's seeing Gideon. Staines claims she intended to ask Gideon for money to get him out of debt before he loses his house and everything in it, but he also says that she told him—after having made the promise to see her son—that something had come up and because of it, she wouldn't ask Gideon for the money. In the meantime, Richard Davies claims she hadn't asked to see Gideon at all, but just the opposite. He says he wanted her to try to help Gideon with a problem he's having with stage fright and that's why they were going to meet: at *his* suggestion. Gideon supports this claim, more or less. He says his mother never asked to see him, at least not that he was told. All he knows is that his father wanted them to meet so she could help him out with his playing.'

'She played the violin?' Barbara said. 'There wasn't one at the cottage in Henley.'

'Gideon didn't mean that she was going to tutor him. He said there was actually nothing she could do to help him with his problem, other than to "agree" with his father.'

'What's that supposed to mean when it's dancing the polka?'

'I don't know. But I'll tell you this: He doesn't have stage fright. There's something seriously wrong with the man.'

'Like a guilty conscience? Where was he three nights ago?'

'Home. Alone. So he says.' Lynley tossed his notebook on his desk and removed his glasses. 'And that doesn't even begin to address Eugenie Davies' e-mail, Barbara.' He brought her into the picture on that front, saying in conclusion, '*Jete* was the name tagged onto the message. Does that mean anything to you?'

'An acronym?' She considered the possible words that the four letters could begin, with *just* and *eat* coming to mind at once. She followed that thought along the family tree to its cousin, saying, 'Could be Pitchley branching out from his TongueMan handle?'

'What did you get from St Catherine's on him?' Lynley asked her.

'Gold,' she replied. 'St Catherine's confirms Pitchley's claim that he was James Pitchford twenty years ago.'

'How is that gold?'

'Because of what follows,' Barbara replied. 'Before he was Pitchford, he was someone else: He was Jimmy Pytches, sir, little Jimmy Pytches from Tower Hamlets. He changed his name to Pitchford six years before the murder in Kensington Square.'

'Unusual,' Lynley agreed, 'but hardly damning.'

'By itself, right. But when you put two name changes in one lifetime into the same basket as having two blokes jumping out of his kitchen window when the rozzers come to call, you've got something that smells like cod in the sun. So I rang the station over there and asked if anyone remembered a Jimmy Pytches.'

'And?' Lynley asked.

'And listen to this. The whole family're in and out of trouble all the time. Were back then. Still are

118

now. And when Pitchley was Jimmy Pytches all those years ago, a baby died while he was looking after her. He was a teenager at the time, and the investigation couldn't pin anything on him. The inquest finally called it cot death, but not before our Jimmy spent forty-eight hours being held and questioned as suspect number one. Here. Check my notes if you want to.'

Lynley did so, putting his reading glasses back on.

Barbara said, 'A second kid dying while he was in the same house,' as Lynley looked over the information. 'Not quite kosher, is it, sir?'

'If he did indeed murder Sonia Davies and if Katja Wolff carried the can for him,' Lynley began and Barbara interrupted with, 'Perhaps this is why she never said a word once she was arrested, sir. Say she and Pitchford had a thing—she was pregnant, right?—and when Sonia was drowned, they both knew that the cops would look hard at Pitchford because of the other death, once they found out who he really was. If they could play it out as an accident, as negligence—'

'Why would he have drowned the Davies girl?'

'Jealousy over what the family had and he hadn't got. Anger over how they were treating his beloved. He wants to rescue her from her situation, or he wants to get back at people he sees as having what he'll never put his mitts on, so he goes after the kid. Katja takes the fall for him, knowing about his past and thinking she'll get a year or two for negligence while he'd probably get life for premeditated murder. And she never once considers how a jury's going to react to her keeping silent about the death of a disabled toddler. And just think of what was

119

probably going through their heads: shades of Mengele and all that, Inspector, and *she* won't even say what happened. So the judge throws the book at her, she gets twenty years, and Pitchford disappears from her life, leaving her to rot in prison while he becomes Pitchley and makes a killing in the City.'

'And then what?' Lynley said. 'She gets out of prison and then what, Havers?'

'She tells Eugenie what really happened, who really did it. Eugenie tracks down Pitchley the way I tracked down Pytches. She goes to confront him, but she never makes it.'

'Because?'

'Because she gets it in the street.'

'I realise that. But from whom, Barbara?'

'I think Leach might be onto it, sir.'

'Pitchley? Why?'

'Katja Wolff wants justice. So does Eugenie. The only way to get it is to put Pitchley away, which I doubt he'd go for.'

Lynley shook his head. 'How do you explain Webberly, then?'

'I think you already know the answer to that.'

'Those letters?'

'It's time to hand them over. You've got to see they're important, Inspector.'

'Havers, they're more than ten years old. They're not an issue.'

'Wrong, wrong, *wrong*.' Barbara pulled on her sandy fringe in sheer frustration. 'Look. Say Pitchley and Eugenie had something going. Say *that's* the reason she was in his street the other night. Say he's been to Henley to see her on the sly and during a tryst he's come across those letters.

120

He's gone round the bend with jealousy, so he gives her the chop and then takes down the superintendent.'

Lynley shook his head. 'Barbara, you can't have it all ways. You're twisting the facts to fit a conclusion. But they don't fit it, and it doesn't fit the case.'

'Why not?'

'Because it leaves too much unaccounted for.' Lynley ticked off the items. 'How could Pitchley have maintained an affair with Eugenie Davies without Ted Wiley's knowledge since Wiley appears to have kept close tabs on the comings and goings at Doll Cottage? What did Eugenie have to confess to Wiley, and why did she die the night before the scheduled confession? Who is *Jete*? Who was she meeting at those pubs and hotels? And what do we do about the coincidence of Katja Wolff's release from prison and two hit and runs in which the victims are significant people in the case that put her away?'

Barbara sighed, her shoulders slumping. She said, 'Okay. Where's Winston? What's he got to say about Katja Wolff?'

Lynley told her about Nkata's report on the German woman's movements from Kennington to Wandsworth on the previous night. He ended with, 'He was confident that both Yasmin Edwards and Katja Wolff are hiding something. When he got the word about Webberly, he passed the message back that he wanted to have another chat with them.'

'So he thinks there's a connection between the hit and runs as well.'

'Right. And I agree. There *is* a connection, Havers. We just haven't seen it clearly.' Lynley

121

stood, handed Barbara her notes, and began gathering up material from his desk. He said, 'Let's get on to Hampstead. Leach's team must have something we can work with by now.'

*　　　*　　　*

Winston Nkata sat in front of the Hampstead police station for a good five minutes before he clambered out of his car. Because of a four car pile-up on the huge roundabout just before the crossing to Vauxhall Bridge, it had taken him more than ninety minutes to get from South London. He was glad of that. Sitting in the car while firemen, paramedics, and traffic police sorted out the tangle of metal and injured bodies had given him the time he needed to come to terms with the balls-up he'd made of his interview with Katja Wolff and Yasmin Edwards.

He'd cocked it up brilliantly. He'd shown his hand. He'd charged like a bull from the pen exactly sixty-seven minutes after opening his eyes that morning, galloping from his parents' flat to Kennington at the earliest hour he'd deemed reasonable. Snorting and pawing the ground, eager to lower his horns and attack, he'd ridden up in that creaking lift with a soaring sense of being about to break the case. And he'd gone to great lengths to assure himself that his mission to Kennington was indeed all about the case. Because if he could reveal Katja Wolff's little something on the side in such a way as to create a fissure in her and Yasmin's relationship, then what was to prevent Yasmin Edwards from admitting what he already knew in his bones to be true: that Katja

122

Wolff had not been home on the night of the murder of Eugenie Davies?

He intended nothing more than that, he'd told himself. He was just a cop carrying out his duties. Her flesh meant nothing: smooth and taut, the colour of newly minted pennies. Her body was of no account either: lithe and firm, with a waist dipping in over welcoming hips. Her eyes were only windows: dark like the shadows and trying to hide what they couldn't hide, which was anger and fear. And that anger and fear were meant to be used, to be used by him to whom she was nothing, just a dyke who'd chopped her husband one night and had taken up with a baby killer.

It wasn't his responsibility to sort out why Yasmin Edwards would bring that baby killer into her home where her own child lived, and Nkata knew it. But he did tell himself that, aside from providing them the break they needed in the investigation, it would also be for the best if the crack he was able to produce in the women's relationship led to a break-up that would take Daniel Edwards out of the reach of a convicted killer.

He shut his ears to the thought that the boy's own mother also was a convicted killer. After all, she'd struck out against an adult. There was nothing in her background to indicate she had it in for children.

So he was filled with the righteousness of his cause when he rang the buzzer at Yasmin Edwards' door. And when there was no answer at first, he merely used the lack of response as a spur. It dug into the sides of his reason for being there, and he rang again till he forced a reply.

123

Nkata was a man who'd encountered prejudice and hatred for most of his life. One couldn't be a member of a minority race in England and not be the recipient of hostility in a hundred subtle forms every day. Even at the Met, where he'd assumed performance counted for more than epidermal hue, he'd learned to watch himself, never allowing others in too close, never completely letting down his guard lest he pay the price of presuming that a familiarity of discourse meant an equality of mind. That was not the case, no matter how things looked to the uninitiated observer. And wise was the black man who remembered that.

Because of all this, Nkata had long thought himself incapable of the sort of judgement that he'd learned to experience at the hands of others. But after his morning interview in the Doddington Grove Estate, he'd learned that his vision was just as narrow and just as fully capable of leading him to ill-founded conclusions as was the vision of the most illiterate, badly dressed, and ill-spoken member of the National Front.

He'd seen them together. He'd seen the way they greeted each other, the way they talked together, the way they walked like a couple to Galveston Road. He'd known Wolff was a woman whose life partner was another woman. So when they'd gone into that house and shut the door, he'd allowed an embrace silhouetted against the window to provoke his imagination into running from its pen like an untamed pony. A lesbian meeting another woman and trotting off with her for seclusion together meant only one thing. So he had believed. So he had let his belief colour his second interview in Yasmin Edwards' flat.

Had he not known how thoroughly he'd cocked things up right then, he would have been informed soon enough when he phoned the number on the business card that Katja had handed him. Harriet Lewis herself confirmed the story: Yes, she was Katja Wolff's solicitor. Yes, she had been with her on the previous evening. Yes, they had gone to Galveston Road together.

'You leave after quarter of an hour?' Nkata asked her.

She said, 'What's this about, Constable?'

'What sort of business'd you engage in in Galveston Road?' he asked her.

'None that's any business of yours,' the solicitor had said, just as Katja Wolff promised she would.

'How long's she been a client of yours?' he tried next.

'Our conversation is over,' she'd said. 'I work for Miss Wolff, not for you.'

So he was left with nothing except the knowledge that he'd done everything wrong and that he'd have to explain himself to the one person he sought to emulate: DI Lynley. And when the traffic snarled up near Vauxhall Bridge, then stopped altogether as sirens blared and lights flashed up ahead, he was grateful not only for the diversion a smash-up provided but also for the time he would be handed to decide how to tell the tale of the last twelve hours.

Now, he looked at the front of the Hampstead police station and forced himself out of his car. He walked inside, showed his ID, and trudged to do the penance his actions called for.

He found everyone in the incident room, where the morning meeting was just breaking up. The

125

china board was filled with the day's list of actions and the men and women assigned to them, but the hush among the constables leaving told Nkata that they'd been informed about what had happened to Webberly.

DI Lynley and Barbara Havers remained behind, comparing two computer sheets. Nkata joined them, saying, 'Sorry. Pile-up at Vauxhall Bridge,' to which Lynley replied, looking up over his spectacles, 'Ah. Winston. How did it go?'

'Couldn't shake either one of them from what they'd already said.'

'Damn,' Barb muttered.

'Did you speak to Edwards alone?' Lynley asked.

'Didn't need to. Wolff was meeting with her solicitor, 'Spector. That's who the bird was. Solicitor confirmed when I rang her.' He didn't add more, but his face must have shown something of his chagrin because Lynley examined him a long moment during which Nkata felt all the misery of a child who's displeased his parent.

'You sounded quite sure when we spoke,' Lynley remarked, 'and when you're feeling sure, you're usually right. Are you certain you spoke to the solicitor, Winnie? Wolff could have given you the number of a friend to play the rôle of solicitor when you rang her.'

'She gave me her business card,' Nkata said. 'And what solicitor of your acquaintance's going to lie for a client when the answer the cops want is either yes or no? But I still think the women are hiding something. I just went at it wrong to suss out what it is.' And then because his admiration for Lynley would always override his need to look good in the inspector's eyes, he added, 'But I cocked it

126

up with my whole approach. Whoever talks to them next, better not be me.'

Barbara Havers said supportively, 'Well, God knows I've done that more than once, Winnie,' and Nkata shot her a grateful look. She *had* cocked up and it had cost her a suspension from duty, her previous rank, and probably the chance to rise in the Met. But she'd at least brought down a killer by the end of that case, while he'd done nothing more than complicate matters.

Lynley said, 'Yes. Well. Haven't we all. No matter, Winston. We'll sort things out,' although he did sound disappointed to Nkata's ears, which wasn't half of what his own mum was going to sound when he told *her* what had happened.

'Jewel,' she'd say, 'what were you *thinking,* son?'

And that was a question he preferred not to answer.

He brought himself round to listening to the update he'd missed from the morning's briefing. The BT records from Eugenie Davies' phone had been matched up with names and addresses. And the callers on her answer machine had likewise been identified. The woman who named herself Lynn had emerged as one Lynn Davies—

'A relation?' Nkata asked.

'Still to be discovered.'

—with an address that put her close to East Dulwich.

'Havers will handle that interview,' Lynley said. He went on to report that the unidentified male caller on the answer machine who'd angrily demanded that Mrs Davies pick up the phone and talk to him was one Raphael Robson, whose address in Gospel Oak put him closer to the scene

127

of the murder than anyone else, other than J.W. Pitchley, of course. 'I'll take on Robson next,' Lynley went on, and he added to Nkata, 'I'd like you there as well,' as if already knowing that he would need to bolster Nkata's faltering sense of competence.

Nkata said, 'Right,' as Lynley went on to explain that the BT records had also confirmed Richard Davies' story of phone calls taken from and made to his former wife. They'd begun in early August, round the time that their son had had his problem at Wigmore Hall and they'd continued up to the morning before Eugenie Davies' death when Davies had made a brief call to her. There were plenty of calls from Staines as well, Lynley told him. So both men's stories were being corroborated by the evidence they had at hand.

'A word, you three?' came from the doorway upon the conclusion of Lynley's remarks. They swung round to see that DCI Leach had returned to the incident room, and he had a scrap of paper in his hand that he gestured with as he said, 'In my office, if you will,' after which he vanished, expecting them to follow.

'Where've you got to tracing the kid Wolff had while she was in prison?' Leach asked Barbara Havers when they joined him.

Barbara said, 'I got side-tracked onto Pitchley once I stopped in for his photo yesterday. I'm onto that today. But nothing's telling us that Katja Wolff even wants to know where the kid ended up, sir. If she wanted to find him, the first person she would've talked to is the nun. Which she hasn't done.'

Leach made a dismissive noise in his throat.

'Check it out, all the same.'

'Right,' Barbara said. 'D'you want it before or after I track down Lynn Davies?'

'Before. After. Just do it, Constable,' Leach said irritably. 'We've had a report from across the river. Forensic have analysed the paint chips they found on the body.'

'And?' Lynley asked.

'We're going to have to adjust our thinking. SO7 says the paint shows cellulose mixed with thinners to water it down. That doesn't match up with anything that's been used on cars for at least forty years. They're telling us the chips came from something old. Think nineteen-fifties at the latest, they're saying.'

'Nineteen-*fifties*?' Barbara asked incredulously.

'That explains why last night's witness thought of a limousine,' Lynley said. 'Cars were big in the fifties. Jaguars. Rolls Royces. Bentleys were enormous.'

'So someone ran her down in his classic auto?' Barbara Havers asked. 'Now *that's* desperation.'

'Could be a taxi,' Nkata pointed out. 'Taxi out of use, got sold to someone who fixed it up and uses it now for his regular motor.'

'Taxi, classic car, or golden chariot,' Barbara said, 'everyone we've got under the microscope's out of the running.'

'Unless one of them borrowed a car,' Lynley noted.

'We can't discount that possibility,' Leach concurred.

'Are we back to square one, then?' Barbara asked.

'I'll get someone to start checking it out. That

129

and repair shops catering for old cars. Although we can't expect much body damage on something manufactured in the fifties. Cars were like tanks then.'

'But they had chrome bumpers,' Nkata said, 'massive chrome bumpers that could've got mashed.'

'So we'll need to check out old parts shops as well.' Leach made a note. 'It's easier to replace than to repair, especially if you know the cops are looking.' He phoned into the incident room and allocated that assignment, after which he rang off and said to Lynley, 'It still could be a blind coincidence.'

Lynley said, 'Do you think that, sir?' in a measured tone that told Nkata the DI was looking for something beneath whatever reply the DCI might give.

'I'd like to. But I do see how it puts one in blinkers: thinking what we want to think in this situation.' He gazed at his telephone as if willing it to ring. The others said nothing. Finally, he murmured, 'He's a good man. He may have stepped wrong now and then, but which of us hasn't? Stepping wrong doesn't make him less of what he is.' He looked at Lynley and they seemed to communicate something that Nkata couldn't understand. Then he said, 'Get on with it, you lot,' and they left him.

Outside, Barbara Havers spoke to Lynley. 'He knows, Inspector.'

Nkata said, 'Knows what? Who?'

Barbara said, 'Leach. He knows Webberly's got a connection with the Davies woman.'

' 'Course he knows it. They worked on that old

case together. Nothing new there. And we already knew it as well.'

'Right. But what we didn't know—'

'That'll do, Havers,' Lynley said. The two of them exchanged a long look before Barbara said airily, 'Oh. Right. Well, I'm off, then,' and with a friendly nod at Nkata, she walked towards her car.

In the immediate aftermath of this brief exchange, Nkata felt the unspoken reprimand in Lynley's decision to keep from him what was obviously a new piece of information which he and Barbara had uncovered. Nkata realised he deserved to be left in the dark in this way—God knew he'd certainly not shown he possessed the requisite level of skill to do the *right* thing with a valuable new fact—but at the same time he thought he'd been circumspect enough with his recitation of his morning's cock-up so as not to be thought of as a complete incompetent. That obviously hadn't been the case.

Nkata felt all the misery of his position. He said, ' 'Spector, you want me off this now?'

'Off what, Winston?'

'The case. You know. 'f I can't talk to two birds without making a mess of things . . .' He shrugged.

In reply Lynley looked completely confused, and Nkata knew he'd have to go further, admitting what he preferred to keep buried. He directed his gaze to Barbara, who'd climbed into her soup tin car and was in the process of revving the Mini's sorely tried engine. He said, 'I mean, 'f I don't know what to *do* with a fact when I got a fact, I guess I c'n see how you might not want me to *have* a fact in the first place. But that doesn't give me a full hand, which c'n make me less effective, right?

131

Not that I showed how 'ffective I was this morning, of course. So what I'm saying's . . . if you want me off the case—'

'Winston,' Lynley cut in firmly. 'A hair shirt might be appropriate, given the circumstance—whatever it is—but I assure you, the cat o' nine tails can be dispensed with.'

'What?'

Lynley smiled. 'You've a brilliant career ahead of you, Winnie. No blots on your copy book, unlike the rest of us. I'd like to see you keep it that way. Do you understand?'

'That I cocked things up? That another cock-up'd mean a formal—'

'No. That I'd like to keep you in the clear should . . .' Uncharacteristically, Lynley paused in what seemed like the search for a phrase that would explain something without revealing what he was explaining. He settled on, 'Should our procedures come under scrutiny later on, I'd prefer them to be mine and not yours,' and he made the statement with such delicacy that Nkata followed it with a leap to comprehension once he put Lynley's words together with what Barbara Havers had inadvertently revealed just before leaving them.

He said in disbelief, 'Holy God. You onto something you're keeping quiet about?'

Lynley said wryly, 'Job well done. You didn't hear that from me.'

'Barb knows 'bout it?'

'Only because she was there. I'm responsible, Winston. I'd like to keep it that way.'

'Could it take us to the killer, what you're on to?'

'I don't think so. But yes, it may do.'

'Is it evidence?'

132

'Let's not discuss that.'

Nkata couldn't believe what he was hearing. 'Then you got to turn it in! You got to 'stablish the chain. You can't not hand it over 'cause you think . . . What *do* you think?'

'That the hit and runs are probably connected but that I need to see exactly how they're connected before I make a move that could destroy someone's life. What's left of it. It's my decision, Winnie. And to protect yourself, I suggest you don't ask any more questions.'

Nkata studied the DI, not believing that Lynley, of all people, should be operating in a grey area. He knew that he could insist and end up in there with him—with Barbara as well—but he was ambitious enough to heed the wisdom in the inspector's words. Still, he said, 'Wish you wouldn't go at it like this, man.'

'Objection noted,' Lynley said.


# CHAPTER SEVENTEEN

Libby Neale decided to call in sick with the flu. She knew Rock Peters would have a conniption and threaten to withhold her week's pay—not that that actually *meant* anything since he was currently three weeks behind paying her anyway—but she didn't care. When she'd parted from Gideon the previous night, she'd hoped he'd come down to her flat after the cop left him and when he didn't, she slept so badly that she was as good as sick anyway. So calling it the flu wasn't that much of a lie.

She wandered around her flat in sweats for the

first three hours after she got up, mostly pounding the heels of her palms together and straining her ears to hear any sound from above to indicate that Gideon was stirring. She didn't get very far. Finally, she gave up the attempt at eavesdropping on him—not that it was *really* eavesdropping when all you were listening for was the sound of movement to indicate that someone was basically all right—and she decided to make sure in person that he was doing okay. He'd been a wreck yesterday *before* the cop got there. Who the hell knew what condition he'd been in once the cop left?

Should've gone to him then, she told herself. And while she made an earnest attempt not to ponder the reason that she *hadn't* gone to him once the cop departed, the thought of what she should have done in the first place led inexorably to the why of why she hadn't.

He'd spooked her. He'd been so not there. She'd talked to him in the kite shed and after that in the kitchen and he'd answered her—sort of—but still he'd been so somewhere else in his head that she'd wondered if he maybe needed to be committed or something. Just for a while. And then wondering *that* had made her feel so disloyal that she couldn't really face him, or at least that was what she told herself when she spent the evening watching old movies on Sky TV and eating two very large bags of cheddar cheese popcorn which she could have done without thank you very much and finally going to bed alone where she fought with the sheets and blankets all night when she wasn't having a soon-to-be-major-motion-picture nightmare.

So after spinning her wheels pacing the floor, browsing in the refrigerator for the bag of celery that was supposed to make her feel less guilty about the cheddar cheese popcorn, and watching Kilroy yacking with women who'd married men young enough to be their sons and—in two cases—their frigging grandsons, she went upstairs to search out Gideon.

She found him on the floor in the music room, sitting beneath the window seat with his back against the wall. He had his legs drawn up to his chest, with his chin resting upon his knees like some kid who's been disciplined by a ticked-off parent. All around him were scattered papers, which turned out to be Xerox copies of newspaper articles, all of them covering the same subject. He'd been back to the Press Association's news library.

He didn't look at her when she came into the room. He was focused on the stories surrounding him, and she wondered if he even heard her. She said his name, but he didn't stir, other than to begin a gentle rocking.

Breakdown, she thought with alarm. Complete crack up. He looked like someone who'd lost it. He was wearing exactly what he'd had on yesterday, so she figured he hadn't slept all night either.

'Hey,' she said quietly, 'what's up, Gideon? You been back down to Victoria? Why'n't you tell me? I'd've gone with you.'

She scanned the papers that fanned around him, overlarge sheets on which newspaper clippings had been photocopied every which way. She saw that the British papers—in keeping with the country's general bent towards xenophobia—had gone after the nanny with a rusty hatchet. If she wasn't 'the German' in every article, she was 'the former Communist whose family lived particularly well'—

135

not to mention *suspiciously* well, Libby thought sardonically—'under Russian domination'. One paper had unearthed the news that her grandfather had been a member of the Nazi party while another had found a picture of her father, who'd evidently been a cardholding, jackbooted, *Sieg heil!* shouting member of the Hitler Youth, if that's what it was called.

The tireless ability of the press to milk a story for its every frigging ounce of liquid was totally amazing. It looked to Libby like the life of everyone even moderately involved with the death of Sonia Davies and the trial and conviction of her killer had been dissected by the tabloids at one time or another. So Gideon's home teacher had come under the microscope, as had the lodger, as well as Rafe Robson, both of Gideon's parents, and his grandparents, too. And long after the verdict it seemed that anyone who'd wanted to make a buck had sold *his* version of the story to the papers.

Thus, people had crawled out from under rocks to comment on life as a nanny—NEWSREADER: I WAS A NANNY AND IT WAS HELL blared one headline—and those who had no experience as nannies had experience with Germans they wanted to reveal—A RACE APART, FORMER BERLIN GI SAYS announced another. But what Libby noticed most of all was the number of stories that dealt with Gideon's family having had a nanny for his sister in the first place.

They went at the topic from several angles: There was the group who chose to dwell on what the German nanny was paid (a pittance, so no wonder she finally offed the poor kid, like in a rage or something) compared to what something called

136

'a well-trained Norland Nanny' was paid (a fortune that prompted Libby to seriously consider a change in career, pronto), crafting their nasty little articles in such a way as to suggest that the Davies family had gotten to the max what they'd paid for with their skinflint pennies. Then there was the group who chose to dwell on speculating what purposes were being served when a mother made the decision to 'work outside the home.' And then there was the group who chose to dwell on what it did to parental expectation, responsibility, and devotion when a family was burdened with a disabled child. Battle lines were drawn all over the place on the topic of how to deal with the birth of a Down's Syndrome baby, and all the options taken by parents of such children were given a good airing: give them up for adoption, put them away at the Government's expense, devote your life to them, learn to cope by asking the aid of outside agencies, join a support group, soldier on with upper lips stiff, treat the child like any other, and on and on.

Libby found that she couldn't begin to imagine what it had been like for all of them when little Sonia Davies had died. Her birth would have been tough to deal with, but to love her—because they must have loved her, right?—and then to lose her and then to have every detail of what went into her existence and the existence of her family displayed for public entertainment and consumption . . . Whew, Libby thought. How did *anyone* deal with that?

Not well, if Gideon was anything to go by. He'd changed his position so his forehead was balanced on his knees. He continued to rock.

'Gideon,' she asked him, 'you all right?'

'I don't want to remember now that I remember,' he replied numbly. 'I don't want to think. And I can't stop either. Remembering. Thinking. I want to rip my brain from my head.'

'I can buy that,' Libby assured him. 'So why don't we dump all this stuff in the trash? You been reading it all night?' She bent to the papers and began to gather them. 'No wonder you can't get your mind off it, Gid.'

He grabbed her wrist, crying out, 'Don't!'

'But if you don't want to think—'

'No! I've been reading and reading and I want to know how anyone could continue to exist, could even *want* to exist . . . Look at it all, Libby. Look. Just look. I'm understanding it all now, you see? And I just can't cope with the understanding.'

Libby looked again at the papers and saw them the way that Gideon must have seen them, coming upon them twenty years after the fact of being protected from the knowledge of what that time had been like for his family. Particularly she saw the thinly veiled attacks on his parents in the light he would be seeing them. And she made the leap that he no doubt had already made from what the papers had printed: His mother had left them because of *this*, she had disappeared for nearly twenty years because she had no doubt begun to believe herself as ill-suited for parenthood as the newspapers had made her out to be. It seemed that Gideon was finally understanding his past. Little wonder that he was inches away from flipping out.

She was about to say all of this when he got to his feet. He took two steps, then swayed. She leapt up and grabbed him by the arm.

138

He said, 'I've got to see Cresswell-White.'

'Who? That attorney?'

He headed out of the room, fumbling in his pocket and bringing out his keys. The thought of him driving alone across London spurred Libby to follow. At the front door, she snatched his leather jacket from the coat rack, and she trailed him along the sidewalk to his GPS. As he attempted to insert the key in the lock with a hand that trembled like an octogenarian's, she threw the jacket over his shoulders and said, 'You're *not* driving. You'd get in a wreck before you got to Regent's Park.'

'I've got to get to the Temple.'

'Fine. Cool. Whatever. I'll drive.'

During the drive, Gideon said not a word. He merely stared straight ahead, his knees knocking together spasmodically.

He got out the moment she turned off the ignition in the area of the Temple. He set off down the street. Libby locked the car and trotted to catch up, reaching him as he crossed over at the end and entered that holy of legal holies.

Gideon led her to the place she'd accompanied him previously: to a building that was part brick and part stone, sitting on the edge of a little park. He went in through the same narrow doorway, where black wooden slats on the wall were painted in white with the names of the lawyers who had offices inside.

They had to cool their heels in reception before Cresswell-White had a break in his schedule. They sat in silence on the black leather sofas, both of them staring alternately at the Persian carpet and the brass chandelier. Around them, telephones rang constantly and quietly as a group working in

139

an office directly opposite the sofas fielded calls.

After forty minutes of pondering the crucial issue of whether the oak chest in reception had been built to store chamber pots, Libby heard someone say, 'Gideon,' and roused herself to see that Bertram Cresswell-White had himself come out to take them back to his corner office. Unlike their previous visit—which had been scheduled in advance—no coffee was on offer this time, although a fire was lit and it was doing at least something to cut the chill that pervaded the room.

The lawyer had been working hard at some task or another, for a computer's monitor was still glowing with a page of typescript and half a dozen books were open on his desk along with what looked like pretty ancient files. Among these, a black and white photograph of a woman lay. She was blonde with close-cropped hair, a bad complexion, and an expression saying 'Don't mess with me'.

Gideon saw the picture and said, 'Are you trying to get her out?'

Cresswell-White closed the file, gestured them to the leather chairs near the fireplace and said, 'She would have been hanged if I'd had my way and the law were different. She's a monster. And I've made the study of monsters my avocation.'

'What'd she do?' Libby asked.

'Killed children and buried their bodies on the moors. She liked to make audiotapes as she tortured them, she and her boyfriend.' Libby swallowed. Cresswell-White glanced at his watch with some meaning but tempered this action with, 'I heard about your mother, Gideon. On Radio Four News. I'm terribly sorry. I expect that's something to do with why you've come. How can I help you?'

'With her address.' Gideon spoke as if he'd thought of nothing else since first getting into his car in Chalcot Square.

'Whose?'

'You have to know where she is. You were the one who put her away so you would've been told when they let her out, and I know she's out. That's why I've come. I need her address.'

Libby thought, Hold *on* here, Gid.

Cresswell-White gave his version of that same reaction. He knotted his eyebrows, saying, 'Are you asking me for Katja Wolff's address?'

'You have it, don't you? You have to have it. I don't expect they'd let her out without telling you where she went.'

'Why do you want it? I'm not saying I do have it, by the way.'

'She's owed.'

Libby thought, This is *really* the limit. She said quietly but with what she hoped was gentle urgency, 'Gideon. Gosh. The police're handling this, aren't they?'

'She's out now,' Gideon said to Cresswell-White as if Libby hadn't spoken. 'She's out and she's owed. Where is she?'

'I can't tell you that.' Cresswell-White leaned forward, his body if not his hands reaching for Gideon. 'I know you've had a very bad shock. Your life has probably been one long effort to recover from what she put you through. God knows the time that she spent in prison doesn't mitigate your suffering one iota.'

'I've got to find her,' Gideon said. 'It's the only

way.'

'No. Listen to me. It's the wrong way. Oh, it feels right and I know that feeling: You'd climb back into the past if you could and you'd tear her limb from limb *before* the fact, just to prevent her from doing the harm she eventually did your family. But you'd gain as little as I gain, Gideon, when I hear the jury's verdict and I know that I've won but all the time I've lost because nothing can bring a dead child back to life. A woman who takes the life of a child is the worst kind of demon because she can *give* life if she chooses. And to take a life when you can give life is a crime that's compounded and one for which no sentence will ever be long enough and no punishment—even death—ever good enough.'

'There's got to be reparation,' Gideon said. He didn't sound so much stubborn as desperate. 'My mother's dead, don't you see? There's got to be reparation and this is the only way. I don't have a choice.'

'You do,' Cresswell-White said. 'You can choose not to meet her at the level she operates on. You can choose to believe what I'm telling you because what I'm telling you comes from decades of experience. There is no vengeance for this sort of thing. Even death was no vengeance when death was both legal and possible, Gideon.'

'You don't understand.' Gideon closed his eyes and for a moment, Libby thought he'd start crying. She wanted to do something to prevent him breaking down and humiliating himself further in the eyes of this man who did not really know him and could not therefore know what he'd been going through for two long months. But she also wanted to do something to smooth things over, on the off

142

chance that something bad might accidentally happen to the German chick in the next few days, in which case Gideon would be the first person they'd be talking to after this little conversation in the Temple. Not that she really thought Gideon'd *do* anything to anyone. He was just talking; he was just looking for something to make him feel like his world wasn't falling apart.

Libby said to the lawyer in a low voice, 'He's been up all night. And he's been having nightmares on the nights he *can* sleep. He saw her, see, and—'

Cresswell-White sat up and took notice of this, saying, 'Katja Wolff?' Has she contacted you, Gideon? The terms of her parole prevent her from contacting any member of the family, and if she violates those terms, we can see to it—'

'No, no. His mom,' Libby interrupted. 'He saw his mom. But he didn't know who she was because he hadn't seen her since he was a little kid. And that's been eating at him since he heard she was . . . you know, killed.' She glanced cautiously at Gideon. His eyes were still closed, and his head was shaking as if he wanted to negate everything that had happened to bring him to this position of begging a lawyer he didn't even know to violate whatever it was he would have to violate in order to give out the information that Gideon wanted. That wasn't going to happen, and Libby knew it. Cresswell-White sure as hell wasn't going to hand the German nanny over to Gideon on a platter and risk his own reputation and career for having done so. Which was just as well and damn lucky to boot. All Gideon needed to really mess up his life at this point was access to the woman who'd killed his sister and maybe killed his mom as well.

143

But Libby knew how he felt, or at least she thought she knew. He felt like he'd blown his chance for some kind of redemption for some kind of sin the punishment for which was not being able to play his violin. And that's what it all boiled down to after all: that violin.

Cresswell-White said, 'Gideon, Katja Wolff's not worth the time it would take to locate her. This is a woman who showed no remorse, who was so certain of her exoneration that she offered no defence of her actions. Her silence said, "Let them prove they have a case," and only when the facts piled up—those bruises, those fractures left to heal *untreated* on your sister's body—and she heard the verdict and the sentence did she decide a defence might be in order. Imagine that. Imagine what kind of person lies behind that simple refusal to cooperate—to answer the most *basic* of questions—when a child in her care has died. She didn't even weep once she made her initial statement. And she won't weep now. You can't expect that from her. She is not like us. Abusers of children are never like us.'

Libby watched anxiously as Cresswell-White spoke, looking for a sign that what the lawyer was saying was somehow making an impression on Gideon. But she was left with a growing sense of despair when Gideon opened his eyes, got to his feet, and spoke.

He said, as if Cresswell-White's words meant nothing to him. 'This is what it is: I didn't understand, but now I do. And I've got to find her.' He walked towards the door of the office, raising his hands to his forehead as if he wanted to do what he'd said earlier: rip the brain from his head.

144

Cresswell-White said to Libby, 'He's not well.'

To which she responded, 'Well, *duh*,' as she went after Gideon.

\*　　　\*　　　\*

Raphael Robson's home in Gospel Oak was set off one of the busier roads in the district. It turned out to be an enormous, ramshackle Edwardian building in need of renovation, the front garden of which was hidden behind a yew hedge and gravelled over to make it into a parking space. When Lynley and Nkata arrived, three vehicles were standing in front of house: a dirty white van, a black Vauxhall, and a silver Renault. Lynley took quick note of the fact that the Vauxhall wasn't old enough to qualify as their hit-and-run vehicle.

A man came round the side of the house as they approached the front steps. He headed towards the Renault without noticing them. When Lynley called out, he stopped in his tracks, car keys extended to unlock his vehicle. Was he Raphael Robson? Lynley asked him and produced his identification.

The man was an unappealing sort with a serious comb-over of dun-coloured hair that began just above his left ear and made his skull look as if someone were water-colouring a lattice across it. He was patchy skinned from far too many holidays in the Mediterranean in August, and his shoulders bore a liberal sprinkling of dandruff. He gave a glance to Lynley's warrant card and said yes, he was Raphael Robson.

Lynley introduced Nkata and asked Robson if there was somewhere they could have a word with

145

him, out of the noise of cars whooshing by just beyond the hedge. Robson said yes, yes, of course. If they'd follow him . . . ?

'The front door's warped,' he said, 'We haven't replaced it yet. We'll need to go in through the back.'

*Through the back* took them along a brick path that led into a good sized garden. This was overgrown with weeds and grass, edged by herbaceous borders long gone to ruin and dotted with trees that hadn't been pruned in years. Beneath them, wet fallen leaves were rotting to join their brothers from seasons past in the soil. In the midst of all the chaos and decay, however, a newish building stood. Robson saw both Lynley and Nkata giving this a look-over and he said, 'That was our first project. We do furniture in there.'

'Building it?'

'Restoring it. We mean to do the house as well. Doing up furniture and selling it gives us something of a kitty to work from. Restoring a place like this—' with a nod at the imposing edifice—'takes a fortune. Whenever we get enough saved to do a room, we do it. It's taking forever, but no one's in a hurry. And there's a certain camaraderie that develops when everyone's behind a project, I think.'

Lynley wondered at the word *camaraderie*. He'd been thinking Robson's *us* referred to his wife and family, but 'developing camaraderie' suggested something else. He considered the vehicles he'd seen in front of the building and said, 'This is a commune, then?'

Robson unlocked the door and swung it open onto a passageway with a wooden bench running along its wall and adult sized wellingtons lined up beneath it and hooks holding jackets on the wall above it. He said, 'That sounds like something from the summer-of-love era. But yes, I suppose you could call it a commune. Mostly it's a group with shared interests.'

'Which are?'

'Making music and turning this house into something we can all enjoy.'

'Not restoring furniture?' Nkata asked.

'That's merely a means to an end. Musicians don't make enough money to finance a restoration like this one without something else to fall back on.'

He allowed them into the passage before him, shutting the door when they were inside and locking it scrupulously behind them. He said, 'This way,' and led them into what might once have been the dining room but now was a musty combination of draughting room, store room, and office, with water-stained wallpaper covering the upper half of the walls and battered wainscoting covering the lower half. A computer was part of the office function that the room was serving. From where he stood, Lynley could see the telephone line that was plugged in to it.

He said, 'We've tracked you through a message you left on the answer machine of a woman called Eugenie Davies, Mr Robson. This was four days ago. At eight-fifteen in the evening.'

Next to Lynley, Nkata got out his leather notebook and his propelling pencil, twisting it to produce a micro-millimetre of lead. Robson watched him do this then walked to a worktable on which a set of blueprints was spread. He smoothed

147

his hand over the top one as if to study it, but he answered the question with the single word. 'Yes.'

'Do you know she was murdered three nights ago?'

'Yes. I know.' His voice was low and his hand grasped a blueprint that was still rolled up. His thumb played along the rubber band that held it formed into a tube. 'Richard told me,' he said, lifting his gaze to Lynley. 'He'd been to tell Gideon when I arrived for one of our sessions.'

'Sessions?'

'I teach the violin. Gideon's been my pupil since childhood. He isn't any longer, of course; he's no one's pupil. But we play together three hours a day when he's not recording, rehearsing, or touring. You've heard of him, doubtless.'

'I was under the impression he hasn't played in several months.'

Robson's hand had reached out to touch the opened blueprint again, but he hesitated and did nothing more with the gesture. He said on a heavy sigh, 'Sit down, Inspector. You as well, Constable,' and he turned back to them. 'It's important not only to keep up appearances in a situation like Gideon's, but it's also important to go on normally as much as possible. So I still turn up for our daily three hours together and we keep hoping that when enough time passes, he'll be able to go back to the music.'

'"We?"' Nkata raised his head to look for the answer.

'Richard and I. Gideon's father.'

Somewhere in the house, a scherzo began. Dozens of energetic notes ran riot on what sounded like a harpsichord at first but then

148

abruptly changed to an oboe and then just as abruptly altered to a flute. This was accompanied by an increase in volume and the sudden rhythmic pounding of several percussion instruments. Robson went to the door and shut it, saying, 'Sorry. Janet's gone a bit mad over the electric keyboard. She's enthralled with anything a computer chip can do.'

'And you?' Lynley asked.

'I haven't the money for a keyboard.'

'I meant computer chips, Mr Robson. Do you use this computer? I see it has a telephone connection.'

Robson's gaze flicked to it. He crossed the room and sat at a chair that he drew out from the sheet of plywood which served as a desk top. At this, Lynley and Nkata also sat, unfolding two metal chairs and swinging them into position so that, with Robson, they formed a triangle near the computer.

'We all use it,' Robson said.

'For e-mail? Chat rooms? Surfing the net?'

'I mostly use it for e-mail. My sister's in Los Angeles. My brother's in Birmingham. My parents have a house on the Costa del Sol. It's an easy way for us to stay in contact.'

'Your address is . . . ?'

'Why?'

'Curiosity,' Lynley said.

Robson recited it, looking puzzled. Lynley heard what he'd suspected he'd hear when he saw the computer sitting in the room. *Jete* was Robson's online name and consequently part of his e-mail address.

'You've been fairly distressed about Mrs Davies, it seems,' he said to the violinist. 'Your message on

149

her answer machine was agitated, Mr Robson, and the last e-mail you sent her looked a bit frantic as well. "I must see you. I'm begging." Had you had some sort of falling out?'

Robson's seat was a desk chair that swivelled, and he used it to rotate, to examine the computer's empty staring screen as if he could see his last message to Eugenie Davies there. He said, 'You'd be checking everything. Of course. I see that,' as if speaking to himself and not them. Then he went on in a normal tone with, 'We parted quite badly. I said some things that . . .' He removed a handkerchief from his pocket, pressing it to his forehead where perspiration had begun to bead. 'I expected I'd have a chance to apologise. We always think that, don't we? Even as I drove away from the restaurant—and I was in a real fury, I admit it—I didn't drive off thinking That's it, I'm done with this business forever, she's a blind silly cow and that's the end of it. What I thought was, Oh God, she looks rotten, she's thinner than ever, why can't she see what that *means*, for God's sake.'

'Which was what?' Lynley asked.

'That she'd made a decision in her head, yes, and it probably sounded like a sensible one to her. But her body was rebelling against that decision, which was her . . . I don't know . . . I suppose it was her *spirit's* way of trying to tell her to stop, to carry things not one inch farther. And you could *see* the rebellion in her. Believe me, you could actually see it. It wasn't just that she'd let herself go. God knows she'd done that years ago. She'd been quite lovely but to see her—especially as she was in these last few years—you'd never have realised how men would at one time slow down in the street as they

150

passed her.'

'What decision had she made, Mr Robson?' Lynley asked as Nkata scratched his head and tried to look patient.

Robson said, 'Come with me. I want to show you something,' by way of answer. He took them from the house, out the same way they'd come in, out into the garden. He headed towards the building where he'd said the commune worked on their furniture.

The building comprised a single large room in which battered pieces stood in various stages of restoration. It smelled strongly of sawdust, turpentine, and wood stain, and a patina of the dust that comes from heavy sanding lay like a gauze veil on everything. Footprints tracked back and forth across the dirty floor, from a workbench above which a set of newly cleaned tools gleamed with oil to a three-legged wardrobe that listed tiredly, sanded down to bare walnut, disembowelled, and awaiting the next stage of rejuvenation.

'Here's my guess,' Robson said. 'Tell me how it matches to reality. I did a wardrobe for her. Cherry wood, it was. First rate. Beautiful. Not the sort of thing you see every day. I did her a commode as well, early eighteenth century. Oak. And a washstand. Victorian. Ebony with a marble top. One of the drawer pulls is missing but you wouldn't want to replace it because you couldn't match it and anyway leaving it without the pull actually gives it more character. The wardrobe took the longest, because you don't ever want to refinish a piece unless there is no hope for it. You just want to restore it. So it was six months before I had it the way I wanted it and no one—' he nodded at the house to indicate his housemates—'was pleased that I was working on that instead of something we could make a profit on.'

Lynley frowned at this, knowing that there were lines upon lines being written by Robson and wondering how adept he himself would be to read between them in the time they had. He said, 'You had a falling out with Mrs Davies because of a decision she'd made. But I can't think her decision was about selling the pieces of furniture you'd done for her. Am I right?'

Robson's shoulders dropped slightly, as if he'd been hoping that Lynley wouldn't be able to confirm what he himself suspected. He'd been clutching his handkerchief, and now he looked down at it as he said, 'So she didn't keep them, did she? She didn't keep any of the pieces I gave to her. She sold them all and gave the money to charity. Or she just gave the furniture itself away. But she didn't keep it. That's what you're telling me.'

'She had no antiques in her house in Henley, if that's what you're wondering,' Lynley said. 'Her furniture was—' He looked for the right word to convey the manner in which Eugenie Davies' house in Friday Street had been furnished. 'Spartan,' he said.

'Just like a nun's cell, I expect.' Robson's words were bitter. 'That's how she punished herself. But it wasn't enough, that sort of deprivation, so she was ready to take it to the next level.'

'What would that be?' Nkata had given up writing during Robson's recitation of the antiques he'd given to Eugenie Davies. *The next level,*

152

however, clearly promised more.

'Wiley,' Robson said. 'The bloke from the book shop. She'd been seeing him for several years, but she'd decided it was time to . . .' Robson shoved his handkerchief into his pocket and gave his attention to the listing wardrobe. To Lynley's eyes, the piece didn't look even salvageable, with its missing leg and its gaping interior that showed a large jagged hole in its back, very much as if someone had taken an axe to it. 'She was going to marry him if he asked her. She said that she believed—she *felt*, she said, with women's bloody intuition, she said—that they were heading towards it. I told her that if a man didn't bother to make an attempt . . . In three years, if he didn't try to make a move on her . . . God, I'm not talking about rape. Not shoving her into a wall and feeling her up. But just . . . He hadn't even tried to get close to her. He hadn't even talked about *why* he hadn't tried. They just went on their picnics, took their walks, rode the bus on those stupid pensioners' days out . . . And I tried to tell her that it wasn't normal. It wasn't red-blooded. So if she made it permanent with him, if she actually made herself his partner and took herself out of the *sodding* running . . .' Robson ran out of steam. His eyes became red-rimmed. 'But I suppose that's what she wanted. To take up life with someone who couldn't begin to give her anything complete, who couldn't begin to give her what a man can give to a woman when she means everything to him.'

Lynley examined Robson as he spoke, saw the misery in the lines that etched their painful history on his patchy-skinned face. 'When was the last time you saw Mrs Davies?'

'A fortnight ago. Thursday.'

'Where?'

'Marlow. The Swan and Three Roses. Just outside of town.'

'And you didn't see her again? Did you speak to her?'

'On the phone twice. I was trying to . . . I'd reacted badly to what she'd told me about Wiley and I knew it. I wanted to make things right between us. But it just got worse because I still wanted to talk to her about it, about him, about what it meant that he never . . . never once in three years . . . But she didn't want to hear. She didn't want to see. "He's a good man, Raphael," she kept saying, "and it's time now."'

'Time for what?'

Robson continued as if Nkata hasn't asked the question, as if he himself were a silent Cyrano who'd waited long for an opportunity to unburden himself. He said, 'I didn't disagree that it was time. She'd punished herself for years. She wasn't in prison but she may as well have been because she made her life a prison anyway. She lived one step away from solitary confinement, in complete self-denial, surrounding herself with people with whom she had nothing in common, always volunteering for the worst jobs, and all of it so that she could pay and pay and pay.'

'For what?' Nkata had been standing close to the door as he wrote, as if hoping a near contact with the outside environment might spare his fine wool charcoal suit from the worst of the dust that permeated the work room's air. But now he took a step closer to Robson, and he cast a glance towards Lynley who indicated with his hand that they would

154

wait for the violinist to continue. Silence on their part was as useful a tool as silence on his part was revealing.

Robson finally said, 'When she was born, Eugenie didn't love her instantly the way she thought she was supposed to love her. At first she was just exhausted because the birth had been difficult and all she wanted was to recover from it. And that's not unnatural when a woman's been in labour so long—thirty hours, it was—and she's got nothing left in her even to cuddle a new born. That is not a sin.'

'I wouldn't disagree,' Lynley said.

'And they didn't know at first anyway, about the baby. Yes of course there were signs, but labour had been rough. She didn't come out pink and perfect like a birth that's been orchestrated for a Hollywood production. So the doctors didn't know till she was examined and then . . . Good God, *anyone* would be slaughtered by the news. Anyone would have to adjust and that takes time. But she thought she should have been different, Eugenie. She thought she should have loved her at once, felt like a fighter, had plans how to care for her, known what to do, what to expect, how to *be*. When she couldn't do that, she hated herself. And the rest of them didn't make it easier for her to accept the baby, did they, especially Richard's father—that mad bastard—who expected another prodigy from them and when he got the reverse . . . There was just too much for Eugenie to cope with. Sonia's physical problems, Gideon's needs—which were mounting daily and what else could you expect when it comes to dealing with a prodigy?—mad Jack's raving, Richard's second failure—'

155

'Second failure?' Lynley asked.

'Another damaged child, if you can believe it. He'd had an earlier one. From another marriage. So when a second one was born . . . It was terrible for all of them but Eugenie couldn't see that it was normal to feel the anguish at first, to curse God, to do whatever one *has* to do to get through a bad time. Instead she heard her bloody father's voice, "God speaks to us directly. There is no mystery in His message. Examine your soul and your conscience to read God's handwriting therein, Eugenie." That's what he wrote to her, if you can believe it. That was his blessing and comfort on the birth of that pathetic little baby. As if an infant were a punishment from God. And there was no one to talk her out of feeling like that, do you see? Oh there was the nun, but she talked about God's will as if the entire situation were predetermined and Eugenie was meant to understand that, accept it, not to rage against it, grieve about it, feel whatever despair she needed to feel and then just get *on* with life. So then when the baby died . . . and the way she died . . . I expect there were moments when Eugenie had actually thought "better she be dead than have to live like this, with doctors and operations and lungs failing and heart barely beating and stomach not working and ears not hearing and not even being able to shit properly for the love of God . . . Better she be dead." And then, she actually was dead. It was as if someone had heard her and granted a wish that wasn't a real wish at all but just an expression of one moment's despair. So what was she to feel but guilt? And what was she to do to make reparation but deny herself everything that might mean comfort?'

156

'Until Major Wiley came along,' Lynley noted.

'I suppose so.' Robson's words were hollow. 'Wiley was a new beginning for her. Or at least that's how she said she thought of it.'

'But you disagreed.'

'I think he was just another form of imprisonment. But worse than before because he'd be wearing the guise of something new.'

'So you argued about it.'

'And then I wanted to apologise,' Robson added. 'I was desperate to apologise—don't you see— because we'd shared years of friendship, the two of us, Eugenie and I, and I couldn't see sending them down the drain because of Wiley. I wanted her to know that. That's all. For whatever it was worth.'

Lynley set these words against what he'd learned from both Gideon and Richard Davies. 'She ended contact with her family long ago, but not with you, then? Were you and Mrs Davies once lovers, Mr Robson?'

Colour flared into Robson's face, an unattractive smearing of crimson that battled with the various patches of his damaged skin. 'We met twice a month,' he said in answer.

'Where?'

'In London. In the country. Wherever she wanted. She asked for news of Gideon, and I provided it. That was the extent of what she and I had together.'

The pubs and hotels in her diary, Lynley thought. Twice each month. But it didn't make sense. Her meetings with Robson didn't follow the pattern that Robson himself described as being the path of Eugenie Davies' life. If she had been intent upon punishing herself for the transgression of

157

human despair, for the unspoken wish—so horribly granted—to be delivered from the struggle to care for a fragile daughter, why had she even allowed herself news of her son, news that might comfort her, might keep her in touch? Wouldn't she have denied herself that?

There was a piece missing somewhere, Lynley concluded. And his instincts told him that Raphael Robson knew exactly what that missing piece was.

He said, 'I can understand part of her behaviour, but I can't understand all of it, Mr Robson. Why cut out contact with her family but maintain contact with you?'

'As I said. It was how she punished herself.'

'For something she'd thought but never acted on?'

It seemed that the answer to this simple question should have come easily to Raphael Robson. Yes or no. He'd spent years knowing the dead woman, after all. He'd engaged in regular meetings with her. But Robson didn't answer at first. He took a plane from among the tools instead, and he appeared to examine it with his long and thin musician's hands.

'Mr Robson?' Lynley said.

Robson moved across the room to a window so covered in dust that it looked nearly opaque. He said, 'She'd sacked her. It was Eugenie's decision. That began everything. So she blamed herself.'

Nkata looked up. 'Katja Wolff?

Robson said, 'Eugenie was the one who said the German girl had to go. If she hadn't made that decision . . . if they hadn't rowed . . .' He made an aimless gesture. 'We can't relive a single moment, can we? We can't unsay things, and we can't undo

158

things. We can only sweep up the pieces of the mess we make of our lives.'

True enough, Lynley thought, but the statements were also useful generalities that weren't going to take them one inch closer to the truth. He said, 'Tell me about that time, before the baby was murdered. As you remember it, Mr Robson.'

'Why? What's that got to do with—'

'Humour me.'

'There isn't much to tell. It's a grubby little story. The German girl got herself pregnant, and she was badly out of sorts. She was sick each morning and half the time sick at noon and at night. Sonia demanded someone's full time attention, but Katja couldn't give it. She tried, God knows, but she got weaker and weaker. Not enough sleep. And she couldn't eat without sicking everything up. She was up with Sonia night after night, and she was trying to sleep when she got the chance. But she slept when she was meant to be doing something else once too often, and Eugenie sacked her. She snapped, then, did Katja. Sonia fussed too much one evening. And that was that.'

'Did you give evidence at the trial?' Nkata asked.

'Yes. I was there. Yes. I gave evidence.'

'Against her?'

'I just testified to what I'd seen, where I'd been, what I knew.'

'For the prosecution?'

'Ultimately, I suppose. Yes.' Robson shifted on his feet and waited for another question, his gaze on Lynley as Nkata wrote. When Lynley said nothing and the silence among them lengthened, Robson finally spoke. 'What I'd seen was practically nothing. I'd been giving Gideon some instruction, and the first I knew that something was wrong was when Katja began screaming from the bathroom. People came charging from all corners of the house, Eugenie dialled nine-nine-nine, Richard tried the kiss of life.'

'And the fault went down to Katja Wolff,' Nkata noted.

'There was too much chaos to find fault anywhere at first,' Robson said. 'Katja was screaming that she hadn't left the baby alone, so it seemed as if she'd had some sort of seizure and died in an instant when Katja's back was turned, when she was reaching for a towel. Something like that. Then she said she'd been on the phone for a minute or two. But that fell through when Katie Waddington denied it. Then came the post mortem. It became clear how Sonia died and that there had been earlier . . . earlier incidents that no one knew about and . . .' He opened his hands as if saying, The rest is as it was.

Lynley said, 'Wolff is out of prison, Mr Robson. Have you heard from her?'

Robson shook his head. 'I can't think she'd want to talk to me.'

'Talking might not be what she has in mind,' Nkata said.

Robson looked from him to Lynley. 'You're thinking Katja might have killed Eugenie.'

Lynley said, 'The investigating officer from that period of time was run over last night as well.'

'Good God.'

'We're thinking everyone needs to take care till we get to the bottom of what happened to Mrs Davies,' Lynley said. 'She had something to tell Major Wiley, by the way, according to him. Would you have any idea what that was?'

'None at all,' Robson said, shaking his head but all the same saying the words far too quickly for Lynley's liking. As if realising that the speed of his reply was more revealing than the reply itself, Robson went on to say, 'If there was something she wanted to reveal to Major Wiley, she didn't tell me. You see, Inspector.'

Lynley didn't see. At least he didn't see what Robson hoped he would see. Instead, he saw a man holding something back. He said, 'As Mrs Davies' close friend, I'd think there might be something you've not yet considered, Mr Robson. If you reflect on your most recent meetings with her and especially the last one when the two of you rowed, I expect a detail like a chance remark might give us an indication of what she wanted to tell Major Wiley.'

'There's nothing. Really. I can't say . . .'

Lynley pressed on. 'If what she had to tell Major Wiley is the reason she was killed—and we can't dismiss that possibility, Mr Robson—anything you can remember is vital.'

'She might have wanted him to know about Sonia's death and what led up to her death. Perhaps she believed she needed to tell him why she'd left Richard and Gideon. She might have felt she needed his forgiveness for having done that before they could proceed with each other.'

'Would that have been like her?' Lynley asked. 'The confessional bit before carrying on with a relationship, I mean.'

'Yes,' Robson said and his affirmation seemed genuine. 'Confession would have been exactly like Eugenie.'

Lynley nodded and thought this over. Part of it made sense, but he couldn't escape a simple fact that had announced itself through Robson's helpful revelation: They hadn't mentioned to Robson that Major Wiley had been in Africa twenty years ago and hence hadn't known the circumstances of Sonia Davies' death.

But if Robson knew that, he probably knew more. And whatever that more was, Lynley was willing to wager it led to the death in West Hampstead.

## *Gideon*

### 1 NOVEMBER

*I object, Dr Rose. I am not avoiding anything. You might question my pursuit of the truth with regard to my sister's death, you might remark that it serves the powerful interests of distraction for me to spend half a day to-ing and fro-ing round Cheltenham, and you might scrutinise my reasons for lolling round the Press Association Office for another three hours, copying and reading the cuttings about the arrest and the trial of Katja Wolff. But you cannot accuse me of avoiding the very activity you yourself assigned me in the first place.*

*Yes, you told me to write what I remember, which is what I've done. And it seems to me that until I get beyond this business of my sister's death, it's going to throw up a block to any other memories that I might have. So I may as well get through all this. I may as well learn what happened back then. If this endeavour is an elaborate subconscious foil to what I* am supposed to remember—whatever the hell that is—then we'll know that eventually, won't we? And in the meantime, you'll be all the richer for the countless appointments that you and I shall have had together. I may even become your patient for life.

And don't tell me you sense my frustration, please, because I'm obviously frustrated because just when I think I'm on to something, you sit there asking me to think about the process of rationalisation and to ponder what that could mean in my current pursuit.

I'll tell you what rationalisation means: It means that I am consciously or unconsciously sidestepping the reason for my loss of music. It means that I am setting up an elaborate maze to thwart your attempts to help me.

So you see? I am completely aware of what I might be doing. And now I ask you to let me do it.

I've been to Dad's. He wasn't there when I arrived, but Jill was. She's decided to paint his kitchen, and she'd brought a selection of paint cards with her, which she'd spread out on the kitchen table. I told her I'd come to go through some old paperwork that Dad keeps in the Granddad Room. She gave me one of those conspiratorial looks that suggest two people are in agreement on a subject that's going undiscussed, and from that I concluded that Dad's museum of devotion to his father is going to be packed away when he and Jill have a home of their own. She won't have told Dad this, naturally. Jill's way is not to be so direct.

To me she said, 'I hope you've got your gum boots with you.' I smiled but made no reply, instead taking myself to the Granddad Room and closing the door behind me.

I don't frequent this spot very often. It makes me

*uneasy to surround myself with such overwhelming evidence of my father's devotion to his father. I suppose I think that Dad's fervour for his father's memory is somewhat misguided. True, Granddad survived a prison camp, countless deprivations, forced labour, torture, and conditions suited more to an animal than a man, but he ruled my father's life with derision—if not with an iron fist—both before and after the war, and I have never been able to understand why Dad clings to his memory instead of burying him once and for all. It was because of Granddad, after all, that our lives were defined as they were defined in Kensington Square: Dad's superhuman employment history was because Granddad could not support himself, his own wife, and their standard of living; Mother's going out to work—despite having given birth to a handicapped child—was because the income Dad brought in to care for his own parents and the house and my music and my education was not sufficient; my own pursuit of music was encouraged and supported financially in the first place because Granddad decreed it would be so . . . And on top of all this always I can hear Granddad's accusation:* Freaks, Dick! You produce nothing but freaks.

*So within the room, I avoided the display of Granddad memorabilia. I went instead to the desk from which Dad had taken the picture of Katja Wolff and Sonia, and I opened the first of its drawers, which was filled to the top with papers and folders.*

*What were you looking for? you ask me.*

*Something to make me certain about what happened. Because I'm* not *certain, Dr Rose, and with every piece of information I dig up, I find myself becoming that much less certain.*

164

*I've remembered something about my parents and Katja Wolff. It's been triggered by my conversation with Sarah-Jane Beckett and by what followed, which was those additional hours in the Press Association Library. I found a diagram among those cuttings, Dr Rose, a drawing of sorts that showed the previously healed injuries that Sonia had sustained over time. There was a fractured clavicle. There was a dislocated hip. An index finger had healed from a break, and a wrist showed evidence of a hairline fracture. I felt nausea overcome me when I read all this. In my mind one question rang out: How could Sonia have been injured by Katja—by anyone— without the rest of us knowing that something had happened to her?*

*The papers said that under cross examination, the prosecution's expert witness—a physician specialising in child abuse cases—admitted that an infant's bones, more easily given to fractures, are also more easily given to healing from those fractures without the intervention of a doctor. He admitted that, as he was not a specialist in the skeletal anomalies of the Down's Syndrome child, he could not deny that the fractures and dislocations that Sonia had sustained might have been connected to her disability. But under re-examination by the prosecution, he drove home the point that was central to his testimony: A child whose body is undergoing trauma is going to react to that trauma. For that reaction to go unnoticed and for that trauma to go untreated, someone is being derelict in his duty.*

*And still Katja Wolff said nothing. Given an opportunity to rise to her own defence—even to talk about Sonia's condition, her operations, and all the attendant problems she had that made her difficult and fussy and a source of nearly constant and inconsolable crying—Katja Wolff remained silent in the dock as the prosecutor for the Crown savaged her 'callous indifference to the suffering of a child', her 'single-minded self-interest', and 'the animosity that had sprung up between the German and her employer'.*

*And that's when I remembered, Dr Rose.*

*We're having breakfast, which we eat in the kitchen and not the dining room. Only the four of us are present: Dad, my mother, Sonia, and I. I'm playing with my Weetabix, lining up slices of banana like cargo on a barge despite having been told to eat it and not to play, and Sonia is sitting in her highchair while Mother spoons baby food into her mouth.*

*Mother says, 'We can't keep putting up with this, Richard,' and I look up from my Weetabix barge because I think she's cross that I'm still not eating and I think I'm about to be scolded. But Mother continues. 'She was out till half past one again. We gave her a curfew, and if she can't stick to it—'*

*'She has to have some evenings off,' Dad says.*

*'But not the following morning as well. We did have an agreement, Richard.'*

*And I understand from this that Katja is meant to be with us at breakfast, is meant to be feeding Sonia. She has failed to get up and go to my sister, so Mother is doing Katja's job.*

*'We're paying her to care for the baby,' Mother says. 'Not to go dancing, not to go to the cinema, not to watch television, and certainly not to advance her love life under our roof.'*

*That's what I've remembered, Dr Rose, that remark about Katja's love life. And I've also remembered what my parents said next.*

166

'She's not interested in anyone in this house, Eugenie.'

'Please don't expect me to believe that.'

I look between them—first at Dad then at my mother—and I feel something in the air that I can't identify, perhaps a sense of unease. And into this unease comes Katja in a rush. She is filled with apologies for having slept through her morning alarm.

'I please to feed the little one,' she says in her English which must become more broken whenever she's under stress.

My mother says, 'Gideon, would you take your cereal to the dining room, please?' and because of the undercurrents in the kitchen, I obey. But I pause to listen just out of sight and I hear my mother say, 'We've already had one talk about your morning duties, Katja,' and Katja says, 'Please to let me feed the baby, Frau Davies,' in a clear firm voice.

It is the voice of someone unafraid of her employer, I realise now, Dr Rose. And that voice suggests there are very good reasons for Katja not to be afraid.

So I went to my father's flat. I said my hellos to Jill. I dodged certificates, display cases, and trunks containing my grandfather's belongings, and I homed in on my grandmother's desk, which Dad has used as his for years.

I was looking for something that could confirm the connection between Katja and the man who'd made her pregnant. Because I'd finally come to see that if Katja Wolff maintained silence, she could have done so for only one possible reason: to protect someone. And that someone had to be my father, who had kept her photo for more than twenty years.

167

_I did not progress far in my search._

In the drawer that I'd opened, I discovered an accordion file of correspondence. Among the letters therein—most of which comprised subjects having to do with my career—there was one from a solicitor with a north London address. Her client Katja Veronika Wolff had authorised Harriet Lewis, to contact Richard Davies with regard to monies owed her. Since the terms of her parole forbade her to contact any member of the Davies family personally, Miss Wolff was using this legal channel as a conduit through which the matter could be satisfactorily settled. If Mr Davies would be so kind as to phone Ms Lewis at the above listed number at his earliest convenience, this matter of money could be handled expeditiously and to everyone's satisfaction. Ms Lewis remained yours truly, et cetera.

I studied this letter. It was less than two months old. The language in it did not appear to contain the sort of veiled threat one would expect from a solicitor with future litigation on his mind. It was all straightforward, pleasant, and professional. As such, it fairly screamed the question Why?

I was pondering the possible answers to this question when Dad arrived at the flat. I heard him come in. I heard his voice and Jill's coming from the kitchen. Shortly afterwards, his footsteps marked his progress from the kitchen to the Granddad Room.

When he opened the door, I was still sitting there with the accordion file open on the floor at my feet and the letter from Harriet Lewis in my hand. I made no attempt to hide the fact that I was going through my father's belongings, and when he crossed the room, saying sharply, 'What are you doing, Gideon?'

168

my reply was to hand him the letter and say, 'What's behind this, Dad?'

He flicked his gaze over it. He returned it to the accordion file and returned the file to the drawer before he replied.

'She wanted to be paid for the time she spent in remand prior to the trial,' he said. 'The first month of the remand period constituted the notice we'd given her, and she wanted her money for that month as well as interest on it.'

'All these years later?'

'Perhaps a more pertinent remark would be: "After she murdered Sonia?"' He pushed the desk drawer shut.

'She was very sure of her place with our family, wasn't she? She never expected to be sacked.'

'You've no idea what you're talking about.'

'Have you answered that letter, then? Have you phoned those solicitors as requested?'

'I've no intention of doing anything to revisit that period, Gideon.'

I nodded at the drawer where he'd returned the letter. 'Someone apparently doesn't think so. Not only that, but despite what someone's supposed to have done to devastate your life, someone apparently has no compunction about re-entering it even via a solicitor. I don't understand why, unless there was something more between you than employer and employee. Because don't you think a letter like that indicates a sense of confidence that someone in Katja Wolff's position ought not to have with regard to you?'

'What the hell are you getting at?'

'I've remembered my mother talking to you about Katja. I've remembered her suspicions.'

169

'You've remembered rubbish.'

'Sarah-Jane Beckett says James Pitchford wasn't interested in Katja. She says he wasn't actually interested in women at all. That leaves him out of the equation, Dad, which brings it down to you or Granddad, the only other men in the house. Or Raphael, I suppose, although I think both you and I know where Raphael's true affections lay.'

'What are you implying?'

'Sarah-Jane says Granddad was fond of Katja. She says he hung about when she was nearby. But somehow I can't see Granddad managing more than calf-love. And that leaves you.'

'Sarah-Jane Beckett was a jealous cow,' Dad replied. 'She set her sights on Pitchford the day she walked into the house. One pear-shaped syllable out of his heavily tutored mouth and she thought she'd encountered the Second Coming. She was a social climber of the first order, Gideon, and before Katja entered our lives, nothing stood between her and the top of the mountain, which was that fool Pitchford. The last thing she'd have wanted was to see a relationship developing where she herself wanted one. And I assume you have enough basic human psychology under your belt to be able to think that one through.'

I was forced to do just that, sifting back through my time in Cheltenham to weigh what Sarah-Jane had said, placing it in the balance against what Dad was claiming now. Had there been a vindictive satisfaction in Sarah-Jane's comments about Katja Wolff? Or had she simply tried to accommodate a request that I myself had made? Surely, had I called upon her with no desire other than to re-establish a connection with her, she wouldn't have brought up

170

Katja or that period of time on her own. And didn't the very cause of jealousy dictate that the object of the passion be derided at every opportunity? So if it was base jealousy that she felt, wouldn't she have sought to bring up the subject of Katja Wolff herself? And no matter what Sarah-Jane had felt for Katja Wolff twenty years ago, why would she still be wallowing in that feeling now? Tucked away in Cheltenham in her smartly decorated house, wife, mother, collector of dolls, she had little need to dwell on the past, hadn't she?

Into my thoughts, Dad said roughly, 'All right. That's it, then,' in a tone that brought an abrupt end to my reflections. 'This has gone on long enough, Gideon.'

'What?' I said.

'This mucking about. This contemplation of your navel. I'm at my limit with it all. Come with me. We're going to deal with this head-on.'

I thought he meant to tell me something I'd not yet heard, so I followed him. I expected him to take me into the garden the better to have a confidential talk far out of earshot of Jill, who remained in the kitchen contentedly setting up paint samples along the window sill. But instead he went to the door of the flat, and from there to the street. He strode to his car that was parked midway between Cornwall Gardens and Gloucester Road. He said, 'Get in,' as he unlocked it. And when I hesitated, 'God damn it, Gideon. You heard me. Get the hell in.'

I said, 'Where are we going?' as he started the engine.

He jerked the car into reverse and negotiated his way out of the space. We shot up Gloucester Road in the direction of those wrought iron gates that mark the entrance to Kensington Gardens. 'We're going where we should have gone in the first place,' he replied.

He headed east along Kensington Road, driving in a way that I'd never seen him do. He veered round taxis and buses and once leaned on the horn when two women dashed across the street near the Albert Hall. A sharp left at Exhibition Road took us into Hyde Park. He gained even more speed along South Carriage Drive and maintained it the length of Park Lane afterwards. It wasn't until we'd got beyond Marble Arch that I realised where he was taking me. But I said nothing till he'd finally parked the car in the Portman Square underground carpark, where he always went when I performed nearby.

'What's the point in this, Dad?' I asked him, trying for patience where I had fear.

'You're going to get past this nonsense,' he told me. 'Are you man enough to come with me or have you lost your bollocks along with your nerve?'

He shoved open his door and stood waiting for me. I felt my insides go liquid at the thought of what the next few minutes might hold. But I got out of the car anyway. And we walked side by side along Wigmore Street, heading in the direction of Wigmore Hall.

How did that feel? you ask me. What were you experiencing, Gideon?

I was experiencing heading there that night. Only that night I'd been alone because I'd come directly from Chalcot Square.

I'm walking along the street, and I haven't a clue what's in store for me. I'm nervous, but not more than usual before a performance. I've mentioned that, haven't I? My nerves? Funny, I can't remember having nerves when I ought to have had them:

*performing in public the very first time as a six year old, performing several times thereafter as a seven year old, playing for Perlman, meeting Menuhin . . . What was it about me then? How was I so capable of taking things in my stride? I lost that naïve confidence somewhere along the line. So this night on the way to Wigmore Hall is no different to all those other nights I've lived through, and my expectation is that the nervous anticipation that precedes this concert will pass as it usually does, the moment I lift the Guarneri and the bow.*

*I walk along and I think about the music, revisiting it in my head as I usually do. I haven't had a flawless rehearsal of this piece—never have had one—but I'm telling myself that muscle memory will guide my playing past the sections that have given me difficulty.*

*Particular sections? you ask. The same sections each time?*

*No. That's what's always been so peculiar about* The Archduke. *I never know which part of the piece is going to trip me up. It's been a field not cleared of landmines, and no matter how slowly I've progressed over the rough terrain, I've always managed to encounter an explosive.*

*So I move along the street, dimly hear the after-work crowd at one of the pubs I pass, and think about my music. My fingers actually find the notes although I carry the violin in its case, and in doing this, they somewhat calm my anxiety, which I mistakenly take as a sign that all will be well.*

*I arrive ninety minutes early. Just before I round the corner to access the artists' entrance behind the concert hall, I can see up ahead extending over the pavement the covered glass entry of the hall itself,*

173

peopled at this moment only by pedestrians hurrying home from work. I run through the first ten measures of the Allegro. I tell myself what a simple good thing it is, really, to play music with two friends like Beth and Sherrill. I have no idea of what will happen to me in those ninety minutes that are left of my career. I am, if you will, an innocent lamb on his way to be slaughtered, without a sense of danger and somehow lacking the ability to scent blood in the air.

On the way to the hall with Dad, I recalled all this. But there was no real immediacy to my trepidation because I knew already how the next few minutes would play out.

As I did that night, we rounded the corner into Welbeck Street. We hadn't spoken since emerging from the underground car park. I took Dad's silence to mean grim determination. He probably took mine as acquiescence to the plan instead of resignation to what I knew would be the outcome.

At Welbeck Way, we turned again, walking towards the red double doors above which the words Artistes Entrance are hewn into the stone pediment. I was thinking about the fact that Dad hadn't pondered his plan quite through. There would probably be people in the ticket booth at the front of the hall, but at this time of day the artistes' entrance would be locked with no one near it to open it should we knock. So if Dad really wanted me to relive that night of The Archduke, he was going at it wrong, and he was about to be thwarted.

I was on the point of telling him this when my steps faltered, Dr Rose. First they faltered, then they stopped altogether, and nothing on earth could have prompted me to continue walking.

Dad took my arm and said, 'You won't get

174

*anywhere by running away, Gideon.'*

*He thought I was afraid, of course, overcome by anxiety, and unwilling to place myself into the jeopardy that the music ostensibly represented. But it wasn't fear that paralysed me. It was what I saw right in front of me, what I couldn't believe that I hadn't been able to dredge out of my mind before this moment, despite the number of times that I had played at Wigmore Hall in the past.*

*The blue door, Dr Rose. The same blue door that has flashed periodically in my memory and in my dreams. It stands at the top of a flight of ten steps, right next to the artistes' entrance for Wigmore Hall.*

*It's identical to the door I've seen in my mind: bright blue, cerulean blue, the blue of a highland summer sky. It has a silver ring in the centre, two security locks, and a fanlight above it. Beneath that window is a lighting fixture, mounted centrally above the door. There is a railing along the steps, and this is painted like the door itself: that bright, clear, unforgettable blue that I had forgotten nonetheless.*

*I saw that the door appeared to lead to a residence: There were windows next to it, with curtains hanging in them, and from below in Welbeck Way I could see that there were pictures of some sort hanging high on the walls. I felt a surge of excitement the likes of which I haven't felt in months—perhaps in years—as I realised that behind that door might very well lie the explanation for what had happened to me, the cause of my troubles, and the cure.*

*I jerked myself out of Dad's grasp and bounded up those steps. Just as you have told me to do in my imagination, Dr Rose, I tried that door although I* could see before I did so that it could be opened only from the exterior by means of a key. So I knocked upon it. I pounded upon it. And it was opened.

There my hopes for rescue ended. For the door was opened by a Chinese woman so small that at first I thought she was a child. I also thought she was wearing gloves till I saw that her hands were covered in flour. I had never seen her before.

She said, 'Yes?' and looked at me politely. When I said nothing, her gaze shifted down to my father who waited at the foot of the steps. 'May I help you?' she asked, and she moved subtly as she spoke, placing her hip and the bulk of her weight—what little of it there was—behind the door.

I had no idea what to ask her. I had no idea why her front door had been haunting me. I had no idea why I'd gone bolting up the stairs so sure of myself, so damnably certain that I was nearing an end to my troubles.

So I said, 'Sorry. Sorry. There's been a mistake,' although I added in what I already knew was a fruitless possibility, 'Do you live here alone?'

Certainly, I knew this was the wrong question the moment after I asked it. What woman in her right mind is going to tell a strange man on her doorstep that she lives alone even if she does? But before she could offer a reply to the question, I heard a man's voice asking from somewhere behind her, 'Who is that, Sylvia?' and I had my answer. I had more than that because a moment after he asked the question, the man swung the door open wider and peered out. And I didn't know him any more than I knew Sylvia: a large bald gentleman with hands the size of most people's skulls.

'Sorry. Wrong address,' I told him.

176

*'Who d'you want?' he asked.*

*'I don't know,' I replied.*

*Like Sylvia, he looked from me to my father. He said, 'Not the way it sounded from the thrashing you gave to the door just now.'*

*'Yes. I'd thought . . .' What had I thought? That I was about to be given the gift of clarity? I suppose so.*

*But there was no clarity in Welbeck Way. And when I said to Dad later, once the blue door was closed upon us, 'It's part of the answer. I swear that it's part,' his reply was a thoroughly disgusted, 'You don't even know the damn question.'*

## CHAPTER EIGHTEEN

'Lynn Davies?' Barbara Havers produced her warrant card for the woman who'd answered the door of the yellow stucco building. It stood at the end of a line of terraced houses in Therapia Road, a split level Victorian conversion in an East Dulwich quadrant that Barbara had discovered was defined by two cemeteries, a park, and a golf course.

'Yes,' the woman replied, but she said the word as a question, and she cocked her head to one side, puzzled, when she looked at Barbara's identification. She was Barbara's own height—which made her short—but her body looked fit under her simple clothing of blue jeans, trainers, and a fisherman's sweater. She would be the sister-in-law of Eugenie Davies, Barbara concluded, for Lynn looked about the same age as the dead woman, although the wiry hair that spilled round

177

her shoulders and down her back was only just beginning to grey.

'Could I have a word?' Barbara asked her.

'Yes, yes, of course.' Lynn Davies opened the door wider and admitted Barbara into an entrance whose floor was covered by a small, hooked rug. An umbrella stand stood in a corner there, next to it a rattan coat rack from which two identical raincoats hung, both bright yellow and edged in black. She took Barbara to a sitting room, where a bay window overlooked the street. In the alcove that the window comprised, an easel held a heavy sheet of white paper that bore smears of colour in the unmistakable style of finger painting. More sheets of paper—these completed works of art— hung on the walls of the alcove, stuck higgledy piggledy with drawing pins. The sheet on the easel was not a finished work, but it was dry, and it looked as if the artist had been startled in the midst of its creation, for three fingers of paint lurched down towards one corner while the rest of the piece was done in happy, irregular swirls.

Lynn Davies said nothing as Barbara gave a look towards the alcove. She merely waited quietly.

Barbara said to her, 'You're related to Eugenie Davies by marriage, I expect.'

To which Lynn Davies said, 'Not quite. What's this about, Constable?' and her brow furrowed in apparent concern. 'Has something happened to Eugenie?'

'You're not Richard Davies' sister?'

'I was Richard's first wife. Please. Tell me. I'm getting rather frightened. Has something happened to Eugenie?' She clasped her hands in front of her, tightly, so that her arms made a perfect V along her torso. 'Something must have done because why else would you be here?'

Barbara readjusted her thinking, from Richard's sister to Richard's first wife to everything implied by *Richard's first wife.* She watched Lynn as she explained the whys and wherefores of New Scotland Yard's visit.

Lynn was olive skinned, with darker crescents like coffee stains under her deep brown eyes. This skin paled slightly when she learned about the details of the hit and run in West Hampstead. She said, 'Dear God,' and walked to an ancient three piece suite. She sat, staring in front of her but saying to Barbara, 'Please . . .' then nodding to the armchair next to which dozens of children's books were neatly stacked, *How the Grinch Stole Christmas* placed seasonably on the top.

'I'm sorry,' Barbara said. 'I can see it's a shock.'

'I didn't know,' Lynn said. 'And it must have been in the papers, mustn't it? Because of Gideon. And because of . . . of how you say that she died. But I didn't see them—the papers—because I've not been coping as well as I thought I would and . . . Oh God. Poor Eugenie. To have it all end like this.'

This didn't seem at all to be the reaction of an embittered first wife thrown over for a second. Barbara said, 'You knew her quite well, then.'

'I've known Eugenie for years.'

'When did you see her last?'

'Last week. She came to the service for my daughter. That's why I haven't seen . . . why I didn't know . . .' Lynn rubbed the palm of her right hand hard against her thigh, as if this action could quell something within her. 'Virginia, my daughter, died

179

quite suddenly last week, Constable. I knew it could happen at any time. I'd known that for years. But somehow one is never quite as prepared as one hopes to be.'

'I'm sorry,' Barbara said.

'She was painting as she did each afternoon. I was in the kitchen making our tea. I heard her fall. I came running out. And that was . . . What do they call it, Constable? *It.* The great, long-expected visitation arrived, and I wasn't with her. I wasn't even there to say goodbye.'

Like Tony, Barbara thought, and it jolted her to have her brother shoot into her mind when she hadn't prepared herself to greet him. It was just like Tony, who had died alone without a single member of the family at his bedside. She didn't like to think about Tony, about his lingering illness or the hell that his death had brought into her family. She said only, 'Kids aren't meant to die before their parents, are they,' and she felt an attendant tightness in her throat.

'The doctors said she was dead before she hit the floor,' Lynn Davies told her. 'And I know they mean to comfort me. But when you've spent most of your life caring for a child like Virginia—always and forever a little one no matter how large she grew—your world is still wrenched to pieces when she's taken, especially if you've simply stepped out of the room to see to her tea. So I haven't been able to read a paper—much less a novel or a magazine—and I haven't turned on the telly or the radio because although I'd like to distract myself, if I do that there's a chance I'll stop feeling and what I feel right now—at this moment, if you can understand what I'm saying—is how I stay

180

connected to her. If you can understand.' Lynn's eyes filled as she spoke.

Barbara gave her a moment as she herself adjusted to what she was learning. Among the information she was indexing in her mind was the unimaginable fact that Richard Davies had apparently fathered not one but two disabled children. For what else could Lynn Davies possibly mean when she described her daughter as forever a little one? 'Virginia wasn't—' Barbara searched for a word. There *had* to be a euphemism somewhere, she thought with frustration, and if she were from America—that great land of political correctness— she would probably have known it. 'She wasn't well?' she settled on saying.

'My daughter was disabled from birth, Constable. She had the body of a woman and the mind of a three-year-old child.'

'Oh. Hell. I'm sorry to hear that.'

'Her heart wasn't right. We knew from the first it would fail her eventually. But her spirit was strong, so she surprised everyone and lived thirty-two years.'

'Here at home with you?'

'It wasn't an easy life for either of us. But when I consider what might have been, I have no regrets. I gained more than I lost when my marriage ended. And ultimately, I couldn't blame Richard for asking for the divorce.'

'And then he remarried and had another . . .' Again, there was no useful catch phrase. Lynn supplied her own, saying, 'A child imperfect as we measure perfection. Yes. Richard had another, and those who believe in a vengeful God might argue that he was being punished for having abandoned

181

us, Virginia and me. But I don't think that's how God works. Richard wouldn't have asked us to leave in the first place if I'd only agreed to have more children.'

'*Asked* you to leave?' What a prince among men, Barbara thought. Here was something for a bloke to be proud of: having asked his wife and his retarded child to find themselves new digs.

Lynn hastened to explain. 'We lived with his parents, in the house he himself had grown up in. So when it came time to part, it didn't make sense that Virginia and I should stay with Richard's parents while Richard left. And, anyway, that was part of the problem: Richard's parents. His father was completely unmoveable on the subject of Virginia. He wanted her put away. He insisted on it. And Richard was . . . It was so important to him to have his father's approval. So he was won over to that way of thinking, about putting Virginia into a home. But I wouldn't hear of it. After all, this was . . .' Her eyes again showed her pain, and she stopped for a moment before saying with simple dignity, 'She was our child. She hadn't asked to be born the way she was. Who were we to think we could chuck her away? And that's what Richard himself thought at first. Until his father changed his mind.' She looked again to the alcove, to the bright smeared paintings that decorated it, saying, 'He was a terrible man, Jack Davies was. I know he'd suffered horribly in the war. I know his mind was a ruin and he couldn't be blamed for the ugliness inside him. But to hate an innocent child so much that she wasn't allowed to be in the same room with him . . .? That was wrong, Constable. That was terribly wrong.'

182

'It sounds like hell,' Barbara acknowledged.

'A form of it. "Thank God she doesn't spring from *my* blood," he used to say. And Richard's mother would murmur, "Jack, Jack, you don't actually mean that," when all the time you could see that if there was a single way that he could wipe Virginia's existence from this planet, he would have gladly made the attempt without a second thought.' Lynn's lips trembled. 'And now she's gone. Wouldn't Jack be happy now.' She shoved her hand into the pocket of her blue jeans and brought out a crumpled tissue, which she pressed beneath her eyes, saying, 'I'm terribly sorry. Forgive me for running on in this way. I shouldn't be . . . God, how I miss her.'

'It's okay,' Barbara said. 'You're trying to cope.'

'And now Eugenie,' Lynn Davies said. 'How can I help with what's happened to Eugenie? That's why you've come, isn't it? Not just to tell me but to ask for my help?'

'You and Mrs Davies had a bond, I expect. Through your children.'

'Not at first. It was when her little Sonia died that we met. Eugenie simply turned up on my doorstep one day. She wanted to talk. I was happy to listen.'

'You saw her regularly then?'

'Yes. She dropped round often. She needed to talk—what mother wouldn't in those circumstances?—and I was glad to be here for her. She felt she couldn't talk to Richard, you see, and while there was a Catholic nun she was close to, the nun wasn't a mother, was she? And that's what Eugenie needed: another mother to talk to, and especially the mother of a special child. She was

183

grieving terribly, and there was no one in that household who could understand how she felt. But she knew about me and she knew about Virginia because Richard had told her shortly after they married.'

'Not before they married? That's odd.'

Lynn smiled resignedly. 'That's Richard, Constable Havers. He paid maintenance till Virginia reached adulthood, but he never saw her once she and I left him. I did think he might come to the funeral. I let him know when she died. But he sent flowers and that was that.'

'Brilliant,' Barbara muttered.

'He is who he is. Not a bad man, but not a man equipped to cope with a handicapped child. And not everyone is. At least I'd had some practical training in nursing while Richard . . . well, what did he have but his brief career in the army? And anyway, he wanted to carry on the family name, which meant, naturally, that he would have to find a second wife. And that actually turned out to be the right thing to do, didn't it, because Eugenie gave him Gideon.'

'The jackpot.'

'In a way. But I expect the burden of giving birth to a prodigy is an enormous one. A different set of responsibilities but just as heavy.'

'Eugenie didn't say?'

'She never spoke much of Gideon. And then, when she and Richard divorced, she never spoke of Gideon at all. Or of Richard. Or of any of them. Mostly, when she came, she helped me with Virginia. She loved the parks, Virginia did, the cemeteries as well. It was our special joy to take a ramble in Camberwell Old Cemetery. But I didn't like to do it without someone else with us, to help keep an eye on Virginia. If I was there with her alone, I had to fix my attention on her and I got no pleasure from the afternoon. But with Eugenie there, it was easier. She would watch her. I would watch her. We could talk, bask in the sun, read the gravestones. She was very good to us.'

'Did you speak to her the day of Virginia's funeral?' Barbara asked.

'Of course. Yes. But we didn't speak of anything that could help your enquiry, I'm afraid. Just about Virginia. The loss. How I was coping. Eugenie was a great comfort to me. Indeed, she'd been a comfort for years. And Virginia . . . She actually came to *know* Eugenie. To recognise her. To—' Lynn stopped. She rose and went to the alcove where she stood in front of the easel on which her daughter's final painting marked her quick passage from life into death. She said in a contemplative voice, 'Yesterday I did several of these myself. I wanted to *feel* what had given her such joy. But I couldn't reach that place. I tried painting after painting till my hands were black from all the colours I'd mixed together, and still I couldn't feel it. So I finally saw how blessed she actually had been: to be eternally a child who asked so little of life.'

'There's a lesson in that,' Barbara agreed.

'Yes. Isn't there.' She studied the painting.

Barbara stirred in her seat, wanting to bring Lynn Davies back. She said, 'Eugenie'd been seeing a bloke in Henley, Mrs Davies. A retired army bloke called Ted Wiley. He owns the book shop across the street from her house. Did she ever speak of him?'

Lynn Davies turned from the painting. 'Ted Wiley? A book shop? No. She never talked of Ted Wiley.'

'Of anyone else she might have been involved with?'

Lynn thought about this. 'She was careful with what she revealed about herself. She'd always been that way. But I think . . . I don't know if this is any help, but the last time we spoke—this would be before I rang to tell her about Virginia's passing— she mentioned . . . Well, I don't know if it actually meant anything. At least I don't know if it meant she'd become involved.'

'It might be of help,' Barbara told her. 'What did she say?'

'It wasn't so much what she said but the way she said it. There was a lightness to her voice that I'd never heard before. She asked me if I believed that one could fall in love where one wasn't expecting to find love. She asked me if I thought that years could pass and one could suddenly look upon someone in a light entirely different from the way one had looked on him in the past. She asked me if I thought love could grow from that, from that new way of looking. Could she have been talking about the army man? Someone she'd known for years but never thought of as a lover till now?'

Barbara wondered about this. It did seem likely. But there was something more to consider: Eugenie Davies' whereabouts at the time of her death and the address in her possession suggested something else.

She said, 'Did she ever mention James Pitchford?'

Lynn shook her head.

'What about Pitchley? Or Pytches, perhaps?'

'She didn't mention anyone by name. But that's how she was: a very private person.'

A very private person who'd ended up murdered, Barbara thought. And she wondered if the dead woman's need for privacy was at the core of her killing.

\*　　　\*　　　\*

DCI Eric Leach listened to the sister in charge of the intensive care unit at Charing Cross Hospital as she essentially told him the worst. *No change* was what they said when the doctors were handing over the reins of someone's condition to God, fate, nature, or time. It was not what they said when someone made some sort of progress, side-stepped the grim reaper, or achieved a sudden and miraculous recovery. Leach hung up the phone and turned from his desk, brooding. He brooded not only over what had happened to Malcolm Webberly but also over his own inadequacies and what they were doing to his ability to anticipate the investigation's twists and turns.

He had to deal with the problem of Esmé. That much was clear. How to deal with it would come to him soon. But *that* he had to deal with it was obvious. Because had he not been distracted by Esmé's fears about her mum's new boyfriend—not to mention by his own feelings about Bridget having found a replacement for him—he surely would have remembered that J.W. Pitchley, aka James Pitchford had also once been Jimmy Pytches whose ties to an infant's death in Tower Hamlets had long ago been the subject of the London tabloids' delight. Not when that infant died, of course, that situation having sorted itself out soon enough after the post mortem. But years later, after another child died in Kensington.

Once that pug-like Yard woman had revealed this titbit, Leach had remembered it all. He'd tried to tell himself that he'd deleted the information from his memory banks because it hadn't amounted to anything but aggro for Pitchford during the investigation into the Davies baby's death. But the truth was, he should have remembered it, and it was down to Bridget and Bridget's boyfriend and especially Esmé's anxiety over Bridget's boyfriend that he hadn't. And he couldn't afford not to remember what he needed to remember about that long ago case. Because it was seeming to him more and more probable that that case had a link to this one which was unlikely to be easily severed.

A PC popped his head into his office doorway, saying, 'We've got that bloke from West Hampstead you were asking for, sir. D'you want him in an interview room?'

'Got his brief with him?'

'What else?' he said. 'I don't expect he takes a dump in the morning without checking with his solicitor to see how many sheets of toilet paper he's got a right to use.'

'Make it an interview room, then,' Leach said. He didn't like allowing solicitors to think they'd somehow intimidated him, and showing Pitchley-Pitchford-Pytches into his office felt like something that would do just that.

He took a few minutes to make the call that would release Pitchley's motor to him. There was

188

nothing more to be gained by holding the Boxster, and it seemed to Leach that their possession of past details about James Pitchford and Jimmy Pytches was more likely to chisel information from the man than was their continuing to hold on to his car.

After the call, he grabbed a cup of coffee and went to the interview room where Pitchley-Pitchford-Pytches—Leach was beginning to think of him as P-Man for simple ease of keeping track of all his names—and his solicitor were waiting, seated at the interview table. Azoff was smoking despite the sign expressly forbidding it, his way of sneering 'bugger you for ten pence,' while P-Man was working his hands through his hair like someone trying to rolf his brain.

'I've advised my client to say nothing,' Azoff began, eschewing anything that might have gone for a greeting. 'He's cooperated thus far with no sign on your part of recompensing him in any way.'

'Recompensing?' Leach said incredulously. 'What d'you think this is, man? We're running a murder enquiry here, and if we need your boy to assist us, we're going to bloody well have him.'

'I see no reason to carry on with these meetings if he's not going to be charged with something,' Azoff countered.

At which, P-Man looked up, mouth open, his face a veritable picture of 'what the hell are you *saying,* you berk?' Leach liked this because a man who was innocent would hardly look at his solicitor like a back-alley thug with a garrote in his hand just because the lawyer said the words 'charge him'. A man who was innocent would wear an expression saying, 'Yeah. Got *that,* Jack?' and he'd direct that

189

expression at the cop. But P-Man wasn't doing that, which made Leach more certain than ever that he needed to be broken. He wasn't sure what breaking him would actually achieve, but he was more than willing to try it.

He said, 'Well. Right. Mr Pytches,' quite affably.

To which Azoff said, 'Pitchley,' with an irritation that he underscored with a gust of tobacco smoke blown into the air, carrying on it the accompanying olfactory tincture of advanced halitosis.

Leach said, 'Ah. Doesn't know it all, then, does he?' to P-Man with a nod at the solicitor. 'Got some nooks and crannies in the skeleton cupboard you've not shone a torch into, yes?'

P-Man sank his head into his hands, body language for his sudden realisation that his bollocksed up life had just become a degree more bollocksed up. 'I've told you everything I can tell you,' he said, sidestepping the Jimmy Pytches issue. 'I've not seen that woman—I've not seen *any* of them—since six months after the trial. I moved on. Well, what else could I do? New house, new life—'

'New name,' Leach said. 'Just like before. But Mr Azoff here doesn't seem to know that a bloke like you with a past like yours has a way of getting sucked into events, Mr Pytches. Even when he thinks he's weighted that past in concrete boots and chucked it into the Thames.'

'What the hell are you on about, Leach?' Azoff said.

'Get rid of that shit burner you've got in your mouth, and I'll do what I can to elucidate,' Leach said. 'This is a non-smoking area and I presume that reading is one of your talents, Mr Azoff.'

Azoff took his time about removing the cigarette

190

from his mouth, and he took even more time to dislodge its ash against the sole of his shoe, carefully so as to preserve the remaining tobacco for his later pleasure. During this performance, P-Man, unbidden, unspooled most of his story for the solicitor. At the end of a recitation that was as brief and as positively slanted as possible, P-Man said, 'I've not mentioned this cot death business before because there was no need, Lou. And there's *still* no need. Or at least there wouldn't be if this—' a jerk of his head at Leach indicated that the demonstrative pronoun was as close as P-Man intended to come to dignifying Leach's presence by actually giving him a name—'hadn't made up his mind to something that bears no relationship whatsoever to the truth.'

'Pytches,' Azoff said, and while he sounded thoughtful as he said the name, his narrowing eyes suggested that his thoughts had less to do with absorbing a new piece of information than they had to do with what he planned as a disciplinary measure for a client who continued to withhold facts from him, making him look like a fool each time he was forced to face the police. 'You say *another* kid who died, Jay?'

'Two kids and a woman,' Leach reminded him. 'And counting, by the way. Another victim got hit last night. Where were you, Pytches?'

'That's not fair!' P-Man cried. 'I haven't seen a single one of those people ... I haven't talked to ... I don't know *why* she had my address with her ... And I certainly don't believe—'

'Last night,' Leach repeated.

'Nothing. *Nowhere.* At home. Where the hell else would I be when you've got my car?'

191

'Picked up by someone, perhaps,' Leach said.

'Who? Someone I supposedly joined for a nice dash round London for a quick hit and run?'

'I don't think I mentioned it was hit and run.'

'Don't make yourself out to be so bloody clever. You said another victim. You said another hit. You can't expect me to think you meant hitting someone with a cricket bat, can you? Else why would I be here?'

He was getting hot under the collar. Leach liked that. He also liked the fact that P-Man's brief was just cheesed off enough to let him twist in the wind for a minute or two. That could be distinctly useful.

He said, 'Good question, Mr Pytches.'

'Pitchley,' P-Man said.

'What have you seen of Katja Wolff lately?'

'Kat—' P-Man halted himself. 'What about Katja Wolff?' he asked, quietly cautious.

'I had a look through ancient history this morning and I found you never gave evidence at her trial.'

'I wasn't asked to give evidence. I was in the house but I didn't see anything and there was no reason—'

'But the Beckett woman did. The boy's teacher. Sarah-Jane she was called. My notes—have I mentioned that I keep all my records from investigations?—show that you and she were together when the kid got the chop. You were together, which must mean you both saw everything or nothing at all, but in any event—'

'I didn't see *anything*.'

'—in any event,' Leach continued forcefully, 'Beckett gave evidence while you stayed mum. Why was that?'

'She was the boy's teacher. Gideon. The brother. She saw more of the family. She saw more of the little girl. She saw what kind of care Katja gave her, so she must have thought she had something to contribute. And listen, I wasn't *asked* to give evidence. I spoke to the police, I gave my statement, I waited for more but I wasn't asked.'

'Convenient, that.'

'Why? Are you trying to suggest—'

'Plug it,' Azoff said finally. And to Leach, 'Get to the point or we're off.'

'Not without my motor,' P-Man said.

Leach fished in his jacket pocket and brought out the release form for the Boxster. He laid it on the table between himself and the two other men. He said, 'You were the only one from that house who didn't give evidence against her, Mr Pytches. I'd've thought she'd've dropped in to say thank you now that she's out of the coop.'

'What're you *on* about?' P-Man cried.

'Beckett gave character evidence. Talked to us and to everyone else about which wires in Katja Wolff's circuits were fraying. Bit of temper here. Dash of impatience there. Other things to do when the baby needed looking after. Not always on her toes the way a properly trained nanny would be. And then getting herself in the club . . .'

'Yes? So? What about it?' P-Man said. 'Sarah-Jane saw more than I saw. She talked about that. Am I supposed to be her conscience or something? Twenty odd years after the fact?'

Azoff intervened. 'We're looking for a point to this confab, DCI Leach. If there isn't one, we'll have that paperwork and be off.' He reached for it.

Leach pressed his fingers along its edge. 'The

193

point is Katja Wolff,' he said. 'And our boy's ties to her.'

'I have no ties to her,' P-Man protested.

'I'm not sure about that. Someone got her pregnant, and I'm not putting a fiver on the Holy Ghost.'

'Don't blame that on me. We lived in the same house. That's all. We nodded on the staircase. I might have given her the odd lesson with her English and, yes, I might have *admired* . . . Look. She was attractive. She was sure of herself, confident, not the way you'd expect a foreigner who didn't even speak the language to feel or act. That's always nice to see in a woman. And for God's sake, I'm not blind.'

'Had a bit of a thing with her, then. Tip-toeing round the house at night. Once or twice behind the garden shed, and ooops, look what happened.'

Azoff slapped his hand on the table between them. He said, 'Once, twice, eighty-five times. If you're not intending to talk about the case in hand, we're off. You got that?'

'This *is* the case in hand, Mr Azoff, especially if our boy spent the last twenty years brooding about a woman he diddled and then didn't do a thing to help once she'd—A—got herself up the spout thanks to him and—B—got herself charged with murder. He might want to make amends for that. And what better way than to give a hand in a spot of revenge. Which she might think she's owed, by the way. Time passes a bit slow inside, you know. And you'd be dead surprised to see the way that slow time makes a killer decide *she's* the injured party.'

'That's . . . that is *utterly* . . . that's preposterous,'

194

P-Man sputtered.

'Is it?'

'You know it is. What's supposed to have happened?'

'Jay—' Azoff counselled.

'She's supposed to have tracked me down, rung my bell one night, and said, "Hello, Jim. Know we haven't seen each other for twenty, but how about helping me rub out a few people? Just for a laugh, this is. Not too busy, are you?" Is that how you picture it, Inspector?'

'Shut up, Jay,' Azoff said.

'No! I've spent half my life scouring the walls when *I'm* not the one who's pissed on them and I'm tired of it. I'm God damn bloody tired. If it's not the police, then it's the papers. If it's not the papers, it's—' He stopped himself.

'Yes?' Leach leaned forward. 'Who is it, then? What's the nasty you've got back there, Mr P? Something beyond that cot death, I reckon. You're a real man of mystery, you are. And I'll tell you this much: I'm not finished with you.'

P-Man sank back in his chair, his throat working. Azoff said, 'Odd. I don't hear a caution, Inspector. Forgive me if I lapsed into momentary unconsciousness sometime during this meeting, but I don't recall having heard a caution yet. And if I *won't* be hearing one in the next fifteen seconds, it's my suggestion that we make our farewells now, heartrending though those farewells may be.'

Leach shoved the Boxster's paperwork at them. He said, 'Don't plan any holidays, Mr P.' And to Azoff, 'Keep that fag unlit till you're on the street or I'll have you.'

'Cor. Blimey. I'm ackshully pissing me pants,

195

guv'nor,' Azoff said.

Leach started to speak, then stopped himself. Then he said, 'Get out,' and saw to it that they did just that.

*       *       *

J.W. Pitchley, aka TongueMan, aka James Pitchford, aka Jimmy Pytches said his goodbye to Lou Azoff in front of the Hampstead police station, and he knew that this was a final one. Azoff was cheesed off about the Jimmy Pytches revelation, more cheesed off than he'd been by the James Pitchford revelation, and despite the fact that he'd been declared blameless of the death of both children first as Pytches and then as Pitchford, that wasn't 'the issue', as Azoff put it. He wasn't about to put himself in the position of getting sucker punched again by something that his client was withholding from him, Azoff said. How'd he think it felt, sitting in there with a sodding copper who'd probably not even passed his bleeding O-levels for Christ's sake, and having the rug pulled out without even knowing there was a rug in the room? This effing situation wasn't *on*, Jay. Or is it James? Or Jimmy? Or someone else, for that matter?

It wasn't someone else. He wasn't someone else. And even if Azoff hadn't said, 'You'll get my final bill by special courier tomorrow,' he himself would have put the full stop to their legal dealings. No matter that he handled the labyrinth that was Azoff's tricky financial position. He could find someone else in the City equally talented at moving Azoff's money round faster than the Inland

196

Revenue could track it.

So he said, 'Right, Lou,' and he didn't bother to try to talk the solicitor out of quitting. He couldn't blame the poor sod, really. Who could expect someone to want to play defence on a team that wouldn't give directions to the pitch?

He watched Azoff wind his scarf round his neck and fling its end over his shoulder, like the denouement of a play that had already gone on far too long. The solicitor made his exit, and Pitchley sighed. He could have told Azoff that sacking him had not only already crossed his mind but had also planted itself there half way through the interview with DCI Leach, but he decided to let the solicitor have his moment. The drama of quitting on the streets of Hampstead was meagre compensation for having endured the ignominy of ignorance to which Pitchley's omission of certain facts had recently exposed him. But it was all that Pitchley had to offer at the moment, so he offered it and stood, head bowed, while Azoff railed and till Azoff did his bit with the scarf. 'I'll get on to a bloke I know who'll see you right with your money,' he told the solicitor.

'You do just that,' Azoff said. He made no similar offer on his part: recommending another solicitor willing to take on a client who asked him to work in the dark. But then Pitchley didn't expect him to. Indeed, he'd given up expecting anything.

That hadn't always been the case, although if it couldn't be said that he'd had expectations years ago, it *could* be said that he'd possessed dreams. She'd told him hers in that breathless, confiding, cheerful whisper, after hours when they had their English lessons and their chats at the top of the

197

house, one ear to the speaker from the baby's room so that if she stirred, if she cried, if she needed her Katja, her Katja would be there, fast as could be. She said, 'There are these fashion-for-clothes schools, yes? For design of what to wear. Yes? You see? And you see how I make these fashion drawings, yes? This is where I study when the money is saved. Where I come from, James, clothing . . . Oh, I cannot say, but your colours, your *colours* . . . And see at this scarf I have bought. This is Oxfam, James. Someone gave it away!' And she would bring it out and whirl it like an eastern dancer, a length of worn silk with its fringe coming loose but to her a fabric to be turned into a sash, a belt, a drawstring bag, a hat. Two such scarves and she had a blouse. Five and a motley skirt emerged. 'This I am meant to do,' she would say, and her eyes were bright and her cheeks were flushed and the rest of her skin was velvet milk. All London wore black, but never Katja. Katja was a rainbow, a celebration of life.

And because of all that, he had dreams himself. Not plans as she had, not something spoken, but something held on to like a feather that will soil and be useless for flight if grasped too tightly or for too long.

He wouldn't move quickly, he'd told himself. They were both young. She had her schooling ahead of her and he wanted to establish himself in the City before taking on the sort of responsibilities that came with marriage. But when the time was right . . . Yes, she was the one. So completely different, so completely capable of *becoming,* so eager to learn, so willing—no, so *desperate*—to escape who she'd been in order to achieve who she

198

believed she could become. She was, in effect, his female counterpart. She didn't know that yet and she never would if he had his way, but in the unlikely event that she discovered that fact, she was a woman who would understand. We all have our hot air balloons, he would tell her.

Had he loved her? he wondered. Or had he merely seen in her his best chance for a life where her foreign background would cast a useful shadow in which he could hide? He didn't know. He'd never got a chance to find out. And at a distance of two decades, he still didn't know how it might have worked out between the two of them. But what he did know without a single doubt was that at long last he'd had enough.

With the Boxster in his possession, he began the drive that he knew was a journey that had been long in coming. It took him across London, first dropping down out of Hampstead and veering in the direction of Regent's Park, then wending his way eastward, ever eastward, to arrive in that Hades of postal codes: E3 where his nightmares had their roots.

Unlike many areas of London, Tower Hamlets had not become gentrified. Films made here did not feature actors who batted their eyelashes, fell in love, lived arty lives, and lent an air of genteel down-at-heel glamour to the place, thus resulting in its renaissance at the hands of yuppies in Range Rovers yearning to be trendy. For the word *renaissance* implied that a place had once seen better times to which an infusion of cash would return it. But to Pitchley's eyes, Tower Hamlets had been a dump from the moment its first building had its initial foundation stone set into

199

place.

He'd spent more than half his life trying to scrub the grime of Tower Hamlets from beneath his fingernails. He'd worked at jobs not fit for man or beast since his ninth birthday, squirrelling away whatever he could towards a future he wanted but couldn't quite define. He'd endured bullying at a school where learning took a distant seventh place to tormenting teachers, demolishing ancient and nearly useless equipment, graffitiing every available inch, shagging birds on the stairwells, setting fires in the dust bins, and pinching everything from the third formers' sweets money to the Christmas collection taken each year to give a decent meal to the area's homeless drunks. In that environment, he'd forced himself to learn, a sponge for *whatever* might get him out of the inferno that he'd come to assume was his punishment for a transgression he'd committed in a previous lifetime.

His family didn't understand his passion to be free of the place. So his mother—unmarried as she always had been and would be to her grave—smoked her fags all day at the window of the council flat, collected the dole like it was owed to her for doing the nation the favour of breathing, raised the six offspring that were got by four fathers, and wondered aloud how she'd managed to produce such a git as Jimmy, all neat and tidy like he actually thought he was something other than a yobbo in disguise.

'Lookit '*im*, will you?' she'd ask his siblings. 'Too good for us, our Jim. Wha's it to be today, laddie?'—as she looked him over—'Riding to the 'ounds, are we?'

He'd say, 'Aw, Mum,' and feel misery climbing

from his navel up his chest and into his jaws.

'Tha's all right, lad,' she'd reply. 'Just pinch one of them nice doggies so we'll 'ave a watcher round these ol' digs, okay? Tha'd be nice, now, woul'n't it, kids? 'Ow'd you like our Jimmy to pinch us a dog?'

'Mum, I'm not going fox hunting,' he'd say.

And they'd laugh. Laugh and laugh till he wanted to thrash the lot of them for being so useless.

His mother was the worst because she set the tone. She might have been clever. She might have been energetic. She might have been capable of doing something with her life. But she got herself a baby—Jimmy himself—when she was fifteen and that's when she learned that if she kept having them, she'd be paid. Child allowance was what they called it. What Jimmy Pytches called it was Government Chains.

So he made his life's purpose the demolition of his past, taking every odd job he could get his mitts on as soon as he was able to do so. What the job was didn't matter to him: cleaning windows, scrubbing floors, vacuuming carpets, walking dogs, washing cars, babysitting. He didn't care. If he was paid to do it, do it he would. Because although money couldn't buy him better blood, it could get him miles from the blood that threatened to drown him.

Then came that cot death, that God awful moment when he went into her bedroom because it was long past the time she generally woke up from her nap. And there she was like a plastic doll, with one hand curled to her mouth like she'd been trying to help herself *breathe*—for God's sake—and her tiny fingernails were blue were blue were bluest

201

of blue and he knew right then that she was a goner. Crikey, he'd been in the sitting room, hadn't he? He'd been right next door. He'd been watching Arsenal. He'd been thinking, Lucky day, this is, the brat's well away and I won't have to fuss with her during the game. He'd *thought* that—the brat—but he didn't mean it, never would have said it, actually smiled when he saw her in her push chair at the local grocery with her mum. He never thought 'the brat' then. Just, Here's lit'le Sherry and her mum. Hello, Chubbychops. Because that's what he called her. He called her a nonsense name, Chubbychops.

Then she was dead and the police were there. Questions and answers and tears all round. And what kind of monster was *he* who watched Arsenal while a baby was dying and who even to this *day* remembered the score?

There were whispers, of course. There were rumours as well. Both fuelled his passion to be gone forever. And forever was what he thought he'd achieved, a kind of eternal paradise defined by a Dutch-fronted house in Kensington, the kind of house so grand it had a medallion carved 1879 on its gable. And this house was peopled as grandly as it was situated, much to his delight. A war hero, a child prodigy on the violin, a for-God's-sake *governess* for that child, a foreign nanny . . . Nothing could have been more different to where he'd come from: Tower Hamlets via a bedsit in Hammersmith and a fortune spent on learning everything from how to say *haricots verts* and knowing what it meant to how to use cutlery instead of one's fingers for moving bits of food round one's plate. So when he'd finally reached Kensington Square, no one knew. Least of all Katja who would never have known, having not had a lifetime of instruction on what it meant to say *lounge* at an inopportune time.

And then she'd got pregnant, the worst sort of getting pregnant. Unlike his mum, who'd carried on during her pregnancies as if growing a child inside her body were nothing more than a minor inconvenience causing her to switch to a different set of clothes for a few months, Katja'd had no easy time of it, which made her condition impossible to hide. And from that pregnancy had risen everything else, including his own past, threatening to seep from the splitting pipes of their life in Kensington Square like the sewage it was.

Even after all that, he'd thought he could escape it again. James Pitchford, whose past had hung over him like Damocles' sword, just waiting to be smeared across the tabloids as Lodger Once Investigated in Cot Death, just waiting to be revealed as Jimmy Pytches: all aitches dropped and tee-aitches said as effs, Jimmy Pytches the subject of laughter for trying to be better than he was. So he changed again, morphed himself into J.W. Pitchley, ace investor and financial wizard, but running, always running, and always to run.

Which brought him to Tower Hamlets now: a man who'd come to accept the fact that to escape what he could not bear to face, he could kill himself, he could change his identity yet again, or he could flee forever, not only the teeming city of London but everything that London—and England—represented.

He parked the Boxster near the tower block that had been his childhood home. He looked round and saw that little had changed, including the presence of local skin heads, three of them this time, who smoked in the doorway of a nearby shop, watching him and his car with studied attention. He called out to them, 'Want to make ten quid?'

One of them spat a gob of yellowish sputum into the street. 'Each?' he said.

'All right. Each.'

'What's to do, then?'

'Keep an eye on the motor for me. See that no one touches it. OK?'

They shrugged. Pitchley took this for assent. He nodded at them saying, 'Ten now, twenty later.'

'Let's 'ave it,' said their leader and he slouched over for the cash.

As he handed the ten pound note over to the thug, Pitchley realised the bloke might well be his youngest half brother, Paul. It had been more than twenty years since he'd seen little Paulie. What an irony it would be if he were handing over what went for extorted dosh to his own brother without either of them knowing who the other was. But that was the case for most of his siblings now. For all he knew, there might even be more of them than the five there were when he did his runner.

He entered the tower block estate: a patch of dead lawn, chalk hopscotch squares drawn drunkenly on the uneven tarmac, a deflated football with a knife gouge in it, two shopping trolleys overturned and rendered wheel-less. Three little girls were attempting to inline skate on one of the concrete paths, but its condition was as bad as the tarmac's, so they'd get about two and a half yards of even ground to glide on before they had to clomp over or around a spot where the concrete looked as if the bomb squad might want to come to have a look for a UXB.

Pitchley made his way to the lift and found that it was out of service. A block lettered sign informed him of this, hanging on old chrome doors long ago decorated by the resident spray paint artists.

He set off up the stairs, seven flights of them. She loved—as she said—' 'aving me bit of a view.' This was important since she never did anything but stand, sit, lounge, smoke, drink, eat, or watch telly in that sagging-seat chair that had stood forever next to the window.

He was out of breath by the second floor. He had to pause on the landing and breathe deeply of its urine scented air before climbing upwards. When he got to the fifth floor, he stopped again. By the seventh, his arm pits were dripping.

He rubbed down his neck as he walked to the door of her flat. He never suffered a moment's doubt that she would be there. Jen Pytches would move her arse only if the building were going up in flames. And even then, she'd complain about it: 'Wha' abou' me programme on the telly?'

He rapped on the door. From within he heard the sound of chatter, television voices that marked the time of day. Chat shows in the morning, afternoon and it was snooker—God only knew why—and evening brought the soaps.

No answer to his knock, so he rapped again, louder this time, and he called out, 'Mum?' He tried the door and found it unlocked. He opened it a crack and said, 'Mum?' again.

She said, 'Who's it, then? That you, Paulie? You been to the job centre already, 'ave you? Don' think so, lad. Don' be trying to pull the wool over, you go' tha', son? I wasn' born this morning.' She

205

coughed the deep, phlegm-cursed cough of the forty-year smoker, as Pitchley used the tips of his fingers to move the door inward.

He slipped inside and faced his mother. It was the first time he'd seen her in twenty-five years.

'Well,' she said. She was by the window as he thought she would be, but no longer the woman he remembered from his childhood. Twenty-five years of not stirring a muscle unless forced to do so had made his mother into a great mound of a woman wearing stretch trousers and a jumper the size of a parachute. He wouldn't have known her at all had he passed her on the street. He wouldn't have known her now had she not said, 'Jim. Wha's a dolly to make of this sor' 'f surprise?'

He said, 'Hello, Mum,' and he looked round the flat. Nothing had changed. Here was the same U-shaped blue sofa, there were the lamps with the misshapen shades, up on the walls were the same set of pictures: each little Pytches sitting on the knee of his or her own dad on the only occasion Jen had managed to make any of them act like fathers. God, seeing them brought it back in a rush: the risible exercise of all the kids lined up and Jen pointing to the pictures, saying, 'Here's your dad, Jim. He was called Trev. But I called him my little fancy boy.' And, 'Yours was Derek, Bonnie. Look at the neck on that bloke, will you, dear? Couldn't put me 'ands *anywhere* near round his neck. Oooh. Wha' a man your dad was, Bon.' And on down the line, the same recitation, given once a week lest any of them forget.

'Wha' you want then, Jim?' his mother asked him. She gave a grunt as she reached for the telly's remote. She squinted at the screen, made some

206

sort of mental note about what it was she was watching, and pushed the button to mute the sound.

'I'm off,' he said. 'I wanted you to know.'

She kept her gaze level on him and said, 'You *been* off, lad. How many years? So wha's this off that's different from that?'

'Australia,' he said. 'New Zealand. Canada. I don't know yet. But I wanted to tell you I'm making it permanent. Cashing in everything. Starting over. I wanted you to know so you could tell the others.'

'Don' think they been losing sleep wondering where you wanked off to,' his mother said.

'I know. But all the same . . .' He wondered how much his mother knew. As far as he could recall, she didn't read a newspaper. The nation might go to hell in a wicker basket—politicians on the take, the Royals stepping down, the Lords taking up weapons to fight off the Commons' plans for their demise, sports figures dying, rock stars taking overdoses of designer drugs, trains crashing, bombs exploding in Piccadilly—and none of it had ever mattered, so she wouldn't know what had happened to one James Pitchford and what had been done to stop more from happening.

'Old times, I suppose,' he settled on saying. 'You're my mum. I thought you had a right.'

She said, 'Fetch me fags,' and nodded to a table by the sofa where a packet of Benson and Hedges spilled out onto the cover of *Woman's Weekly*. He took them to her and she lit up, watching the screen of the television where the camera was offering a bird's eye view of a snooker table with a player bent over it studying a shot like a surgeon with a scalpel in his hand.

207

'Old times,' she repeated. 'Good of you, Jim. Cheers, then.' And she pushed the sound button on the remote.

Pitchley shifted on his feet. He looked round for something that would do as employment. She wasn't really who he'd come to see, anyway, but he could tell that she wasn't about to part with any information on his siblings if he asked her directly. She owed him nothing and both of them knew it. One didn't spend a quarter of a century pretending that one's past had never occurred, only to come calling from the blue with the hope one's mum might decide to be helpful.

He said, 'Look, Mum. I'm sorry. It was the only way.'

She waved him off, cigarette smoke creating a filmy snake in the air. And seeing that cast him back through time, to this very room, to his mum on the floor, to the baby coming fast and her smoking one fag after another because *where* was the ambulance they'd rung for, God damn it, didn't they have the right to get their needs seen to? And he'd been there with her, alone when it happened, *Don't leave me, Jim. Don't leave me, lad.* And the thing was slimy like an uncooked cod and bloody and still attached to the cord and she smoked, she *smoked* all the way through it and the smoke rose into the air like a snake.

Pitchley strode into the kitchen to rid himself of the memory of his ten-year-old self with a bloody newborn in his terrified hands. Three twenty-five in the morning, it had been. Brothers and sister asleep, neighbours asleep, the whole sodding world indifferent, deep in their beds, dreaming their dreams.

He'd never much liked children after that. And the thought of producing one himself . . . The older he became, the more he'd realised he didn't need that drama twice in one lifetime.

He went to the sink and turned on the water, thinking that a drink or a splash on his face would drive the memory out of his head. As he reached for a glass, he heard the flat door open. He heard a man's voice say, 'You made a right cock up of *that* one, di'n't you? How many times I got to tell you to shut your gob when it comes to jollying the customers?'

Another man said, 'I di'n't mean no harm. Birds always like a bit of oiling, don't they?'

To which the first said, 'Bollocks. We lost them, you yob.' And then, ' 'lo, Mum. How's going wha's going?'

'We got a visitor,' Jen Pytches said.

Pitchley drank down his water and heard the footsteps cross the small sitting room and come into the kitchen. He placed his glass into the grimy sink and turned to face his two younger brothers. They filled the room, big men like their father with watermelon heads and hands the size of dustbin lids. Pitchley felt in their presence as he'd always felt—intimidated as the dickens. And he did what he'd always done at the first sight of those hulking creatures: He cursed the fate that had inspired his mother to couple with a veritable midget when she got him and to choose an all-in wrestler—or so it seemed—to father his brothers.

'Robbie', he said as a hello to the elder one. And 'Brent', to the younger. They were dressed identically in boots and blue jeans topped with bomber jackets on which the words *Rolling Suds*

209

were printed front and back. They'd been working, Pitchley concluded, attempting to keep alive the mobile car-wash business that he himself had initiated when he was thirteen years old.

Robbie took the lead, as always. 'Well, well, well. Lookit wha' we got here, Bren, our big bro. And don't he look a real pitcher in them fancy trousers?'

Brent snickered and chewed on his thumbnail and waited, as always, for direction from Rob.

Pitchley said, 'You win, Rob. I'm shoving off.'

'Shoving off like how?' Robbie went to the fridge and pulled out a can of beer which he tossed to Brent, calling out, 'Ma! You want somethin' in there? Eat? Drink?'

She said, 'Cheers, Rob. Woul'n't say no to a bite o' that pork pie from yesterday. You see't there, luv? On the top shelf? Go' to eat it 'fore it goes off.'

'Yeah. Go' it,' Rob called back. He plopped the crumbling remains of the pie onto a plate and shoved it at Brent, who disappeared for a moment as he delivered it to their mother. Rob ripped the ring-pull from his beer can and flicked it into the kitchen sink, pumping the beer directly into his mouth. He finished it in one long go and began on Brent's, which the younger man had foolishly left behind.

'So,' Rob said. 'Shoving off, are you? And where'bouts you shoving off to, Jay?'

'I'm emigrating, Rob. I don't know where. It doesn't matter.'

'Matters to me.'

Of course, Pitchley thought. For where else would the money come from when he placed a bad

210

bet, when he crashed another car, when he fancied a holiday by the sea? Without Pitchley there to write out the cheques when Robbie had a financial itch that wanted scratching, life as he'd known it was going to be different. He'd actually have to make a proper go of Rolling Suds, and if the business failed—as it had been threatening to do for years under Rob's quixotic management—then there would be no fallback position. Well, that was life, Rob, Pitchley thought. The milk cow's dried up, the golden egg's broken, the rainbow's vanishing permanently. You might've tracked me from East London to Hammersmith to Kensington to Hampstead and all points in between when you fancied, but you are going to be hard pressed to track me across the sea.

He said again, 'I don't know where I'll end up. Not yet.'

'So wha's the point in all this, then?' Robbie indicated Pitchley and his presence in their shabby childhood flat by raising the empty can to him. 'Can't be ol' times now, can it, Jay? Ol' times's the least of what you'd want to come round to have a chat about, I 'xpect. You'd like to forget them, you would, Jay. But here's the ringer. Some of us can't. We don't got the *wherewithal*. So everything we been through stays right up 'ere, circling round and round.' He used the can again, but this time to indicate the alleged movement in his head. Then he shoved both the cans into the plastic grocery bag that hung from the handle of one of the kitchen drawers and had long done service as the family dust bin.

'I know,' Pitchley said.

'You know, you know,' his brother mocked. 'You

211

don't know nowt, Jay, and don't you forget it.'

Pitchley said for the thousandth time to his brother, 'I didn't ask you to take them on. What you did—'

'Oh *no*. You di'n't ask. You just said, "You saw what they wrote 'bout me, Rob!" Tha's what you said. "They're gonna end up pulling me limb to limb," you said. "I'm gonna be nothing when this is over."'

'I may have said that but what I meant was—'

'Bugger what you meant!' Robbie kicked a cupboard door. Pitchley flinched.

'Wha's this, then?' Brent had returned, having pinched their mother's packet of Benson and Hedges. He was lighting up.

'This yob's doing another runner and claims he don't know where he's going. How'd you like that?'

Brent blinked. 'Tha's shit, Jay.'

'Bloody right tha's shit.' Rob jabbed his finger into Pitchley's face. 'I did time for you. I did six months. You know wha' it's like inside? Lemme tell you.' And the catalogue began, the same dreary recitation that Pitchley had heard every time his brother wanted more money. It started with the reason for Robbie's run-in with the law: beating up the journalist who'd unearthed Jimmy Pytches from the carefully constructed past of James Pitchford, who'd not only printed the story pulled from a snout at the Tower Hamlets station but had the audacity to follow it up with another despite being warned off by Rob, who stood to gain nothing—'*sod all*, Jay, you hear me?'—for taking up arms to protect the reputation of a brother who'd *deserted* them years ago. 'Us lot never came *near* to you till you needed us, Jay, and then you

212

bled us dry,' Robbie said.

His capacity for rewriting history was amazing, Pitchley thought. He said, 'You came near me back then because you saw my picture in the paper, Rob. You saw a chance to put me in your debt. Bash a few heads. Break a few bones. All in the cause of keeping Jimmy's past hidden. He'll like that, he will. He's 'shamed of us. An' if we keep him thinkin' we're 'bout to pop out of his cupboard at any time, he'll pay, stupid git. He'll pay and he'll pay.'

'I sat in a cell,' Robbie roared. 'I shat in a bucket. You go' that, mate? I go' done over in the *shower,* Jay. And wha'd *you* get?'

'You!' Pitchley cried. 'You and Brent. That's what I got. The two of you breathing down my neck ever since, hands out for the dosh, regular as rain in the winter.'

'Can't wash cars in the rain, can we, Jay?' Brent offered.

'Shut up!' Rob threw the rubbish sack at Brent. 'Blood and guts, you're so *fucking* stupid.'

'He said—'

'Shut up! I heard wha' he said. Don' you know what he meant? He meant we're leeches. Tha's what he's saying. Like we owe him and not the reverse.'

'I'm not saying that.' Pitchley reached in his pocket. He brought out his chequebook, where inside was the incomplete cheque he'd been writing when the cop had shown up at his house. 'But I am saying that it's ending now because I'm leaving, Rob. I'll write this last cheque and after that you're on your own.'

'Fuck that shit!' Rob advanced on him. Brent

213

took a hasty step back towards the sitting room. Jen Pytches called, 'Wha's goin' on, you lot?'

'Rob and Jay—'

'Shut up! Shut up! Christ on the cross! Why're you such a bleeding git, Brent?'

Pitchley took out a biro. He clicked out the ink. But before he could put pen to paper, Rob was on him. He ripped the chequebook from Pitchley's hand and threw it against the wall where it hit a rack of mugs which crashed to the floor.

'Hey!' Jen shouted.

Pitchley saw his life flash before him.

Brent dived into the sitting room.

'Bloody stupid wanker,' Rob hissed. His hands went for the lapels of Pitchley's jacket. He jerked Pitchley forward. His head snapped back. 'You don't understand fuck all, you git. You never did.'

Pitchley closed his eyes and waited for the blow, but it didn't come. Instead, his brother released him as savagely as he'd taken hold of him, shoving him backwards against the kitchen sink.

'I di'n't do nowt wanting your stupid money,' Rob said. 'You handed it over, yeah, right. An' I was glad to take it, yeah. But you're the one what go' out the chequebook every time you saw my mug. "Give the bloody git a thousand or two and he'll disappear." Tha's wha' you thought. And then you blamed *me* for takin' the hand out when the hand out was nothing but guilt money in the first place.'

'I didn't do anything to feel guilty—'

Rob's hand chopped the air, silencing Pitchley. 'You pr'tended we didn't *exist*, Jay. So don't blame me for wha' you did.'

Pitchley swallowed. There was nothing more to

214

say. There was too much truth in Robbie's claim and too much falsehood in his own past.

From the sitting room, the sound of the television rose, Jen raising the volume to drown out whatever her oldest two sons were doing in the kitchen. None of my business, her action said.

Right, Pitchley thought. All of their lives had been none of her business.

He said, 'I'm sorry. It was the only way I knew to make a life, Rob.'

Rob turned away. He went back to the fridge. He brought out another beer and opened it. He raised it to Pitchley in a mocking, farewell salute. He said, 'I only ever wanted to be your brother, Jim.'

### *Gideon*

*2 NOVEMBER*
*It seems to me that the truth about James Pitchford and Katja Wolff lies between what Sarah-Jane said about James's indifference to women and what Dad said about James's besottedness with Katja. Both of them had reason to twist the facts. If Sarah-Jane had disliked Katja and wanted James for herself, she'd not be likely to admit it if the Lodger had shown a preference elsewhere. And as for Dad . . . If he was responsible for Katja's pregnancy, he'd hardly be likely to confess that to me, would he? Fathers tend not to reveal that sort of thing to their sons.*

*You listen to me with that expression of calm tranquillity on your face, and* because *that expression is so calm so tranquil so unjudging so open to receive*

215

*whatever it is that I choose to maunder on about, I can see what you're thinking, Dr Rose: He's* clinging *to the fact of Katja Wolff's pregnancy, as the only means currently available to him to avoid . . .*

What, *Dr Rose? And what if I'm not avoiding anything?*

*That could be the case precisely, Gideon. But consider that you've come up with no memory relating to your music in quite some time. You've offered very few memories of your mother. Your grandfather in your childhood has all but been deleted from your brain, as has your grandmother. And Raphael Robson—as he was in your childhood—has barely warranted a passing mention.*

*I can't* help *the way my brain is connecting the dots, can I?*

*Of course not. But in order to stimulate associative thoughts, one needs to be in a mental position in which the mind is free to roam. That's the point of becoming quiet, becoming restful, choosing a place to write and writing undisturbed. Actively pursuing the death of your sister and the subsequent trial—*

*How can I go on to something else when my mind is* filled *with this? I can't just clear my brain, forget about it, and pursue something else. She was* murdered, *Dr Rose. I'd forgotten she was murdered. God forgive me, but I'd even forgotten she existed. I can't just set that to one side. I can't simply jot down details about playing* ansiosamente *as a nine year old when I was meant to play* animato, *and I can't dwell upon the psychological significance of misinterpreting a piece of music like that.*

*But what about the blue door, Gideon? you inquire, still reason incarnate. Considering the part that that door has played in your mental process,*

216

*would it help if you reflected upon it and wrote about it rather than what you've been told by others?*

*No, Dr Rose. That door—if you will pardon the pun—is closed.*

*Still, why not shut your eyes for a few moments and visualise that door again? you recommend. Why not see if you can put it into a context quite apart from Wigmore Hall? As you describe it, it appears to be an exterior door to a house or a flat. Could it be possible that it has nothing to do with Wigmore Hall? Perhaps it's the colour that you might think and write about for a time and not the door itself. Perhaps it's the presence of two locks instead of one. Perhaps it's the lighting fixture above it and the entire idea of what light is used for.*

*Freud, Jung, and whoever else occupy the consulting room with us . . . And yes, yes, yes, Dr Rose. I am a field ready for the harvest.*


### 3 NOVEMBER

*Libby's come home. She was gone for three days after our altercation in the square. I heard nothing from her during that time, and the silence from her flat was an accusation, asserting that I'd driven her away through cowardice and monomania. The silence claimed that my monomania was merely a useful shield behind which I could hide so that I didn't have to face my failure with Libby herself, my failure to connect with a human being who had been dropped into my lap by the Almighty for the sole purpose of allowing me to form an attachment to her.*

*Here she is, Gideon, the Fates or God or Karma had said to me on that day when I agreed to let the basement flat to the curly-haired courier who needed*

217

*a refuge from her husband. Here's your opportunity to resolve what has plagued you since Beth left your life.*

*But I had allowed that singular chance for redemption to slip through my fingers. More than that, I had done everything in my power to avoid having that chance in the first place. For what better way to circumvent intimate involvement with a woman than to subvert my career, thereby giving myself an exigent focal point for all my endeavours? No time to talk about our situation, Libby darling. No time to consider the oddity of it. No time to consider why I can hold your naked body, feel your soft breasts against my chest, feel the mound of your pubis pressing against me, and experience nothing but the raging humiliation of experiencing nothing. Indeed, there is no time for anything at all but resolving this plaguing persistent pernicious question regarding my music, Libby.*

*Or is the consideration of Libby right now a blind that helps cloud whatever it is that the blue door represents? And how the hell am I to know?*

*When Libby returned to Chalcot Square, she didn't bang on my door or phone me. Nor did she announce her presence through the means of either the Suzuki's engine gunning explosively outside or pop music blaring from her flat. The only way I knew that she was back at all was from the sudden sound of the old pipes clanging from within the walls of the building. She was having a bath.*

*I gave her forty minutes' leeway once the pipes were silent. Then I went downstairs, outside, and down the steps to her front door. I hesitated before knocking, almost giving up the idea of trying to mend my fences with her. But at the last moment when I thought, To hell with it, which I realise was my way of turning tail*

218

and running away, I found that I didn't want to be at odds with Libby. If nothing else, she'd been such a friend. I missed that friendship, and I wanted to make sure I still had it.

Several knocks were required to get a response. Even when she did answer, she asked, 'Who is it?' from behind the closed door although she knew very well that I was the only person likely to be calling on her in Chalcot Square. I was patient with this. *She's upset with me*, I told myself. *And, all things considered, that's her right.*

When she opened the door, I said the conventional thing to her. 'Hullo. I was worried about you. When you disappeared . . .'

'Don't lie,' was her reply, although she didn't say it unkindly. She'd had time to dress, and she was wearing something other than her usual garb: a colourful skirt that dangled to her calves, a black sweater that reached her hips. Her feet were bare, although she had a gold chain round her ankle. She looked quite nice.

'It's not a lie. When you left, I thought you'd gone to work. When you didn't come back . . . I didn't know what to think.'

'Another lie,' she said.

I persisted, telling myself, *The fault is mine. I'll take the punishment.* 'May I come in?'

She stepped back from the door in a movement that was not unlike a complete body shrug. I walked into the flat and saw that she'd been assembling a meal for herself. She had it laid out on the coffee table in front of the futon that serves as her sofa, and it was completely unlike her usual fare of take-away Chinese or curry: a grilled chicken breast, broccoli, and a salad of lettuce and tomatoes.

219

I said, 'You're eating. Sorry. Shall I come back later?' and I hated the formality that I heard in my voice.

She said, 'No problem as long as you don't mind if I eat in front of you.'

'I don't mind. Do you mind being watched while you eat?'

'I don't mind.'

It was a conversational check and counter check. There were so many things that she and I could talk about and so many things that we were avoiding.

I said, 'I'm sorry about the other day. About what happened. Between us, that is. I'm going through a bad patch just now. Well, obviously, you know that already. But until I see it through, I'm not going to be right for anyone.'

'Were you before, Gideon?'

I was confused. 'Was I what?'

'Right for anyone.' She went back to the sofa, tucking her skirt beneath her as she sat, an oddly feminine movement that seemed completely out of character.

'I don't know how to answer that honestly and be honest with myself,' I said. 'I'm supposed to say Yes, I was right in the past and I'll be right again. But the truth of the matter is that I might not have been. Right, that is. I might not ever have been right for anyone, and I might never be. And that's all I know just now.'

She was drinking water, I saw, not Coke as had been her preference since I had known her. She had a glass with a slice of lemon floating amidst the ice cubes, and she took this up as I was speaking and she watched me over the rim as she drank. 'Fair enough,' she said. 'Is that what you've come to tell me?'

220

'As I said, I was worried about you. We didn't part on good terms. And when you left and didn't return . . . I suppose I thought you might have . . . Well, I'm glad you're back. And well. I'm glad you're well.'

'Why?' she asked. 'What did you think I might have done? Jumped into the river or something?'

'Of course not.'

'Then?'

I didn't see at the moment that this was the wrong road to be travelling down. Idiotically, I turned into it, assuming it would take us to the destination that I had in mind. I said, 'I know your position in London is tenuous, Libby. So I wouldn't blame you for . . . well, for doing whatever you felt you needed to do to shore it up. Especially since you and I parted badly. But I'm glad you're back. I'm awfully glad. I've missed having you here to talk to.'

'Gotcha,' she said with a wink, although she didn't smile. 'I get it, Gid.'

'What?'

She took up her knife and fork and cut into the chicken. Despite the fact that she'd been in England for several years at this point, I noted that she still ate like an American, with that inefficient shifting about of the knife and the fork from one hand to the other. I was dwelling on this fact when she answered me. 'You think I've been with Rock, don't you?'

'I hadn't really . . . well, you do work for him. And after you and I had that row . . . I know that it would be only natural to . . .' I wasn't sure how to complete the thought. She was chewing her chicken slowly, and she was watching me flailing round verbally, perhaps determined not to do a single thing to help me.

She finally spoke. 'What you thought was that I was back with Rock, doing what Rock wants me to

221

do. *Fucking him, basically, whenever he wants it. And totally putting up with him fucking everyone else he comes across. Right?'*

*'I know he holds the whip hand, Libby, but since you've been gone, I've been thinking that if you consult a solicitor who specialises in immigration law—'*

*'Bullshit what you've been thinking,' she scoffed.*

*'Listen. If your husband is continuing to threaten you with going to the Home Office, we can—'*

*'It is what you think, isn't it?' She set down her fork. 'I wasn't with Rock Peters, Gideon. Sure. It's hard for you to believe. I mean, why* wouldn't *I go running back to some complete asshole, since that's, like, my basic m.o. In fact, why wouldn't I move right in with him and put up with his shit all over again? I've been doing* such *a totally good job of putting up with yours.'*

*'You're still angry, then.' I sighed, frustrated with my inability to communicate with anyone, it seemed. I wanted to get us past this, but I didn't know where I wanted to get us* to. *I couldn't offer Libby what she had blatantly wanted from me for months, and I didn't actually know what else I could offer her that would satisfy, not only at that moment but in the future. But I wanted to offer her something. 'Libby, I'm not right,' I said. 'You've seen that. You know it. We've not talked about the worst of what's wrong with me, but you know because you've experienced . . . You've seen . . . You've been with me . . . at night.' God, it was excruciating trying to say it outright.*

*I hadn't taken a seat when she herself had, so I paced across the sitting room to the kitchen and back again. I was waiting for her to rescue me.*

*Have others done that before? you enquire.*

222

*Done . . . what?*

*Rescued you, Gideon. Because, you see, often we wait for what we're used to from people. We develop the expectation that one person will give us what we've traditionally received from others.*

*God knows there have been few enough others, Dr Rose. There was Beth, of course. But she reacted with wounded silence, which is certainly not what I wanted from Libby.*

*And from Libby, what was it that you wanted?*

*Understanding, I suppose. An acceptance that would make further conversation—and a fuller admission—unnecessary. But what I got was a statement that told me clearly she was going to give me none of that.*

*She said, 'Life isn't all about you, Gideon.'*

*I said, 'I'm not implying that it is.'*

*She said, 'Sure you are. I'm gone for three days and you assume that I've totally freaked because we can't get something going between us. You figure that I've run back to Rock and he and I are bumping woolies all because of you.'*

*'I wouldn't say that you were having relations with him because of me. But you have to admit that you wouldn't have gone to him in the first place if we hadn't . . . if things had gone differently for us. For you and me.'*

*'Geez. You are, like, deaf as a stone, aren't you? Have you even been listening to me? But then, why would you when we're not discussing you.'*

*'That's not fair. And I have been listening.'*

*'Yeah? Well, I said I wasn't with Rock. I saw him, sure. I went to work every day so I saw him. And I could've gotten back with him if I wanted but I didn't want. And if he wants to phone the Feds—or whoever*

223

*it is that you guys phone—then he's going to do it and that'll be it: a one way ticket to San Francisco. And there is, like, absolutely zilch that I can do about it. And that's the story.'*

*'There's got to be a compromise. If he wants you as he seems to want you, perhaps you can get some counselling that would enable you to—'*

*'Are you out of your mind? Or are you just freaked out that I might start wanting something from you?'*

*'I'm only trying to suggest a solution to the immigration problem. You don't want to be deported. I don't want you to be deported. Clearly, Rock doesn't want you to be deported because if he did, he would have done something to alert the authorities—it's the Home Office, by the way—and they would have already come for you.'*

*She had cut into her chicken again and she had lifted a forkful of meat to her mouth. But she hadn't taken it. Instead, she held the fork suspended while I spoke and when I had finished, she laid the fork back onto her plate and stared at me for a good fifteen seconds before saying anything. And then what she said made no sense at all, 'Tap dancing,' were her words.*

*I said, 'What?'*

*'Tap dancing, Gideon. That's where I went when I left here. That's what I do. I tap dance. I'm not very good but it doesn't matter because I don't, like, do it to be good. I do it because I get hot and sweaty and I have fun and I like the way it makes me feel when I'm done.'*

*I said, 'Yes. I see,' although I didn't, actually. We were talking about her marriage, we were talking about her status in the UK, we were talking about our own difficulties—at least we were trying to—and what*

224

*tap dancing had to do with all this was unclear to me.*

*'There's this very nice chick at my tap dancing class, an Indian girl who's taking the class on the sly. She invited me home to meet her family. And that's where I've been. With her. With them. I wasn't with Rock. Didn't even think of going to Rock. What I thought was what would be best for me. And that's what I did, Gid. Just like that.'*

*'Yes. Well. I see.' I was a broken record. I could sense her anger, but I didn't know what to do with it.*

*'No. You don't see. Everyone in your itty bitty world lives and dies and breathes for you, and that's the way it's always been. So you figure that what's going on with me is the exact same deal. You can't get it up when we're together and I'm just so totally* bummed *about it that I rush off to the biggest dickhead in London and do the nasty with him because of you. You think I'm saying Gid doesn't want me, but good old Rock does, and if some total asshole* wants *me that makes me okay, that makes me real, that makes me really exist.'*

*'Libby, I'm not saying any of that.'*

*'You don't have to. It's the way you live, so it's the way you think everyone else lives, too. Only in your world, you live for that stupid violin instead of for another person and if the violin* rejects *you or something, you don't know who you are any more. And that's what's going on, Gideon. But my life is, like, totally* not *about you. And yours isn't about your violin.'*

*I stood there wondering how we'd reached this point. I couldn't think of a clear response. And in my head all I could hear was Dad saying, This is what comes of knowing Americans, and of all Americans, the worst are Californians. They don't converse. They*

225

*psychologise.*

*I said, 'I'm a musician, Libby.'*

*'No. You're a person. Like I'm a person.'*

*'People don't exist outside what they do.'*

*''Course they do. Most people exist just fine. It's only people who don't have any real insides—people who've never taken the time to find out who they really are—that fall to pieces when stuff doesn't turn out the way they want it to.'*

*'You can't know how this . . . this situation . . . between us is going to turn out. I've said that I'm in the middle of a bad patch, but I'm coming through it. I'm working at coming through it every day.'*

*'You are so not listening to me.' She threw down her fork. She'd not eaten half of her meal, but she carried her plate over to the kitchen, dumped the chicken and broccoli into a plastic bag, and flung that bag into the fridge. 'You don't have anything to turn to if your music goes bad. And you think I don't have anything to turn to if you and me or Rock and me or me and anything goes bad either. But I'm not you. I have a life. You're the person who doesn't.'*

*'Which is why I'm trying to get my life back. Because until I do, I won't be good for myself or for anyone.'*

*'Wrong. No. You never had a life. All you had was the violin. Playing the violin wasn't ever who you are. But you made it who you are and that's why you're nothing right now.'*

*Gibberish, I could hear Dad scoffing. Another month in this charming creature's company and what's left of your mind will turn to porridge. This is what comes of a steady diet of McDonald's, television chat shows, and self-help books. If, of course, the dear thing can read, which is a supposition that's still*

226

left open to serious doubt, Gideon.

With Dad in my head and Libby in front of me, I didn't stand a chance. The only course that seemed open to me was a dignified exit, which I attempted to make, saying, 'I think we've said all we need to on the subject. It's safe to say that this is just going to be one area in which we disagree.'

'Well, let's make sure we only say what's safe,' was Libby's retort. ' 'Cause if things get, like, too scary for us, we might actually be able to change.'

I was at the door, but this parting shot of hers was going so far wide of the mark that I had to correct her. I said, 'Some people don't need to change, Libby. They might need to understand what's happening to them, but they don't need to change.'

Before she could answer, I left her. It seemed crucial that I have the last word. Still, as I closed the door behind me—and I did it carefully so as not to betray anything that she might take as an adverse reaction to our conversation—I heard her say, 'Yeah. Right, Gideon,' and something scraped viciously across the wooden floor, as if she'd kicked the coffee table.


## 4 NOVEMBER

I am the music. I am the instrument. She sees fault in this. I do not. What I see is the difference between us, that difference which Dad has been attempting to point out from the moment he and Libby met. Libby has never been a professional, and she's not an artist. It's easy for her to say that I am not the violin because she has never known what it is to have a life that is inextricably entwined with an artistic performance. Throughout her life, she's had a series of jobs, work

227

*that she's gone to and then left at the end of the day. Artists do not live that sort of life. Assuming that they do or can displays an ignorance which must give one pause to consider.*

*To consider what? you want to know.*

*To consider the possibilities. For Libby and me. Because there for a time, I had thought . . . Yes. There seemed to be a rightness in our knowing each other. There seemed to be a distinct advantage in the fact that Libby didn't know who I was, didn't recognise my name when she saw it that day on her courier parcel, didn't appreciate the facts of my career, didn't care whether I played the violin or made kites and sold them in Camden Market. I liked that about her. But now I see that being with someone who* understands *my life is crucial if I am going to* live *my life.*

*And that need for understanding was what prompted me to seek out Katie Waddington, the girl from the convent that I remembered sitting in the kitchen in Kensington Square, Katja Wolff's most frequent visitor.*

*Katja Wolff was one half of the two KWs, Katie informed me when I tracked her down. Sometimes, she said, when one has a close friendship, one makes the mistake of assuming it will be there forever, unchanging and nurturing. But it rarely is.*

*It was no big problem to locate Katie Waddington. Nor was it any big surprise to discover that she'd followed a life course similar to what she'd suggested would be her mission two decades earlier. I located her by means of the telephone directory, and I found her in her clinic in Maida Vale. It's called Harmony of Bodies and Minds, this clinic, and it's a name which I suppose is useful to disguise its main*

228

*function: sex therapy. They don't come right out and cell it sex therapy because who would have the nerve to engage in it if that were the case? Instead, they call it 'relationship therapy', and an inability to take part in the sexual act itself is called 'relationship dysfunction'.*

*'You'd be astonished to know how many people have problems with sex,' Katie informed me in a fashion that sounded personally friendly and professionally reassuring. 'We get at least three referrals every day. Some are due to medical problems: diabetes, heart conditions, post operative trauma. That sort of thing. But for every client with a medical problem, there are nine or ten with psychological troubles. I suppose that's not surprising, really, given our national obsession with sex and the pretence we maintain that sex isn't our national obsession. One only has to look at the tabloids and the glossies to know the level of interest everyone has in sex. I'm surprised not to find more people in therapy struggling with all this. God knows I've never encountered anyone without some sort of issue with sex. The healthy ones are those who deal with it.'*

*She took me down a corridor painted in warm, earthy colours, and we went to her office, which opened onto a terrace where a profusion of pot plants provided a verdant backdrop for a comfortable room of overstuffed furniture, large cushions, and a collection of pottery ('South American', she informed me) and baskets ('North American . . . lovely, aren't they? They're my guilty pleasure. I can't afford them but I buy them anyway. I suppose there are worse vices in life.'). We sat and took stock of each other. Katie said in that same warm, personally friendly and professionally reassuring voice, 'Now. How can I help*

229

*you, Gideon?'*

*I realised that she thought I'd come to solicit her skills, and I hastened to disabuse her of the notion. Nothing in her area of speciality was required, I told her heartily. I'd really come for some information about Katja Wolff, if she didn't mind. I would recompense her for her time since I'd be using up what would otherwise be someone's appointment. But as to having . . . shall we say* difficulties *of the sort she was used to dealing with . . . ? Har, har. Chuckle. Well, at the moment there was no need for* that *sort of intervention.*

*Katie said, 'Brilliant. So glad to hear it,' and she settled more comfortably into her armchair. This was high backed and upholstered in autumn colours similar to those which decorated the waiting room and the corridor. It was also extremely sturdy, a quality that would be necessary considering Katie's size. For if she'd had a tendency to fat as a twentysomething university student sitting in the kitchen in Kensington Square, now she was downright obese, of a size that would no longer fit into a seat at the cinema or on a plane. But she was still dressed in hues that flattered her colouring, and the jewellery she wore was tasteful and looked expensive. Nonetheless, it was difficult for me to imagine how she managed to get around. And, admittedly, I couldn't picture anyone telling their innermost libidinous secrets to her. It was obvious others hadn't shared my aversion, however. The clinic looked like a thriving enterprise, and I'd managed to get in to see Katie only because a regular client had cancelled minutes before I phoned.*

*I told her that I was trying to refresh some memories of my childhood, and I'd remembered her. I'd recalled that she'd often been in the kitchen when*

230

*Katja Wolff was feeding Sonia, and as I had no idea of Katja's whereabouts, it seemed to me that she— Katie—might be able to fill in the gaps where my memories were dim.*

*Thankfully, she didn't ask why I'd developed this sudden interest in the past. Nor did she, from her place of professional wisdom, comment upon what it might mean that I had gaps in my recollections in the first place. Instead, she said, 'People at Immaculate Conception used to call us the two KWs. "Where are the KWs?" they'd ask. "Someone fetch the KWs to have a look at this."'*

*'So you were close friends.'*

*'I wasn't the only one who sought her out when she first accepted a room at the convent,' she explained. 'But our friendship . . . I suppose it* took. *So yes, we were close at the time.'*

*There was a low table next to her chair, and on it stood an elaborate bird cage with two budgerigars inside, one a brilliant blue and the other green. As Katie spoke, she unfastened the door of the cage, and took the blue bird out, grasping him in her large fat fist. He squawked in protest and took a nip at her fingers. She said, 'Naughty,* naughty, *Joey,' and picked up a tongue depressor that lay on the table next to the cage. For a grim moment I thought she meant to use it to swat the little bird. But instead she used it to massage his head and neck in a way that calmed him. Indeed, it appeared to hypnotise him, and it did much the same for me, since I watched in fascination as the bird's eyes eased shut. Katie opened her palm, and he sank into it contentedly.*

*'Therapeutic,' Katie told me as she went on with the massage, using the tips of her fingers once the bird was gentled. 'Lowers the blood pressure.'*

'I didn't know that birds had high blood pressure.'

She laughed quietly. 'Not Joey's. Mine. I've morbid obesity, to state the obvious. Doctor says I'll die before I'm fifty if I don't shed sixteen stone. "You weren't born fat," he tells me. "No, but I've lived it," I tell him. It's hell on one's heart, and what it does to one's blood pressure doesn't bear mentioning. But we all have to go some way. I'm just choosing mine.' She ran her fingers along Joey's folded right wing. In response—eyes still closed—he stretched it out. 'That's what attracted me to Katja. She was someone who made choices, and I loved that about her. Probably because in my own family everyone just went into the restaurant business without thinking there might be something else out there to do with their lives. But Katja was someone who grabbed at life. She didn't just accept what was thrust upon her.'

'East Germany,' I acknowledged. 'The balloon escape.'

'Yes. That's an excellent example. The balloon escape and how she engineered it.'

'Except she wasn't the one who built the balloon, was she? Not from what I've been told.'

'No, she didn't build it. That's not what I meant by engineered. I meant how she convinced Hannes Hertel to take her with him. How she blackmailed him, actually, if what she told me was true, and I expect it was because why would someone lie about something so unflattering? But nasty as her plan might have been, she had real nerve to go to him and to make the threat. He was a big man—six foot three or four to hear her tell it—and he could have done her serious harm had he a mind to do so. He could have killed her, I expect, and gone on his way over the wall and disappeared from there. It was a calculated

232

risk on her part, and she took it. That's how much she wanted life.'

'What sort of risk?'

'The threat, you mean?' Katie had gone on to Joey's other wing, which he'd stretched out as cooperatively as he had done the first. Inside the cage, the second budgerigar had skittered along one of the perches and was watching the massage session with one bright eye. 'She threatened to alert the authorities if Hannes didn't take her with him.'

'That's not a story that's ever come out, is it?'

'I expect I'm the only person she ever told, and she probably didn't realise. We'd both been drinking, and when Katja got pissed—which wasn't often, mind you—she'd say or do things that she couldn't even remember twenty-four hours later. I never mentioned the Hannes situation to her after she told me about it, but I admired her for it because it spoke of the lengths she was willing to go to. And as I had to go to my own lengths—' She indicated the office and the clinic itself, so many steps removed from her family's restaurant business—'it made us sisters, after a fashion.'

'You lived at the convent as well?'

'God no. Katja did. She worked for the sisters—in their kitchen, I think—in exchange for her room while she was learning English. But I lived behind the convent. There were lodgings for students at the bottom of the grounds. Right on the District line, so the noise was ghastly. But the rent was cheap, and the location—near to so many colleges—made it convenient. Several hundred students lived there then, and most of us knew of Katja.' Here she smiled. 'Had we not known of her, we would have taken notice of her eventually. What she could do with a jumper,

233

*three scarves, and a pair of trousers was quite remarkable. She had an innovative mind when it came to fashion. That's what she wanted to do, by the way. And she would have done, had things not turned out so badly for her.'*

*This was exactly where I wanted the conversation to head.*

*'She wasn't really qualified to be my sister's nanny, was she?' I asked.*

*Katie was stroking the budgerigar's tail feathers now. 'She was devoted to your sister,' Katie said. 'She loved her. She was brilliant with her. I never saw her be anything other than absolutely tender and gentle towards Sonia. She was a godsend, Gideon.'*

*That wasn't what I expected to hear, and I closed my eyes, trying to find a picture in my mind of Katja and Sonia together. I wanted a picture that squared with what I'd said to the ginger-haired policeman, not one that squared with what Katie was claiming.*

*I said, 'You would have seen them together mostly in the kitchen, though, when she was feeding Sonia,' and I kept my eyes closed, trying to conjure that picture at least: the old red and black lino squares on the floor, the table scarred with the semi-circles of cups placed down on unprotected wood, the two windows set below the level of the street and the bars that fronted them. Odd that I could remember the sight of feet passing by on the pavement above those kitchen windows, but I could not at that moment envisage a scene in which something might have happened that would confirm what I'd later reported to the police.*

*Katie said, 'I did see them in the kitchen. But I saw them at the convent as well. And in the square. And elsewhere. Part of Katja's job was to stimulate her* senses and—' Here she cut herself off, stopped stroking the bird, and said, 'But you already know all this, I suppose.'

I murmured vaguely, 'As I said, my memory . . . ?'

That seemed to be enough because she went on. 'Ah. Yes. Right. Well, all children, disabled or not, benefit from sensory stimulation, and Katja saw to it that Sonia had a variety of experiences. She worked with her in developing motor skills and she saw to it that she was exposed to the environment beyond the home. She was limited by your sister's health, but when Sonia was able to cope with it, Katja would take her out and about. And if I was free, I went as well. So I saw her with Sonia, not every day but several times a week, for the entire time your sister was . . . well, alive. And Katja was very good to Sonia. So when everything happened as it happened . . . Well, I still find it a bit difficult to understand.'

So thoroughly different was this account to anything I'd heard or read in the papers that I felt compelled to attempt a frontal assault. 'This doesn't square at all with what I've been told.'

'By whom?'

'By Sarah-Jane Beckett for one.'

'That doesn't surprise me,' Katie said. 'You can take everything Sarah-Jane says with a pinch of salt. They were oil and water, Katja and she. And there was James to consider. He was wild about Katja, completely over the moon every time she so much as looked his way. Sarah-Jane didn't much like that. It was only too obvious that she'd earmarked James for herself.'

This was down-the-rabbit-hole stuff, Dr Rose, this bit about James the Lodger. No matter where, how, or to whom I turned, the story seemed to turn as well.

235

*And it turned in subtle ways, just a variation here and a little twist there but enough to throw me off my stride and make me wonder in whose words I could believe.*

*Perhaps in no one's, you point out to me. Each person sees things in his own way, Gideon. Each person develops a version of past events that he can live with, and put to the rack, that's the version that he tells. Ultimately, it becomes his truth.*

*But what is Katie Waddington trying to live with, twenty years after the crime? I can understand what Dad is trying to live with, what Sarah-Jane Beckett is trying to live with. But Katie . . .? She wasn't a member of the household. She had no interest in anything other than her friendship with Katja Wolff. Right?*

*Yet it had been Katie Waddington's evidence that as much as anything, had sealed Katja Wolff's fate. I'd read that in the newspaper cutting where the words* Nanny Lied to Police *had formed a mammoth headline. In her only statement to the investigators Katja had claimed that a phone call from Katie Waddington had taken her from the bathroom for no more than a minute on the night Sonia drowned. But Katie Waddington had, under oath, sworn that she was at an evening class at the same moment that that phone call had ostensibly been made. Her testimony had been supported by the records of the class instructor. And a serious blow had been dealt to Katja's nearly non-existent defence.*

*But wait. God. Had Katie too wanted James the Lodger? I wondered. Had she orchestrated events somehow in order to make James Pitchford available to her?*

*As if she perceived the subject festering in my*

236

mind, Katie continued with the theme she'd begun, 'Katja wasn't interested in James. She saw him as someone who could help her with her English, and I suppose she used him, if it comes down to it. She saw that he wanted her to spend her free time with him, and she was happy to do it, so long as that free time was spent in language tutorials. James went along with that. I suppose he hoped she'd fall in love with him eventually if he was good enough to her.'

'So he could have been the man who made her pregnant.'

'As payment for the language lessons, d'you mean? I doubt it. Sex in exchange for anything wouldn't have been Katja's style. After all, she could have had sex with Hannes Hertel to get him to take her in the hot air balloon. But she chose a different route entirely, and one that could have got her badly hurt.' Katie had ceased petting the blue budgerigar, and she watched the bird as he slowly regained his senses. His tail feathers returned to normal first, then his wings, and finally his eyes, which opened. He blinked as if wondering where he was.

I said, 'Then she was in love with someone other than James. You must know who.'

'I don't know that she was in love with anyone.'

'But if she was pregnant—'

'Don't be naïve, Gideon. A woman doesn't need to be in love to become pregnant. She doesn't even need to be willing.' She returned the blue bird to the cage.

'Are you suggesting . . .' I couldn't even say it, so horrified was I at the thought of what could have happened and at whose hands.

'No, no,' Katie said hastily. 'She wasn't raped. She would have told me. I do believe that. What I meant was that . . .' A marked hesitation during which Katie took the green bird from the cage and began to give it the same massage as she'd given the other. 'As I said, she drank a bit. Not a lot and not often. But when she did . . . well, I'm afraid she forgot things. So there was every chance that she herself didn't know . . . That's the only explanation I've ever been able to come up with.'

'Explanation for what?'

'For the fact that I didn't know she was pregnant,' Katie said. 'We told each other everything. And the fact that she never told me she was pregnant suggests to me that she didn't know herself. Unless she wanted to keep the identity of the father a secret, I suppose.'

I didn't want to head in that direction, and I didn't want her to do so. I said, 'If she drank on her evenings off and one time ended up with someone she didn't even know, she might not have wanted that to come out. It would only have made her look worse, wouldn't it? Especially when she went to trial. Because they talked about her character at the trial, as I understand.' Or at least, I thought, Sarah-Jane Beckett had done.

'As to that,' Katie said, ceasing her stroking of the green bird's head for a moment, 'I wanted to be a character witness. Despite her lie about the telephone call, I thought I could do that much for her. But I wasn't allowed to. Her barrister wouldn't call me. And when the Crown Prosecutor discovered that I hadn't even known she was pregnant . . . You can imagine what he made of that when he was questioning me: How could I declare myself Katja Wolff's closest friend and an authority on what she was and wasn't capable of doing if she'd never trusted me enough to reveal she was pregnant?'

'I see how it went.'

*'Where it went was murder. I thought I could help her. I wanted to help her. But when she asked me to lie about that phone call—'*

*'She asked you to lie?'*

*'Yes. She asked me. But I just couldn't do it. Not in court. Not under oath. Not for anyone. That's where I had to draw the line, and it ended our friendship.'*

*She lowered her gaze to the bird in her palm, its right wing extended now to receive the touch that the other bird had been given. Intelligent little creature, I thought. She'd not yet mesmerised it with her caress, but the bird was already cooperating.*

*'It's odd, isn't it?' she said to me. 'One can earnestly believe one has a particular type of relationship with another person, only to discover it was never what one thought in the first place.'*

*'Yes,' I said. 'It's very odd.'*

# CHAPTER NINETEEN

Yasmin Edwards stood at the corner of Oakhill and Galveston Roads with the number fifty-five burning into her brain. She didn't want any part of what she was doing, but she was doing it anyway, compelled by a force that seemed at once outside herself and integral to her being.

Her heart was saying Go home, girl. Get away from this place. Go back to the shop and go back to pretending.

Her head was saying Nope, time to know the worst.

And the rest of her body was heaving between her head and her heart, leaving her feeling like a thick blonde heroine from a thriller film, the sort who tiptoes through the dark towards that creaking door while the audience shouts at her to stay away.

She'd stopped at the laundry before leaving Kennington. When she'd not been able to cope any longer with what her mind had been insisting for the past several days, she'd shut up the shop and picked up the Fiesta from the car park on the estate with the intention of heading to Wandsworth straight off. But at the top of Braganza Street, where she had to wait for the traffic to clear before she could turn into Kennington Park Road, she'd caught a glimpse of the laundry tucked between the grocery and the electrical shop, and she'd decided to pop round and ask Katja what she wanted for dinner.

No matter that she knew in her heart this was just an excuse to check up on her lover. She *hadn't* asked Katja about dinner before they'd parted that morning, had she? The unexpected visit from that bloody detective had rattled them away from their regular routine.

So she found a spot to park and she ducked into the shop, where she saw to her relief that Katja was at work: in the back, bending over a steaming iron that she was gliding along someone's lace-edged sheets. The combination of heat, humidity, and a smelly jungle of unwashed laundry made the shop feel like the tropics. Within ten seconds of entering the place, Yasmin felt dizzy, sweat beading on her forehead.

She'd never met Mrs Crushley, but she recognised the laundry owner from the attitude she projected from her sewing machine when Yasmin approached the counter. She was of the England-

240

fought-the-war-for-the-likes-of-you generation, a woman too young to have done service during any conflict in recent history but just old enough to remember a London that was largely Anglo-Saxon in origin. She said sharply, 'Yes? What d' you want?', her glance darting all over Yasmin's person, her face looking like she smelled something bad. Yasmin wasn't carrying laundry, which made her suspect to Mrs Crushley. Yasmin was black, which went a good distance towards making her dangerous as well. She could have a knife in her kit, after all. She could have a poisoned dart taken from a fellow tribesman tucked away in her hair.

She said politely, 'If I could have a word with Katja . . . ?'

'*Katja?*' Mrs Crushley declared, sounding as if Yasmin had asked if Jesus Christ happened to be working that day. 'What you want with her, then?'

'Just a word.'

'Don't see as I need to allow that, do I? 'Nough that I'm employing her, i'n't it, without her taking social calls all day.' Mrs Crushley lifted the garment she was working on—a man's white shirt—and she used her crooked teeth to bite off a bit of thread from a button she'd been replacing.

At the back of the shop, Katja raised her head. But for some reason, rather than smile a greeting immediately, she looked beyond Yasmin to the door. And *then* she looked back at Yasmin and smiled.

It was the sort of thing anyone might have done, the sort of thing Yasmin once wouldn't have noticed. But now she found that she was acutely attuned to everything about Katja's behaviour. There were meanings everywhere; there were

241

meanings within meanings. And that was down to that filthy detective.

She said to Katja, 'Forgot to ask about your tea this morning,' with a wary glance at Mrs Crushley.

Mrs Crushley snorted, saying, 'Asking her about her *tea*, is it? In my day we ate wha' was put in front of us.'

Katja approached. Yasmin saw that she was soaked through with sweat. Her azure blouse clung to her torso like hunger. Her hair lay limply against her skull. But she'd never looked like this before— used up and bedraggled—at the end of a day since working at the laundry, and seeing her so now when the day was not even half over fired all of Yasmin's suspicions once again. If she *never* came home looking such a mess, Yasmin reasoned, she had to be going somewhere else before returning to the Doddington Grove Estate.

She'd come to the laundry just to check up on Katja, to make sure she hadn't bunked off and put herself in a bad place with her probation officer. But like most people who tell themselves they're merely sating their curiosity or doing something for someone else's benefit, Yasmin received more information than she wanted.

She said, 'Wha' about it, then?' to Katja, her lips offering a smile that felt like a contortion. 'Got any thoughts? I could do us lamb with couscous, if you like. That stew thing, remember?'

Katja nodded. She wiped her forehead on her sleeve and used her cuff against her upper lip. She said, 'Yes. This is good. Lamb is good, Yas. Thank you.'

And they stood there after that, perfectly mute. They exchanged a look as Mrs Crushley watched

242

them both over her half-moon glasses. She said, 'Go' the information you was wanting, Missie Fancy Hairdo, I believe. Then best take your leave.'

Yasmin pressed her lips together to keep herself from making a choice between saying, 'Where? *Who?*' to Katja or 'Shit yourself, white cunt,' to Mrs Crushley. Katja spoke instead. She said quietly, 'I must get back to work, Yas. See you tonight?'

'Yeah. All right,' Yasmin replied and she left without asking Katja what time.

What time was the ultimate trap she could have set, the trap that went beyond having a look at Katja's appearance. With Mrs Crushley sitting there, knowing what hour Katja got off work, it would have been easy to ask exactly when Katja would return from the laundry that evening and to watch for Mrs Crushley's expression if the time didn't match up with Katja's hours of employment. But Yasmin didn't want to give the nasty sow the pleasure of drawing an inference of any kind about her relationship with Katja, so she went on her way and drove to Wandsworth.

Now she stood on the street corner in the frigid wind. She examined the neighbourhood, and she set it down next to Doddington Grove Estate, which did not gain from the comparison. The street was clean, like it'd been swept. The pavement was clear of debris and fallen leaves. There were no stains from dog urine on the lamp posts and no piles of dog shit in the gutters. The houses were free of graffiti and displayed white curtains in the windows. No laundry hung dispiritedly from balconies, because there were no balconies: just a long row of terraced houses all well taken care of by their inhabitants.

Someone could be happy here, Yasmin thought. Someone could make a special life here. She began to walk cautiously down the pavement. No one was about, but she still felt watched. She adjusted the button at the top of her jacket and pulled out a scarf to cover her hair. She knew it was a stupid thing to do. She knew it marked her: scared, less than, and worried about. But she did it anyway because she wanted to feel safe, at ease, and confident here, and she was willing to try anything to get that way.

When she reached Number Fifty-five, she hesitated at the gate. She wondered at this final moment if she could really go through with it, and she asked herself if she really wanted to know. She cursed the black man who'd brought her to this moment, loathing not only him but herself: him for passing her the information in the first place, herself for making something out of it.

But she had to know. She had too many questions that a simple knock on the door might answer. She couldn't leave until she'd confronted the fears that she'd too long been trying to ignore.

She opened the gate into an untidy front garden. The path to the door was flagstones and the door itself was shiny red with a polished brass knocker in the centre. Autumn bare shrub branches arched over the porch, and a wire milk basket held three empty bottles, one of which had a note sticking out of it.

Yasmin bent to grasp this note, thinking at the last moment that she wouldn't actually have to face . . . to see . . . Perhaps the note would tell her. She unrolled it against her palm, and read the words: 'We're switching to two skimmed, one silver top

244

from now on, please.' That was all. The handwriting gave away nothing. Age, sex, race, creed. The message could have been penned by anyone.

She played her fingers into her palms, encouraging her hand to lift and do its work. She took a step back and looked at the bay window, in the hope that she might see something there that might save her from what she was about to do. But the curtains were like the others in the street: swathes of material that invited some little light into the room and against which a silhouette could be seen at night. But during the day, they protected the room within from outside watchers. So Yasmin was left with the door again.

She thought, Bugger this. She had a *right* to know. She marched to the door and rapped the knocker forcefully against the wood.

She waited. Nothing. She rang the bell. She heard it sounding right near the door, one of those fancy bells that played a tune. But the result was the same. Nothing.

Yasmin didn't want to think she'd come all the way from Kennington to learn nothing. She didn't want to think what it would be like, continuing with Katja as if she didn't have any doubts. It was better to know: good or bad. Because if she knew, then she'd have a clear sense of what she was meant to do next.

His card weighed in her pocket like a four by two inch sheet of pure lead. She'd first looked at it, turning it over and over in her hands, as the hours passed last night without Katja coming home. She'd phoned, of course. She'd said, 'Yas, I'll be late,' and she'd said, 'It's a bit complicated for the phone. Tell you later, shall I?' when Yasmin had asked what was up. But *later* hadn't come when Yasmin expected and after several hours, she'd got out of bed, gone to the window, tried to use the darkness to understand something of what was happening, and finally gone to her jacket where she'd found that card he'd given her in the shop.

She'd stared at the name: Winston Nkata. African, that was. But he sounded West Indies when he wasn't being dead careful to sound plod. A phone number was printed on the bottom, to the left of the name, a Met number that she'd sooner die than ring. A pager number was across from it, in the right corner. 'You page me,' he'd said. 'Day or night.'

Or had he said that? In any case, what did it matter because she wasn't about to grass to a cop. Not in this lifetime. She wasn't that stupid. So she'd shoved the card into her jacket pocket where she felt it now, a little piece of lead growing hot, growing heavy, weighing her right shoulder down with the pull of it, drawing her like metal to a magnet and the magnet was an action she *wouldn't* take.

She stepped away from the house. She backed down the flagstone path to the pavement. She felt behind her for the gate, and backed through it as well. If someone intended to peer through those curtains as she departed, then she damn well intended to see who it was. But that didn't happen. The house was empty.

Yasmin made her decision when a DHL delivery van rumbled into Galveston Road. It puttered along as the driver looked for the correct address and when he had the right house, he left the van

246

running as he trotted up to the door to make his delivery three houses away from where Yasmin stood. She waited as he rang the bell. Ten seconds and that door was opened. An exchange of pleasantries, a signature on a clipboard, and the delivery man trotted back to his van and went on his way, passing Yasmin where she stood on the pavement, giving her a glance that registered only *female, black, bad face, decent body, good for a shag.* Then he and his van were gone. But possibility was not.

Yasmin walked towards the house where he'd made the delivery. She rehearsed her lines. She paused out of sight of the window identical to the window on Number Fifty-five and she took a moment to scribble that address—Number Fifty-five, Galveston Road, Wandsworth, on the back of the detective's card. Then she removed her headscarf and refashioned it into a turban. She took her earrings off and shoved the brass and beads of them into her pocket. And although her jacket was buttoned to the neck, she undid it and unclipped her necklace—just for good measure—depositing it into her shoulder bag, redoing her jacket, and flattening its collar to a humble and unfashionable angle.

Garbed as well as she could be for the part, she entered the garden of the DHL house and rapped hesitantly on its front door. There was a spy hole in it, so she lowered her head, took her bag from her shoulder and held it awkwardly like a handbag in front of her. She arranged her features as best she could to portray humility, fear, worry, and a desperate eagerness to please. In a moment, she heard the voice.

'Yes? What can I do for you?' It came from behind the closed door but the *fact* of it told Yasmin she'd cleared the first hurdle.

She looked up. 'Please, can you help me?' she asked. 'I have come to clean your neighbour's house, but she is not at home. Number Fifty-five?'

'She works during the day,' the voice called back.

'But I do not understand . . .' Yasmin held up the detective's card. She said, 'If you see . . . Her husband wrote it all down . . .?'

'Husband?' The locks on the door were released and the door itself was opened. A middle-aged woman stood there, a pair of scissors in her hand. Seeing Yasmin's gaze go to the scissors and her expression alter, the woman said, 'Oh. Sorry. I was opening a parcel. Here. Let me have a look at that.'

Yasmin willingly handed over the card. The woman read the address.

'Yes. I see. It certainly does say . . . But you said her husband?' And when Yasmin nodded, the woman turned the card over and read the front of it, just exactly what Yasmin herself had read and read again on the previous night: Winston Nkata, Detective Constable, Metropolitan Police. A phone number and a pager number. Everything on the complete up and up.

'Well, of course, the fact that he's a policeman . . .' the woman said thoughtfully. But then, 'No. There's a mistake, I'm sure. No one named Nkata lives there.' She handed the card back.

'You are sure?' Yasmin asked, drawing her eyebrows together, attempting to look her most pathetic. 'He said I should clean . . .'

'Yes, yes, my dear girl. I'm sure that he did. But he's given you the wrong address for some reason.

248

No one named Nkata lives in that house or ever has done. It's been lived in for years by a family called McKay.'

'McKay?' Yasmin asked. And her heart felt lighter. Because if there was a partner to Harriet Lewis the solicitor as Katja had claimed, then her fears were groundless.

'Yes, yes, McKay,' the woman said. 'Noreen McKay. And her niece and nephew. Very nice woman, she is, very pleasant, but she isn't married. Never has been as far as I know. And certainly not to someone called Nkata, if you know what I mean and no offence intended.'

'I . . . yes. Yes. I see.' Yasmin whispered because that was all she could force from herself upon learning the full name of the occupant of Number Fifty-five. 'I do thank you, madam. Thank you very much indeed.' She backed away.

The woman came forward. 'See here, are you all right, Miss?' she asked.

'Oh yes. Yes. Just . . . When one expects work and is disappointed . . .'

'I'm awfully sorry. If I hadn't had my own cleaner here yesterday, I'd not mind letting you have a go with my house. You seem decent enough. May I have your name and number on the chance my woman doesn't work out? She's one of those Filipinos, and they can't always be relied on, if you know what I mean.'

Yasmin raised her head. What she wanted to say battled with what she needed to say, given the situation. Need won. There were other considerations beyond insult right now. She said, 'You are very kind, madam,' and she called herself Nora and recited eight digits at random, all of

249

which the woman eagerly wrote onto a pad that she took from a table by the door.

'Well,' she said as she wrote the last number with a flourish. 'Our little encounter might turn out all for the best.' She offered a smile. 'You never know, do you?'

How true, Yasmin thought. She nodded, went back to the street, and returned to Number Fifty-five for a final look at it. She felt numb and for a moment she encouraged herself to believe that the numbness was a sign of not caring about what she'd just learned. But she knew the reality was that she was in shock.

And between the time of the shock's wearing off and the rage's setting in, she hoped she'd have five minutes to decide what to do.

*     *     *

Winston Nkata's pager went off while Lynley was reading the action reports that DCI Leach's team had been sending in to the incident room for compilation during the morning. In the absence of both eyewitnesses and evidence at the crime scene beyond the paint chips, the vehicle used in the first hit and run was what was left as the murder squad's focus. But according to the activities reports, the town's body shops were proving to be fallow ground so far, as were the parts shops where something like a chrome bumper might possibly be purchased to replace one damaged in an accident.

Lynley looked up from one of the reports to see Nkata scrutinising his pager and contemplatively fingering his facial scar. He took off his reading glasses and said, 'What is it, Winnie?' and the

250

constable replied, 'Don't know, man.' But he said it slowly, as if he had his thoughts on the subject, after which he went to a phone on a nearby desk where a WPC was entering data into the computer.

'I think our next step is Swansea, sir,' Lynley had said to DCI Leach by mobile once they'd completed their interview with Raphael Robson. 'It seems to me that we've got all the principals in hand at this point. Let's run their names through the DVLA and see if one of them has an older car registered, in addition to what they're driving round town. Start with Raphael Robson and see what he has. It could be in a lock-up somewhere.'

Leach had agreed. And this is what the WPC at the computer was doing at the moment: contacting the vehicle department, plugging in names, and looking for ownership of a classic—or simply an old—car.

'We can't discount the possibility that one of our suspects just has access to cars—old or otherwise,' Leach had pointed out. 'Could be the friend of a collector, for instance. Friend of a car salesman. Friend of someone who works as a mechanic.'

'And we also can't discount the possibility that the car was stolen, recently purchased from a private party but not registered, or brought over from Europe to do the job and already returned with no one the wiser,' Lynley said. 'In which case the DVLA will be a dead end. But in the absence of anything else . . .'

'Right,' Leach said. 'What've we got to lose?'

Both of them knew that what they had to lose was Webberly, whose condition had altered perilously in Charing Cross Hospital.

'Heart attack,' Hillier had said tersely from

intensive care. 'Just three hours ago. Blood pressure went down, heart started acting dodgy, then . . . bam. It was massive.'

'Jesus Christ,' Lynley said.

'Used those things on him . . . what're they . . . electrical shocks . . .'

'Those paddles?'

'Ten times. Eleven. Randie was there. They got her out of the room but not before the alarms and the shouting and . . . It's a *bloody* mess, this.'

'What are they telling you, sir?'

'He's monitored every which way to Sunday. IVs, tubes, machines, wires. Ventricular fibrillation, this was. It could happen again. Anything could.'

'How's Randie?'

'Coping.' Hillier didn't give Lynley a chance to inquire about anything else. Instead, he went on gruffly as if wishing to dismiss a topic that was too frightening to entertain, 'Who've you brought in for questioning?' He wasn't happy when he learned that Leach's best efforts had failed to gain anything substantial from Pitchley-Pitchford-Pytches upon his third interview. He was also not pleased to learn that the equally best efforts of the teams who were working the sites of the two hit and runs had uncovered nothing more useful than what they had already known about the car. He *was* moderately satisfied with the news from forensic about the paint chips and the age of the vehicle. But information was one thing; an arrest was another. And he Goddamn wanted a bloody arrest.

'Do you have that message, Acting Superintendent?'

Lynley took a deep breath and put the heightened level of Hillier's acerbity down to his understandable dread about Webberly. He did indeed have the message, he told the AC steadily. Was Miranda really all right, though? Was there anything he could . . .? Had Helen at least managed to get her to eat something?

'She's gone to Frances,' Hillier said.

'Randie?'

'Your wife. Laura's got exactly nowhere, can't even budge her from her bedroom, so Helen's decided to try her hand. Good woman, there.' Hillier harrumphed. He would, Lynley knew, never venture any closer to a compliment.

'Thank you, sir.'

'Get on with things. I'm staying here. I don't want Randie alone should anything . . . should she be asked to decide . . .'

'Right. Yes, sir. That's the best idea, isn't it?'

Now, Lynley watched Nkata. Curiously, the constable was protecting his phone conversation from eavesdroppers with a broad shoulder lifted to shield the mouthpiece of the receiver. Lynley frowned at this, and when Nkata rang off, he said, 'Get anything?'

Rubbing his hands together, the DC said, 'Hope so, man. Bird who lives with Katja Wolff's asking for another word. That's who paged. Think I ought . . .?' He nodded towards the doorway, but the motion seemed more a bow to obligation than an actual request for direction because the constable's fingers began tapping against the pocket of his trousers as if eager to dig out his car keys.

Lynley reflected upon what Nkata had already told him about his most recent interview with both women. 'Did she say what she wanted?'

'Just a word. Said she didn't want to talk on the

253

phone.'

'Why not?'

Nkata shrugged and shifted his weight from one foot to the other. 'Villains, man. You know how they are. Always like to be the ones pulling the strings.'

That certainly rang an authentic note. If a convict was going to grass on a mate, that convict generally named the time, the place, and the circumstances under which the grassing would occur. It was a power play that acted as a salve to their conscience when they lived the part of no honour among thieves. But lags rarely bore love for cops, and caution suggested that a cop be wise to the fact that a villain liked nothing better than to throw spanners if he could, with the size of the spanners generally matching the proportions of his animosity for the police.

He said, 'What's she called again, Winnie?'

'Who?'

'The woman who paged you. Wolff's flat mate.' And when Nkata told him, Lynley asked what crime had sent Yasmin Edwards to prison.

'Knifed her husband,' Nkata said. 'Killed him. She was in five years. But I got the 'pression he beat her up a lot. She's got a bad face, 'spector. Scarred up. She and Wolff live with her son. Daniel. Ten, eleven years old. Nice kid. Should I ...?' Again the anxious nod at the door.

Lynley pondered the wisdom of sending Nkata south of the river again on his own. His very zeal to take on the task gave Lynley pause. On the one hand, Nkata would be eager to make up for his earlier gaffe. On the other hand, he was inexperienced, and the appetite he had for again

254

confronting Yasmin Edwards suggested the potential for a loss of objectivity. As long as the potential was there, Nkata—not to mention the case itself—was in jeopardy. Just as Webberly had been, Lynley realised, all those years ago in another investigation.

They kept coming full circle to that other murder, he thought. There had to be a reason for that.

He said, 'Has she got an axe to grind, this Yasmin Edwards?'

'With me, you mean?'

'With cops in general.'

'Could have, yeah.'

'Mind how you go, then.'

Nkata said, 'Will do,' and he hastened out of the incident room, car keys already in his palm.

When the constable was gone, Lynley sat at a desk and put on his glasses. The situation they were in was maddening. He'd been involved in cases before in which they'd had mounds of evidence but no one to whom it could be attached. He'd been involved in cases in which they'd had motives leaping out from the wallpaper in the sitting room of every suspect they questioned but no evidence they could apply to the suspects. And he'd been involved in cases in which the means and the opportunity to kill could be applied left, right, and centre and all that was missing was clarity on the motive. But this . . .

How was it possible that two people could be hit and abandoned on populated streets without *someone* seeing something other than a black vehicle? Lynley wondered. And how was it possible that the first victim could actually be dragged from point A to point B in Crediton Hill once the hit took place without someone noticing what was going on?

The moving of the body was an important detail, and Lynley fetched the latest report from forensic to examine what they'd come up with from evidence taken from Eugenie Davies' body. The forensic pathologist would have combed it, probed it, studied it, and analysed it. And if there was a trace of evidence left on it—this despite the rain of the evening—the forensic pathologist would have found it.

Lynley flipped through the paperwork. Nothing under her fingernails, all blood on the body her own, remnants of earth fallen from tyres bearing no telling characteristics like minerals peculiar to one part of the country, granules caught up in her hair similar to those on the street itself, two hairs on her body—one grey and one brown—which, under analysis—

Lynley's interest sharpened. Two hairs, two different colours, an analysis. Surely this amounted to something. He read the report, frowning, wading through descriptions of cuticle, cortex, and medulla and celebrating the initial conclusion offered by SO7: The hairs were mammalian in origin.

But when he continued, fighting his way through the morass of technical terms from the *macrofibrillar ultrastructure of the medullary cells* to *the electrophoretic variants of the structural proteins,* he found that the results of the forensic examination of the hairs was inconclusive. How the hell could that possibly be?

He reached for a phone and punched in the number of the forensic lab across the river. After speaking to three technicians and a secretary, he was finally able to pin someone down who explained in layman's terms why a study of hair, made in this century of science so advanced that a microscopic particle of *skin*—for God's sake—could identify a killer, would offer inconclusive results.

'Actually,' Dr Claudia Knowles told him, 'we have no way of telling if the hairs even came from the killer, Inspector. They could well be from the victim, you know.'

'How can that be?'

'First, because we have no scalp attached to either of them. Second—and here's the trickier part—because there's a vast variation in features even within hairs that come from *one* individual. So we could take dozens of samples of your victim's hair and still not be able to match them to the two hairs found on her body. And all the time they could still be hers. Because of the possible variations. Do you see what I mean?'

'But what about DNA typing? What's the point of combing for hairs in the first place if we can't use them—'

'It's not that we can't use them,' Dr Knowles interrupted. 'We can and we will. But even then, what we'll learn—and this isn't done overnight, which I'm sure you're already aware of—is whether the hairs did come from your victim. Which will help you, of course. But if the hairs *didn't* come from her, you'll be helped only as far as knowing that someone was close enough to her body either before or after her death to have left a hair or two on it.'

'What about two people being close enough to

257

her body to leave a hair? Since one hair was grey and one was brown?'

'That could have happened. But even then, you see, we can't discount the possibility that prior to her death she embraced someone who quite innocently left a hair behind in the process. And even if we *have* the DNA typing in front of us, to prove that she couldn't have embraced anyone who is currently in her life, what do we do with that typing, Inspector, without someone on the other end giving us a sample to match it to?'

God. Yes. That was the problem. That would always be the blasted problem. Lynley thanked Dr Knowles and rang off, flinging the report to one side. They needed a break.

He read through the notes of his interviews again: what Wiley had said, what Staines had said, what Davies, Robson, and the younger Davies had said. There had to be something he was overlooking. But he couldn't dig it out of what he had written.

All right, he thought. Time to try another tack.

He left the station and made the quick drive to West Hampstead. He found Crediton Hill a short distance from Finchley Road, and he parked at the top end, got out, and began to pace. The street was lined with cars and it possessed that uninhabited air of a place where all the occupants leave for work each morning not to return till night.

Chalk marks on the tarmac indicated the spot where Eugenie Davies' body had lain, and Lynley stood upon these and gazed down the street in the direction the deadly vehicle would have come. She'd been hit and then driven over several times, which seemed to indicate that she'd either not been

258

thrown as Webberly had or that she'd been thrown directly in front of the car, making the act of driving back and forth over her an easy piece of business. Then she'd been dragged to one side, her body half shoved beneath a Vauxhall.

But why? Why would her killer risk being seen? Why not just drive off and leave her lying in the middle of the road? Of course, putting her to one side might have served the purpose of keeping her from being noticed at once in the dark and the rain, thereby assuring she'd be dead when someone finally did find her. But it was such a risk to get out of the car at all. Unless the killer had a reason for doing so . . .

Such as living in the neighbourhood? Yes. It was possible.

But was anything else?

Lynley went on to the pavement, pacing along and thinking about every variation he could come up with on the theme of killer-victim-motive, killer-moving-the-broken-body, and killer-getting-out-of-the-car. All he could come up with was her handbag: something she'd carried inside it, something the killer had wanted, had known she'd have with her, had needed to obtain.

But the bag had been found beneath another car in the street, in a spot where it was unlikely that a killer—working in haste and in the darkness—would have seen it. And its contents were in order as far as anyone could tell. Unless, of course, the killer had removed a single item—like a letter, perhaps?—and then thrown the bag beneath the car where it ultimately had been found.

Lynley paced and considered this and felt as if a Greek chorus had taken up residence in his head, reciting not only all the possibilities but also the consequences of his choosing one of them and investing an ounce of belief in it. He walked several yards past several houses, past the autumn coloured hedges that edged their gardens. He was just about to turn back and walk to his car when something glittering on the pavement caught his eye, quite near a yew hedge that looked more recently planted than the others in the street.

He bent to this like Sherlock Holmes redeemed. But it proved to be just a shard of glass that, along with a few other shards, had been swept from the pavement into the flower bed where the hedge was planted. He took a pencil from his jacket pocket and turned the shards over, then dug round in the earth and found a few more. And because he'd never felt quite so much without resources as he was feeling in this investigation, he took out his handkerchief and collected them all.

Back in his car, he phoned home, seeking Helen. It was hours since she'd turned up at Charing Cross Hospital, hours since she'd trekked to Webberly's house to see what could be made of Frances. But she wasn't there. And she wasn't at work in Chelsea with St James. This, he decided, was not a good sign.

He drove to Stamford Brook.

*       *       *

In Kensington Square, Barbara Havers parked where she'd parked before: by the line of bollards that prevented traffic entering the square from the north in Derry Street. She walked to the Convent of the Immaculate Conception, but instead of

260

going to the door straightaway and requesting to speak with Sister Cecilia Mahoney once again, she lit a cigarette and ventured farther along the pavement to the distinguished, brick, Dutch-gabled house where so much had happened two decades in the past.

It was the tallest building on its side of the street: five floors with a basement which was accessed by a narrow stairway that curved down from the flagstone-covered front garden. Two brick pillars topped with white stone finials sided the wrought-iron entrance gate, and Barbara swung this gate open, entered, closed it behind her, and stood looking up at the house.

It was quite a contrast to Lynn Davies' small dwelling on the other side of the river. With its french windows and balconies, its creamy woodwork, its solemn pediments and dog-toothed cornices, its fanlights and its stained glass windows, it—and the neighbourhood that surrounded it—couldn't have been more different to the environment in which Virginia Davies had lived her life.

But there was another difference besides the obvious physical one, and Barbara thought about it as she surveyed the house. Inside had lived a terrible man, in Lynn Davies' words, a man who couldn't bear to be in the same room as a grandchild who was, in his eyes, not what she should have been. The child had been unwelcome in this house, she'd been an object of continual loathing, so her mother had taken her away forever. And old Jack Davies—terrible Jack Davies—had been appeased. More, he'd been gratified, as it happened, because when his son got

261

round to marrying again, Jack's next grandchild turned out to be a musical genius.

Delight all round at that one, Barbara thought. The kid picked up a fiddle, made his mark, and gave the name Davies the glory it deserved. But then came the *next* grandchild's birth, and old Jack Davies—terrible Jack Davies—was made to look imperfection in the face again.

But on this second go with a defective child, things were more dicey for Jack. Because if old Jack Davies drove *this* mother off with his relentless demands to 'keep her out of my sight, put that creature *away* somewhere', chances were that this mother would take her other child with her. And that would mean goodbye Gideon and goodbye to basking vicariously in the glory of everything Gideon stood to accomplish.

When Sonia Davies was drowned in her bath, had the police even known about Virginia? Barbara wondered. And if they had, had the family managed to keep old Jack's attitude to her under wraps? Probably.

He'd gone through a horrific time in the war, he'd never recovered, he was a military hero. But he also sounded like a man who was five notes short of a full sonata, and how was anyone to know how far a man like that would go when he'd been thwarted?

Barbara went back to the pavement, closing the gate behind her. She flipped her cigarette into the street and retraced her steps to the Convent of the Immaculate Conception.

This time round, she found Sister Cecilia Mahoney in the enormous garden behind the main building. With another nun, she was raking up leaves from a mammoth sycamore tree that could have shaded an entire hamlet. They'd so far made five piles of leaves, which formed colourful mounds across the lawn. In the distance where a wall marked the end of the convent's property and protected it from the trains of the District line that rumbled above ground throughout the day, a man in a boiler suit and a knitted hat was tending a fire where some of the gathered leaves were burning.

'You need to have a care with that sort of thing,' Barbara said to Sister Cecilia as she joined her on the lawn. 'One wrong move and all of Kensington'll go up in smoke. I don't expect you want that.'

'With no Wren to build its replacement,' Sister Cecilia noted. 'Yes. We're being quite careful, Constable. George doesn't leave the fire unattended. And I'm thinking it's George who's got the better bargain. We do the gathering and he makes the offering that God receives with pleasure.'

'Pardon?'

The nun drew her rake along the lawn, its tines snaring a cluster of leaves. 'Biblical allusion, if you'll pardon me. Cain and Abel. Abel's fire produced smoke that went heavenward.'

'Oh. Right.'

'You don't know the Old Testament?'

'Just the lying, knowing, and begetting parts. And I've got most of those memorised.'

Sister Cecilia laughed and took her rake to lean it against a bench that encircled the sycamore at the garden's centre. She returned to Barbara, saying, 'Sure there was a great deal of lying and begetting going on in those days, wasn't there, Constable? But then, they had to set about it,

263

didn't they, since they'd been told to populate the world.'

Barbara smiled. 'Could I have a word?'

'Of course. You'll be preferring to have it inside the convent, I expect.' Sister Cecilia didn't wait for a reply. She merely said to her companion, 'Sister Rose, if I can leave you to this for a quarter of an hour . . . ?' and when the other nun nodded, she led the way to a short flight of concrete steps which took them to the back door of the dun brick building.

They walked down a lino-floored corridor to a door marked *visitors' room*. Here, Sister Cecilia knocked and when there was no reply, she swung the door open saying, 'Would you like a cup of tea, Constable? A coffee? I think we've a biscuit or two.'

Barbara demurred. Just conversation, she told the nun.

'You don't mind if I . . . ?' Sister Cecilia indicated an electric kettle, which stood on a chipped, plastic tray along with a tin of Earl Grey tea and several mismatched cups and saucers. She plugged the kettle in and fetched from the top of a small chest of drawers a box of sugar cubes, three of which she popped into a cup, saying serenely to Barbara, 'Sweet tooth. But God forgives small vices in us all. I would feel less guilty, though, if you'd be taking a biscuit at least. They're Weight Watchers. Oh but sure, I don't mean to imply that you're needing to—'

'No offence taken,' Barbara interrupted. 'I'll have one.'

Sister Cecilia looked mischievous. 'They do come in packets of two, Constable.'

264

'Hand them over, then. I'll cope.'

With her tea made and her biscuits in their little packet on a separate saucer, Sister Cecilia was prepared to join Barbara. They sat on two vinyl-covered chairs next to a window that overlooked the garden where Sister Rose was still raking leaves. A low veneer table separated them, its surface holding a variety of religious magazines and one copy of *Elle,* heavily thumbed.

Barbara told the nun that she'd met Lynn Davies and asked if Sister Cecilia knew about this earlier marriage and this additional child of Richard Davies.

Sister Cecilia confirmed that she had long known, that she'd learned about Lynn and that 'poor dear mite of hers' from Eugenie shortly after Gideon's birth. 'It came as quite a shock to Eugenie, to be sure, Constable. She'd not known Richard was even divorced, and she spent some time reflecting on what it meant that he hadn't told her prior to their marriage.'

'I expect she felt betrayed.'

'Oh, it wasn't the personal side of the omission that concerned her. At least, if it was, she didn't discuss that part of it with me. It was the spiritual and religious implications that Eugenie wrestled with during those first years after Gideon's birth.'

'What sort of implications?'

'Well, the holy Church recognises marriage as a permanent covenant between a man and a woman.'

'So was Mrs Davies concerned that if the Church saw her husband's first marriage as his legitimate one, her own marriage would be considered bigamous? And the kids from that marriage illegitimate?'

Sister Cecilia took a sip of tea. 'Yes and no,' she replied. 'The situation was complicated by the fact that Richard himself wasn't Catholic. He wasn't actually anything, poor man. He hadn't been married in any church in the first place, so Eugenie's real question was whether he'd lived in sin with Lynn and if the child from that union— who would thus be conceived in sin—bore the mark of God's judgement upon her. And if that were the case, did Eugenie herself run the risk of calling down God's judgement upon herself as well?'

'For having married a man who'd "lived in sin", d'you mean?'

'Ah no. For not herself having married him in the Church.'

'The Church wouldn't allow it?'

'It was never a question of what the Church would or would not allow. Richard didn't want a religious ceremony, so they never had one. Just the civil procedure at the register office.'

'But as a Catholic, wouldn't Mrs Davies have wanted a Church wedding as well? Wouldn't she have been obliged to have one? I mean, for everything to be on the up and up with God and the Pope.'

'That's how it is, my dear. But Eugenie was Catholic only as far as it went.'

'Meaning?'

'Meaning that she received some sacraments, but not others. She accepted some beliefs, but not others.'

'When you join up, aren't you supposed to swear on the Bible or something that you'll abide by the rules? I mean, we know that she wasn't brought up

Catholic, so does the Church take on members who abide by some rules and not by others?'

'You must remember that the Church has no secret police to make certain its members are walking the straight and narrow, Constable,' the nun replied. She took a bite from her biscuit and munched. 'God has given us each a conscience so that we can monitor our own behaviour. Isn't it true, of course, that there are many topics on which individual Catholics part ways with Holy Mother the Church, but whether that puts their eternal salvation into jeopardy is something that only God could tell us.'

'Yet Mrs Davies seemed to believe that God gets even with sinners during their lifetime, if she thought that Virginia was God's way of dealing with Richard and Lynn.'

'Sure it is that when a misfortune befalls someone, people often interpret it that way. But consider Job. What was his sin that he was so tried by God?'

'Knowing and begetting on the wrong side of the sheets?' Barbara asked. 'I can't remember.'

'You can't remember because there was no sin. Just the terrible trials of his faith in the Almighty.' Sister Cecilia took up her tea, wiping the biscuit crumbs from her fingers onto the nubby material of her skirt.

'Is that what you told Mrs Davies, then?'

'I pointed out that had God wished to punish her, He certainly wouldn't have started out by giving her Gideon—a perfectly healthy child—as the first fruit of her marriage to Richard.'

'But as to Sonia?'

'Did she consider that child her punishment

267

from God for her sins?' Sister Cecilia clarified. 'She never said as much. But from the way she reacted when she was told about the wee one's condition . . . And then when she stopped attending Church entirely once the baby died . . .' The nun sighed, brought her cup to her lips and held it there as she considered how to reply. She finally said, 'We can only surmise, Constable. We can only take the questions she asked with regard to Lynn and Virginia and infer from them how she herself might have felt and what she might have believed when she was faced with a similar trial.'

'What about the rest of them?'

'The rest?'

'The rest of the family. Did she mention how they felt? About Sonia? Once they knew . . . ?'

'She never said.'

'Lynn says she left in part because of Richard Davies' dad. She says he had a few cogs not working but the ones that did work were nasty enough for her to be glad the rest were misfiring. If a cog misfires. But I expect you know what I mean.'

'Eugenie didn't talk about the household.'

'She didn't mention anyone wanting to get rid of Sonia? Like Richard? Or his dad? Or anyone?'

Sister Cecilia's blue eyes widened over the biscuit she'd raised to her lips. She said, 'Mary and Joseph. No. *No.* This was not a house of evil people. Troubled people, perhaps, as we're all troubled from time to time. But to want to be rid of a baby so desperately that one of them might have . . . ? No. I can't think that of any of them.'

'But someone did kill her, and you told me yesterday that you didn't believe it was Katja Wolff.'

'Didn't and don't,' the nun affirmed.

'But someone had to have done the deed unless you believe that the hand of God swept down and held that baby under the water. So who? Eugenie herself? Richard? Granddad? The lodger? Gideon?'

'He was eight years old!'

'And jealous that a second child had come to take the spotlight off him?'

'She could hardly do that.'

'But she could take everyone's attention from him. She could take up their time. She could take most of their money. She could tap the well till the well was dry. And if it went dry, where would that leave Gideon?'

'No eight-year-old child thinks that far into the future.'

'But someone else might have, someone who had a vested interest in keeping him front and centre in the household.'

'Yes. Well. I don't know who that someone might be.'

Barbara watched the nun place half her biscuit onto the saucer. She watched as Sister Cecilia went to the kettle and switched it on for a second cup of tea. She weighed her preconceived notions about nuns with what information she'd gathered from this one and the air with which Sister Cecilia had parted with it. She concluded that the nun was telling her everything she knew. In their earlier interview, Sister Cecilia had said that Eugenie stopped attending church when Sonia died. So she—Sister Cecilia—would no longer have had the opportunity she'd once had for heart-to-heart chats of the sort that passed along crucial information.

She said, 'What happened to the other baby?'

'The other . . . ? Oh. Are you speaking of Katja's child?'

'My DCI wants me to track him down.'

'He's in Australia, Constable. He's been there since he was twelve years old. And as I told you when we first spoke, if Katja wished to find him, she'd have come to me at once upon her release. You must believe me. The terms of the adoption asked the parents to provide annual updates about the child, so I've always known where he was and I'd have provided Katja with that information any time she asked for it.'

'But she didn't?'

'She did not.' Sister Cecilia headed for the door. 'If you'll excuse me for a moment, I'll fetch something you might want to see.'

The nun left the room just as the electric kettle brought the water to a boil and clicked off. Barbara rose and brewed a second cup of Earl Grey for Sister Cecilia, scoring another packet of the biscuits for herself. She'd crammed these down her throat and added the three cubes of sugar to Sister Cecilia's tea when the nun returned, a manila envelope in her hand.

She sat, knees and ankles together, and spread the contents of the envelope on her lap. Barbara saw they consisted of letters and photographs, both snap shots and studio portraits.

'He's called Jeremy, Katja's son,' Sister Cecilia told her. 'He'll be twenty in February. He was adopted by a family called Watts, along with three other children. They're in Adelaide now, all of them. He favours his mother, I think.'

Barbara took the photos that Sister Cecilia

270

offered her. In them, she saw that the nun had maintained a pictorial record of the child's life. Jeremy was fair and blue-eyed, although the blond hair of his childhood had darkened to stripped pine in his adolescence. He'd gone through a gawky period round the time his family had taken him and his siblings to Australia, but once he'd passed through that, he was handsome enough. Straight nose, square jaw, ears flat against his skull, he would do for an Aryan, Barbara thought.

She said, 'Katja Wolff doesn't know that you have these?'

Sister Cecilia said, 'As I told you, she wouldn't ever see me. Even when it came time to arrange for Jeremy's adoption, she wouldn't speak to me. The prison acted as our go-between: The warden told me Katja wanted an adoption and the warden told me when the time had arrived. Sure, I don't know if Katja ever *saw* the baby. All I know is that she wanted him placed with a family at once, and she wanted me to see to it, as soon as was possible after the birth.'

Barbara handed the pictures back, saying, 'She didn't want him to go to the father?'

'Adoption was what she wanted.'

'Who was the dad?'

'We didn't speak—'

'Got that. I know. But you *knew* her. You knew all of them. So you must have had an idea or two. There were three men in the house that we know of: the Granddad, Richard Davies, and the lodger, who was a bloke called James Pitchford. There were four, if you count Raphael Robson, the violin teacher. Five, if you want to count Gideon and think Katja might have liked to have at them

271

young. He was precocious in one way. Why not in another?'

The nun looked affronted. 'Katja was not a child molester.'

'She might not have seen it as molestation. Women don't, do they, when they're initiating a male. Hell, there are tribes where it's *customary* for older women to take young boys in hand.'

'Be that as it may, this was not a tribe. And Gideon was certainly not the father of that baby. I doubt—' and here the nun blushed hotly—'I doubt that he would been capable of the act.'

'Then whoever it was, he must have had reason to keep his part in it under wraps. Else why not come forward and lay claim to the kid once Katja got her twenty year sentence? Unless, of course, he didn't want to be known as the man who put a killer in the club.'

'Why does it have to be someone from the house at all?' Sister Cecilia asked. 'And why is it important to know?'

'I'm not sure it is important,' Barbara admitted. 'But if the father of her baby is somehow involved with everything else that happened to Katja Wolff, then he might be in danger right now. If she's behind two hit and runs.'

'*Two . . .?*'

'The officer who headed the investigation into Sonia's death was hit last night. He's in a coma.'

Sister Cecilia's fingers reached for the crucifix she wore round her neck. They curled round it and held on fast as the nun said, 'I cannot believe Katja had anything to do with that.'

'Right,' Barbara said. 'But sometimes we end up having to believe what we don't want to believe.

That's the way of the world, Sister.'

'It is not the way of my world,' the nun declared.


*Gideon*

<u>*6 NOVEMBER*</u>

*I've been dreaming again, Dr Rose. I'm standing on the stage at the Barbican, with the lights blindingly bright above me. The orchestra is behind me, and the maestro—whose face I cannot see—taps on his lectern. The music begins—four measures from the cellos—and I lift my instrument and prepare to join in. Then from somewhere in the vast hall, I hear it: A baby has begun crying.*

*It echoes through the hall, but I'm the only person who seems to notice. The cellos continue to play, the rest of the strings join them, and I know that my solo will be fast upon us.*

*I cannot think, I cannot play, I cannot do anything but wonder why the maestro won't stop the orchestra, won't turn to the audience, won't demand that someone have the simple courtesy to take the screaming child out of the auditorium so that we can concentrate on our playing. There is a full measure's rest before I'm to begin my solo, and as I wait for it to arrive, I keep glancing out to the audience. But I can see nothing because of the lights, and they are far more blinding than lights ever are in an actual auditorium. Indeed, they're the sort of lights one imagines to be shone upon a suspect who is under interrogation.*

*I begin. Of course, it isn't right. It isn't in the right key. To my left, the lead violin stands abruptly and I*

273

*see that he's Raphael Robson. I want to say, 'Raphael, you're playing! With an audience, you're playing!' but the rest of the violins follow his lead and leap to their feet as well. They begin to protest to the maestro, as do the cellos and the basses. I hear all their voices. I try to drown them out with my playing and I try to drown the baby out, but I cannot. I want to tell them that it's not me, it's not my fault, and I say, 'Can't you hear? Can't you hear it?' as I continue to play. And I watch the maestro as I do so, because he's continuing to direct the orchestra as if they'd never stopped playing in the first place.*

*Raphael then approaches the maestro, who turns to me. And he is my father. 'Play!' he snarls. And I'm so surprised to see him there where he should not be that I back away and the darkness of the auditorium envelops me.*

*I begin to search for the screaming baby. I go up the aisle, feeling my way in the dark, until I hear that the crying is coming from behind a closed door.*

*I open this door. Suddenly, I am outside, in daylight, and in front of me is an enormous fountain. But this is not an ordinary fountain because standing in the water are a minister of some sort dressed all in black and a woman in white who is holding the yowling infant to her bosom. As I watch, the minister submerges them both—the woman and the child that she holds—in the water, and I know that the woman is Katja Wolff and that she's holding my sister.*

*Somehow, I know I must get to that fountain, but my feet become too heavy to lift. So I watch and when Katja Wolff emerges from the water, she emerges alone.*

*The water makes her white dress cling to her and through the material her nipples show as does her*
274

*pubic hair, which is thick, dark as night, and coiling coiling coiling over her sex which still glistens through the wet dress she's wearing as if she's not wearing a dress at all. And I feel that stirring within me, that rush of desire I haven't felt in years. The throb begins and I welcome it and I no longer think of the concert I've left or the ceremony I've witnessed in the water.*

*My feet are freed. I approach. Katja cups her breasts in her hands. But before I can reach the fountain and her, the minister blocks my way and I look at him and he is my father.*

*He goes to her. He does to her what I want to do, and I am forced to watch as her body draws him in and begins to work him as the water slaps languidly against their legs.*

*I cry out, and I awaken.*

*And there it was between my legs, Dr Rose, what I hadn't been able to manage in . . . how many years? . . . since Beth. Throbbing, engorged, and ready for action, all because of a dream in which I was nothing but a voyeur of my father's pleasure.*

*I lay there in the darkness, despising myself, despising my body and my mind and what both of them were telling me through the means of a dream. And as I lay there, a memory came to me.*

*It is Katja, and she has come into the dining room where we're having dinner. She's carrying my sister who is dressed for bed, and it's very clear that she's excited about something because when Katja Wolff is excited, her English becomes more broken. She says, 'See! See you must what she has done!'*

*Granddad says irritably, 'What is it now?' and there's a moment that I recognise as tension while all the adults look at each other: Mother at Granddad, Dad at Gran, Sarah-Jane at James the Lodger. He—*

275

James—is looking at Katja. And Katja is looking at Sonia.

She says, 'Show them, little one,' and she sets my sister on the floor. She puts her on her bum but she doesn't prop her up as she's had to do in the past. Instead, she balances her carefully and removes her hands, and Sonia remains upright.

'She sits alone!' Katja announces proudly. 'Is this not a dream?'

Mother gets to her feet, saying, 'Wonderful, darling!' and goes to cuddle her. She says, 'Thank you, Katja,' and when she smiles, her face is radiant with delight.

Granddad makes no comment at all because he doesn't look to see what Sonia has managed to do. Gran murmurs, 'Lovely, my dear,' and watches Granddad.

Sarah-Jane Beckett makes a polite comment and attempts to draw James the Lodger into conversation. But it's a vain attempt because James is fixated on Katja, the way a starving dog might fixate on a rare piece of beef.

And Katja herself is fixated on my father. 'See how lovely is she!' Katja crows. 'See what learns she and how quickly! What a good big girl is Sonia, yes. Every baby can thrive with Katja.'

Every baby. *How had I forgotten those words and that look? How had it escaped me till now: what those words and that look really meant? What they* had *to have meant, because everyone freezes the way people freeze when a motion picture is reduced to a single frame. And a moment later—in the breath of a second—Mother picks up Sonia and says, 'We're all quite sure that's the case, my dear.'*

*I saw it then, and I see it now. But I didn't*

276

*understand because what was I, seven years old? What child that young can comprehend the full reality of the situation in which he's living? What child that young can infer from a single simple statement graciously said a woman's sudden understanding of a betrayal that has occurred and is continuing to occur within her own home?*

### 9 NOVEMBER
*He kept that picture, Dr Rose. Everything I know goes back to the fact that my father kept that single picture, a photograph that he himself must have taken and hidden away because how else could it possibly have come to be in his possession?*

*So I see them, on a sunny afternoon in the summer, and he asks Katja to step into the garden so that he can take a photo of her with my sister. Sonia's presence, cradled in Katja's arms, legitimises the moment. Sonia is the excuse despite the fact that she is cradled in such a way that her face isn't visible to the camera. And that's an important detail as well because Sonia isn't perfect. Sonia is a freak, and a picture of Sonia whose face bears the manifestations of the congenital syndrome that afflicts her—oblique palpebral fissures, I have learned they are called, epicanthal folds, and a mouth that is disproportionately small—will serve as a constant reminder to Dad that he created for the second time in his life a child with physical and mental imperfections. So he doesn't want to capture her face on film, but he needs her there as an excuse.*

*Are he and Katja lovers at the time? Or do they both just think about it then, each of them waiting for some sign from the other that will express an interest*

277

*that cannot yet be spoken? And when it happens between them for the first time, who makes the move and what is the move that signals the direction they will soon be taking?*

*She goes out for a breath of air on a stifling night, the kind of August night in London when a heat wave hits and there's no escaping the oppressive atmosphere created by polluted air hanging too long over the city, which is daily heated by the scorching sun and further poisoned by the diesel lorries that belch exhaust fumes along the streets. Sonia is asleep at long last, and Katja has ten precious minutes to herself. The darkness outside makes a false promise of deliverance from the heat trapped inside the house, so she walks out into it, out into the garden behind the house, which is where he finds her.*

*'Terrible day,' he says. 'I'm burning up.'*

*'I too,' she replies, and she watches him steadily. 'I too burn, Richard.'*

*And that is enough. That final statement and especially the use of his Christian name constitute implicit permission, and he needs no other invitation. He surges towards her, and it begins between them, and this is what I see from the garden.*

## CHAPTER TWENTY

Libby Neale had never been to Richard Davies' flat, so she didn't know what to expect when she drove Gideon there from the Temple. Asked about it, she might have guessed that he'd be living high out of very deep pockets. He'd been making such a deal about Gideon's not playing the violin for the

278

past four months, it seemed reasonable to conclude that he needed a hefty income that only cash from Gideon on a regular basis could provide.

So she said, 'This is *it?*' when Gideon told her to pull in at a parking space on the north side of a street called Cornwall Gardens. She looked at the neighbourhood with a vague sense of disappointment, taking in buildings that were—okay—*genteel* enough but dilapidated to the max. True, there were some decent looking places crammed in here and there, but the rest of them looked like they'd seen better days in another century.

It got worse. Gideon, without replying to her question, led the way to a building that looked like prayers were holding it up. He used a key on a front door so warped away from the jamb that using a key in the first place seemed like an unnecessary courtesy applied to spare the door's feelings. A credit card would have done as well. When they were inside, he led her upstairs to a second door. This one wasn't warped, but someone had decorated it with a trail of green spray paint in the shape of a Z, like an Irish Zorro had come to call.

Gideon said, 'Dad?' as he swung the door open and they entered his father's flat. He said to Libby, 'Wait here,' which she was glad to do as he ducked into a kitchen that was just off the living room. The place gave her the major creeps. It was so not the kind of place she'd thought Richard Davies would've set himself up in.

First off, what was with the colour scheme? Libby wondered. She was no decorator—leave that to her mom and her sister who were into Feng Shui

279

in a major way. But even she could tell that the colours in this place were guaranteed to make anyone want to take a leap from the nearest bridge. Puke green walls. Diarrhoea brown furniture. And weirdo art like that nude woman shown from neck to ankles with pubic hair looking like the inside of a toilet going through the flush cycle. What did *that* mean? Above the fireplace—which for some reason was filled with books—a circular display of tree branches had been pounded. These looked like they'd been made into walking sticks because they were sanded down and had holes punched through them and leather thongs threaded through the holes like wrist straps. But how weird to have them there in the first place.

The only thing in the room that Libby saw and had expected to see were pictures of Gideon. There were tons of those. And they were all unified by the same boring theme: the violin. Surprise, surprise, Libby thought. Richard couldn't *possibly* have a shot of Gideon doing something he might *like* to do. Why show him flying kites on Primrose Hill? Why take a picture of him helping some kid from the East End learn how to hold a violin if he *himself* wasn't holding it, playing it, and making a bang-up salary for doing so? Richard, Libby thought, needed his butt kicked. He was so *not* helping Gideon get better.

She heard a window in the kitchen creak open, heard Gideon shout for his father in the direction of the garden that she'd seen to the left of the building itself. Richard obviously wasn't out there, though, because after thirty seconds and a few more shouts, the window closed. Gideon came back through the living room and headed down the hall.

He didn't say, 'Wait here,' this time, so Libby followed him. She'd had enough of the creepoid living room.

He worked through the place back to front, saying, 'Dad?' as he opened a bedroom door and then a bathroom door. Libby followed. She was about to tell him it was sort of obvious that Richard wasn't at home so why was Gideon yelling for him like he'd lost his hearing in the last twenty-four hours when he shoved on another door, swung it wide, and revealed the icing on the cake of the flat's overall weirdness.

Gideon ducked through the doorway and she trailed him, saying, 'Whoops! Oh, sorry,' when she first caught a glimpse of the uniformed soldier standing just inside. It took her a moment to realise the soldier wasn't Richard playing dress-up with the hope of spooking the hell out of them. It was instead a mannequin. She approached it gingerly and said, 'Geez. What the hell . . . ?' and glanced at Gideon. But he was already at a desk at the far side of the room, and he had its fold-down front opened and was rooting through all its cubbyholes, looking so intense that she figured he wouldn't hear her even if she asked what she wanted to ask, which was what the hell Richard was *doing* with this weirdo piece of crap in his house and did Gid think Jill knew about it?

There were display cases as well, the kinds that you saw in museums. And these were filled with letters, medals, commendations, telegrams, and all sorts of junk that upon inspection appeared to have come from World War II. On the walls were pictures from the same era, all showing a dude in

281

the army. Here he was on his stomach, squinting down the barrel of a rifle like John Wayne in a war movie. There he was running alongside a tank. Next he was seated cross-legged on the ground, at the front of a pack of similar dudes with their weapons slung over their bodies all casual, like having an AK47—or whatever it had been in those days—across your shoulder was pretty much par for the course. It wasn't what *anyone* with a grain of sense would show himself doing today. Not unless he was part of some neo-Nazi freedom fighter let's-get-rid-of-everyone-who's-not-a-WASP group.

Libby felt queasy. Getting out of this place in the next thirty seconds didn't seem like such a bad idea.

Behind her, the drawers slammed shut and other drawers opened. Paperwork shuffled. Things flopped to the floor. She turned and watched what Gideon was doing, thinking, Richard's *really* going to blow a fuse over this one, but then not much caring because Richard was reaping what Richard had spent a long time sowing.

She said, 'Gideon. What are we looking for?'

'He's got her address. He has to have it.'

'That doesn't make sense.'

'He knows where she is. He's seen her.'

'Did he tell you that?'

'She's written to him. He *knows*.'

'Gid, did he *tell* you that?' Libby didn't think so. 'Hey, why would she write to him? Why would she try to see him? Cresswell-White said she can't contact you guys. Her parole will be screwed up if she does. She's just spent twenty years in the joint, right? You think she wants to go back for three or four more?'

282

'He knows, Libby. And so do I.'

'Then what are we doing here? I mean, if *you* know . . .' Gideon was making less and less sense by the hour. She thought fleetingly of his psychiatrist. Libby knew the shrink's name, Dr Something Rose, but that was all. She wondered if she should phone every Dr Rose in the book—how many could there be?—and say, Look, I'm a friend of Gideon Davies. I'm getting freaked out. He's acting too weird. Can you help out?

Did psychiatrists make house calls? And more to the point, did they take it seriously if a friend of a patient called and said it looked like things were getting out of hand? Or did they then think the friend of the patient should be the next patient? Shit. Hell. *What* should she do? Not call Richard, that's for sure. He wasn't exactly playing the rôle of Mr Sympathy By The Bucketful.

Gideon had dumped out each of the desk drawers on the floor and had done a thorough job of searching through their contents. The only thing left was a letter holder on top of the desk, which for some bizarre reason—but by then, who was counting them?—he went for last, opening envelopes and throwing them onto the floor after glancing at their contents. But the fifth one he came to, he read. Libby could see it was a card with flowers on the front and a printed greeting inside along with a note. His hand dropped hard as he read the message.

She thought, He's found it. She crossed the room to him. She said, 'What? She, like, *wrote* to your dad?'

He said, 'Virginia.'

She said, 'What? Who? Who's Virginia?'

283

His shoulders shook and his fist grabbed onto the card like he wanted to strangle it and he said again, 'Virginia. *Virginia.* God damn him. He lied to me.' And he began to cry. Not tears but sobs, heaves of his body like *everything* was trying to come up and out of him: the contents of his stomach, the thoughts in his mind, and the feelings of his heart.

Tentatively, Libby reached for the card. He let her take it from him and she ran her gaze over it, looking for what had caused Gideon's reaction. It said:

*Dear Richard,*
*Thank you for the flowers. They were much appreciated. The ceremony was a brief one, but I tried to make it something Virginia herself would have liked. So I filled the chapel with her finger paintings and put her favourite toys round her coffin before the cremation.*
*Our daughter was a miracle child in many ways, not only because she defied medical probability and lived thirty-two years but also because she managed to teach so much to anyone who came into contact with her. I think you would have been proud to be her father, Richard. Despite her problems, she had your tenacity and your fighting spirit, no poor gifts to pass on to a child.*
*Fondly,*
*Lynn*

Libby re-read the message and understood. *She had your tenacity and your fighting spirit, no poor gifts to pass on to a child.* Virginia, she thought.

284

Another kid. Gideon had another sister and she was dead, too.

She looked at Gideon, at a loss for what to say. He'd been taking so many body blows in the past few days that she couldn't even begin to think where to start with the psychic salve that might soothe him.

She said hesitantly, 'You didn't know about her, Gid?' And then, 'Gideon?' again when he didn't reply. She reached out and touched his shoulder. He sat unmoving except for the fact that his whole frame was trembling. It was *vibrating,* almost, beneath his clothes.

He said, 'Dead.'

She said, 'Yeah. I read that in the note. Lynn must've been . . . Well, obviously, she says "our daughter" so she was her mom. Which means your dad was married before and you had a half-sister as well. You didn't know?'

He took the card back from her. He heaved himself off the chair and clumsily shoved the card back into its envelope, stuffing this into the back pocket of his trousers. He said in a voice that was low, like someone talking while hypnotised, 'He lies to me about everything. He always has. And he's lying now.'

He walked through the litter he'd left on the floor, like a man without vision. Libby trailed him, saying, 'Maybe he didn't lie at all,' not so much because she wanted to defend Richard Davies— who probably would have lied about the second coming of Christ if that was the way to get what he wanted—but because she didn't want Gideon to have to deal with anything else. 'I mean, if he never told you about Virginia, it wouldn't have

285

necessarily been a lie. It might've just been one of those things that never came up. Like, maybe he never had the opportunity to talk about her or something. Maybe your mom didn't want her discussed. Too painful? All's I'm saying is that it doesn't have to mean—'

'I knew,' he said. 'I've always known.'

He went into the kitchen with Libby on his heels, chewing on this one. If Gideon knew about Virginia, then what was with him? Freaked out because she'd died, too? Distraught because no one had told him she'd died? Outraged because he'd been kept from the funeral? Except it looked like Richard himself didn't go, if the note was an indication of anything. So what was the lie?

She said, 'Gid—' but stopped herself when he began punching numbers into the phone. Although he stood with one hand pressed to his stomach and one foot tapping against the floor, his expression was grim, the way a man looks when he's made up his mind about something.

He said into the phone, 'Jill? Gideon. I want to speak to Dad . . . No? Then where . . . ? . . . I'm at the flat. No, he's not here . . . I checked there. Did he give you any idea . . . ?' A rather long pause while Richard's lover either wracked her brains or recited a list of possibilities at the end of which Gideon said, 'Right. Mothercare. Fine . . . Thanks, Jill,' and listened some more. He ended with, 'No. No message. No message at all. If he rings you, in fact, don't tell him I phoned. I wouldn't want to . . . Right. Let's not worry him. He's got enough on his mind.' Then he rang off. 'She thinks he's gone off to Oxford Street. Supplies, she says. He wants an intercom for the baby's room. She hadn't yet got

286

one because she intended the baby to sleep with them. Or with her. Or with him. Or with *someone*. But she didn't intend her to be alone. Because if a baby gets left alone, Libby, if a child goes untended for a while, if the parents aren't vigilant, if there's a distraction when they don't expect one, if there's a window open, if someone leaves a candle lit, if anything at all, then the worst can happen. The worst *will* happen. And who knows that better than Dad?'

'Let's go,' Libby said. 'Let's get out of here, Gideon. Come on. I'll buy you a latte, okay? There's got to be a Starbucks nearby.'

He shook his head. 'You go. Take the car. Go home.'

'I'm not going to leave you here. Besides, how would you get—'

'I'll wait for Dad. He'll drive me back.'

'That could be hours. If he goes back to Jill's and she starts labour and then she has the baby, it could be days. Come on. I don't want to leave you hanging around this place alone.'

But she couldn't move him. He wouldn't have her there, and he wouldn't go with her. He would, however, speak to his father. 'I don't care how long it takes,' he told her. 'This time, I don't really care at all.'

Reluctantly, then, she agreed to the plan, not liking it but also seeing that there wasn't much she could do about it. Besides, he seemed calmer after talking to Jill. Or at least he seemed moderately more himself. She said, 'Will you call me, then, if you need anything?'

'I won't be needing anything,' he replied.

Helen herself answered the door when Lynley knocked at Webberly's house in Stamford Brook. He said, 'Helen, why are you still here? When Hillier told me you'd come over from the hospital, I couldn't believe it. You shouldn't be doing this.'

'Whyever not?' she asked in a perfectly reasonable voice.

He stepped inside as Webberly's dog came bounding from the direction of the kitchen, barking at full volume. Lynley backed towards the door while Helen took the dog by the collar and said, 'Alfie, no.' She gave him a shake. 'He doesn't sound like a friend, but he's quite all right. All bark and bluster.'

'So I noticed,' Lynley said.

She looked up from the animal. 'Actually, I was talking about you.' She released the Alsatian once he'd settled. The dog sniffed round Lynley's trouser turn-ups, accepted intrusion, and trotted back towards the kitchen. 'Don't lecture me, darling,' Helen said to her husband. 'As you see, I have friends in high places.'

'With dangerous teeth.'

'That's true.' She gave a nod to the door, and said, 'I didn't think it would be you. I was hoping for Randie.'

'She still won't leave him?'

'It's a stalemate. She won't leave her father; Frances won't leave the house. None of us have been able to move either of them. I thought when we got word about the heart attack . . . Surely, she'll want to go to him, I thought. She'll force herself. Because he may die and not to *be* there if he dies . . . But no.'

'It's not your problem, Helen. And considering the kinds of days you've been having . . . You need to get some rest. Where's Laura Hillier?'

'She and Frances had a row. Frances more than Laura, actually. One of those don't-look-at-me-as-if-I-were-a-monster sort of conversations that start out with one party trying to convince the other party that she's not thinking what the other party is determined to believe she thinks she's thinking because at some level—would that be subconsciously?—she actually *is* thinking it.'

Lynley tried to wade through all this, saying, 'Are these waters too deep for me, Helen?'

'They may require life belts.'

'I thought I might be of help.'

Helen had walked into the sitting room. There an ironing board had been set up and an iron was sending steam ceilingward, which told Lynley—much to his astonishment—that his wife was actually in the process of seeing to the family laundry. A shirt lay across the board itself, one arm the subject of Helen's most recent ministrations. From the look of the wrinkles that appeared to have been permanently applied to the garment, it seemed that Lynley's wife hadn't exactly found a new calling in life.

She saw his glance and said, 'Yes. Well. I'd hoped to be helpful.'

'It's brilliant of you. Really,' Lynley replied supportively.

'I'm not doing it properly. I can see that. I'm sure there's a logic to it—an order or something?—but I've not yet worked it out. Sleeves first? Front? Back? Collar? I do one part and the other part—

289

which I've already done—wrinkles up again. Can you advise?'

'There must be a laundry nearby.'

'That's terrifically helpful, Tommy.' Helen smiled ruefully. 'Perhaps I should stick to pillowcases. At least they're flat.'

Where's Frances?'

'Darling, no. We can't possibly ask her to—'

He chuckled. 'That's not what I meant. I'd like to talk to her. Is she upstairs?'

'Oh. Yes. Once she and Laura had their argument, it was tears all round. Laura dashed out, absolutely sobbing. Frances tore up the stairs looking grim-faced. When I checked on her, she was sitting on the floor in a corner of her bedroom, clutching onto the curtains. She asked to be left alone.'

'Randie needs to be with her. She needs to be with Randie.'

'Believe me, Tommy, I've made that point. Carefully, subtly, straightforwardly, respectfully, cajolingly, and every other way I could think of, save belligerently.'

'That could be what she needs. Bellicosity.'

'Tone might work—although I doubt it—but volume I guarantee will get you nowhere. She asks to be left alone each time I go up to see her and while I'd rather not leave her alone, I keep thinking I ought to respect her wishes.'

'Let me have a go, then.'

'I'll come as well. Have you any further news of Malcolm? We haven't had word from the hospital since Randie phoned, which is good, I suppose. Because surely Randie would have phoned at once if . . . Is there no change, Tommy?'

'No change,' Lynley said. 'The heart complicates things. It's a waiting game.'

'Do you think they might they have to decide . . . ?' Helen paused on the staircase above him and looked back, reading in his expression the answer to her uncompleted question. 'I'm so terribly sorry for all of them,' she said. 'For you as well. I do know what he means to you.'

'Frances needs to be there. Randie can't be asked to do it alone, if it comes to that.'

'Of course she can't,' Helen said.

Lynley had never been upstairs in Webberly's home, so he allowed his wife to show him the way to the master bedroom. The first floor of the house was dominated by scents: potpourri from bowls on a three-tier stand that they passed at the top of the stairs, orange spice from a candle burning outside the bathroom door, lemon from polish used on the furniture. But the scents were not strong enough to cover the stronger odour of air overheated, overweighed with cigar smoke, and so long stale that it seemed only rainfall—violent and long—within the walls of the house would be enough to cleanse it.

'Every window is shut,' Helen said quietly. 'Well, of course, it's November so one wouldn't expect . . . But still . . . It must be so difficult for them. Not just for Malcolm and Randie. They can get away. But for Frances, because she must so want to be . . . to be *cured*.'

'One would think,' Lynley agreed. 'Through here, Helen?'

Only one of the doors was closed and Helen nodded when he indicated it. He tapped on its white panels and said, 'Frances? It's Tommy. May I come in?'

No reply. He called out again, a little louder this time, following that with another rap on the door. When she didn't respond, he tried the knob. It turned, so he eased the door open. Behind him, Helen said, 'Frances? Will you see Tommy?'

To which Webberly's wife finally said, 'Yes,' in a voice that was neither fearful nor resentful at the intrusion, just quiet and tired.

They found her not in the corner where Helen last had seen her but sitting on an undecorated straight-backed chair that she'd drawn up to look at her reflection in a mirror above the dressing table. On the table, she'd laid out hair brushes, hair slides, and ribbons. She was running two ribbons through her fingers as they entered, as if studying the effect that their colour had against her skin.

She was undoubtedly wearing, Lynley saw, what she'd been wearing when she'd phoned her daughter on the previous night. She had on a quilted pink dressing gown belted at the waist, and an azure nightdress beneath it. She hadn't combed her hair despite the brushes laid out before her, so it was still asymmetrically flattened by her head's pressure into her pillow, as if an invisible hat were perched on it.

She looked so colourless that Lynley thought at once of spirits despite the hour of the day: gin, brandy, whisky, vodka, or anything else to bring some blood to her face. He said to Helen, 'Would you bring up a drink, darling?' And to Webberly's wife, 'Frances, you could do with a brandy. I'd like you to have one.'

She said, 'Yes. All right. A brandy.'

Helen left them. Lynley saw a linen chest

292

extended across the foot of the bed and he dragged this over to where Frances sat so that he could speak at her level rather than down at her like a lecturing uncle. He didn't know where to begin. He didn't know what would do any good. Considering the length of time that Frances Webberly had spent inside the walls of this house, paralysed by inexplicable terrors, it didn't seem likely that a simple declaration of her husband's peril and her daughter's need could convince her that her fears were groundless. He was wise enough to know that the human mind did not work that way. Common logic did not suffice to obliterate demons that lived within the tortuous caves of a woman's psyche.

He said, 'Can I do anything, Frances? I know you want to go to him.'

She'd raised one of the ribbons against her cheek, and she lowered this slowly to the top of the table. 'Do you know that,' she said, not a question but a statement. 'If I had the heart of a woman who knows how to love her husband properly, I would have gone to him already. Directly they phoned from casualty. Directly they said, "Is this Mrs Webberly? We're phoning you from Charing Cross Hospital. Casualty. Is this a relative of Malcolm Webberly that I'm speaking to?" I would have gone. I wouldn't have waited to hear a word more. No woman who loves her husband would have done that. No real woman—no adequate woman— would have said, "What's happened? Oh God. *Why's* he not here? Please tell me. The dog came home but Malcolm wasn't *with* him and he's left me, hasn't he? He's left me, he's left me at last." And they said, "Mrs Webberly, your husband's alive. But we would like to speak to you. Here, Mrs

Webberly. Can we send a taxi for you? Is there someone who can bring you down to the hospital?" And that was good of them, wasn't it, to pretend like that? To ignore what I'd said. But when they rang off, they said, "We've got a real nutter here. Poor bloke, this Webberly. No wonder the old sod was out on the streets. Probably *threw* himself in front of the car."' Her fingers curled round a navy ribbon, and her nails sank into it, making gullies in the satin.

Lynley said, 'In the middle of the night when you have a shock, you don't weigh your words, Frances. Nurses, doctors, orderlies, and everyone else at a hospital would know that.'

'"He's your *husband*," she said. "He's cared for you all these miserable years and you *owe* this to him. And to Miranda. Frances, you owe it to her. You must pull yourself together because if you don't and if something should happen to Malcolm while you're not there . . . and if, God, if he should actually die . . . Get up, get up, get *up* Frances Louise because you and I know there is nothing God help me *nothing at all* that's wrong with you. The spotlight's *off* you. Accept that fact." As if she knew what it's like. As if she's actually spent time in my world, in this world, right inside here—' Savagely, she rapped her temple—'instead of in her own little space where everything's perfect, always has been, always will be world without end amen. But it's not like that for me. That is not how it is.'

'Of course,' Lynley said. 'We all look at the world through the prisms of our own experiences, don't we? But sometimes in a moment of crisis, people forget that. So they say things and do things . . . It's all for an end that everyone wants but no

294

one knows how to reach. How can I help you?'

Helen came back into the room then, a wine glass in her hand. It was half-filled with brandy and she placed it on the dressing table and looked towards Lynley with 'What now?' on her face. He wished he knew. He had very little doubt that with every decent intention in the world Frances's sister had already run through the repertoire. Certainly, Laura Hillier had tried reasoning with Frances first, manipulating her second, inducing guilt in her third, and uttering threats fourth. What was probably needed—a slow process of getting the poor woman once again used to an external environment of which she'd been terrified for years—was something that none of them could manage and something for which they had no time.

What now? Lynley wondered along with his wife. *A miracle, Helen.*

He said, 'Drink some of this, Frances,' and lifted the glass for her. When she'd done so, he laid his hand on hers. He said, 'What exactly have they told you about Malcolm?'

Frances murmured, ' "The doctors want to speak to you," she said. "You must go to the hospital. You must be with him. You must be with Randie." ' For the first time, Frances moved her gaze from her reflection. She looked at the joining of her hand with Lynley's. She said, 'If Randie's with him, that's nearly all he would want. "What a brave, new world that's been given to us," he said when she was born. That's why he said she'd be called Miranda. And she was perfect to him. Every way perfect. Perfect as I couldn't hope to be. Ever. Not ever. Daddy's got a princess.' She reached for the wine glass where Lynley had placed it. She started to pick it up but stopped herself and said, 'No. No. That's not it. Not a princess. Not at all. Daddy's found a queen.' Her eyes remained motionless, on the brandy in the glass, but their rims slowly reddened as tears pooled against them.

Lynley's glance met Helen's where she stood just beyond Frances's right shoulder. He could read her reaction to this and he knew it matched his own. Escape was called for. To be in the presence of a maternal jealousy so strong that it wouldn't loosen its grip upon someone even in the midst of a life-and-death crisis . . . It was more than disconcerting, Lynley thought. It was obscene. He felt like a voyeur.

Helen said, 'If Malcolm's anything at all like my father, Frances, I expect what he's felt is a special responsibility towards Randie, because she's a daughter and not a son.'

To which Lynley added, 'I saw that in my own family. The way my father was with my older sister wasn't in the least the way he was with me. Or with my younger brother, for that matter. We weren't as vulnerable, in his eyes. We needed toughening up. But I think what all that means is—'

Frances moved the hand that had been beneath his. She said, 'No. They're right. What they're thinking at the hospital. The queen is dead and he can't cope now. He threw himself under that car last night.' Then for the first time she looked directly at Lynley. She said it again, 'The queen is finally dead. There's no one to replace her. Certainly not me.'

And Lynley suddenly understood. He said, 'You knew,' as Helen began to say, 'Frances, you must *never* believe—', but Frances stopped her by getting

296

to her feet. She went to one of the two bedside tables, and she opened its drawer and set it on the bed. From the very back, tucked away as far as possible from the other contents, she took a small, white square of linen. She unfolded it like a priest in a ritual, shaking it first then smoothing it out against the counterpane on the bed.

Lynley joined her there. Helen did likewise. The three of them looked down on what was a handkerchief, ordinary save for two details: In one corner were twined the initials *E* and *D*, and directly in the centre of the material lay a rusty smear which described a little drama from the past. He cuts his finger his palm the back of his hand doing something for her . . . sawing a board pounding a nail drying a glass picking up the pieces of a jar accidentally smashed on the floor . . . and she quickly removes a handkerchief from her pocket her handbag the sleeve of her sweater the cup of her bra and she presses it upon him because he never remembers to carry one himself. This piece of linen finds its way into the pocket of his trousers his jacket the breast of his coat where he forgets about it till his wife preparing the laundry the dry cleaning the sorting of old things to go to Oxfam finds it sees it knows it for what it is and keeps it. For how many years? Lynley wondered. For how many blasted God awful years in which she asked nothing about what it meant, giving her husband the opportunity to tell the truth, whatever that truth was, or to lie, fabricating a reason that might have been perfectly believable or at least something that she could cling to in order to lie to herself.

Helen said, 'Frances, will you let me get rid of

297

this?' and she placed her fingers not on the handkerchief itself but right next to it, as if it were a relic and she a novitiate in some obscure religion in which only the ordained could touch the blessed.

Frances said, 'No!' and grabbed it. 'He loved her,' she said. 'He loved her and I knew it. I saw it happening, as if it was a study of the whole *process* of love being played out in front of me. Like a television drama. And I kept waiting, you see, because right from the first I knew how he felt. He had to talk about it, he said. Because of Randie . . . because these poor people had lost a little girl not so much younger than our own Randie, and he could see how horrible it was for them, how much they suffered, especially the mother and "No one seems to want to *talk* to her about it, Frances. She has no one. She's existing in a bubble of grief—no, an infected boil of grief—and not one of them is trying to lance it. It feels inhuman, Frances, *inhuman*. Someone must help her before she breaks." So he decided to be the one. He would put that killer in gaol, by God, and he would not rest, Frances dear, till he had that killer signed, sealed, and delivered to justice. Because how would *we* feel if someone—God forbid—harmed our Randie? We would stay up nights, wouldn't we, we would search the streets, we would not sleep and we would not eat and we would not even darken our own doorstep for days on end if that's what it took to find the monster that hurt her.'

Lynley released a slow breath, realising that he'd been holding it the entire time that Frances had been speaking. He felt so far out of his depth that drowning looked like the only option. He glanced at his wife for some sort of guidance and saw that

298

she'd raised her fingers to her lips. And he knew it was sorrow that Helen felt, sorrow for the words that had gone too long unspoken between the Webberlys. He found himself wondering what was actually worse: years of enduring the iron maiden of imagining or seconds of experiencing the quick death of knowing.

Helen said, 'Frances, if Malcolm hadn't loved you—'

'Duty.' Frances began to refold the handkerchief carefully. She said nothing more.

Lynley said, 'I think that's part of love, Frances. It's not the easy part. It's not that first rush of excitement: wanting and believing something's been written in the stars and aren't we the lucky ones because we've just looked heavenwards and got the message. It's the part that's the choice to stay the course.'

'I gave him no choice,' Frances said.

'Frances,' Helen murmured, and Lynley could tell from her voice just exactly how much her next words cost her, 'believe me when I say that you don't have that power.'

Frances looked at Helen then, but of course could not see beyond the structure that Helen had built to live in the world she'd long ago created for herself: the fashionable haircut, the carefully tended and unblemished skin, the manicured hands, the perfect slim body weekly massaged, in the clothes designed for women who knew what elegance meant and how to use it. But as to seeing Helen herself, as to knowing her as the woman who'd once taken the quickest route out of the life of a man she'd dearly loved because she could not cope with staying a course that had altered too

299

radically for her resources and her liking . . . Frances Webberly did not know that Helen and thus could not know that no one understood better than Helen that one person's condition—mental, spiritual, psychological, social, emotional, physical or any combination thereof—could never really control the choices another person made.

Lynley said, 'You need to know this, Frances. Malcolm didn't throw himself under that car. Eric Leach phoned him to tell him about Eugenie Davies, yes, and I expect you read about her death in the paper.'

'He was distraught. I thought he'd *forgotten* about her and then I knew he hadn't. All these years.'

'Not forgotten her, true,' Lynley said, 'but not for the reasons you think. Frances, we don't forget. We can't forget. We don't walk away untouched when we hand our documents to the CPS. It doesn't work that way. But the fact of our remembering is just that, because that's what the mind does. It just remembers. And if we're lucky, the remembering doesn't turn into nightmares. But that's the best we can hope for. That's part of the job.'

Lynley knew he was walking a fine line between truth and falsehood. He knew that whatever Webberly had experienced in his affair with Eugenie Davies and in the years that had followed that affair probably went far beyond mere memory. But that couldn't be allowed to matter at the moment. All that mattered was that the man's wife understand one part of the last forty-eight hours. So he repeated that part for her, 'Frances, he didn't throw himself into the traffic. He was hit by a car.

300

He was hit deliberately. Someone tried to kill him. And within the next few hours or days, we're going to know if that someone succeeded because he may die. He's had a serious heart attack as well. You've been told that, haven't you?'

A sound escaped her. It was something between the excruciating groan of a woman giving birth and the fearful moan of an abandoned child. 'I don't want Malcolm to die,' she said. 'I'm so afraid.'

'You're not alone in that,' Lynley replied.

\*       \*       \*

The fact that she had an appointment at a woman's shelter was what kept Yasmin Edwards steady between the time she phoned the pager number on Constable Nkata's card and the time she was able to meet him at the shop. He'd said he'd have to drive down from Hampstead to see her so he couldn't swear what time he'd get there but he would come as soon as possible, madam, and in the meantime if she began to worry that he wasn't coming at all or he'd forgotten or had got waylaid in some way, she could ring his pager again and he'd let her know where he was on the route, if that would suit her. She'd said she could come to him or meet him somewhere. She said, in fact, she'd prefer it that way. He'd said no, it was best that he come to her.

She'd nearly changed her mind then. But she thought about Number Fifty-five, about Katja's mouth closing over hers, about what it meant that Katja could still slide down and down and down to love her. And she said, 'Right. I'll be at the shop, then.'

In the meantime, she kept her appointment at the shelter in Camberwell. Three sisters in their thirties, an Asian lady, and an old bag married for forty-six years were the residents. Among them were shared countless bruises along with two black eyes, four split lips, a stitched-up cheek, a broken wrist, one dislocated shoulder, and a perforated eardrum. They were like beaten dogs recently let off the chain: cowering and undecided between flight and attack.

Do *not* let any one do this to you, Yasmin wanted to shout at the women. The only thing that kept her from shouting was the scar on her own face and her badly set nose, both of which told the tale of what she herself had once allowed to be done to her.

So she flashed them a smile, said, 'C'mon over here, you gorgeous tomatoes.' She spent two hours at the women's shelter, with her make-up and her colour swatches, with her scarves, her scents, and her wigs. And when she finally left them, three of the residents had got used to smiling again, the fourth had actually managed a laugh, and the fifth had begun to raise her eyes from the floor. Yasmin considered it a good day's work.

She returned to the shop. When she arrived, the cop was striding up and down in front of it. She saw him check his watch and try to peer round the metal security door that she lowered over the shop front whenever she wasn't there. Then he looked at his watch again and took his beeper from his leather belt and tapped it.

Yasmin pulled up in the old Fiesta. When she opened her door, the detective was there before she put a foot on the pavement.

302

'This some kind of joke?' he demanded. 'You think messing in a murder 'vestigation's something you can have fun with, Missus Edwards?'

'You said you didn't know how long—' Yasmin stopped herself. What was *she* making excuses for? She said, 'I had a 'pointment. You want to help me unload the car or you want to chew my bum?' She thrust out her chin as she spoke, only hearing her final words for their double meaning after she'd said them. Then she wouldn't give him the pleasure of her embarrassment. She faced him squarely— tall woman, tall man—and waited for *him* to go for the crude. *Hey, baby, I'll chew on more'n your bum, you give me the chance.*

But he didn't do that. Wordlessly, he went to the Fiesta's hatch back and waited for her to come round and unlock it.

She did so. She shoved her cardboard box of supplies into his arms and topped it with the case of lotions, make-up, and brushes. Then she smacked the hatch of the Fiesta closed and strode to the shop, where she unlocked the metal door and yanked it upwards, using her shoulder against it as she usually did when it stuck midway.

He said, 'Hang on,' and put his burdens on the ground. Before she could stop it from happening, his hands—broad and flat and black with pale oval nails neatly trimmed to the tips of his fingers— planted themselves on either side of her. He heaved upwards as she pushed, and with a sound like *eeeerrreeek* of metal on metal, the door gave way. He stayed where he was, right behind her, too close by half, and said, 'That needs seeing to. 'Fore much longer, you won't be able to slide it at all.'

She said, 'I c'n cope,' and she grabbed up the

303

metal box of her make-up because she wanted to be doing something and because she wanted him to know she could manage the supplies, the door, and the shop itself just fine on her own.

But once inside, it was like before. He seemed to fill the place. He seemed to make it his. And that irritated her, especially since he did nothing at all to give the impression that he meant to intimidate or at least to dominate. He merely set the cardboard box onto the counter, saying gravely, 'I wasted nearly an hour waiting for you, Missus Edwards. I hope you 'ntend to make it worth my while now you're finally here.'

'You getting *nothing*—' She swung round. She'd been putting away her make-up case as he spoke, and her reaction was reflex, pure as the bell and those Russian dogs.

*Now don't go playing Miss Ice Cubes, Yas. Girl got blessed with a body like yours, she need to use it to her bes' a'vantage.*

So *You getting* nothing *off me* was what she'd intended to hurl at the cop. No kiss-and-don't-tell by the airing cupboard, no grope in the lap at the dinner table, no peeling back blouses and easing down trousers and no no no hands separating rigid legs. *Come on, Yas. Don't fight me on this.*

She felt her face freeze. He was watching her. She saw his gaze on her mouth, and she watched it travel to her nose. She was marked by what went for love from a man and he read those marks and she would never be able to forget it.

He said, 'Missus Edwards,' and she hated the sound and she wondered why she'd kept Roger's name. She'd told herself she'd done it for Daniel, mother and son tied together by a name when they

304

couldn't be tied by anything else. But now she wondered if she'd really done it to flay herself, not as a constant reminder of the fact that she'd killed her husband but as a way of doing penance for having hooked up with him in the first place.

She'd loved him, yes. But she'd soon learned that there was nothing whatsoever to be gained from loving. Still, the lesson hadn't stuck, had it? For she'd loved again and look where she was now: facing down a cop who would see this time the very same killer but an entirely different sort of corpse.

'You had something to tell me.' DC Winston Nkata reached into the pocket of the jacket that fit him hand-to-a-leather-glove, and he brought out a notebook, the same one he'd been writing in before, with the same propelling pencil clipped to it.

Seeing this, Yasmin thought of the lies he'd already recorded and how bad it was going to be for her if she decided to clean house now. And the image of cleaning house opened her mind to the rest of it: how people could look on a person and because of her face, her speech, and the way she decided to carry herself, how people could reach a conclusion about her and cling to it in the face of all evidence to the contrary and why? Because people were just so desperate to believe.

Yasmin said, 'She wasn't at home. We weren't watching the telly. She wasn't there.'

She saw the detective's chest slowly deflate, as if he'd been holding his breath since the moment he'd arrived, betting against his own respiration that Yasmin Edwards had paged him that morning with the express intention of betraying her lover.

'Where was she?' he asked. 'She tell you, Missus

Edwards? What time d'she get home?'

'Twelve-forty-one.'

He nodded. He wrote steadily and tried to look cool but Yasmin could see it all happening in his head. He was doing the maths. He was matching the maths to Katja's lies. And underneath that, he was celebrating the fact that his gamble had won him the jackpot he'd bet for.

## CHAPTER TWENTY-ONE

Her final words to him were, 'And let's not forget, Eric. *You* wanted the divorce. So if you can't cope with the fact that I've got Jerry now, don't let's pretend it's Esmé's problem.' And she'd looked so flaming triumphant about it all, so filled with look-at-me-I've-found-someone-who-actually-wants-me-boyo that Leach found himself cursing his twelve-year-old daughter—God forgive him—for being capable of manipulating him into talking to her mother in the first place. 'I've got a right to see other people,' Bridget had asserted. 'You were the one who gave it to me.'

'Look, Bridg,' he'd said. 'It's not that I'm jealous. It's that Esmé's in a state because she thinks you'll remarry.'

'I intend to remarry. I *want* to remarry.'

'All right. Fine. But she thinks you've already chosen this bloke and—'

'What if I have? What if I've decided it feels good to be wanted? To be with a man who doesn't have a thing about breasts that droop a bit and lines of character on my face. That's what he calls

306

them by the way, Eric, lines of character.'

'This is on the rebound,' Leach tried to tell her.

'Do *not* inform me what this is. Or we'll get into what your behaviour is: midlife idiocy, extended immaturity, adolescent stupidity. Shall I go on? No? Right. I didn't think so.' And she turned on her heel and left him. She returned to her classroom in the primary school where ten minutes before Leach had motioned to her from the doorway, having dutifully stopped to speak to the head teacher first, asking if he could have a word, please, with Mrs Leach. The head teacher had remarked how irregular it was that a parent should come calling on one of the teachers in the midst of the school day, but when Leach had introduced himself to her, she'd become simultaneously cooperative and compassionate, which told Leach that the word was out not only about the pending divorce but also about Bridget's new love interest. He felt like saying, 'Hey. I don't give a toss that she's got a new bloke,' but he wasn't so sure that was the case. Nonetheless, the fact of the new bloke at least allowed him to feel less guilty about being the one who'd wanted to separate and, as his wife stalked off, he tried to keep his mind fixed on that.

He said, 'Bridg, listen. I'm sorry,' to her retreating back, but he didn't say it very loudly, he knew she hadn't heard him, and he wasn't sure what he was apologising about anyway.

Still, as he watched her retreat, he did feel the blow to his pride. So he tried to obliterate his regrets about how they'd parted, and he told himself he'd done the right thing. Considering how quickly she'd managed to replace him, there wasn't much doubt their marriage had been dead long before he'd first mentioned the fact.

Yet he couldn't help thinking that some couples managed to stay the course no matter what happened to their feelings for each other. Indeed, some couples swore that they were 'absolutely desperate to grow together' when all the time the only real glue that kept them adhered to each other was a bank account, a piece of property, shared offspring, and an unwillingness to divide up the furniture and the Christmas decorations. Leach knew men on the force who were married to women they'd loathed forever. But the very thought of putting their children, their possessions—not to mention their pensions—at risk had kept them polishing their wedding rings for years.

Which thought led Leach ineluctably to Malcolm Webberly.

Leach had known that something was up from the phone calls, from the notes scribbled, shoved into envelopes, and posted, from the oft distracted manner in which Webberly engaged in a conversation. He'd had his suspicions. But he'd been able to discount them because he hadn't known for certain till he saw them together, seven years after the case itself when quite by chance he and Bridget had taken the kids to the Regatta because Curtis'd had a project at school—The Culture and Traditions of Our Country . . . Jesus . . . Leach even remembered the bloody name of it!—and there they were, the two of them, standing on that bridge that crossed the Thames into Henley, his arm round her waist and the sunlight on them both. He didn't know who she was at first, didn't remember her, saw only that she was good looking and that they comprised that unit which calls itself In Love.

How odd, Leach thought now, to recall what he'd felt at the sight of Webberly and his Lady Friend. He realised that he'd never considered his superior officer a real breathing man before that moment. He realised that he'd seen Webberly in rather the same manner as a child sees a much older adult. And the sudden knowledge that Webberly had a secret life felt like the blow an eight year old would take should he walk in on his dad in flagrante with a neighbour.

And she'd looked like that, the woman on the bridge, as familiar as a neighbour. In fact, she looked so familiar that for a time Leach expected to see her at work—perhaps a secretary he'd not yet met?—or maybe emerging from an office in the Earl's Court Road. He'd reckoned that she was just someone Webberly had happened to meet, happened to strike up a conversation with, happened to discover an attraction to, happened to say to himself 'Oh, why not, Malc? No need to be such a bloody Puritan,' about.

Leach couldn't remember when or how he'd sussed out that Webberly's lover was Eugenie Davies. But when he had done, he hadn't been able to keep mum any longer. He'd used his outrage as an excuse for speaking, no little boy fearful that Dad would leave home again but a full grown adult who knew right from wrong. My God, he'd thought, that an officer from the murder squad— that his own partner—should cross the line like that, should take the opportunity to gratify himself with someone who'd been traumatised, victimised, and brutalised both by tragic events and the aftermath of those events . . . It was inconceivable.

Webberly had been, if not deaf to the subject, at least willing to hear him out. He hadn't made a comment at all till Leach had recited every stanza of the ode to Webberly's unprofessional conduct that he'd been composing. Then he'd said, 'What the hell do you think of me, Eric? It wasn't like that. This didn't start during the case. I hadn't seen her for years when we began to . . . Not till . . . It was at Paddington Station. Completely by chance. We spoke there for ten minutes or less, between trains. Then later . . . Hell. Why am I explaining this? If you think I'm out of order, put yourself up for transfer.'

But he hadn't wanted that.

Why? he asked himself.

Because of what Malcolm Webberly had become to him.

How our pasts define our presents, Leach thought now. We're not even aware that it's happening, but every time we reach a conclusion, make a judgement, or take a decision, the years of our lives are stacked up behind us: all those dominoes of influence that we don't begin to acknowledge as part of defining who we are.

He drove to Hammersmith. He told himself he needed a few minutes to decompress from the scene with Bridget, and he did his decompressing in the car, wending his way south till he was in striking distance of Charing Cross Hospital. So he finished the journey and located intensive care.

He couldn't get in to see him, he was told by the sister in charge when he walked through the swinging doors. Only family were allowed in to see

310

the patients in the ICU. Was he a member of the Webberly family?

Oh yes, he thought. And of long standing, although he'd never truly admitted that to himself and Webberly hadn't ever twigged the idea. But what he said was, 'No. Just another officer. The superintendent and I used to work together.'

The nurse nodded. She remarked how good it was that so many members of the Met had stopped by, had phoned, had sent flowers, and had stood by with offers of blood for the patient. 'Type B,' she said to him. 'Do you happen to be . . .? Or O, which is universal, but I expect you know that.'

'AB negative.'

'That's very rare. We wouldn't be able to use it in this case, but you ought to be a regular donor, if you don't mind my saying.'

'Is there anything . . .?' He nodded in the direction of the rooms.

'His daughter's with him. His brother-in-law as well. There's really nothing . . . But he's holding his own.'

'Still hooked up to the machines?'

She looked regretful. 'I'm awfully sorry. I can't exactly give out . . . I do hope you understand. But if I may ask . . . Do you pray . . .?'

'Not regularly.'

'Sometimes it helps.'

But there was something more useful than prayer, Leach thought. Like cracking the whip over the murder team and at least making progress towards finding the bastard who did this to Malcolm. And he could do that.

He was about to nod a goodbye to the nurse when a young woman wearing a track suit and

311

untied trainers emerged from one of the rooms. The nurse called her over, saying, 'This gentleman's asking after your dad.'

Leach hadn't seen Miranda Webberly since her childhood, but he saw now that she'd grown up to look very much like her father: same stout body, same rust-coloured hair, same ruddy complexion, same smile that crinkled round her eyes and produced a single dimple on her left cheek. She looked like the sort of young woman who didn't bother with fashion magazines and he liked her for that.

She spoke quietly about her father's condition: that he hadn't regained consciousness, that there'd been 'a rather serious crisis with his heart' earlier that day but now he had stabilised thank God, that his blood count—'I think it was the white cells? But maybe the other . . . ?' indicated a point of internal bleeding that they were going to have to locate soon since right now they were tranfusing him but that would be a waste of blood if he was losing it from somewhere inside.

'They say he can hear, even in a coma, so I've been reading to him,' Miranda confided. 'I hadn't thought to bring anything from Cambridge, so Uncle David went out and bought a book about narrow boating. I think it's the first thing that came to hand. But it's terribly dull and I'm afraid it'll send *me* into a coma before much longer. And I can't think it'll make Dad wake up because he's longing to hear how things turn out. Of course, he's in a coma mostly because they want him a coma. At least, that's what they're telling me.'

She seemed eager to make Leach feel comfortable, to let him know how much his

312

pathetic effort to be of help was appreciated. She looked exhausted, but she was calm, with no apparent expectation that someone—other than herself—should rescue her from the situation in which she was involved. He liked her more.

He said, 'Is there someone who could take over from you here? Give you a chance to get home for a bath? An hour's kip?'

'Oh, yes, of course,' she said and she fished in her track suit top and brought out a rubber band that she used to discipline her steel wool hair. 'But I want to be here. He's my dad, and . . . He can hear me, you see. He knows I'm with him. And if that's a help . . . I mean, it's important that someone going through what he's going through know he's not alone, don't you think?'

Which implied that Webberly's wife wasn't with him. Which suggested a volume or two of what the years had been like since Webberly had made his decision not to leave Frances for Eugenie.

They'd talked about it the single time that Leach himself had brought up the subject. He couldn't remember now *why* he'd felt compelled to venture into such a private area of another man's life, but something had happened—a veiled remark? a phone conversation with a subtext of hostility on Webberly's part? a departmental party to which Webberly had shown up alone for the dozenth time?—and that something had prompted Leach to say, 'I don't see how you can act the lover of one and be the lover of the other. You could leave Frances, Malc. You know that. You've got someplace to go.'

Webberly hadn't responded at first. Indeed, he hadn't responded for days. Leach thought he might

313

never respond at all till two weeks later when Webberly's car was in for repair and Leach had dropped him off at his home because it was not so far out of his way. Half past seven in the evening, and she was in her pyjamas when she came to the door and flung it open, crowing, 'Daddy! Daddy! Daddy!' and dashing down the path to be caught up in her father's arms. Webberly had buried his face in her crinkly hair, had blown noisy kisses against her neck, had elicited more crows of joy from her.

'This is my Randie,' he'd said to Leach. 'This is why.'

Leach said to Miranda now, 'Your mum's not here, then? Gone home for a rest has she?'

She said, 'I'll tell her you were here, Inspector. She'll be so glad to know. Everyone's been so . . . so *decent*. Really.' And she shook his hand and said that she would get back to her dad.

'If there's something I can do . . . ?'

'You've done it,' she assured him.

But on the way back to the Hampstead station, Leach didn't feel that way. And once inside, he began pacing round the incident room as he reviewed one report after another, most of which he'd already read. He said to the WPC on the computer, 'So what's Swansea given us?'

She shook her head. 'Every car owned by every principal's a late model, sir. There's nothing earlier than ten years old.'

'Who owns that one?'

She referred to a clipboard, ran her finger down the page. 'Robson,' she said. 'Raphael. He's got a Renault. Colour is . . . let me see . . . silver.'

'Blast. There's got to be something.' Leach

314

considered another way to approach the problem. He said, 'Significant others. Go there.'

She said, 'Sir?'

'Go through the reports. Get all the names. Wives, husbands, boyfriends, girlfriends, teenagers who drive, flatmates, anyone and everyone connected to this who has a driving licence. Run their names through the DVLA and see if any of them have a car that fits our profile.'

'All of them, sir?' the constable said.

'I believe we speak the same language, Vanessa.'

She sighed, said, 'Yes, sir,' and returned to work as one of the newer constables came barrelling into the room. He was called Solberg, a wet-behind-the-ears DC who'd been eager to prove himself from day one on the murder squad. He was trailing a sheaf of paperwork behind him, and his face was so red, he looked like a runner at the end of a marathon.

He cried out, 'Guv! Check this out. Ten days ago, and it's hot. It's hot.'

Leach said, 'What're you on about, Solberg?'

'A bit of a complication,' he replied.

*　　　*　　　*

Nkata decided to turn to Katja Wolff's solicitor after his conversation with Yasmin Edwards. She'd said, 'You got what you want, now get out, Constable' once she'd watched him write 12:41 in his notebook, and she'd refused to speculate on where her lover had been on the night Eugenie Davies had died. He'd thought about pushing her—You lied once, madam, so what's to say you aren't lying again and do you know what happens

315

to lags who get ticks by their names as accessories to murder?—but he hadn't done so. He hadn't had the heart, because he'd seen the emotions running across her face while he was questioning her, and he had an idea of how much it had cost her to tell him the little she'd already told. Still, he'd not been able to stop himself from considering what would happen if he asked her why: Why was she betraying her lover and, more important, what was the significance of that betrayal? But that wasn't his business, was it? It couldn't be his business because he was a copper and she was a lag. And that's the way it was.

So he'd closed his notebook. He'd intended to turn on his heel and get out of her shop with a simple yet pointed, 'Cheers, Missus Edwards. You did the right thing.' But he didn't say that. Instead what he'd said was, 'You all right, Missus Edwards?' and found himself taken aback at the gentleness he felt. It was wrong as hell to feel gentle towards such a woman in such a situation, and when she said, 'Just get out,' he took the course of wisdom and did just that.

In his car, he'd slipped from his wallet the card that Katja Wolff had handed him early that morning. He'd removed the *A to Z* from his glove compartment and looked up the street in which Harriet Lewis had her office. As luck would have it, the solicitor's office was in Kentish Town, which meant the other side of the river and yet another drive through London. But wending his way there gave him time to plan an approach likely to dislodge information from the lawyer. And he knew he needed a decent approach because the proximity of her office to HM Prison Holloway suggested that Harriet Lewis had more than one villain as a client, which suggested in turn that she wasn't likely to be easily finessed into revealing anything.

When at last he pulled to the kerb, Nkata discovered that Harriet Lewis had set herself up in humble offices between a newsagent and a grocery displaying limp broccoli and bruised cauliflower out on the pavement. A door was set at an oblique angle to the street, abutting the door to the newsagent's, and on its upper half of translucent glass was printed *Solicitors* and nothing more.

Directly inside, a staircase covered in thinning red carpet led up to two doors which faced each other on a landing. One of the doors was open, revealing an empty room with another adjoining it and a wide-planked wooden floor frosted with dust. The other door was closed, and a business card was tacked to the panels with a drawing pin. Nkata scrutinised this card and found it identical to the one Katja Wolff had given to him. He lifted it with the edge of his fingernail and looked beneath it. There was no other card. Nkata smiled. He had the opening he wanted.

He entered without knocking and found himself in a reception room as unlike the neighbourhood, the immediate environment, and the suite across the landing as he could have imagined. A Persian rug covered most of the polished floor, and on it sat a reception desk, sofa, chairs, and tables of a severely modern design. They were all sharp edges, wood, and leather and they should have argued with not only the rug, but also the wainscoting and the wallpaper, but instead they suggested just the right degree of daring one would hope for when one hired a solicitor.

'May I help you?' The question came from a middle-aged woman who sat at the desk in front of a keyboard and monitor, wearing tiny earphones from which she appeared to have been taking dictation. She was done up in professional navy-and-cream, her hair short and neat and just beginning to grey in a streak that wove back from above her left temple. She had the darkest eyebrows Nkata had ever seen, and in a world in which he was used to being looked at with suspicion by white women, he'd never encountered a more hostile stare.

He produced his identification and asked to speak to the solicitor. He didn't have an appointment, he told Mrs Eyebrows before she could ask, but he expected Miss Lewis—

'*Ms* Lewis,' the receptionist said, removing her earphones and setting them aside.

—would see him once she was told he was calling about Katja Wolff. He laid his card on the desk and added, 'Pass that to her if you like. Tell her we talked on the 'phone this morning. I 'xpect she'll remember.'

Mrs Eyebrows made a point of not touching the card till Nkata's fingers had left it. Then she picked it up, saying, 'Wait here, please,' and went through to the inner office. She came out perhaps two minutes later and repositioned the earphones on her head. She resumed her typing without a glance in his direction, which might have caused his blood to start heating had he not learned early in life to take white women's behaviour for what it usually was: obvious and ignorant as hell.

So he studied the pictures on the walls—old

318

black and white head shots of women that put him in mind of days when the British Empire stretched round the globe—and when he was done inspecting these, he picked up a copy of *Ms* from America and engrossed himself in an article about alternatives to hysterectomies that seemed to be written by a woman who was balancing on her shoulder a chip the size of the Blidworth Boulder.

He did not sit, and when Mrs Eyebrows said to him meaningfully, 'It will be a while, Constable, as you've come without an appointment,' he said, 'Murder's like that, i'n't it? Never does let you know when it's coming.' And he leaned his shoulder against the pale striped wallpaper and gave it a smack with the palm of his hand, saying, 'Very nice, this is. What d'you call the design?'

He could see the receptionist eyeing the spot he'd touched, looking for grease marks. She made no reply. He nodded at her pleasantly, snapped his magazine more fully open, and rested his head against the wall.

'We've a sofa, Constable,' Mrs Eyebrows said.

'Been sitting all day,' he told her and added, 'Piles,' with a grimace for good measure.

That appeared to do it. She got to her feet, disappeared into the inner office once again, and returned in a minute. She was bearing a tray with the remains of afternoon tea on it, and she said that the solicitor was ready to see him now.

Nkata smiled to himself. He bet she was.

Harriet Lewis, dressed in black as she had been on the previous evening, was standing behind her desk when he entered. She said, 'We've had our conversation already, Constable Nkata. Am I going to have to ring for counsel?'

319

'You feeling the need?' Nkata asked her. 'Woman like you, 'fraid to go it alone?'

'"Woman like me,"' she mimicked, 'no bloody fool. I spend my life telling clients to keep their mouths shut in the presence of the police. I'd be fairly stupid not to heed my own advice, now wouldn't I?'

'You'd be stupider—'

'More stupid,' she said.

'—stupider,' he repeated, 'to find yourself dis'tangling your way out of a charge of obstruction in a police inquiry.'

'You've charged no one with anything. You haven't a leg to stand on.'

'Day's not over.'

'Don't threaten me.'

'Make your phone call, then,' Nkata told her. He looked round and saw that a seating area of three chairs and a coffee table had been fashioned at one end of the room. He sauntered over, sat down, and said, 'Ah. Whew. Nice to take a load off at the end of the day,' and nodded at her telephone. 'Go ahead. I got the time to wait. My mum's a fine cook and she'll keep dinner warm.'

'What's this about, Constable? We've already spoken. I have nothing to add to what I've already told you.'

'Don't have a partner, I notice,' he said, ' 'less she's hiding under your desk.'

'I don't believe I said there was a partner. You made that assumption.'

'Based on Katja Wolff's lie. Number Fifty-five Galveston Road, Miss Lewis. Care to speculate with me on that topic? Tha's where your partner's s'posed to live, by the way.'

320

'My relationship with my client is privileged.'

'Right. You got a client there, then?'

'I didn't say that.'

Nkata leaned forward, elbows on knees. He said, 'Listen to what I say, then.' He looked at his watch. 'Seventy-seven minutes ago Katja Wolff lost her alibi for the time of a hit and run in West Hampstead. You got that straight? And losing that alibi sends her straight to the top of the class. My experience, people don't lie 'bout where they were the night someone goes down 'less they got a good reason. This case, the reason looks like she was involved. Woman who was killed—'

'I know who was killed,' the solicitor snapped.

'Do you? Good. Then you also proba'ly know that your client might've had an axe she wanted to grind with that individual.'

'That idea's laughable. If anything, the complete opposite is the truth.'

'Katja Wolff wanting Eugenie Davies to stay alive? Why's that, Miss?'

'That's privileged information.'

'Cheers. So add to your privileged information this bit: Last night a second hit and run happened in Hammersmith. Round midnight this one was. The officer who first put Katja away. He's not dead, but he's hanging on the edge. And you got to know how cops feel 'bout a suspect when one of their own goes down.'

This piece of news seemed to make the first dent in Harriet Lewis's armour of calm. She adjusted her spine microscopically and said, 'Katja Wolff is not involved in any of this.'

'So you get paid to say. And paid to believe. So your partner would proba'ly say and proba'ly

321

believe if you had a partner.'

'Stop harping on that. You and I both know that I'm not responsible for a piece of misinformation passed to you by a client when I'm not present.'

'Right. But you are present now. And now that it's clear you got no partner, p'rhaps we need to dwell on why I was told that you had.'

'I have no idea.'

'Don't you.' Nkata took out his notebook and his pencil, and he tapped the pencil against the notebook's leather cover for emphasis. 'Here's what it's looking like to me: You're Katja Wolff's brief, but you're something else 's well, something tastier and something that's lying just the other side of what's on the up and up in your business. Now—'

'You're incredible.'

'—word of that gets out, you start looking bad, Miss Lewis. You got some code of ethics or other, and solicitor playing love monkeys with her client isn't part of that code. Fact, it starts looking like that's *why* you take on lags in the first place: Get'em when they're at their lowest, you do, and it's plain sailing when you want to pop 'em in bed.'

'That's outrageous.' Harriet Lewis finally came round from behind her desk. She strode across the room, took position behind one of the chairs in the grouping by the coffee table, and gripped onto its back. 'Leave this office, Constable.'

'Let's play at this,' he said reasonably, settling back into his chair. 'Let's think out loud.'

'Your sort's not even capable of doing it silently.'

Nkata smiled. He gave himself a point. He said, 'Stick with me, then, all the same.'

'I've no intention of speaking with you further.

322

Now leave, or I'll see to it you're brought to the attention of the PCA.'

'What're you going to complain 'bout? And how's it likely to look when the story gets out that you couldn't cope with one lone copper come to talk to you about a killer? And not jus' any killer, Miss Lewis. A baby killer, twenty years put away.'

The solicitor made no reply to this.

Nkata pressed on, nodding in the direction of Harriet Lewis's desk. 'So you phone up Police Complaints right now, and you shout harassment and you file whatever you want to file. And when the story finds it way to the papers, you watch and see who gets the smear.'

'You're blackmailing me.'

'I'm telling you the facts. You c'n do with them what you want. What I want is the truth about Galveston Road. Give me that and I'm gone.'

'Go there yourself.'

'Been there once. Not going again without ammunition.'

'Galveston Road has *nothing* to do with—'

'Miss Lewis? Don't play me like a fool.' Nkata nodded at her telephone. 'You making that call to the PCA? You ready to file your complaint 'gainst me?'

Harriet Lewis appeared to consider her options as she let out a breath. She came round the chair. She sat. She said, 'Katja Wolff's alibi lives in that house, Constable Nkata. She's a woman called Noreen McKay, and she's unwilling to step forward and clear Katja from suspicion. We went there last night to talk to her about it. We weren't successful. And I very much doubt you'll be.'

'Why's that?' Nkata asked.

323

Harriet Lewis smoothed down her skirt. She fingered a minute length of thread that she found at the edge of a button on her jacket. 'I suppose you'd call it a code of ethics,' she finally said.

'She's a solicitor?'

Harriet Lewis stood. 'I'm going to have to phone Katja and request her permission to answer that question,' she said.

*　　*　　*

Libby Neale went straight to the refrigerator when she got home from South Kensington. She was having a major white jones, and she considered herself deserving of having the attack taken care of. She kept a pint of vanilla Häagen-Dazs in the freezer for just such emergencies. She dug this out, ferreted a spoon from the utensil drawer, and prised open the lid. She'd gobbled up approximately one dozen spoonfuls before she was even able to think.

When she finally did think, what she thought was *more white*, so she rustled through the trash under the kitchen sink and found part of the bag of cheddar popcorn that she'd thrown away in a moment of disgust on the previous day. She sat on the floor and proceeded to cram into her mouth the two handfuls of popcorn that were left in the bag. From there, she went to a package of flour tortillas, which she'd long kept as a challenge to herself to stay away from anything white. These, she found, weren't exactly white any longer as spots of mould were growing on them like ink stains on linen. But mould was easy enough to remove and if she ingested some by mistake, it couldn't hurt, could it? Consider penicillin.

She rustled a cube of Wensleydale from its wrapper and sliced enough for a quesadilla. She plopped the cheese slices onto the tortilla, topped that with another, and slapped the whole mess into a frying pan. When the Wensleydale was melted and the tortilla was browned, she took the treat from the fire, rolled it into a tube, and settled herself on the kitchen floor. She proceeded to shove the food into her mouth, eating like a victim of famine.

When she'd polished off the quesadilla, she remained on the floor, her head against one of the cupboard doors. She'd needed that, she told herself. Things were getting too weird and when things got too weird, you had to keep your blood sugar high. There was no telling when you'd need to take action.

Gideon hadn't walked her from his father's flat to his car. He'd just shown her to the door and shut it behind her. She'd said, 'You going to be okay, Gid?' as they'd made their way from the study. 'I mean, this can't be the nicest place for you to wait. Look. Why'n't you come home with me? We can leave a note for your dad, and when he gets back, he can call you and we can drive back over.'

'I'll wait here,' he'd said. And he'd opened the door and shut it without ever once looking at her.

What did it *mean* that he wanted to wait for his dad? she wondered. Was this going to be the Big Showdown between them? She certainly hoped so. The Big Showdown had been a long time coming between Davies father and son.

She tried to picture it, a confrontation provoked, for some reason, by Gideon's discovery of a second sister he hadn't even known he'd had. He'd take that card written to Richard by Virginia's mother and he'd wave it in front of his father's nose. He'd say, '*Tell* me about her, you bastard. Tell me why I wasn't allowed to know *her* either.'

Because that seemed to be the crux of what had set Gideon off when he'd read the card: His dad had denied him another sibling when Virginia had been there all along.

And why? Libby thought. Why had Richard made this move to isolate Gid from his surviving sister? It had to be the same reasons that Richard did everything else: to keep Gid focussed on the violin.

No, no, no. Can't have friends, Gideon. Can't go to parties. Can't play at sports. Can't go to a *real* school. Must practise, play, perform, and provide. And you can't do that if you've got any interests away from your instrument. Like a sister, for example.

God, Libby thought. He was such a shit. He was *so* totally screwing up Gideon's life.

What, she wondered, would that life have been like had he not spent it playing his music? He would have gone to school like a regular kid. He would have played sports, like soccer or something. He would have ridden a bike, fallen out of trees, and maybe broken a bone or two. He would have met his buddies for beer in the evening and gone out on dates and screwed around in girls' pants and been normal. He would be so *not* who he was right now.

Gideon deserved what other people had and took for granted, Libby told herself. He deserved friends. He deserved love. He deserved a family.

326

He deserved a life. But he wasn't going to get any of that as long as Richard kept him under his thumb and as long as no one was willing to take positive action to alter the relationship Gideon had with his frigging father.

Libby stirred at that and realised her scalp was tingling. She rolled her head against the cupboard door so that she could look at the kitchen table. She'd left Gideon's car keys there when she'd dashed into the kitchen to admit defeat to her attack of the whites, and it seemed to her now that her possession of those keys was meant to be, like a sign from God that she'd been sent into Gideon's life to be the one who took a stand.

Libby got to her feet. She approached the keys in a state of pure resolution. She snatched them up from the table before she could talk herself out of it. She left the flat.

## CHAPTER TWENTY-TWO

Yasmin Edwards sent Daniel across the street to the Army Centre, a chocolate cake in his hands. He was surprised, considering how she'd reacted in the past to his lingering round the uniformed men, but he said, 'Wicked, Mum!' and grinned at her and was gone in an instant to make what she'd called a thank you visit to them. 'Good of those blokes to offer you tea time to time,' she told her son, and if Daniel recognised the contradiction in this statement from her earlier fury at the idea of someone pitying her son, he didn't mention it.

Alone, Yasmin sat in front of the television set.

She had the lamb stew simmering because—bloody fool that she was—she was *still* incapable of not doing what she'd said earlier she was going to do. She was also as unable to change her mind or to draw the line as she had been as Roger Edwards' girlfriend, his lover, his wife and then as an inmate in Holloway Prison.

She wondered why now, but the answer lay before her in the hollowness she felt and the budding of a fear that she'd long ago buried. It seemed to her that her entire life had been described and dominated by that fear, a gripping terror of one thing that she'd been entirely unwilling to name, let alone to face. But all the running she'd done from the Bogey Man had only brought her to his embrace yet again.

She tried not to think. She wanted not to ponder the fact that she'd been reduced once more to discovering that there was no sanctuary no matter how determinedly she believed there would be.

She hated herself. She hated herself as much as she'd ever hated Roger Edwards and more—far more—than she hated Katja who'd brought her to this mirror of a moment and asked her to gaze long and gaze hard. It made no difference that every kiss, embrace, act of love, and conversation had been built on a lie she could not have discerned. What mattered was that she, Yasmin Edwards, had even allowed herself to be a party to it. So she was filled with self-loathing. She was consumed by a thousand, 'I should've knowns.'

When Katja came in, Yasmin glanced at the clock. She was right on time, but she would be, wouldn't she, because the one thing Katja Wolff wasn't was blind to what was going on within others. It was a survival technique she'd learned inside. So she'd have read a whole book from Yasmin's visit to the laundry that morning. Thus, she'd be home on the stroke of dinner time, and she'd be prepared.

What she'd be prepared for, Katja wouldn't know. That was the only advantage Yasmin had. The rest of the advantages were all her lover's, and the single most important one was exactly like a beacon that had long been shining although Yasmin had always refused to acknowledge it.

Single-mindedness. That Katja Wolff had always had a goal was what had kept her sane in prison. She was a woman with plans: she always had been. 'You must know what you want and who you will become when you are out of here,' she'd told Yasmin time and again. 'Do not let what they have done to you become their triumph. That will happen if you fail.' Yasmin had learned to admire Katja Wolff for that stubborn determination to become who she'd always intended to become, despite her situation. And then she'd learned to love Katja Wolff for the solid foundation of the future she represented for them both, even while held within prison walls.

She'd said to her, 'You got twenty *years* in here. You think you're going to step outside and start designing clothes when you're forty-five years old?'

'I will have a life,' Katja had asserted. 'I will prevail, Yas. I will have a life.'

That life needed to start somewhere once Katja did her time, made her way through open conditions, proved herself there, and was released into society. She needed a place where she would be safe from notice so that she could begin to build

329

her world again. She wouldn't have wanted any spotlight on her. She wouldn't be able to achieve her dream if she failed to fit easily back into the world. Even then, it would be tough: establishing herself in the competitive arena of fashion when all she was, at best, was a notorious graduate of the criminal justice system.

When she'd first fixed herself up in Kennington with Yasmin, Yasmin had understood that Katja would have to undergo a period of adjustment before she began to fulfil the dreams she'd spoken of. So she'd given her time to reacquaint herself with freedom, and she had not questioned the fact that Katja's talk of goals within prison did not immediately translate to action once she was outside. People were different, she told herself. It meant nothing that she—Yasmin—had begun to work at her new life furiously and single-mindedly the moment she was finally released. She, after all, had a son to provide for and a lover whose arrival she spent years anticipating. She had more incentive to put her world in order so that Daniel first and then Katja afterwards would have the home they both deserved.

But now she saw that Katja's talk had been just that. She had no inclination to make her way in the world because she did not need to. Her spot in the world had long been reserved.

Yasmin didn't move from the sofa as Katja shrugged out of her coat, saying, '*Mein Gott.* I'm exhausted,' and then, seeing her, 'What're you doing in the dark there, Yas?' She crossed the room and switched on the table lamp, homing in as she usually did on the cigarettes that Mrs Crushley wouldn't allow her to smoke anywhere near the laundry. She lit up from a book of matches that she took from her pocket and tossed down on the coffee table next to the packet of Dunhills from which she'd scored the cigarette. Yasmin leaned forward and picked up the matches. *Frère Jacques Bar and Brasserie* were the words printed on it.

'Where's Daniel?' Katja said, looking round the flat. She stepped into the kitchen and took note of the fact that the table was set only for two because the next thing she said was, 'Has he gone to a mate's for dinner, Yas?'

'No,' Yasmin said. 'He'll be home soon.' She'd set it up that way to make sure she didn't cave in to her cowardice at the final moment.

'Then why's the table—' Katja stopped. She was a woman who had the discipline not to betray herself, and Yasmin saw her use that discipline now, silencing her own question.

Yasmin smiled bitterly. Right, she told her lover in silence. Didn't think little Pinky would open her eyes, did you, Kat? And if she opened them or had them opened, didn't expect *her* to make a move, make the *first* move, put herself *out* there alone and afraid, did you, Kat? ' 'Cause you had five years to suss out how to get inside her skin and make her feel like she had a future with you. 'Cause even then you knew that if anyone ever made this little bitch start seeing possibilities where there wasn't a hope in hell of planting one, she'd give herself over to that worthless cow and do anything it took to make her happy. And that's what you needed, isn't it, Kat? That's what you were counting on.

She said, 'I been to Number Fifty-five.'

Katja said guardedly, 'You've been where?' And those v's were present in her voice again, those once charming hallmarks of her dissimilarity.

'Number Fifty-five Galveston Road. Wandsworth. South London,' Yasmin said.

Katja didn't reply, but Yasmin could see her thinking despite the fact that her face was the perfect blank she'd learned to produce for anyone looking her way in prison. Her expression said, Nothing going on inside here. Her eyes, however, locked too tightly on Yasmin's.

Yasmin noticed for the first time that Katja was grimy: Her face was oily and her blonde hair clung in spears to her skull. 'Didn't go there tonight,' she noted evenly. 'Decided to shower at home, I s'pose.'

Katja came nearer. She drew in deeply on her cigarette, and Yasmin could see that still she was thinking. She was thinking it could all be a trick to force her into admitting something that Yasmin was only guessing at in the first place. She said, 'Yas,' and put out her hand and grazed it along the line of plaits that Yasmin had drawn back from her face and tied at the nape of her neck with a scarf. Yasmin jerked away.

'Didn't need to shower there, I s'pose,' Yasmin said. 'No cunt juice on your face tonight. Right?'

'Yasmin, what are you talking about?'

'I'm *talking* about Number Fifty-five, Katja. Galveston Road. I'm talking about what you *do* when you go there.'

'I go there to meet my solicitor,' Katja said. 'Yas, you heard me tell that detective so this morning. Do you think I'm lying? Why would I lie? If you wish to phone Harriet and ask her if she and I went there together—'

'*I* went there,' Yasmin announced flatly. 'I *went*

332

there, Katja. Are you listenin' to me?'

'And?' Katja asked. Still so calm, Yasmin thought, still so sure of herself or at least still so capable of looking that way. And why? Because she knew that no one was at home during the day. She believed that anyone ringing the bell would have no luck learning who lived within. Or perhaps she was just buying time to think how to explain it all away.

Yasmin said, 'No one was home.'

'I see.'

'So I went to a neighbour and asked who lives there.' She felt the betrayal swelling inside her, like a balloon too inflated that climbed to her throat. She forced herself to say, 'Noreen McKay,' and she waited to hear her lover's response. What's it going to be? she thought. An excuse? A declaration of misunderstanding? An attempt at a reasonable explanation?

Katja said, 'Yas . . .' Then she murmured, 'Bloody hell,' and the Englishism sounded so strange coming from her that Yasmin felt, if only for an instant, as if she were talking to a different person entirely to the Katja Wolff she'd loved for the last three of her years in prison and all of the five years that had followed them. 'I do not know what to say,' she sighed. She came round the coffee table and joined Yasmin on the sofa. Yasmin flinched at her nearness. Katja moved away.

'I packed your things,' Yasmin said. 'They're in the bedroom. I didn't want Dan to see . . . I'll tell him tomorrow. He's used to you not being here some nights anyway.'

'Yas, it wasn't always—'

Yasmin could hear her voice go higher as she said, 'There's dirty clothes to be washed. I put

333

them separate in a Sainsbury's bag. You can do them tomorrow or borrow a washing machine tonight or stop at a launderette or—'

'Yasmin, you must hear me. We were not always . . . Noreen and I . . . We were not always together as you're thinking we were. This is something . . .' Katja moved closer again. She put her hand on Yasmin's thigh, and Yasmin felt her body go rigid at the touch and that tensing of muscles, that hardening of joints brought too much back, brought everything back, shot her into her past where the faces overhung her . . .

She leaped to her feet. She covered her ears. 'Stop it! You burn in hell!' she cried.

Katja held out her hand but didn't rise from the sofa. She said, 'Yasmin, listen to me. This is something I cannot explain. It's here inside and it's been here forever. I cannot get it out of my system. I try. It fades. Then it comes back again. With you, Yasmin, you must listen to me. With you, I thought . . . I hoped . . .'

'You used me,' Yasmin said. 'No thinking, no hoping. *Using,* Katja. Because what you thought was if things looked like you moved on from her, she'd finally have to step forward and say who she really was. But she didn't do that when you were inside. And she didn't do that when you came out. But you keep thinking she's going to do that, so you set up with me to force her hand. Only that's not how it works 'less she knows what you're up to and with who, right? And it sure's *hell* don't work 'less you give her a taste now and then of what she's missing.'

'That is not how it is.'

'You telling me you haven't done it, the two of

334

you? You haven't been with her since you got out? You haven't been slithering over there after work, after dinner, even after you been with me and say you can't sleep and need a walk and know I won't wake up till morning and I can see it *all* now, Katja. And I want you gone.'

'Yas, I have no place to go.'

Yasmin breathed out a laugh. 'I expect one phone call'll sort that out.'

'Please, Yasmin. Come. Sit. Let me tell you how it has been.'

'How it's *been* is you waiting. Oh, I d'n't see't at first. I thought you're trying to adjust to outside. I thought you're getting ready to make a life for yourself—for you and me and Dan, Katja—but all the time you were waiting for her. You were *always* waiting. You were waiting to make yourself part of *her* life and once you got there, everything in yours'd be taken care of just fine.'

'That's not how it is.'

'No? Really? You make one move to get yourself together since you been out? You phone up design schools? You talk to anyone? You walk into one of those Knightsbridge shops and offer yourself as a 'prentice?'

'No. I have not done that.'

'And we both know why. You don't need to make a life for yourself if she does it for you.'

'That is not the case.' Katja rose from the sofa, crushing out her cigarette in the ashtray, spilling ash onto the table top where it lay like the remnants of disappointed dreams. 'I make my own life as always,' she said. 'It's different from the life I thought I'd have, yes. It's different from the life I spoke of inside, yes. But Noreen doesn't make

335

that life for me any more than you do, Yasmin. I make it myself. And that is what I have been doing since I was released. That is what Harriet is helping me to do. That is why I spent twenty years in prison and did not go mad. Because I knew—I *knew*—what waited for me when I got out.'

'Her,' Yasmin said. 'She waited, right? So go to her. Leave.'

'No. You must understand. I will make you—'

*Make you, make you, make you.* Too many people had *made her* already. Yasmin clutched her hands to her head.

'Yasmin, I did three evil things in my life. I made Hannes take me over the Wall by threatening to tell the authorities.'

'That's ancient history.'

'It's more than that. Listen. That was my first evil, what I did to Hannes. But I also did not speak up when I once should have spoken. That's the second thing. And then, once—only once, Yas, but once was enough—I listened when I should have covered my ears. And I paid for all of it. Twenty years I paid. Because *I* was lied to. And now others must pay. That's what I have been setting about.'

'No! I won't hear!' In panic, Yasmin dashed to the bedroom where she'd packed up Katja's small wardrobe of bright second-hand clothes—all those clothes that defined who Katja was, a woman who would never wear black in a city where black was everywhere—into a duffel bag that she'd bought for that purpose, shelling out her own money as a way of paying for every mistake she'd made in trust. She didn't want to hear, but more than that, she knew she couldn't afford to hear. Hearing what Katja had to say put her at risk, put her future with

336

Daniel at risk, and she wouldn't do that.

She grabbed the duffel bag and slung it out into the sitting room. She followed it with the Sainsbury's bags of dirty laundry and then the single cardboard box that contained the toiletries and other supplies Katja had brought with her into the flat. She cried out, 'I told him, Katja. He knows. You got that? I told him. I *told*.'

She said, 'Who?'

'You know who. *Him*.' Yasmin drew her fingers down her cheek to indicate the scar that marked the black detective's face. 'You weren't here watching the telly, and he knows.'

'But he is . . . they are . . . all of them . . . Yas, you know they are your enemy. What they did to you when you defended yourself against Roger . . . What they put you through? How could you trust—'

'That's what you were depending on, wasn't it? Old Yas won't ever trust a copper, no matter what he says, no matter what I do. So I'll just set myself up with good old Yas, and she'll protect me when they come calling. She'll follow my lead, just like she did inside. But that's over, Katja. Whatever it was, and I don't much care. It's over.'

Katja looked down at the bags. She said quietly, 'We are so close to ending things after all these—'

Yasmin slammed the bedroom door to cut off her words and to cut herself off from further danger. And then, finally, she began to weep. Over her tears, she could hear the sound of Katja gathering up her belongings. When the flat door opened and closed a moment later, Yasmin knew her lover was gone.

'So it's not about the kid,' Havers said to Lynley, concluding the update of her second visit to the Convent of the Immaculate Conception. 'He's called Jeremy Watts, by the way. The nun's always known where he was; Katja Wolff's always known that she's known. She's gone twenty years without asking about him. She's gone twenty years without talking to Sister Cecilia at all. So it's not about the kid.'

'There's something not natural in that,' Lynley said reflectively.

'There's plenty not natural in all of her,' Havers replied. 'In all of *them*. I mean, what's going on with Richard Davies, Inspector? Okay, all right. Virginia was retarded. He was cut up about that. Who wouldn't be? But never even to see her again ... and to let his *dad* dictate ... And why the hell were he and Lynn living with his dad anyway? Sure, those were impressive digs in Kensington and maybe Richard's a bloke who likes to make an impression. And p'rhaps Mum and Dad might've lost the ancestral pile or something if Richard didn't contribute by living there and paying through the nose or whatever, but still ...'

'The relationship between fathers and sons is always complicated,' Lynley said.

'More than mothers and daughters?'

'Indeed. Because so much more goes unspoken.'

They were in a café in Hampstead High Street, not far from the station in Downshire Hill. They'd rendezvoused there by prior arrangement, Havers phoning Lynley on his mobile as he was setting out from Stamford Brook. He'd told her about Webberly's heart attack, and she'd cursed fervently

338

and asked what she could do. His response had been what Randie's had been when she'd phoned the house from the hospital to share an update with her mother not long before Lynley left: They could do nothing but pray; the doctors were watching him.

She'd said, 'What the hell does "watching him" mean?'

Lynley hadn't replied because it seemed to him that 'watching the patient's progress' was a medical euphemism for waiting for an appropriate moment to pull the plug. Now, across the table from Havers with an undoctored espresso (his) and a coffee loaded with milk and sugar not to mention a *pain au chocolat* (both hers) between them, Lynley dug out his handkerchief from his pocket and spread it out on the table, disclosing its contents.

He said, 'We may be down to this,' and indicated the shards of glass he'd taken from the edge of the pavement in Crediton Hill.

Havers scrutinised them. 'Headlamp?' she asked.

'Not considering where I found them. Swept under a hedge.'

'Could be nothing, sir.'

'I know,' Lynley said gloomily.

'Where's Winnie? What's he come up with, Inspector?'

'He's on Katja Wolff's trail.' Lynley filled her in on what Nkata had reported to him earlier.

She said, 'So are you leaning towards Wolff? Because like I said—'

'I know. If she's our killer, it's not about her son. So what's her motive?'

'Revenge? Could they have framed her,

339

Inspector?'

'With Webberly part of the *they?* Christ. I don't want to think so.'

'But with him involved with Eugenie Davies . . .' Havers had brought her coffee to her lips, but she didn't drink, instead looking at him over the top of it. 'I'm not saying he would've done it deliberately, sir. But if he was involved, he could've been blinded, could've been . . . well, *led* to believe . . . You know.'

'That presupposes the CPS, a jury and a judge were all led to believe as well,' Lynley said.

'It's happened,' Havers pointed out. 'And more than once. You know that.'

'All right. Accepted. But why didn't she speak? If evidence was doctored, if testimony was false, why didn't she *speak?*'

'There's that,' Havers sighed. 'We always come back to it.'

'We do.' Lynley took a pencil from his breast pocket. With it, he moved about the pieces of glass at the centre of his handkerchief. 'Too thin for a headlamp,' he told Havers. 'The first pebble that hit it—on the motorway, for instance—would have smashed to bits a headlamp made of this sort of glass.'

'Broken glass in a hedgerow?' Havers said. 'It's probably from a bottle. Someone coming out of a party with a bottle of plonk under his arm. He's had a few and he staggers. It drops, breaks, and he kicks the shards to one side.'

'But there's no curve, Havers. Look at the larger pieces. They're straight.'

'Okay. They're straight. But if you expect to tie these to one of our principals, I think you're going

340

to be wandering in the outback without a guide.'

Lynley knew she was right. He gathered the handkerchief together again, slipped it into his pocket, and brooded. His fingers played with the top of his espresso cup as his eyes examined the ring of sludge left in it. For her part, Havers polished off her *pain au chocolat*, emerging from the exercise with flakes of pastry on her lips.

He said, 'You're hardening your arteries, Constable.'

'And now I'm going after my lungs.' She wiped her mouth with a paper napkin and dug out her packet of Players. She said in advance of his protest, 'I'm owed this. It's been a long day. I'll blow it over my shoulder, okay?'

Lynley was too dispirited to argue. Webberly's condition was heavy in his mind, weighing only slightly less than Frances's knowledge of her husband's affair. He forced himself away from these thoughts, saying, 'All right. Let's look at everyone again. Notes?'

Havers blew out a lungful of smoke impatiently, 'We've *done* this, Inspector. We don't have a thing.'

'We've got to have something,' Lynley said, putting on his reading glasses. 'Notes, Havers.'

She groused but brought them out of her shoulder bag. Lynley took his from his jacket pocket. They started with those individuals without alibis that could be corroborated.

Ian Staines was Lynley's first offering. He was desperate for money, which his sister had promised to request from her son. But she'd reneged on that promise, leaving Staines in dangerous straits. 'He looks about to lose his home,' Lynley said. 'The night of the death, they rowed. He could have followed her up to London. He didn't get home till after one.'

'But the car's not right,' Havers said. 'Unless he had a second vehicle with him in Henley.'

'Which he may have done,' Lynley noted. 'Parked there previously just in case. Someone has access to a second vehicle, Havers.'

They went on to the multi-named J.W. Pitchley, Havers' prime candidate at this point. 'What the hell,' she wanted to know, 'was his address doing in Eugenie Davies' possession? Why was she heading to see him? Staines says she told him something came up. Was that something Pitchley?'

'Possibly, save for the fact that we can establish no tie between them. No phone tie, internet tie—'

'Snail mail?'

'How did she track him down?'

'Same way I did, Inspector. She figured he'd changed identities once, why not again?'

'All right. But why would she arrange to see him?'

Havers took a different tack from all the possibilities she'd offered earlier in the case. She said, 'Maybe *he* arranged to see her once she'd located him. And she contacted him because . . .' Havers considered the potential reasons, settling on, 'because Katja Wolff just got out of the slammer. If the whole boiling lot of them framed her and she was finally out of prison, they'd have plans to lay, right? About how to deal with her if she came calling?'

'But we're back to that, Havers. An entire household of people framing an individual who then doesn't utter a word in her own defence? *Why?*'

'Fear of what they could do to her? The granddad sounds like a real terror. P'rhaps he got to her in some way. He said, "Play our game or we'll let the world know . . ."' Havers considered this and rejected her own idea, saying. 'Know what? That she was in the club? Big deal. Like anyone cared at that point? It came out that she was pregnant anyway.'

Lynley held up a hand to stop her from dismissing the thought. He said, 'But you could be on to something, Barbara. It could have been, "Play our game or we'll let it out who the father of your baby is."'

'Big deal again.'

'Yes, big deal,' Lynley argued, 'if it's not a case of letting the world know who the father is, but letting Eugenie Davies know.'

'Richard?'

'It wouldn't be the first time the man of the house got entangled with the nanny.'

'What about him, then?' Havers said. 'What about Davies knocking off Eugenie?'

'Motive and alibi,' Lynley pointed out. 'He doesn't have one. He has the other. Although the reverse could be said of Robson.'

'But where does Webberly fit in? In fact, where does he fit in no matter who we go with?'

'He fits in only with Wolff. And that takes us back to the original crime: the murder of Sonia Davies. And that takes us back to the initial group who were involved in the subsequent investigation.'

'P'rhaps someone's just making it look like everything's connected to that period of time, sir. Because isn't it the truth that a more profound connection exists: the romantic one between

343

Webberly and Eugenie Davies? And that takes us to Richard, doesn't it? To Richard or to Frances Webberly.'

Lynley didn't want to think of Frances. He said, 'Or to Gideon, blaming Webberly for the end of his parents' marriage.'

'That's weak.'

'But something's going on with him, Havers. If you met him, you'd agree. And he has no alibi, other than being home alone.'

'Where was his dad?'

Lynley referred to his notes once again. 'With the fiancée. She confirms.'

'But he's got a much better motive than Gideon if the Webberly-Eugenie connection's behind this.'

'Hmm. Yes. I do see that. But to assign him the motive of rubbing out his wife *and* Webberly begs the questions of why he would wait all these years to see to the job.'

'He had to wait till now. This is when Katja Wolff was released. He'd know we'd establish a trail to her.'

'That's nursing a grievance for a hell of a long time.'

'So maybe it's a more recent grievance.'

'More recent . . .? Are you arguing he's fallen in love with her a second time in his life?' Lynley considered his question. 'All right. I think it's unlikely, but for the sake of argument, I'll go with it. Let's consider the possibility that he's had his love for his former wife reawakened. We begin with him divorced from her.'

'Destroyed by the fact that she walked out on him,' Havers added.

'Right. Now, Gideon has trouble with the violin.

344

His mother reads about that trouble in the papers or hears it from Robson. She gets back in touch with Davies.'

'They talk often. They begin to reminisce. *He* thinks they're going to make a go of it again, and he's hot to trot—'

'This is, of course, ignoring the entire question of Jill Foster,' Lynley pointed out.

'Hang on, Inspector. Richard and Eugenie talk about Gideon. They talk about old times, their marriage, whatever. Everything he's felt gets fired up again. He becomes a potato all hot for the oven, only to find out that Eugenie's got someone lined up in her knickers already: Wiley.'

'Not Wiley,' Lynley said. 'He's too old. Davies wouldn't see him as competition. Besides, Wiley told us she had something she wanted to reveal to him. She'd said as much. But she didn't want to reveal it three nights ago—'

'Because she was headed to London,' Havers said. 'To Crediton Hill.'

'To Pitchley-Pitchford-Pytches,' Lynley said. 'The end is always the beginning, isn't it?' He found the reference in his notes that supplied a single piece of information that had been there all along, just waiting for the correct interpretation. He said, 'Wait. When I brought up the idea of another man, Havers, Davies went straight to him. By name, in fact. Without a doubt in his mind. I've got him naming Pytches right here in my notes.'

'Pytches?' Havers asked. 'No. It's not Pytches, Inspector. That can't—'

Lynley's mobile rang. He grabbed it from the table top and held up a finger to stop Havers from continuing. She was itching to do so, however.

345

She'd stubbed out her cigarette impatiently, saying, 'What day did you talk to Davies, Inspector?'

Lynley waved her off, clicked on his mobile, said, 'Lynley,' and turned away from Havers' smoke.

His caller was DCI Leach. 'We've got another victim,' he announced.

* * *

Winston Nkata read the sign—*HM Prison Holloway*—and reflected on the fact that had his life taken a slightly different turn, had his mum not fainted dead away at the sight of her son in a casualty ward with thirty-four stitches closing an ugly slash on his face, he might have ended up in such a place. Not in this place, naturally, which imprisoned only women, but in a place just like it. The Scrubs, perhaps, or Dartmoor or the Ville. Doing time inside because what he'd not been able to manage was doing life outside.

But his mum had fainted. She had murmured, 'Oh, Jewel,' and had slid to the floor like her legs'd turned to jelly. And the sight of her there with her turban askew—so that he could see what he'd never noticed before, that her hair was actually going grey—made him finally accept her not like the indomitable force he thought she was but instead like a real woman for once, a woman who loved and relied on him to make her proud that she'd given birth. And that had been that.

But had the moment not occurred, had his dad come to fetch him instead, flinging him into the back seat of the car with a demonstration of the full measure of the disgust he deserved, the outcome might have been quite different. He might have felt

346

the need to prove he didn't care that he'd become the recipient of his father's displeasure, and he might have felt the need to prove it by upping the stakes in the Brixton Warriors' longtime battle with the smaller upstart Longborough Bloods to secure a patch of ground called Windmill Gardens and make it part of their turf. But the moment had happened, and his life course had altered, bringing him to where he was now: staring at the windowless brick bulk of Holloway Prison inside which Katja Wolff had met both Yasmin Edwards and Noreen McKay.

He'd parked across the street from the prison, in front of a pub with boarded-up windows that looked like something straight out of Belfast. He'd eaten an orange, studied the prison entrance, and meditated on what everything meant. Particularly, he meditated on what it meant that the German woman was living with Yasmin Edwards but messing around with someone else, just as he'd suspected when he'd seen those shadows merging on the curtains in the window of Number Fifty-five Galveston Road.

His orange consumed, he ducked across the street when the heavy traffic in Parkhurst Road was halted at the traffic lights. He approached reception and dug out his warrant card, presenting it to the officer behind the desk. She said, 'Is Miss McKay expecting you?'

He said, 'Official business. She won't be surprised to know I'm here.'

The receptionist said she would phone, if Constable Nkata wanted to have a seat. It was late in the day and whether Miss McKay would be able to see him . . .

'Oh, I 'xpect she'll be able to see me,' Nkata said.

He didn't sit but rather walked to the window where he looked out on more of the vast brick walls. As he watched the traffic passing by in the street, a guard gate raised to accommodate a prison van, no doubt returning an inmate at the end of a day's trial at the Old Bailey. This would have been how Katja Wolff had come and gone during those long ago days of her own trial. She'd have been accompanied daily by a prison officer, who would remain in court with her, right inside the dock. That officer would have ferried her to and from her cell beneath the courtroom, made her tea, escorted her to lunch, and seen her back to Holloway for the night. An officer and an inmate alone, during the most difficult period of that inmate's life.

'Constable Nkata?'

Nkata swung round to see the receptionist holding a telephone receiver out to him. He took it from her, said his name, and heard a woman say in response, 'There's a pub across the street. On the corner of Hillmarton Road. I can't see you in here, but if you wait in the pub, I'll join you in quarter of an hour.'

He said, 'Make it five minutes and I'm on my way without hanging about chatting to anyone.'

She exhaled loudly, said, 'Five minutes, then,' and slammed down the phone at her end.

Nkata went back to the pub, which turned out to be a nearly empty room as cold as a barn where the air was redolent mostly of dust. He ordered himself a cider, and he took his drink to a table that faced the door.

She didn't make it in five, but she arrived under ten, coming through the door with a gust of wind. She looked round the pub, and when her eyes fell upon Nkata, she nodded once and came over to him, taking the long sure strides of a woman with power and confidence. She was quite tall, not as tall as Yasmin Edwards but taller than Katja Wolff, perhaps five foot ten.

She said, 'Constable Nkata?'

He said, 'Miss McKay?'

She pulled out a chair, unbuttoned her coat, shrugged out of it, and sat, elbows on the table and hands fingering back her hair. This was blonde and cut short, leaving her ears bare. She wore small pearl studs in their lobes. For a moment, she kept her head bent, but when she drew in a breath and looked up, her blue eyes fixed on Nkata with plain dislike.

'What do you want from me? I don't like interruptions while I'm at work.'

'Could've caught up with you at home,' Nkata said. 'But here was closer than Galveston Road from Harriet Lewis's office.'

At the mention of the solicitor, her face became guarded. 'You know where I live,' she said cautiously.

'Followed a bird called Katja Wolff there last night. From Kennington to Wandsworth by bus, this was. It was in'ersting to note that she went the whole route and didn't stop once to ask directions. Seems like she knew where she was going good enough.'

Noreen McKay sighed. She was middle-aged—probably near fifty, Nkata thought—but the fact that she wore little make-up served her well. She heightened what she had without looking painted, so her colour seemed authentic. She was neatly dressed in the uniform of the prison. Her white blouse was crisp, the navy epaulets bore their brass ornamentation brightly, and her trousers had creases that would have done a military man proud. She had keys on her belt, a radio as well, and some sort of pouch. She looked impressive.

She said, 'I don't know what this is about, but I've nothing to say to you, Constable.'

'Not even 'bout Katja Wolff?' he asked her. ''Bout what she was doing calling on you with her solicitor in tow? They filing a law suit 'gainst you, or something?'

'As I just said, I've nothing to say, and there's no room for compromise in my position. I've a future and two adolescents to consider.'

'Not a husband, though?'

She brushed one hand through her hair again. It seemed to be a characteristic gesture. 'I've never been married, Constable. I've had my sister's children since they were four and six years old. Their father didn't want them when Susie died—too busy playing the footloose bachelor—but he's started coming round now he's realising he won't be twenty years old forever. Frankly, I don't want to give him a reason to take them.'

'There's a reason, then? What would that be?'

Noreen McKay shoved away from the table and went to the bar instead of replying. There, she placed an order and waited while her gin was poured over two ice cubes and a bottle of tonic set next to it.

Nkata watched her, trying to fill in the blanks with a simple scrutiny of her person. He wondered which part of prison work had first attracted Noreen McKay: the power it provided over other people, the sense of superiority it offered, or the chance it represented to cast a fishing line in waters where the trout had no psychological protection.

She returned to the table, her drink in hand. She said, 'You saw Katja Wolff and her solicitor come to my home. That's the extent of what you saw.'

'Saw her let herself in 's well. She didn't knock.'

'Constable, she's German.'

Nkata cocked his head. 'I got no recollection of Germans not knowing they're s'posed to knock on strangers' doors before walking in on them, Miss McKay. Mostly, I think they know the rules. Especially the ones telling them that they don't have to knock where they already've got themselves well established.'

Noreen McKay lifted her gin and tonic. She drank but made no reply.

Nkata said, 'What I'm wondering 'bout the whole situation is this: Is Katja the first lag you had some rabbit with or was she just one in a line of nellies?'

The woman flushed. 'You don't know what you're talking about.'

'What I'm talking about's your position at Holloway and how you might've used and abused it over the years, and what action the guv'nors might think of taking if word got out you've been doing the nasty where you ought to be just locking the doors. You got how many years in the job? You got a pension? In line for promotion to warden? What?'

She smiled without humour, saying, 'You know, I wanted to be a policeman, Constable, but I've

351

dyslexia and I couldn't pass the exams. So I turned to prison work because I like the idea of citizens upholding the law, and I believe in punishing those who cross the line.'

'Which you yourself did. With Katja. She was doing twenty years—'

'She didn't do all her time at Holloway. Virtually no one does. But I've been here for twenty-four years. So I expect your assumption—whatever it is—has a number of holes in it.'

'She was here on remand, she was here for the trial, she did some time here. And when she went off—to Durham, was it?—she'd be able to list her visitors, wouldn't she? And whose name d'you think I'd find in her records as the one to admit—proba'ly the *only* one to admit aside from her brief—for her visits? And she'd be back in Holloway to do some of her time, I expect. Yeah. I expect that could've been fixed up easy enough from within. What's your job, Miss McKay?'

'Deputy Warden,' she said. 'I imagine you know that.'

'Deputy Warden with a taste for the ladies. You always been bent?'

'That's none of your business.'

Nkata slapped his hand on the table and leaned towards the woman. 'It's all my business,' he told her. 'Now, you want me to troll through Katja's records, find all the prisons she was locked up in, get all the visitors lists she filled out, see your name topping them, and put the thumb screws to you? I c'n do that, Miss McKay, but I don't like to. It wastes my time.'

She lowered her gaze to her drink, turning the glass slowly on the mat beneath it. The pub door opened, letting in another gust of chill evening air and the smell of exhaust fumes from Parkhurst Road, and two men in the uniform of prison workers walked inside. They fixed on Noreen, then on Nkata, then back to Noreen. One smiled and made a low comment. Noreen looked up and saw them.

She breathed an oath and said, 'I've got to get out of here,' beginning to rise.

Nkata closed his hand over her wrist. 'Not without giving me something,' he told her. 'Else I'm going to have to look through those records, Miss McKay. And 'f your name's there, I 'xpect you'll have some real 'xplaining to do to your guv.'

'Do you threaten people often?'

'Not a threat. Just a simple fact. Now sit back down and 'tend to your drink.' He nodded towards her colleagues. 'I 'xpect I'm doing your reputation some good.'

Her face flared with red. 'You completely *despicable*—'

'Chill,' he said. 'Let's talk about Katja. She gave me the go ahead to talk to you, by the way.'

'I don't believe—'

'Phone her.'

'She—'

'She's a suspect in a hit-and-run murder. And a suspect in a second hit and run as well. 'F you can clear her name, you better set to it. She's 'bout two breaths away from getting arrested. And you think we'll be able to keep *that* from the press? Notorious baby killer "helping the police with their enquiries" again? Not likely, Miss McKay. Her whole life's about to go under the microscope. And I 'xpect you know what that means.'

'I can't clear her name,' Noreen McKay said, her fingers tightening on her gin and tonic. 'That's just it, you see? I can't clear her name.'

## CHAPTER TWENTY-THREE

'Waddington,' DCI Leach informed them when Lynley and Havers joined him in the incident room. He was all exultation: his face brighter than it had been in days and his step lighter as he dashed across the room to scrawl *Kathleen Waddington* at the top of one of the china boards.

'Where was she hit?' Lynley asked.

'Maida Vale. And it's the same m.o. Quiet neighbourhood. Pedestrian alone. Night. Black car. *Smash.*'

'Last night?' Barbara Havers asked. 'But that would mean—'

'No, no. This was ten days ago.'

'Could be a coincidence,' Lynley said.

'Not bloody likely. She's a player from before.' Leach went on to explain precisely who Kathleen Waddington was: a sex therapist who'd left her clinic on the night in question after ten o'clock. She'd been hit on the street and left with a broken hip and a dislocated shoulder. When she was interviewed by the police, she'd said the car that hit her was big, 'like a gangster car', that it moved fast, that it was dark, possibly black. Leach said, 'I went through my notes from the other case, the baby drowning. Waddington was the woman who wrecked Katja Wolff's story about being out of the bathroom to take a phone call for a minute or less

354

on the night that Sonia Davies drowned. Without Waddington, it still might have gone down to negligence and a few years in prison. With her showing Wolff up to be a liar . . . It was another nail in the coffin. We need to bring Wolff in. Pass that word to Nkata. Let him have the glory. He's been working her hard.'

'What about the car?' Lynley asked.

'That'll come in due course. You can't tell me she spent two decades inside without having formed more than one association she could depend on when she got out.'

'Someone with an old motor?' Barbara Havers asked.

'Bet on it. I've got a PC going through the significant others right now,' with a jerk of his head towards a female constable sitting at one of the terminals in the room. 'She's picking up every name mentioned in every action report and running each through the system. We'll get our mitts on the prison records as well and run through everyone Wolff had contact with while she was inside. We can do that while we've got her in for questioning. D'you want to page your man and give him the message? Or shall I?' Leach rubbed his hands together briskly.

The PC at the computer terminal rose from her seat at that moment, with a paper in her hand. She said, 'I think I've got it, sir,' and Leach bounded to her with a happy, 'Brilliant. Good work, Vanessa. What've we got?'

'A Humber,' she said.

The vehicle in question was a postwar saloon manufactured in the days when the relationship between petrol consumed and miles covered was not the first thing on a driver's mind. It was smaller than a Rolls Royce, a Bentley, or a Daimler—not to mention less costly—but it was larger than the average car on the street today. And whereas the modern car was manufactured from aluminium and alloy to keep its weight low and its mileage high, the Humber was fashioned from steel and chrome with a front end comprising a toothy sneer of heavy grillwork suitable for scooping from the air everything from winged insects to small birds.

'Excellent,' Leach said.

'Whose is it?' Lynley asked.

'Belongs to a woman,' Vanessa told them. 'She's called Jill Foster.'

'Richard Davies' fiancée?' Havers looked at Lynley. Her face broke into a smile. She said, 'That's it. That's bloody *it*, Inspector. When you said—'

But Lynley interrupted her. 'Jill Foster? I can't see that, Havers. I've met the woman. She's enormously pregnant. She's not capable of this. And even if she were, why would she go after Waddington?'

Havers said, 'Sir . . .'

Leach cut in, 'There's got to be another car, then. Another old one.'

'How likely is that?' the PC said doubtfully.

'Page Nkata,' Leach told Lynley. And to Vanessa, 'Get Wolff's prison records. We need to go through them. There's got to be a car—'

'Hang *on*!' Havers said explosively. 'There's another way to look at this, you lot. Listen. He said Pytches. Richard Davies said Pytches. Not Pitchley or Pitchford, but *Pytches*.' She grasped Lynley's arm for emphasis. 'You said he said Pytches when

356

we were having coffee. You *said* you had Pytches in your notes. When you interviewed Richard Davies? Yes?'

Lynley said, 'Pytches? What's Jimmy Pytches have to do with this, Havers?'

'It was a slip of the tongue, don't you see?'

'Constable,' Leach said irritably, 'what the hell are you on about?'

Havers went on, directing her comments to Lynley. 'Richard Davies wouldn't have made that kind of verbal mistake when he'd just been told his former wife was murdered. He couldn't have *known* J.W. Pitchley was Jimmy Pytches right at that moment. He might have known James Pitchford was Jimmy Pytches, yes, all right, but he didn't think of him as Pytches, he'd never known him as Pytches, so why the hell would he call him that in front of you since you yourself didn't know who Pytches even was at that point? Why would he *ever* call him that, in fact? He wouldn't unless it was on his mind because he'd had to go through what I'd gone through: the records in St Catherine's. And why? In order to locate James Pitchford himself.'

'What is this?' Leach demanded.

Lynley held up a hand, saying, 'Hang on a moment, sir. She's got something. Havers, go on.'

'Too right I've got something,' Havers asserted. 'He'd been speaking to his ex-wife for months. You've got that in your notes. He said it and the BT records corroborate.'

'They do,' Lynley said.

'And Gideon told you they were supposed to meet, he and his mother. Right?'

'Yes.'

'She was supposed to be able to help him get over his stage fright. That's what he said. That's also in your notes. Only they didn't meet, did they? They weren't able to meet because she was killed first. So what if she was killed to *prevent* them from meeting? She didn't know where Gideon lived, did she? The only way she could have found out was from Richard.'

Lynley said thoughtfully, 'Davies wants to kill her, and he sees a way. Give her what she thinks is Gideon's address, arrange a time when they're supposed to meet, lie in wait for her—'

'—and when she goes wandering down the street with the address in her hand or wherever it was, *blam*. He runs her down,' Havers concluded. 'Then he drives over her to finish her off. But he makes it look like it's related to the older crime by taking Waddington out first and Webberly afterwards.'

'Why?' Leach asked.

'That's the question,' Lynley acknowledged. He said to Havers, 'It works, Barbara. I do see that it works. But if Eugenie Davies could help her son regain his music, why would Richard Davies want to stop her? From talking to the man—not to mention from seeing his flat, which is a virtual shrine to Gideon's accomplishments—the only reasonable conclusion is that Richard Davies was determined to get his son playing again.'

'So what if we've been looking at it wrong?' Havers asked.

'In what way?'

'I accept that Richard Davies wants Gideon to play again. If he had an issue with his playing—like jealousy or something, like his kid being more of a success than he is and how can he handle that—

358

then he probably would have done something a long time ago to stop him. But from what we know, the kid's been playing since he was just out of nappies.'

'So it seems.'

'Okay. So what if Eugenie Davies was going to meet Gideon in order to *stop* him ever playing again?'

'Why would she do that?'

'What about *quid pro quo* to Richard? If their marriage ended because of something he'd done—'

'Like putting the nanny in the club?' Leach suggested.

'Or devoting his every waking moment to Gideon and forgetting he had a wife at all, a woman in mourning, a woman with needs . . . She loses a child and instead of having someone to lean on, she has Richard and all he cares about is getting *Gideon* through the trauma so he doesn't freak out and stop playing his music and stop being the son who's admired so much and on the edge of being famous and gratifying his daddy's every dream and what about *her* through all this? What about his mum? She's been forgotten, left to cope on her own, and she never forgets what it was like so when she has the chance to put the screws on Richard, she knows just how to do it: when *he* needs her just like she needed him.' Havers drew a deep breath at the end of all this, looking from the DCI to Lynley for their reaction.

Leach was the one to give it. 'How?'

'How what?'

'How's she supposed to be able to stop her son playing? What's she going to do, Constable: break his fingers? Run *him* down?'

Havers drew a second breath, but she let it out on a sigh. 'I don't know,' she said, her shoulders sagging.

'Right,' Leach snorted. 'Well, when you do—'

'No,' Lynley cut in. 'There's some sense to this, sir.'

'You're joking,' Leach said.

'There's something in it. Following Havers' line of thinking, we've got an explanation of why Eugenie Davies was carrying Pitchley's address that night, and nothing else we've come up with so far gets anywhere near explaining that.'

'Bollocks,' Leach said.

'What other explanation can we come up with? Nothing ties her to Pitchley. No letter, no phone call, no e-mail.'

'She had e-mail?' Leach demanded.

Havers said, 'Right. And her computer—' but she stopped herself abruptly, swallowing the rest of her sentence with a wince.

'*Computer*?' Leach echoed. 'Where the hell's her computer? There's no computer mentioned in your reports.'

Lynley felt Havers look at him, then drop her glance to her shoulder bag where she rooted industriously for something that she probably didn't need. He wondered what would serve them better, truth or lie at this point. He opted for, 'I checked the computer. There was nothing on it. She had e-mail, yes. But there was nothing from Pitchley. So I saw no need—'

'To put it in your report?' Leach demanded. 'What the *hell* kind of police work is that?'

'It seemed unnecessary.'

'*What?* Good Christ. I want that computer in

360

here, Lynley. I want our people on it like ants over ice cream. You're no computer expert. You might have missed . . . God damn it. Have you gone out of your mind? What the *hell* were you thinking?'

What could he say? That he was thinking of saving time? saving trouble? saving a reputation? saving a marriage? He said carefully, 'Getting into her e-mail wasn't a problem, sir. Once we managed that, we could see there was virtually nothing—'

'*Virtually?*'

'Just a message from Robson, and we've spoken to him. He's holding something back, I think. But it's not the fact that he had anything to do with Mrs Davies' death.'

'You know that, do you?'

'It's a gut feeling, yes.'

'The same one that prompted you to hold back—or is it remove?—a piece of evidence?'

'It was a judgement call, sir.'

'You've no place making judgement calls. I want that computer. In here. *Now.*'

'As to the Humber?' Havers ventured delicately.

'Bugger the Humber. And bugger Davies. Vanessa, get those sodding prison records of Wolff's. For all we know, she's got ten people on a string, all with vehicles as old as Methuselah, *all* of them somehow related to this case.'

'That's not what we have,' Lynley said. 'What you've come up with here, the Humber, can lead us—'

'I said *bugger* the Humber, Lynley. We're back to square one as far as you're concerned. Bring in that computer. And when you're done, get on your knees and thank God I don't report you to your superiors.'

361

'It's time you came home with me, Jill.' Dora Foster finished drying the last of the dishes and folded the tea towel neatly over its rack by the sink. She straightened its edges with her usual attention to microscopic detail, and she turned back to Jill, who was resting at the kitchen table, her feet up and her fingers kneading the aching muscles of her lower back. Jill felt as if she were carrying a fifty pound bag of flour in her stomach, and she wondered how on God's holy earth she was going to be able to get herself back into shape for her wedding just two months after the birth. 'Our little Catherine's dropped into position,' her mother said. 'It's a matter of days. Any day now, in fact.'

'Richard's not quite resigned to the plan,' Jill told her.

'You're in better hands with me than you'd be alone in a delivery room with a nurse popping by occasionally to see that you're still among the living.'

'Mum, I know that. But Richard's concerned.'

'I've delivered—'

'He knows.'

'Then—'

'It's not that he thinks you aren't competent. But it's different, he says, when it's your own flesh and blood involved. He says a doctor wouldn't operate on his own child. A doctor couldn't remain objective if something were to happen. Like an emergency. A crisis. You know.'

'In an emergency, we go to hospital. Ten minutes in the car.'

362

'I've told him that. He says anything could happen in ten minutes.'

'Nothing will happen. This entire pregnancy has gone like a dream.'

'Yes. But Richard—'

'Richard isn't your husband.' Dora Foster said it firmly. 'He could have been, but he chose not to be. And that gives him no rights in this decision. Have you pointed that out to him?'

Jill sighed. 'Mum . . .'

'Don't *mum* me.'

'What difference does it make that we're not married just now? We're *getting* married: the church, the priest, down the aisle on Dad's arm, the hotel reception, everything properly seen to. What more do you need?'

'It's not what I need,' Dora said. 'It's what you deserve. And don't tell me again this was your idea because I know that's nonsense. You've had your wedding planned since you were ten years old, from the flowers down to the cake decoration, and as I recall, nowhere in your plans did it ever state there'd be a baby in attendance.'

Jill didn't want to go into that. She said, 'Times change, Mum.'

'But you do not. Oh, I know it's the fashion for women to find themselves a partner rather than a husband. A *partner*, like someone they've gone into the baby making business with. And when they have their babies, they parade them round in public without the slightest degree of embarrassment. I know this happens all the time. I'm not blind. But you aren't an actress or rock singer, Jill. You've always known your own mind, and you've never been one to do something just because it's in

363

vogue.'

Jill stirred on her chair. Her mother knew her better than anyone, and what she was saying was true. But what was also true was the fact that compromise was necessary to have a successful relationship and beyond wanting a child, she wanted to have a marriage that was happy, which she certainly wasn't guaranteed if she forced Richard's hand. 'Well, it's done,' she said. 'And it's too late to change things. I'm not about to waddle down the aisle like this.'

'Which makes you a woman without ties,' her mother said. 'So you can state how and where you want your baby delivered. And if Richard doesn't like it, you can point out to him that, as his preference was not to become your husband in the traditional fashion prior to the baby's birth, he can keep out of the picture until after you're married. Now—' Her mother joined her at the table, where a box of wedding invitations sat waiting to be addressed.—'let's get your bag and take you home to Wiltshire. You can leave him a note. Or you can phone him. Shall I fetch the phone for you?'

'I'm not going to Wiltshire tonight,' Jill said. 'I'll speak to Richard. I'll ask him again—'

'*Ask* him?' Her mother put her hand on Jill's hugely swollen ankle. 'Ask him what? Ask him if you can please have your baby—'

'Catherine's his baby as well.'

'That has nothing to do with this. You're having her. Jill, this isn't at all like you. You've always known your own mind, but you're acting as if you're worried now, as if you might do something to drive him away. That's absurd, you know. He's lucky to have you. Considering his age, he's lucky

364

to have any—'

'Mum.' This was one area that they'd long ago agreed not to discuss: Richard's age and the fact that he was two years older than Jill's own father and five years older than her mother. 'You're right. I know my own mind. It's made up: I'll speak to Richard when he comes home. But I won't go to Wiltshire without speaking to him and I certainly won't go and just leave him a note.' She gave her voice The Edge, a tone she'd long used at the BBC, just the inflection that had been needed to bring every production in on time and on budget. No one argued with her when her voice had The Edge.

And Dora Foster didn't argue with her now. Instead, she sighed. She gazed at the ivory wedding dress that hung beneath its transparent shroud on the door. She said, 'I never thought it would be like this.'

'It'll be fine, Mum.' Jill told herself that she meant it.

But when her mother had departed, she was left with her thoughts, those mischievous companions of one's solitude. They insisted she consider her mother's words carefully, which took her over the ground of her association with Richard.

It didn't *mean* anything that he'd been the one who wished to wait. There had been logic involved in the decision. And they'd taken it mutually, hadn't they? What difference did it make that he'd been the one to suggest it? He'd used sound reasoning. She'd told him she was pregnant, and he'd been joyful at the news, as joyful as she herself had been. He'd said, 'We'll get married. *Tell* me we'll get married,' and she had laughed at the sight of his face looking so much like a little boy's, afraid

365

of being disappointed. She'd said, 'Of course we'll get married,' and he'd pulled her into his arms and led her off into the bedroom.

After their coupling they lay entwined and he talked about their wedding. She'd been filled with bliss, with that gratified and grateful aftermath of orgasm during which everything seems possible and anything seems reasonable, so when he declared that he wanted her to have a *proper* wedding and no rushed affair, she sleepily had said, 'Yes. Yes. A proper wedding, darling.' To which he'd added, 'With a proper gown for you. Flowers and attendants. A church. A photographer. A reception. I want to celebrate, Jill.'

Which, of course, he could not do if they had to shoehorn the planning into the seven months before the baby's birth. And even if they were able to manage that, no amount of shoehorning would fit her into an elegant wedding gown once she had a bump. It was so practical to wait. In fact, Jill realised as she thought about it, Richard had led her right up to the idea so that when he said at the conclusion of her recitation of everything that had to be done in order to produce the kind of wedding he wanted her to have, 'I'd no idea how *many* months . . . Will you be comfortable, Jill, with a wedding that far along into your pregnancy?' she'd been more than ready for his next line of thinking. 'No one ought to enjoy the day more than you. And as you're so small . . .' He put his hand on her stomach as if for emphasis. It was flat and taut, but it wouldn't be, soon. 'D'you think we ought to wait?' he'd suggested.

Why not, she'd thought. She'd waited thirty-seven years for her wedding day. There was no problem waiting a few months more.

But that had been before Gideon's troubles had taken up primary residence in Richard's mind. And Gideon's troubles had brought on Eugenie.

Jill could see now that Richard's preoccupation after Wigmore Hall may have had a secondary source beyond his son's failure to perform that night. And when she set that secondary source next to his apparent reluctance to marry, she felt an uneasiness creep over her, like a fog bank gliding noiselessly onto an unsuspecting shore.

She blamed her mother for this. Dora Foster was happy enough to be on the road to having her first grandchild, but she wasn't pleased with Jill's choice of father although she knew better than to say so directly. Still, she *would* feel the need to voice her objections subtly, and what better way than to create an inroad in Jill's implicit faith in Richard's honour. Not that she actually *thought* in terms of a man doing 'the honourable thing'. She didn't, after all, live in a Hardy novel. When she thought of honour, she merely thought of a man telling the truth about his actions and intentions. Richard said they would marry; ergo, they would.

They could have married at once, of course, once she'd become pregnant. She wouldn't have minded. It was, after all, marriage and children that she'd placed on her list as having to accomplish by her thirty-fifth birthday. She'd never written the word *wedding* and she had seen a wedding only as one of the means she could use to achieve her end. Indeed, had she not been so blissful there in bed after their lovemaking, she probably would have said, 'Bother the wedding, Richard. Let's marry now,' and he would have agreed.

Wouldn't he? she wondered. Just as he'd agreed to the name she'd chosen for the baby? Just as he'd agreed to her mother's delivering the baby? Just as he'd agreed to selling her flat first instead of his? To buying that house she'd found in Harrow? To simply *going* with the estate agent to at least take a look at that house?

What did it mean that Richard was thwarting her at every turn, thwarting her in the most reasonable of fashions, making it seem as if every decision they reached was reached mutually and not a case of her giving in because she was . . . What? Afraid? And if so, of what?

And the answer was there even though the woman was dead, even though she could not come back to harm them, to stand in the way, to prevent what was meant to be . . .

The phone rang. Jill started. She looked round, dazed at first. So deep into her thoughts had she been that she wasn't aware for a moment that she was still in the kitchen and the cordless phone was somewhere in the sitting room. She lumbered to get it.

'Is this Miss Foster?' a woman's voice said. It was a professional voice, a competent voice, a voice such as Jill's own once had been.

Jill said, 'Yes.'

'Miss Jill Foster?'

'Yes. Yes. Who is this please?'

And the answer fractured Jill's world into pieces.

\*      \*      \*

There was something about the way Noreen McKay made the statement—'I can't clear her

368

name'—that gave Nkata pause before lighting the fireworks of celebration. There was a desperation behind the deputy warden's eyes and an incipient panic in the manner in which she downed the rest of her drink in a gulp. He said, 'Can't or won't clear her name, Miss McKay?'

She said, 'I have two teenage children to consider. They're all I have left as family. I don't want a custody battle with their father.'

'Courts're more liberal these days.'

'I also have a career. It's not the one I wanted, but it's the one I've got. The one I've made for myself. Don't you see? If it comes to light that I ever—' She stopped herself.

Nkata sighed. He couldn't take *ever* to the bank and deposit it, one way or the other. He said, 'She was with you, then. Three nights back? Last night as well? Late last night?'

Noreen McKay blinked. She was sitting so straight and tall in her chair that she looked like a cardboard cut-out of herself.

'Miss McKay, I got to know whether I c'n cross her name off.'

'And I've got to know whether I can trust you. The fact that you've come here, right to the prison itself . . . Don't you see what that suggests?'

'Suggests I'm busy. Suggests it doesn't make sense for me to go driving back and forth 'cross London when you're . . . what . . . a mile? two miles? from Harriet Lewis's office.'

'It suggests more than that,' Noreen McKay said. 'It tells me that you're self-interested, Constable, and if you're self-interested, what's to prevent you from passing on my name to a snout, for a nice fifty quid? Or from being the snout yourself, for fifty

369

more? It's a good story to sell to the *Mail*. You've threatened worse already in this conversation.'

'I could do that now, comes down to it. You given me enough already, you have.'

'I've given you what? The fact that a solicitor and her client came to my house one evening? What do you expect the *Mail* to do with that?'

Nkata had to acknowledge that Noreen McKay was making a good point. There was hardly seed for anyone's planting in what little information he had. There was, however, what he knew already and what he could assume from what he knew and what he ultimately could do with *that*. But the truth of the matter, however reluctantly he admitted it to himself, was that he actually needed from her only confirmation and a period of time to go with that confirmation. As for the rest of it, all the whys and the wherefores . . . If the truth were told, he *wanted* them, but he did not need them, not professionally.

He said, 'The hit and run in Hampstead happened round half ten or eleven th' other night. Harriet Lewis says you c'n give Katja Wolff an alibi for the time. She also says you won't, which's what makes me think you and Katja got something between yourselves that's going to make one of you look bad if it gets out.'

'I've said: I'm not going to talk about that.'

'I get that, Miss McKay. Loud and clear. So what about you talking about what you're willing to talk about. What about bare facts with no window dressing on them?'

'What do you mean?'

'Yesses and nos.'

Noreen McKay glanced over at the bar, where her colleagues were downing pints of Guinness.

The pub door opened, and three more prison employees walked in, all of them women in uniforms similar to the deputy warden's. Two of them called out to her and looked as if they were considering a saunter over for an introduction to McKay's companion. Noreen turned from them abruptly and said in a low voice, 'This is impossible. I shouldn't have . . . We've got to get out of here.'

'You running out wouldn't look so good,' Nkata murmured. 'Especially when I jump up and start shouting your name. But yesses and nos, and I'm gone, Miss McKay. Quiet as a mouse and you c'n tell them I'm anyone. Truant officer come to talk about your kids. Scout for Manchester United interested in the boy. I don't care. Just yesses and nos, and you got your life back, whatever it is.'

'You don't *know* what it is.'

' 'Course. Like I said. Whatever it is.'

She stared at him for a moment before saying, 'All right. Ask.'

'Was she with you three nights ago?'

'Yes.'

'Between ten and midnight?'

'Yes.'

'What time d'she leave?'

'We said yesses or nos.'

'Right. Yeah. She leave before midnight?'

'No.'

'She arrive before ten?'

'Yes.'

'She come alone?'

'Yes.'

'Missus Edwards know where she was?'

Noreen McKay moved her gaze at this question, but it didn't appear to be because she was about to

371

lie. 'No,' she said.

'And last night?'

'What about last night?'

'Katja Wolff with you last night? Say, after her solicitor left?'

Noreen McKay looked back at him. 'Yes.'

'She stay? Was she there round half eleven, midnight?'

'Yes. She left . . . It was probably half past one when she left.'

'You know Missus Edwards?'

Her gaze moved again. He saw a muscle tighten in her jaw. She said, 'Yes. Yes, I know Yasmin Edwards. She served most of her time in Holloway.'

'You know she and Katja—'

'Yes.'

'Then what're you doing mixed up with them?' he asked abruptly, abjuring the previous yesses and nos in a sudden need for weapons, a personal need that he could barely acknowledge let alone begin to understand. 'You got some sort of plan, you and Katja? You two using her and her boy for some reason?'

She looked at him but did not reply.

He said, 'These're *people,* Miss McKay. They got lives and they got feelings. If you and Katja're planning to put something down to Yasmin, like laying a trail to her door, making her look bad, putting her at risk—'

Noreen snapped forward, saying in a hiss, 'Isn't it obvious that just the *opposite* has happened? *I* look bad. *I'm* at risk. And why? Because I love her, Constable. That's my sin. You think this is about quirky sex, don't you? The abuse of power.

372

Coercion leading to perversion, and nauseating scenes of desperate women with dildos strapped to their hips mounting desperate women behind bars. But what you don't think is that this is complicated, that it has to do with loving someone but not being able to love her openly so loving her the only way I can and having to know that on the nights we're apart—which are far more than we're together, believe me—she's with someone else, loving someone else, or at least playing at it because that's what *I* want. And every argument we *ever* have has *no* solution because both of us are right in the choices we've made. I can't give her what she wants from me, and I can't accept what she wants to give. So she gives it elsewhere and I take scraps from her and she takes scraps from me, and *that's* how it is, no matter what she says about how and when and for whom things will change.' She leaned back in her chair after the speech, her breath coming jerkily as she fumbled her way into her navy coat once more. She got to her feet and headed for the door.

Nkata followed her. Outside, the wind was blowing ferociously, and Noreen McKay was standing in it. She was breathing like a runner in the light from a street lamp, one hand curled round the pole. She was looking at Holloway Prison across the street.

She appeared to feel, rather than to see, Nkata come up next to her. She didn't look at him when she spoke. 'At first, I was just curious about her. They put her in the medical unit after her trial, which is where I was assigned back then. She was on suicide watch. But I could tell that she had no intention of harming herself. There was this *resolve*

373

about her, this knowing completely who she was. And I found that attractive, compelling really, because while I knew who I was as well, I'd never been able to admit it to myself. Then she went to the pregnancy unit and she could have gone to the mother-and-baby unit after the child was born, but she didn't want that, she didn't want him, and I found that I needed to know what she wanted and what she was made of that she could exist so sure and so alone.'

Nkata said nothing. He blocked some of the wind with his back as he positioned himself before the deputy warden.

'So I just watched her. She was in jeopardy, of course, once she was off the medical unit. There's a form of honour among them, and the worst in their eyes is the killer of babies, so she wasn't safe unless she was with other Category One offenders. But she didn't care that she wasn't safe, and that fascinated me. I thought at first it was because she saw her life as over, and I wanted to talk to her about that. I called it my duty and since I was in charge of the Samaritans at that point—'

'Samaritans?' Nkata asked.

'We have a programme of visits for them here at the prison. If a prisoner wishes to participate, she tells the staff member in charge.'

'Katja wanted to participate?'

'No. Never. But I used that as an excuse to talk to her.' She examined Nkata's face and seemed to read something into his expression because she went on with, 'I am *good* at my job. We've got twelve-step programmes now. We've got an increase in visits. We've got better rehabilitation and easier means for families to see mothers

374

who're doing time. I *am* good at my job.' She looked away from him, into the street where the evening traffic was pouring out towards the northern suburbs. She said, 'She didn't want any of it, and I couldn't understand why. She'd fought deportation to Germany, and I couldn't understand why. She talked to no one unless spoken to first. But all the time she watched. And so she eventually saw me watching her. When I was assigned to her wing—this is later—we started talking. She went first, which surprised me. She said, "Why do you watch me?" I remember that. And what followed. I remember that also.'

'She's holding all the cards, Miss McKay,' Nkata noted.

'This isn't about blackmail, Constable. Katja *could* destroy me, but I know she won't.'

'Why?'

'There are things you just know.'

'We're talking 'bout a lag.'

'We're talking about Katja.' The deputy warden pushed away from the street lamp and approached the traffic lights that would allow her to cross the road and return to the prison. Nkata walked beside her. She said, 'I knew what I was from an early age. I expect my parents knew as well when I played dressing up and dressed like a soldier, a pirate, a fireman. But never like a princess or a nurse or a mum. And that's not normal, is it, and when at last you're fifteen, all you want is what's normal. So I tried it: short skirts, high heels, low necklines, the whole bit. I went after men and I shagged every boy I could get my hands on. Then one day in the paper I saw an ad for women looking for women and I phoned a number. For a joke, I told myself. Just for a lark. We met at a health club and had a swim and went out for coffee and then went to her place. She was twenty-four. I was nineteen. We were together five years, till I went into the prison service. And then . . . I couldn't live that life. It felt like too much of a risk. And then my sister got Hodgkin's and I got her children and for a long time that was enough.'

'Till Katja.'

'I've had scores of bed mates in the form of men, but only two lovers, both of them women. Katja's one of them.'

'For how long?'

'Seventeen years. Off and on.'

'You mean to go on like this forever?'

'With Yasmin in the middle, d'you mean?' She glanced at Nkata, seeming to try to read an answer in his silence. 'If it can be said that we choose where we love, then I chose Katja for two reasons. She never spoke about what put her in prison, so I knew she could hold her tongue about me. And she had an enormous secret she was keeping, which I thought at the time was a lover outside prison. I'll be safe getting involved, I thought. When she leaves, she'll go to her or to him, and I'll have had the chance to get this out of my system so I can live the rest of my life celibate but still knowing I once had *something* . . .' The traffic light in Parkhurst Road changed, and the walking figure altered along with it from red to green. Noreen stepped off the pavement, but looked back over her shoulder as she made a final comment, 'It's been seventeen years, Constable. She's the only prisoner I ever touched . . . that way. She's the only woman I've ever loved . . . this way.'

'Why?' he asked as she began to cross the street.

'Because she's safe,' Noreen McKay said in parting. 'And because she's strong. No one can break Katja Wolff.'

\*     \*     \*

'Bloody hell. This is just brilliant,' Barbara Havers muttered. She was beginning to feel the peril of her own situation: Two months demoted for insubordination and assault on a superior officer, she couldn't afford yet another pot hole on the ill-paved road of her career. 'If Leach tells Hillier about that computer, we're done for, Inspector. You know that, don't you?'

'We're only done for if there's something useful to the investigation on the computer,' Lynley pointed out as he nosed the Bentley into the heavy evening traffic of Rosslyn Hill. 'And there isn't, Havers.'

His utter calm rubbed against the sore of Barbara's apprehension. Their progress to his car had been so rapid after leaving Leach's office that she hadn't had a chance for a cigarette, and she was itching for a hit of tobacco to steady her nerves, which made her irritable as well as afraid. 'You know that, do you?' she asked him. 'And what about those letters? From the superintendent to her? If we need those letters to build a case against Richard Davies . . . for why he went after Webberly . . . for why he made it look like Wolff was after people . . .' She ran her hand through her hair and felt it bristle. She needed to cut it. She'd do that tonight, take the nail scissors to it and do a proper job. Maybe she'd hack it all off and punk it up with hair goo. *That* should serve to distract AC Hillier from the rôle she'd played in evidence tampering.

'You can't have it all ways,' Lynley said.

'What's that s'posed to mean when it's home with its mother?'

'He can't have killed Eugenie because she threatened Gideon's career, Havers, and then gone after Webberly because he'd been harbouring jealousy over his affair with Eugenie. If you go that direction, where does that put Kathleen Waddington?'

'So maybe I'm wrong about Gideon's career,' she said. 'Maybe he ran down Eugenie because she'd taken up with Webberly.'

'No. You're right. His objective was Eugenie, the only person he killed. But he went after Webberly and Waddington as well to focus our attention onto Katja Wolff.' Lynley sounded so certain, so completely unfazed by the danger they were in, that Barbara wanted to smack him. He could afford to be unruffled, she decided. Out from New Scotland Yard on *his* ear, he'd just motor down to the family pile in Cornwall and live out his days like the landed gentry. She, on the other hand, didn't have that option.

'You sound dead bloody sure of yourself,' she groused.

'Davies had the letter, Havers.'

'What letter?' she demanded.

'The letter telling him Katja Wolff was out of prison. He knew I'd suspect her once he showed me that letter.'

'So he knocks down the superintendent and this Waddington bird to make it look like Eugenie's death was for revenge? Katja going after the crowd who sent her away?'

'That's my guess.'

'But maybe it *is* revenge, Inspector. Not Katja's but his. P'rhaps he knew about Eugenie and Webberly. P'rhaps he's always known but just bided his time and eaten himself up with jealousy and vowed that someday—'

'It doesn't work, Havers. Webberly's letters to Eugenie Davies are addressed to Henley. They all postdate her separation from her husband. Davies had no reason to be jealous. He probably never even knew about them.'

'So *why* choose Webberly? Why not someone else from the trial? The Crown Prosecutor, the judge, another witness.'

'I expect Webberly was easier to locate. He's lived in the same house for twenty-five years.'

'But Davies has to know where the others lived if he found Waddington.'

'What others do you mean?'

'The people who testified against her. Robson, for instance. What about Robson?'

'Robson served Gideon. He told me that himself. I don't see Davies doing anything that might hurt his son, do you? Your entire scenario— the one you came up with in Leach's office— depends on the contention that Davies acted to save his son.'

'Okay. All right. Maybe I'm wrong. Maybe it's all to do with Eugenie and Webberly and their affair. Maybe the letters and the computer are pieces of evidence we could've used to prove it. And maybe we're buggered.'

He glanced over at her. 'Barbara, we're not.' Lynley looked at her hands and she realised she was actually wringing them, like the unfortunate, impotent heroine in a melodrama featuring Simon Legree. He said, 'Have one.'

She said, 'What?'

'A cigarette. Have one. You're owed. I can cope.' He even punched in the Bentley's cigarette lighter, and when it popped out, he handed it over, saying, 'Light up. This is a situation you're not likely to find yourself in again.'

'I bloody well hope not,' Havers muttered.

He shot her a look. 'I was talking about smoking in the Bentley, Barbara.'

'Yeah. Well, I wasn't.' She dug out her Players and used the hot coil of the lighter against one. She inhaled deeply and grudgingly thanked her superior for humouring her vice for once. They inched their way south along the high street and Lynley glanced at his pocket watch. He handed his mobile over to Barbara and said, 'Phone St James and ask him to have the computer ready.'

Barbara was about to do as he asked when the mobile rang in her hand. She flipped it on and Lynley nodded at her to take the call, so she said, 'Havers here.'

'Constable?' It was DCI Leach, speaking not so much in a tone as in a snarl. 'Where the hell are you?'

'Heading to fetch the computer, sir.' *Leach*, she mouthed to Lynley, *in another twist*.

'Bugger the computer,' Leach said. 'Get over to Portman Street. Between Oxford Street and Portman Square. You'll see the action when you get there.'

'Portman Street?' Barbara said. 'But, sir, don't you want—'

'Is your hearing as bad as your judgement?'

'I—'

'We've got another hit and run,' Leach snapped.

'*What*?' Barbara said. 'Another? Who is it?'

'Richard Davies. But there're witnesses this time. And I want you and Lynley over there shaking the lot of them through a sieve before they disappear.'

## *Gideon*

### 10 NOVEMBER

*Confrontation is the only answer. He has lied to me. For nearly three quarters of my life, my father has lied. He's lied not with what he said but with what he's allowed me to believe by saying nothing for twenty years: that we—he and I—were the injured parties when my mother left us. But all the time the truth was that she left us because she'd realised why Katja had murdered my sister and why she kept silent about having done so.*

### 11 NOVEMBER

*So this is how it happened, Dr Rose. No memories now, if you will forgive me, no travelling back through time. Just this:*

*I phoned him. I said, 'I know why Sonia died. I know why Katja refused to talk. You bastard, Dad.'*

*He said nothing.*

*I said, 'I know why my mother left us. I know what happened. Do you understand me? Say something, Dad. It's time for the truth. I know what happened.'*

*I could hear Jill's voice in the background. I could
hear her question, and both the tone and the manner
of her question—'Richard? Darling, who on earth is
it?'—told me something of Dad's reaction to what I
was saying. So I was not surprised when he said
harshly, 'I'm coming over there. Don't leave the
house.'*

*How he got to me so quickly, I don't know. All I
can say is that when he entered the house and came
up the stairs at a decisive pace, it seemed that mere
minutes had passed since I had rung off from our
conversation.*

*But I'd seen the two of them in those minutes:
Katja Wolff who grabbed at life, who used a deadly
threat to get out of East Germany and who would
have used death itself if necessary to achieve the end
that she had in mind, and my father who had
impregnated her, perhaps in the hope of producing a
perfect specimen to carry on a family line that began
with himself. He, after all, discarded women when
they failed to produce something healthy. He'd done
that to his first wife, and he'd been more than likely
setting up to do the same to my mother. But he hadn't
been moving fast enough for Katja, Katja who
grabbed at life and who did not wait for what life
provided her.*

*They argued about it.*

When will you tell her about us, Richard?

When the time is right.

But we have no time! You *know* we have no
time.

Katja, don't act like an hysterical fool.

*And then, when the moment came when he could
have taken a stand, he wouldn't speak up to defend
her, excuse her, or commit himself as my mother*

382

*confronted the German girl with the fact of her pregnancy and with the fact of her failure to perform her duties towards my sister because of her pregnancy. So Katja had finally taken matters into her own hands. Exhausted with arguing and with attempting to defend herself, ill from her pregnancy, and feeling deeply betrayed on all sides, she had snapped. She had drowned Sonia.*

*What did she hope to gain?*

*Perhaps she hoped to free my father from a burden she believed was keeping them apart. Perhaps she saw drowning Sonia as her way of making a statement that needed to be made. Perhaps she wished to punish my mother for having a hold on my father that seemed unbreakable. But kill Sonia she did and then she refused, by means of a stoic silence, to acknowledge her crime, my sister's brief life, or what sins of her own had led to the taking of that life.*

*Why, though? Because she was protecting the man she loved? Or because she was punishing him?*

*All this I saw and all this I thought as I waited for my father's arrival.*

*'What is this cock, Gideon?'*

*Those were his first words to me as he strode into the music room where I was sitting in the window seat fighting off the first tentative stabs in my gut that proclaimed me frightened, childish, and cowardly as the time for our final engagement approached. I gestured to the notebook I'd been writing in all these weeks and I hated the fact that my voice was strained. I hated what that strain revealed: about myself, about him, about what I feared.*

*'I know what happened. I've remembered what happened.'*

*'Have you picked up your instrument?'*

383

'You thought I wouldn't work it out, didn't you?'

'Have you picked up the Guarnerius, Gideon?'

'You thought you could pretend for the rest of your life.'

'Damn it. Have you played? Have you tried to play? Have you even looked at your violin?'

'You thought I'd do what I've always done.'

'I've had enough of this.' He began to move, but not to the violin case. Instead, he walked to the stereo system, and as he did so he removed a new CD from his pocket.

'You thought I'd go along with something you told me because that's what I've always done, right? Throw out anything that resembles an acceptable tale and he'll swallow it: hook, line, and sinker.'

He swung round. 'You don't know what you're talking about. Look at yourself. Look what she's done to you with all this psycho-mumbo-jumbo of hers. You've been reduced to a puling mouse afraid of his shadow.'

'Isn't that what you've done, Dad? Isn't that what you did back then? You lied, you cheated, you betrayed—'

'Enough!' He was battling to free the CD from its wrapping, and he tore at it with his teeth like a dog, spitting the shreds of cellophane onto the floor. 'I'm telling you now that there's one way to deal with this, and it's the way you should have dealt with it from the first. A real man faces his fear head on. He doesn't turn tail and run from it.'

'You're running. Right now.'

'Like bloody God damn hell I am.' He punched the button to open the CD player. He jammed the compact disc inside. He hit play and twisted the volume knob. 'You listen,' he hissed. 'You bloody well

384

listen. *And act like a man.'*

*He'd turned up the sound so high that when the music started, I didn't know what it was at first. But my confusion lasted only for a second because he'd chosen* it, *Dr Rose. Beethoven.* The Archduke. *He'd chosen it.*

*The Allegro Moderato began. And it swelled round the room. And over it I could hear Dad's shout.*

'Listen. Listen. *Listen to what's unmade you, Gideon. Listen to what you're terrified to play.'*

*I covered my ears.* 'I can't.' *But still I heard. It. I heard it. And I heard him above it.*

'Listen *to what you're letting control you. Listen to what you've let a simple bloody piece of music do to your entire career.'*

*'I don't—'*

*'Black smudges on a damn piece of* paper. *That's all it is. That's what you've surrendered your power to.'*

*'Don't make me—'*

*'Stop it.* Listen. *Is it impossible for a musician like you to play this piece? No, it's not. Is it too difficult? It is not. Is it even challenging? No, no, no. Is it mildly, remotely, or vaguely—'*

*'Dad!' I pressed my hands to my ears. The room was going black. It was shrinking to a pinpoint of light and the light was blue, it was blue, it was* blue.

*'What it is is weakness made flesh in you, Gideon. You had a bout of nerves and you've transformed yourself into flaming Raphael Robson. That's what you've done.'*

*The piano introduction was nearly complete. The violin was due to begin. I knew the notes. The music was in me. But in front of my eyes I saw only that door. And Dad—my father—continued to rail.*

*'I'm surprised you haven't started sweating like him. That's where you'll be next. Sweating and shaking like a freak who can't—'*

*'Stop it!'*

*And the music. The music. The* music. *Swelling, exploding, demanding. All round me, the music that I dreaded and feared.*

*And in front of me the door, with* her *standing there on the steps that lead up to it, with the light shining down on her, a woman I wouldn't have known in the street, a woman whose accent has faded in time, in the twenty years she has spent in prison.*

*She says, 'Do you remember me, Gideon? It is Katja Wolff. I must speak with you.'*

*I say politely because I do not know who she is but I have been taught through the years to be polite to the public no matter the demands they make upon me because it is the public who attend my concerts who buy my recordings who support the East London Conservatory and what it is trying to do to better the lives of impoverished children children like me in so many ways save for the circumstances of birth . . . I say, 'I'm afraid I have a concert, Madam.'*

*'This will not take long.'*

*She descends the steps. She crosses the bit of Welbeck Way that separates us. I've moved to the red double doors of the artistes' entrance to Wigmore Hall and I'm about to knock to gain admittance when she says she says oh God she says, 'I've come for payment, Gideon,' and I do not know what she means.*

*But somehow I understand that danger is about to engulf me. I clutch the case in which the Guarneri is protected by leather and velvet, and I say, 'As I said, I do have a concert.'*

386

'Not for more than an hour,' she says. 'This I have been told in the front.'

She nods towards Wigmore Street where the box office is, where she apparently has gone at first to seek me out. They would have told her that the performers for the evening had not yet arrived, Madam, and that when they do arrive, they use the back entrance and not the front. So if she cared to wait there, she might have the opportunity to speak to Mr Davies although the box office couldn't guarantee that Mr Davies would have the time to speak to her.

She says, 'Four hundred thousand pounds, Gideon. Your father claims he does not have it. So I come to you because I know that you must.'

And the world as I know it is shrinking shrinking disappearing entirely into a single bead of light. From that bead grows sound and I hear the Beethoven, the Allegro Moderato, The Archduke's first movement, and then Dad's voice.

He said, 'Act like a man, for the love of God. Sit up. Stand up. Stop cowering there like a beaten dog! Jesus! Stop snivelling. You're acting like this is—'

I heard no more because I knew suddenly what all of this was, and I knew what this had always been. I remembered it all in a piece—like the music itself—and the music was the background and the act that went with that music as background was what I had forced myself to forget.

I am in my room. Raphael is displeased, more displeased than he has ever been and he has been displeased, on edge, anxious, nervous, and irritable for days. I have been petulant and uncooperative. Juilliard has been denied me. Juilliard has been listed among the impossibilities that I am growing used to hearing about. This isn't possible, that isn't possible,

387

*trim here, cut there, make allowances for. So I'll show them, I decide. I won't play this stupid violin again. I won't practise. I won't have lessons. I won't perform in public. I won't perform in private, for myself or for anyone. I will show them.*

*So Raphael marches me to my room. He puts on the recording of* The Archduke *and says, 'I'm losing patience with you, Gideon. This is not a difficult piece. I want you to listen to the first movement till you can hum it in your sleep.'*

*He leaves me, shuts the door. And the Allegro Moderato begins.*

*I say, 'I won't, I won't, I won't!' And I upset a table and kick over a chair and slam my body into the door. 'You can't make me!' I shout. 'You can't make me do anything!'*

*And the music swells. The piano introduces the melody. All is hushed and ready for the violin and cello. Mine is not a difficult part to learn, not for someone with natural gifts like myself. But what will be the point of learning it when I cannot go to Juilliard? Although Perlman did. As a boy, he went there. But I will not. And this is unfair. This is* bloody *unfair. Everything about my world is unfair. I will not do this. I will not accept this.*

*And the music swells.*

*I fling open my door. I shout, 'No!' and 'I won't!' into the corridor. I think someone will come, will march me somewhere and administer discipline but no one comes because they are all busy with their own concerns and not with mine. And I'm angry at this because it is my world that is being affected. It is my life that is being moulded. It is my will that is being thwarted and I want to punch my fist into the wall.*

*And the music swells. And the violin soars. And I*

388

*will not play this piece of music at Juilliard or anywhere else because I must remain here. In this house where we're all prisoners. Because of her.*

*The knob is under my hand before I realise it, the panels of the door inches from my face. I will burst in and frighten her. I will make her cry. I will make her pay. I will make them pay.*

*She isn't frightened. But she is alone. Alone in the tub with the yellow ducklings bobbing nearby and a bright red boat that she's slapping at happily with her fist. And she deserves to be frightened, to be thrashed, to be made to understand what she's done to me, so I grab her and shove her beneath the water and see her eyes widen and widen and widen and feel her struggle to sit up again.*

*And the music—that music—swells and swells. On and on it goes. For minutes. For days.*

*And then Katja is there. She screams my name. And Raphael is right behind her yes, because yes, I understand it all now: They have been talking the two of them talking, which is why Sonia has been left alone, and he has been demanding to know if what Sarah-Jane Beckett has whispered is true. Because he has a right to know, he says. He says this as he enters the bathroom on Katja's heels. It is what he's saying as he enters and she screams. He says, '. . . because if you are, it's mine and you know it. I do have the right—'*

*And the music swells.*

*And Katja screams, screams for my father and Raphael shouts, 'Oh my God! Oh my God' but I do not release her. I do not release her even then because I know that the end of my world began with her.*

389

# CHAPTER TWENTY-FOUR

Jill staggered to her bedroom. Her movements were clumsy. She was hampered by her size. She flung open the cupboard that held her clothes, thinking only, Richard, oh my God, *Richard,* and coming round to wonder wildly what she was doing standing incoherently in front of a rack of garments. All she could think was her lover's name. All she could feel was a mixture of terror and a profound self-hatred at the doubts she'd had, doubts that she'd been harbouring and nursing at the very moment that . . . that what? What had *happened* to him?

'Is he *alive?*' she'd cried into the telephone when the voice asked if she was Miss Foster, Miss Jill Foster, the woman whose name Richard carried in his wallet in the event that something . . .

'My God, what's happened?' Jill had continued.

'Miss Foster, if you'll come to the hospital,' the Voice had said. 'Do you need a taxi? Shall I phone one for you? If you'll give me an address, I can ring a mini cab.'

The idea of waiting five minutes—or ten or fifteen—for a cab was inconceivable. Jill dropped the telephone and stumbled for her coat.

Her coat. That was it. She'd come into her bedroom in search of her coat. She shoved through the hanging garments in the cupboard till her hands came into contact with cashmere. She jerked this from its hanger and struggled into it. She fumbled with the horn buttons, miscalculated where they went, and didn't bother to refasten them more precisely when the hem of the coat hung like a lopsided curtain upon her. From her chest of drawers, she took a scarf—the first one that came to hand, it didn't matter—and she wrapped this round her throat. She slammed a black wool cap on her head and snatched up her shoulder bag. She went for the door.

In the lift, she punched for the underground car park, and she willed the little cubicle downwards without its stopping at any other floors. She told herself that it was a *good* sign the hospital had rung her and asked her to come. If the news was bad, if the situation was—could she risk the word?—fatal, they wouldn't have rung her at all, would they? Wouldn't they instead have sent a constable round to speak to her? So what it meant that they had phoned was that he was alive. He *was* alive.

She found herself making bargains with God as she pushed through the doors to the car park. If Richard would live, if his heart or whatever it was would mend, then she would compromise on the baby's name. They would christen her Cara Catherine. Richard could call her Cara at home behind closed doors, among the family, and Jill herself would call her the same. Then outside in the world at large, both of them could refer to her as Catherine. They'd register her at school as Catherine. Her friends would call her Catherine. And Cara would be even more special because it would be what only her parents called her. That was fair, wasn't it, God? If only Richard would live.

The car was parked seven bays along. She unlocked it, praying that it would start and for the first time seeing the wisdom in having something modern and reliable. But the Humber loomed large in her past—her granddad had been its single devoted owner—and when he'd left the vehicle to her in his will, she'd kept it out of love for him and in memory of the countryside drives they'd taken together. Her friends had laughed at it in earlier years and Richard had lectured her about its dangers—no airbags, no headrests, no seatbelts—but Jill had stubbornly continued to drive it and had no intention of giving it up.

'It's safer than what's on the streets these days,' she'd declared loyally whenever Richard had attempted to wrestle from her a promise not to drive it. 'It's like a tank.'

'Just stay out of it till you've had the baby and promise me you won't let Cara anywhere near it,' he had replied.

Catherine, she had thought. Her name is Catherine. But that was before. That was when she thought nothing could happen in an instant the way things happened: things like this that changed everything, making what had seemed so important yesterday less than a bagatelle today.

Still, she'd made the promise not to drive the Humber and she'd kept that promise for the last two months. So she had added reason to wonder if it would start.

It did. Like a dream. But the increase in Jill's size required her to make an adjustment to the heavy front seat. She reached forward and beneath it for the metal lever. She flipped it up and shifted her weight. The seat wouldn't budge.

She said, 'Damn it. Come on,' and tried again. But either the device itself had corroded over the years or something was blocking the track on which the enormous seat ran.

392

Her anxiety rising, she scrabbled her fingers on the floor beneath her. She felt the lever, then the edge of the lever. She felt the seat springs. She felt the track. And then she found it. Something hard and thin and rectangular was blocking the old metal track, wedged in in such a way as to make it virtually immovable.

She frowned. She pulled on the object. She jockeyed it back and forth when it got stuck. She cursed. Her hands became damp with sweat. And finally, finally, she managed to dislodge it. She slid it out, lifted it, and laid it on the broad seat next to her.

It was a photograph, she saw, a picture in a stark, monastic, wooden frame.

## *Gideon*

### *11 NOVEMBER*

*I ran, Dr Rose. I bolted for the music room door and crashed down the stairs. I flung myself into Chalcot Square. I didn't know where I was going or what I intended to do. But I had to be away from my father and away from what he'd inadvertently forced me to face.*

*I ran blindly, but I saw her face. Not as she might have looked in joy or innocence or even in suffering, but in losing consciousness as I drowned her. I saw her head turn side to side, her baby's hair fan out, her mouth gulp fishlike, her eyes roll back and disappear. She fought to stay alive but she couldn't match the strength of my rage. I held her down and held her down, and when Katja and Raphael burst into the*

393

room, she was no longer moving or struggling against me. But still my rage was not satisfied.

My feet pounded the pavement as I tore along the square. I did not head for Primrose Hill, for Primrose Hill is exposed and exposure to anything, anyone, any longer was an unbearable thought to me. So I thundered in another direction, veering round the first corner I came to, charging through the silent neighbourhood till I burst into the upper reaches of Regent's Park Road.

Moments later, I heard him shouting my name. As I stood panting at the junction where Regent's Park and Gloucester Roads meet, he came round the corner, holding his side against a stitch. He raised his arm. He shouted, 'Wait!' I ran again.

What I thought as I ran was a simple phrase: He's always known. For I remembered more, and I saw what I remembered as a series of images.

Katja screams and shrieks. Raphael pushes past her to get to me. Shouts and footsteps rise up the stairs and along the corridor. A voice cries out, 'God damn it!'

Dad is in the bathroom. He tries to pull me away from the tub where my fingers have dug and dug and dug into my sister's fragile shoulders. He shouts my name and slaps my face. He yanks me by the hair, and I finally release her.

'Get him out of here!' he roars, and for the first time he sounds just like Granddad and I am frightened.

As Raphael jerks me into the corridor, I hear others on their way. My mother is calling, 'Richard? Richard?' as she runs up the stairs. Sarah-Jane Beckett and James the Lodger are talking to each other as they hurry down from above. Somewhere

394

*Granddad is bellowing, 'Dick! Where's my whisky? Dick!' And Gran is calling out fearfully from below, 'Has something happened to Jack?'*

*Then Sarah-Jane Beckett is with me, saying, 'What's happened? What's going on?' She takes me from Raphael's fierce grip, saying, 'Raphael, what are you doing to him?' and 'What on earth is she going on about?' in reference to Katja Wolff, who is weeping and saying, 'I do not leave her. For a minute only,' to which comment Raphael Robson is adding nothing at all.*

*After that, I am in my room. I hear Dad cry, 'Don't come in here, Eugenie. Dial nine-nine-nine.'*

*She says, 'What's happened? Sosy! What's happened?'*

*A door shuts. Katja weeps. Raphael says, 'Let me take her downstairs.'*

*Sarah-Jane Beckett goes to stand at the door to my room, where she listens, her head bent, and there she remains. I sit against the headboard of the bed, arms wet to the elbows, shaking now, finally aware of the terrible enormity of what I have done. And all along the music has played, that same music, the cursed* Archduke *that has haunted and pursued me like a relentless demon for the last twenty years.*

That is what I remembered as I ran, and when I crossed the junction, I did not attempt to avoid the traffic. It seemed to me that the only mercy would be if a car or lorry struck me.

None did. I made it to the other side. But Dad was hard on my heels, still shouting my name.

I set off again running, running away from him, running into the past. And I saw that past like a kaleidoscope of pictures: that genial ginger-haired policeman who smelled of cigars and spoke in a *kindly paternal voice . . . that night in bed with my mother holding me holding me holding me and my face pressed firmly into her breasts as if she would do to me what I had done to my sister . . . my father sitting on the edge of my bed, his hands on my shoulders as my hands were on hers . . . his voice saying, 'You're quite safe, Gideon, no one will harm you,' . . . Raphael with flowers, flowers for my mother, flowers of sympathy to assuage her grief . . . and always hushed voices, in every room, for days on end . . .*

*Finally Sarah-Jane leaves the door where she has stood motionless, waiting and listening. She walks to the tape player, where the violin in the Beethoven trio is executing a passage of doublestops. She punches a button and the music blessedly ceases, leaving behind a silence so hollow that I wish only for the music again.*

*Into this silence comes the sound of sirens. They grow louder and louder as the vehicles approach. Although it's probably taken them minutes, it seems like an hour since Dad yanked on my hair and forced me to release the grip I had on my sister.*

*'Up here, in here,' Dad shouts down the stairs as someone lets the paramedics into the house.*

*And then begins the effort to save what cannot be saved, what I know cannot be saved because I was the one who destroyed her.*

*I can't bear the images, the thoughts, the sounds.*

*I ran blindly, wildly, without caring where I was going. I crossed the street and came to my senses directly in front of the Pembroke Castle pub. And beyond it I saw the terrace where the drinkers sit in summer, the terrace that was empty now, but bordered by a wall, a low brick wall onto which I leapt, along which I ran, and from which I sprang, sprang without thinking onto the iron archway of the pedestrian footbridge that spans the railway line thirty feet beneath it. I sprang thinking, This is it how it will be.*

*I heard the train before I saw it. In the hearing, I took my answer. The train wasn't travelling fast, so the engineer would well be able to stop it and I would not die . . . unless I timed my jump with precision.*

*I moved to the edge of the arch. I saw the train. I watched its approach.*

*'Gideon!'*

*Dad was at the end of the footbridge. 'Stay where you are!' he shouted.*

*'It's too late.'*

*And like a baby, I began to cry, and I waited for the moment, the perfect moment, when I could drop onto the tracks in front of the train and enter oblivion.*

*'What are you saying?' he shouted. 'Too late for what?'*

*'I know what I did,' I cried. 'To Sonia. I remember.'*

*'You remember what?' He looked from me to the train, both of us watching its steady approach. He took a single step closer to me.*

*'You know. What I did. That night. To Sonia. How she died. You know what I did to Sonia.'*

*'No! Wait!' This as I moved my feet so that the soles of my shoes overhung the drop. 'Don't do this, Gideon. Tell me what you think happened.'*

*'I drowned her, Dad! I drowned my sister!'*

*He took another step towards me, his hand extended.*

*The train drew closer. Twenty seconds and it would be over. Twenty seconds and a debt would be*

397

*paid.*

*'Stay where you are! For the love of God, Gideon!'*

*'I drowned her!' I cried, and my breath caught on a sob. 'I drowned her and I didn't even* remember. *Do you know what that means? Do you know how it feels?'*

*His glance went to the train then back to me. He took another step forward. 'Don't!' he shouted. 'Listen to me. You didn't kill your sister.'*

*'You pulled me off her. I* remember *now. And that's why Mother left. She left us without a word because she knew what I'd done. Isn't that right? Isn't that the truth?'*

*'No! No, it's not!'*

*'It is. I remember.'*

*'Listen to me. Wait.' His words were rapid. 'You hurt her, yes. And yes, yes, she was unconscious. But, Gideon, son, hear what I'm saying. You didn't drown Sonia.'*

*'Then who—'*

*'I did.'*

*'I don't believe you.' I looked beneath me, to the waiting rail tracks. A single step was all I needed to take, and I would be on the tracks and a moment later it would all be over. A burst of pain then a wiping of the slate.*

*'Look at me, Gideon. For God's sake, hear me out. Don't do this before you understand what happened.'*

*'You're trying to stall.'*

*'If I am, there'll be another train, won't there? So listen to me. You owe it to yourself.'*

*No one had been present, he told me. Raphael had taken Katja down to the kitchen. My mother had gone to ring the emergency number. Gran had gone to*

398

*Granddad to settle him down. Sarah-Jane had taken me to my room. And James the Lodger had disappeared back upstairs.*

*'I could have taken her from the bath just then,' he said. 'I could have given her the kiss of life. I could have used CPR on her. But I held her there, Gideon. I held her down beneath the water until I heard your mother finish her call to emergency.'*

*'That wouldn't have done it. There wouldn't have been enough time.'*

*'There was. Your mother stayed on the phone with emergency till we heard the paramedics pounding on the front door. She relayed emergency's instructions to me. I pretended to do what they directed. But she couldn't see me, Gideon, so she didn't know that I hadn't taken Sonia out of the bath.'*

*'I don't believe you. You've lied to me my whole life. You said nothing. You told me nothing.'*

*'I'm telling you now.'*

*Below me, the train passed. I saw the engineer look up at the last moment. Our eyes met, his widened, and he reached for his radio transmitter. The warning was sent to trains that would follow. My opportunity for oblivion was past.*

*Dad said, 'You must believe me. I'm telling you the truth.'*

*'What about Katja, then?'*

*'What about Katja?'*

*'She went to prison. And we sent her there, didn't we? We lied to the police and she went to prison. For twenty years, Dad. We're to blame for that.'*

*'No. Gideon, she agreed to go.'*

*'What?'*

*'Come back to me. Here. I'll explain.'*

*So I gave him that much: the belief that he'd talked*

399

me away from the tracks when in fact I knew that we were moments away from being joined by the transport police. I climbed back onto the footbridge proper, and I approached my father. When I was close enough to him, he grabbed me as if dragging me from the brink of a chasm. He held me to him, and I could feel the hammering of his heart. I didn't believe anything that he'd told me so far, but I was willing to listen, to bear him out, and to try to see past the façade he wore and to ascertain what facts lay beneath it.

He spoke in a rush, never once releasing me as he told me the story. Believing that I—and not my father—had drowned my sister, Katja Wolff had known instantly that she bore a large part of the responsibility because she had left Sonia alone. If she agreed to take the blame—claiming to have left the child for a minute only while she took a phone call—then Dad would see that she was rewarded. He would pay her twenty thousand pounds for this service to his family. And in the event that she should come to trial for negligence, he would add to that amount another twenty thousand for every year she was inconvenienced thereafter.

'We didn't know the police would build a case against her,' he said into my ear. 'We didn't know about the healed fractures on your sister's body. We didn't know the tabloids would seize the case with such ferocity. And we didn't know that Bertram Cresswell-White would prosecute her like a man with a chance to convict Myra Hindley all over again. In the normal course of events, she might have been given a suspended sentence for negligence. Or at the most five years. But everything went wrong. And when the judge recommended twenty years because of the abuse . . . It was too late.'

I pulled away from him. Truth or lie? I wondered as I studied his face. 'Who abused Sonia?'

'No one,' he said.

'But the fractures—'

'She was frail, Gideon. Her skeleton was delicate. It was part of her condition. Katja's defence counsel put this to the jury, but Cresswell-White tore their experts to pieces. Everything went badly. Everything went wrong.'

'Then why didn't she give evidence in her own defence? Why didn't she talk to the police? Her own lawyers?'

'That was part of the deal.'

'The deal.'

'Twenty thousand pounds if she remained silent.'

'But you must have known—' What? I thought. What must he have known? That her friend Katie Waddington wouldn't lie under oath, wouldn't testify to having made a phone call that she hadn't made? That Sarah-Jane Beckett would paint her in the worst possible light? That the Crown Prosecutor would try her as a child abuser and limn her as the devil incarnate? That the judge would recommend a draconian sentence? What exactly was my father to have known?

I released myself from the hold he had on me. I began to retrace my route from Chalcot Square. He followed closely on my heels, not speaking. But I could feel his eyes on me. I could feel the burn of their penetration. He's made all of this up, I concluded. He has too many answers and they're coming too quickly.

I told him on the front steps to my house. I said, 'I don't believe you, Dad.'

He countered with, 'Why else would she have remained silent? It was hardly in her interests to do so.'

'Oh, I believe that part,' I told him. 'I believe the part about the twenty thousand pounds. You would have paid her that much to keep me from harm. And to keep it from Granddad that your freak of a son had deliberately drowned your freak of a daughter.'

'That's not what happened!'

'We both know it is.' I turned to go inside.

He grabbed my arm. 'Will you believe your mother?' he asked me.

I turned. He must have seen the question, the disbelief, and the wariness on my face because he went on without my speaking.

'She's been phoning me. Since Wigmore Hall, she's been phoning at least twice a week. She read about what happened, she phoned to ask about you, and she's been phoning ever since. I'll arrange a meeting between you, if you like.'

'What good would that do? You said she didn't see—'

'Gideon, for God's sake. Why do you think she left me? Why do you suppose she took every picture of your sister with her?'

I stared at him. I tried to read him. And more than that, I tried to find the answer to a single question that I didn't give voice to: Even if I saw her, would she tell me the truth?

But Dad appeared to see this question in my eyes because quickly he said, 'Your mother has no reason to lie to you, son. And surely the manner of her disappearance from our lives tells you she couldn't bear the guilt of living the pretence that I'd forced her into living.'

402

*'It also might mean that she couldn't bear to live in the same house with a son who'd murdered his sister.'*

*'Then let her tell you that.'*

*We were eye to eye, and I waited for a sign that he was the least apprehensive. But no sign came.*

*'You can trust me,' he responded.*

*And I wanted more than anything to believe that promise.*

## CHAPTER TWENTY-FIVE

Havers said, 'I wish the situation would stop changing direction every twenty-five minutes. If it would, we *might* actually be able to get a handle on this case.'

Lynley made a turn into Belsize Avenue and did a quick recce of the *A to Z* in his brain to plan a route to Portman Street that wouldn't put them in the middle of a traffic jam. Next to him, Havers was continuing to grouse.

'So if Davies is down, who're we on to? Leach must be right. It's got to be back to Wolff with another vintage car in possession of someone she knows that we haven't sussed out yet. That someone loans the car to her—probably not knowing what she wants it for—and she goes gunning for the principals who put her into the nick. Or maybe the two of them go gunning together. We haven't considered that possibility yet.'

'That scenario argues an innocent woman going to prison for twenty years,' Lynley pointed out.

'It's been known to happen,' Havers said.

'But not with the innocent person saying nothing about *being* innocent in the first place.'

'She's from East Germany, former totalitarian state. She'd been in England . . . what? Two years? Three? When Sonia Davies drowned? She finds herself questioned by the local rozzers and she gets paranoid and won't talk to them. That makes sense to me. I don't expect she had the warm fuzzies for the police where she came from, do you?'

Lynley said, 'I agree that she might have been rattled by police. But she would have told *someone* she was innocent, Havers. She would have spoken to her lawyers, surely. But she didn't. What does that suggest to you?'

'Someone got to her.'

'How?'

'Hell, I don't know.' Havers pulled at her hair in frustration, as if this action would dislodge another possibility in her brain, which it did not.

Lynley thought about what Havers had suggested, however. He said, 'Page Winston. He may have something for us.'

Havers used Lynley's mobile to do so. They worked their way down to Finchley Road. The wind, which had been brisk all day, had picked up in force during the late afternoon and now it was hurtling autumn leaves and rubbish along the street. It was also carrying a storm in from the northeast, and as they made a turn from Park Road into Baker Street, drops began to splatter the Bentley's windscreen. November's early darkness had fallen on London, and the lights from passing vehicles coned forward, creating a playing area for the first sheet of rain.

Lynley cursed. 'This'll make a fine mess of the

404

crime scene.'

Havers agreed. Lynley's mobile rang. Havers handed it over.

Winston Nkata reported that unless Katja Wolff's long time lover was lying, the German woman was in the clear. Both for the murder of Eugenie Davies and for the hit and run of Malcolm Webberly. They were together both nights, he said.

Lynley said, 'That's nothing new, Winston. You've told us that Yasmin Edwards confirms that she and Katja—'

This lover wasn't Yasmin Edwards, Nkata informed him. This lover was the deputy warden at Holloway, one Noreen McKay who'd been involved with Katja Wolff for years. McKay hadn't wanted to come forward for obvious reasons, but put on the rack, she'd admitted to being with the German woman on both nights in question.

'Phone her name into the incident room anyway,' Lynley told Nkata. 'Have them run her through the DVLA. Where's Wolff now?'

''Xpect she's home in Kennington,' Nkata said. 'I'm heading over there now.'

'Why?'

There was a pause on Nkata's end before the constable said, 'Thought it best to let her know she's in the clear. I was rough on her.'

Lynley wondered exactly whom the constable meant when he said *her*. 'First phone Leach with the McKay woman's name. Her address as well.'

'After that?'

'See to the Kennington situation. But, Winnie, go easy.'

'Why's that, 'Spector?'

'We've another hit and run.' Lynley brought him

into the picture, telling him that he and Havers were heading to Portman Street. 'With Davies down, we've got a new match. New rules, new players, and for all we know, an entirely new objective.'

'But with the Wolff woman having an alibi—'

'Just go easy,' Lynley cautioned. 'There's more to know.'

When Lynley rang off, he brought Havers into the picture. She said at his conclusion, 'The pickings are getting slim, Inspector.'

'Aren't they just,' Lynley replied.

Another ten minutes and they had made the circuit to come into Portman Street where, had they not known an accident had happened, they would have concluded as much from the flashing lights a short distance from the square and the car park quality of the stationary traffic. They pulled to the kerb, half in a bus lane and half on the pavement.

They trudged through the rain in the direction of the flashing lights, shouldering their way through a crowd of onlookers. The lights came from two panda cars that were blocking the bus lane and a third that was impeding the flow of traffic. The constables from one of the cars were in conversation with a traffic warden in the middle of the street, while those from the other two cars were divided between talking to people on the pavement and wedging themselves into the upper and lower parts of a bus that was itself parked at an angle with one tyre on the kerb. There was no ambulance anywhere in sight. Nor was there any sign of a scene-of-crime team. And the actual point of impact—which certainly had to be where the panda was parked in the traffic lane—had yet to be cordoned off. Which meant that what valuable evidence might be there wasn't being safeguarded and would soon be lost. Lynley muttered a curse.

With Havers on his heels, he squeezed through the crowd and showed his identification to the nearest policeman, a bobby in an anorak. Water dripped from his helmet onto his neck. Periodically, he slapped it away.

'What's happened?' Lynley asked the constable. 'Where's the victim?'

'Off to hospital,' the constable said.

'He's alive, then?' Lynley glanced at Havers. She gave him a thumbs up. 'What's his condition?'

'Damn lucky, I'd say. Last time we had something like this, we were scraping the corpse off the pavement for a week, and the driver wasn't fit to go another hundred yards.'

'You've witnesses? We'll need to speak with them.'

'Oh, aye? How's that?'

'We've a similar hit and run in West Hampstead,' Lynley told him. 'Another in Hammersmith. And a third in Maida Vale. This one today involves a man who's related to one of our earlier victims.'

'Your facts are off,' the constable said.

'What?' Havers was the one to ask.

'This isn't a hit and run.' The constable nodded at the bus, where inside one of his colleagues was taking a statement from a woman in the seat directly behind the driver's. The driver himself was out on the pavement, gesticulating to his left front headlamp and speaking earnestly to another policeman. 'Bus hit someone,' the constable clarified. 'Pedestrian was shoved out from the pavement directly into its path. Lucky he wasn't killed. Mr Nai—' Here he gave a nod to the driver of the bus, 'has good reflexes and the bus had its brakes serviced last week. We've got some bumps and bruises from the sudden stop—this is on the passengers inside—and the victim's got a bone or two broken, but that's the extent of it.'

'Did anyone see who pushed him?' Lynley asked.

'That's what we're trying to find out, mate.'

\*　　　\*　　　\*

Jill left the Humber in a spot marked clearly for ambulances only, but she didn't care. Let them tow, clamp, or fine her. She squirmed out from beneath the steering wheel and walked rapidly to the entrance for accidents and emergencies. There was no receptionist to greet her, just a guard behind a plain wooden desk.

He took a look at Jill and said, 'Shall I ring your doctor, Madam, or is he meeting you here?'

Jill said, 'What?' before she understood the inference that the guard was drawing from her condition, her personal appearance and her frantic state. She said, 'No. No doctor,' to which the man said, 'You *have* no doctor?' in a disapproving tone.

Ignoring him, Jill made a lumbering dash in the direction of someone who looked like a doctor. He was consulting a clipboard and wore a stethoscope round his neck, which gave him an air of authority that the guard did not possess. Jill cried, 'Richard Davies?' and the doctor looked up. 'Where is Richard Davies? I was phoned. I was told to come. He's been brought in and don't tell me . . . you mustn't tell me he's . . . Please. Where *is* he?'

408

'Jill . . .'

She swung round. He was leaning against a jamb whose door opened into what appeared to be some sort of treatment room just behind the guard's desk. Beyond him, she could see trolleys with people lying upon them, covered to their chins in thin pastel blankets, and beyond the trolleys she could see cubicles formed by curtains at the bottom of which the feet of those ministering to the injured, the critically ill, or the dying were only just visible.

Richard was from among the merely injured. Jill felt her knees grow weak at the sight of him. She cried, 'Oh God, I thought you were . . . They said . . . When they *phoned* . . .' and she began to weep, which was utterly unlike her and told her just how terrified she'd been.

He moved to her and they held each other. He said, 'I asked them not to phone you. I told them I'd ring you myself so that you'd know, but they insisted . . . It's their procedure . . . If I'd known how upset . . . Here, Jill, don't cry . . .'

He tried to fish out a handkerchief for her, which was how she first noticed that his right arm was in plaster. And then she noticed the rest of it: the walking cast on his right foot which she could now see beyond the ripped-open seam of his navy trousers, the ugly bruising on one side of his face and the row of stitches beneath his right eye.

'What *happened*?' she cried.

He said, 'Get me home, darling. They want me to spend the night . . . but I don't need . . . I can't think . . .' He gazed at her earnestly. 'Jill, will you take me home?'

She said of course. Had he ever doubted that

409

she'd be there, do what he asked of her, tend to him, nurse him?

He thanked her with a gratitude that she found touching. And when they gathered his things together, she was even more touched to see that he'd managed the shopping he'd gone out to do. He brought five mangled and soiled shopping bags out of the treatment room with him. 'At least I found the intercom,' he said wryly.

They made their way to the car, ignoring the protest of the young doctor and even younger nurse who tried to stop them. Their progress was slow, Richard needing to stop to rest every four paces or so. As they went out of the ambulance entrance, he told her briefly what had happened.

He'd gone into more than one shop, he said, looking for what he had in mind. He ended up making more purchases than he'd expected, and the shopping bags were unwieldy in the crowds out on the pavement.

'I wasn't paying attention, and I should have been,' he told her. 'There were so many people.'

He was making his way along Portman Street to where he'd left his Granada in the underground car park in Portman Square. The pavement was packed: shoppers running for one last purchase in Oxford Street before the shops closed, business people heading for home, streams of students jostling one another, the homeless eager to find doorways for the night and a handout of coins to keep them from hunger. 'You know how it can be in that part of town,' he said. 'It was madness to go there, but I just didn't want to put it off any longer.'

The shove, he said, came out of nowhere just as a Number 74 bus was pulling out from its stop.

Before he knew what was happening, he was hurtling straight into the vehicle's path. One tyre drove over—

'Your *arm*,' Jill said. 'Your arm. Oh Richard—'

'The police said how lucky I was,' Richard finished. 'It could have been . . . You know what might have happened.' He'd paused again in their walk to the car.

Jill said angrily, 'People don't take care any longer. They're in such a *hurry* all the time. They walk down the street with their mobiles fixed to their skulls and they don't even see anyone else.' She touched his bruised cheek. 'Let me get you home, darling. Let me baby you a bit.' She smiled at him fondly. 'I'll make you some soup and soldiers, and I'll pop you into bed.'

'I'll need to be at my own place tonight,' he said. 'Forgive me, Jill, but I couldn't face sleeping on your sofa.'

'Of *course* you couldn't,' she said. 'Let's get you home.' She repositioned the five shopping bags that she had taken from him in Casualty. They *were* heavy and awkward, she thought. It was no wonder he'd been distracted by them.

She said, 'What did the police do with the person who pushed you?'

'They don't know who it was.'

'Don't *know* . . . ? How is that possible, Richard?'

He shrugged. She knew him well enough to understand at once that he wasn't telling her everything.

She said, 'Richard?'

'Whoever it was, he didn't come forward once I was hit. For all I know, he—or she—didn't even know I fell into the traffic. It happened so fast, and

411

just as the bus was pulling away from the kerb. If they were in a rush . . .' He adjusted his jacket over his shoulder where it hung cape-like because he could not fit it over the cast on his arm. 'I just want to forget it happened.'

Jill said, 'Surely someone would have seen something.'

'They were interviewing people when the ambulance fetched me.' He spied the Humber where Jill had left it and lurched towards it in silence. Jill followed him, saying, 'Richard, are you telling me everything?'

He didn't reply until they were at the car. Then he said, 'They think it was deliberate, Jill,' and then, 'Where's Gideon? He needs to be warned.'

Jill hardly knew what she was doing as she opened the car door, flipped the seat forward, and deposited Richard's packages in the back. Jill saw her lover safely into his seat and then joined him behind the wheel of the car. She said, 'What do you mean, deliberate?' and she looked straight ahead at the worm tracks that the rain was making on her windscreen and she tried to hide her fear.

He made no reply. She turned to him. She said, 'Richard, what do you mean by deliberate? Is this connected to—' and then she saw that he was holding in his lap the frame she'd found beneath her seat.

He said, 'Where did you get this?'

She told him and added, 'But I can't understand . . . Where did it come from? Who is she? I don't know her. I don't recognise . . . And surely she can't be . . .' Jill hesitated, not wanting to say it.

Richard did so for her. 'This is Sonia. My daughter.'

412

And Jill felt a ring of ice take a sudden position round her heart. In the half light coming from the hospital entrance, she reached for the picture and tilted it towards her. In it, a child—blonde as her brother had been in childhood—held a stuffed panda up to her cheek. She laughed at the camera as if she hadn't a care in the world. Which she probably hadn't known that she did have, Jill thought as she looked at the picture again.

She said, 'Richard, you never mentioned that Sonia . . . Why has no one ever *told* me . . .? Richard. Why didn't you tell me your daughter was Down's Syndrome?'

He looked at her then. 'I don't talk about Sonia,' he said evenly. 'I never talk about Sonia. You know that.'

'But I needed to know. I ought to have known. I *deserved* to know.'

'You sound like Gideon.'

'What's Gideon to do with . . .? Richard, why haven't you spoken to me about her before? And what's this picture doing in my car?' The stresses of the evening—the conversation with her mother, the phone call from the hospital, the frantic drive—all of it descended upon Jill at once. 'Are you trying to frighten me?' she cried. 'Are you hoping that if I see what happened to Sonia, I'll agree to have Catherine in hospital and not at my mother's? Is that what you're doing? Is that what this is all about?'

Richard tossed the picture into the back seat where it landed on one of the packages. He said, 'Don't be absurd. Gideon wants a picture of her— God only knows why—and I dug that one out to have it reframed. It needs to be, as you probably

413

saw. The frame's banged up and the glass . . . You've seen for yourself. That's it, Jill. Nothing more than that.'

'But why didn't you tell me? Don't you see the risk that we were running? If she was Down's Syndrome because of something genetic . . . We could have gone to a doctor. We could have had blood tests or something. *Something.* Whatever they do. But instead you let me become pregnant and I never knew that there was a chance . . .'

'*I* knew,' he said. 'There was no chance. I knew you'd have the amnio test. And once we were told Cara's fine, what would've been the point of upsetting you?'

'But when we decided to try for a baby, I had the right . . . Because if the tests had shown that something was wrong, I would have had to decide . . . Don't you see that I needed to know from the start? I needed to know the risk so that I'd have time to think it through, in case I *had* to decide . . . Richard, I can't believe you kept this from me.'

He said, 'Start the car, Jill. I want to go home.'

'You can't think I can dismiss this so easily.'

He sighed, raised his head towards the roof and took a deep breath. He said, 'Jill, I've been hit by a bus. The police think someone pushed me deliberately. That means someone intended me dead. Now, I understand that you're upset. You argue that you've a right to be and I'll accept that for now. But if you'd look beyond your own concerns for one moment, you'll see that I need to get home. My face hurts, my ankle's throbbing, and my arm is swelling. We can thrash this out in the car and I can end up back in casualty asking to see a doctor or we can go home and revisit this

414

situation in the morning. Have it either way.'

Jill stared at him till he turned his head and met her gaze. She said, 'Not telling me about her is tantamount to lying.'

She started the car before he could reply, putting it into gear with a jerk. He winced, 'Had I known you'd react this way, I would have told you. Do you think I actually *want* anything to come between us? Now? With the baby due any moment? Do you think I want that? For the love of God, we nearly lost each other tonight.'

Jill moved the car out into Grafton Way. She knew intuitively that something wasn't right, but what she couldn't intuit was whether that something was wrong within her or wrong within the man she loved.

Richard didn't speak till they'd crisscrossed over into Portland Place and headed through the rain in the direction of Cavendish Square. And then he said, 'I must speak to Gideon as soon as possible. He could be in danger as well. If something happens to him . . . after everything else . . .'

The *as well* told Jill volumes. She said, 'This is connected to what happened to Eugenie, isn't it?'

His silence comprised an eloquent response. Fear began to eat away at her again.

Too late Jill saw that the route she'd chosen was going to take them straight past Wigmore Hall. And the worst of it was that there was apparently a concert on tonight, because a glut of taxis were crowding the street there, all of them jockeying to disgorge their passengers directly under the glass canopy. She saw Richard turn from the sight of it.

He said, 'She's out of prison. And twelve weeks to the day that she got out of prison, Eugenie was murdered.'

'You think that German woman . . .? The woman who killed . . .?' And then it was all back before her again, rendering any other discussion impossible: the image of that pitiable baby and the fact that her condition had been hidden, hidden from Jill Foster who'd had a serious and vested interest in knowing all there was to know about Richard Davies and his fathering of children. She said, 'Were you afraid to tell me? Is that it?'

'You knew Katja Wolff was out of prison. We even spoke of that with the detective the other day.'

'I'm not talking about Katja Wolff. I'm talking about . . . You know what I'm talking about.' She swung the car into Portman Square and from there dropped down and over to Park Lane, saying, 'You were afraid that I wouldn't want to try for a baby if I knew. I'd have too many fears. You were afraid of that, so you didn't tell me because you didn't trust me.'

'How did you expect me to give you the information?' Richard asked. 'Was I supposed to say, "Oh by the way, my ex-wife gave birth to a handicapped child?" It wasn't relevant.'

'How can you say that?'

'Because we *weren't* trying for a baby, you and I. We were having sex. Good sex. The best. And we were in love. But we weren't—'

'I wasn't taking precautions. You knew that.'

'But what I didn't know was that you weren't aware that Sonia had been . . . My God, it was in all the papers when she died: the fact that she was drowned, that she was Down's Syndrome and that she was drowned. I never thought I *had* to mention

416

it.'

'I *didn't* know. She died over twenty years ago, Richard. I was sixteen years old. What sixteen-year-old do you know who reads the newspaper and remembers what she's read two decades later?'

'I'm not responsible for what you can and can't remember.'

'But you *are* responsible for making me aware of something that could affect my future and our baby's future.'

'You were going at it without precautions. I assumed you had your future planned out.'

'Are you telling me you think I *entrapped* you?' They'd reached the traffic lights at the end of Park Lane, and Jill pivoted awkwardly in her seat to face him. 'Is that what you're saying? Are you telling me that I was so desperate to have you as a husband that I got myself pregnant to ensure you'd be willing to trot up to the altar? Well, it hasn't exactly worked out that way, has it? I've compromised right, left, and centre for you.' A taxi blared its horn behind her. Jill glanced in the rear view mirror first, then took note that the lights were now green. They edged their way round the Wellington Arch, and Jill was grateful for the size of the Humber that made her more than visible to the buses and more intimidating to the smaller cars.

'What I'm telling you,' Richard said steadily, 'is that I don't want to argue about this. It happened. I didn't tell you something I thought you knew. I may not have mentioned it, but I never tried to hide it.'

'How can you say that when you haven't a single photo of her anywhere?'

'That's been for Gideon's sake. Do you think I'd want him to spend his life looking at his murdered

417

sister? How do you expect that would affect his music? When Sonia was killed, we all went through hell. *All* of us, Jill, including Gideon. We needed to forget, and removing all the pictures of her seemed one way to do it. Now if you can't understand that or forgive it, if you wish to end our relationship because of it—' His voice quavered. He put his hand to his face, pulling on the skin along his jaw, savagely pulling it, saying nothing.

And neither did Jill for the remainder of the journey to Cornwall Gardens. She took the route along Kensington Gore. Seven minutes more and they were parking at a spot midway along the leaf-blown square.

In silence, Jill helped her lover from the car and reached into the back seat to collect the parcels. On the one hand, since they were for Catherine, it made more sense to leave them where they were. On the other hand, since everything was suddenly so unsettled about the future of Catherine's parents, it seemed to send a subtle but unmistakable message to take them inside to Richard's flat. Jill scooped them up. She also scooped up the photo that had been the cause of their argument.

Richard said, 'Here. Let me take something,' and offered his good hand.

She said, 'I can manage.'

'Jill . . .'

'I can manage.' She walked to Braemar Mansions, the decrepit building yet another reminder of how she was compromising with her fiancé. Who would want to live in such a place? she wondered. Who would be willing to purchase a flat in a building that was falling apart at the seams? If

418

she and Richard waited to sell his flat before they tried to sell her own, they'd be forever denied their house, their garden, and their place to be a family with Catherine. Which was, perhaps, what he had wanted all along.

He never remarried, she told herself. Twenty years since his divorce—sixteen? eighteen? oh, it didn't even *matter*—and he'd never taken another woman into his life. And now, on this day, on this night during which he himself could have died, he thought of her. Of what had happened to her and why and what he must now do to safeguard . . . whom? Not Jill Foster, not his pregnant companion, not their unborn child, but his son. Gideon. His son. His *bloody* son.

Richard came up behind her, as she mounted the steps to the building. He reached round her and unlocked the door, pushing it open so that she could enter the unlit hall with its cracking tiles on the floor and its wallpaper sagging from its mildewed walls. It seemed a further affront that there was no lift and only a partial curve in the staircase to serve as a landing should someone wish to rest while ascending. But Jill didn't want to rest. She climbed to the first floor and let her lover struggle up behind her.

He was breathing heavily when he reached the top. She would have felt repentant to have left him fumbling upwards with only the rickety railing to assist in a climb made awkward by the plaster on his leg—but she thought the lesson was a good one for him.

'My building has a lift,' she said. 'People want lifts, you know, when they're looking for flats. And how much do you actually expect to get for this place, compared with what we could get for mine? We could move house, then. We could *have* a house. And then you'd have the time to paint, redecorate, whatever it might take to make this place saleable.'

'I'm exhausted,' he said. 'I can't continue like this.' He shouldered past her and limped to the door of his flat.

She said, 'That's convenient, isn't it?' as they went inside and Richard closed the door behind them. The lights were on. Richard frowned at this. He walked to the window and peered out. 'You never continue what you want to avoid.'

'That's not true. You're becoming unreasonable. You've had a fright, we've both had a fright, and you're reacting to that. When you've had a chance to rest—'

'Don't tell me what to do!' Her voice rose shrilly. She knew at heart that Richard was right, that she was being unreasonable, but she couldn't stop. Somehow all the unspoken doubts she'd been harbouring for months were mingling with her unacknowledged fears. Everything was bubbling up inside her, like noxious gases looking for a fissure through which they could seep. 'You've had your way. I've given it and given it. And now you're going to give me mine.'

He didn't move from the window. 'Has all of this come from seeing that ancient picture?' he asked and extended his hand to her. 'Give it to me, then. I want to destroy it.'

'I thought you meant it for Gideon,' she cried.

'I did, but if it's going to cause this kind of trouble between us . . . Give it to me, Jill.'

'No. I'll give it to Gideon. Gideon's what's

420

important, after all. How Gideon feels, what he does, when he plays his music. He's stood between us from the very first—my God, we even *met* because of Gideon—and I don't intend to displace him now. You want Gideon to have this picture, and he shall have it. Let's phone him at once and tell him we've got it.'

'Jill. Don't be a fool. I haven't told him you know he's afraid to play, and if you phone him about the picture, he's going to feel betrayed.'

'You can't have it all ways, my darling. He wants the picture and he shall have it tonight. I'll take it over to him myself.' She picked up the phone and began to punch the number.

'Jill!' Richard said and started to approach her.

'What're you going to take over to me, Jill?' Gideon asked.

They whirled round at the sound of his voice. He was standing in the doorway to the sitting room, in the dim passage that led to the bedroom and to Richard's study. He held a square envelope in one hand and a floral card in the other. His face was the colour of sand, and his eyes were ringed by the circles of insomnia.

'What were you going to take over to me?' he repeated.

### Gideon

<u>12 NOVEMBER</u>
*You sit in your father's leather arm chair, Dr Rose, watching me as I stumble through the recitation of the dreadful facts. Your face remains as it always is—*

421

*interested in what I'm saying but without judgement—and your eyes shine with a compassion that makes me feel like a child in desperate need of comfort.*

*And that is what I have become: phoning you and weeping, begging that you see me at once, claiming that there is no one else whom I can trust.*

*You say, Meet me at the office in ninety minutes.*

*Precise, like that. Ninety minutes. I want to know what you are doing that you cannot meet me there this minute.*

*You say, Calm yourself, Gideon. Go within. Breathe deeply.*

*I need to see you* now, *I cry.*

*You tell me that you're with your father, but you will be there as soon as you can. You say, Wait on the steps if you get there ahead of me. Ninety minutes, Gideon. Can you remember that?*

*So now we are here and now I tell you everything that I have remembered on this terrible day. I end it all by saying, How is it possible that I forgot all this? What sort of monster am I that I wasn't able to remember* anything *of what happened all those years ago?*

*It's clear to you that I have finished my recitation, and that is when you explain things to me. You say in your calm and dispassionate voice that the memory of harming my sister and believing myself to have killed her was something that was not only horrific but associatively connected to the music playing when I committed the act. The act was the memory I repressed, but because music was connected to it, I ultimately repressed the music as well. Remember, you say, that a repressed memory is like a magnet, Gideon. It attracts to it other things that are* associated with the memory and pulls them in, repressing them also. The Archduke *was intimately related to your actions that night. You repressed those actions—and it appears that everyone either overtly or subtly* encouraged *you to repress them—and the music got drawn into the repression.*

But I've always been able to play everything else. Only The Archduke defeated me.

*Indeed, you say. But when Katja Wolff appeared unexpectedly at Wigmore Hall and introduced herself to you, the complete repression was finally triggered.*

Why? *Why?*

*Because Katja Wolff, your violin,* The Archduke, *and your sister's death were all associatively connected in your mind. That's how it works, Gideon. The main repressed memory was your belief that you had drowned your sister. That repression drew to it the memory of Katja, the person most associated with your sister. What followed Katja into the black hole was* The Archduke, *the piece that was playing that night. Finally, the rest of the music—symbolised by the violin itself—followed that single piece you'd always had trouble playing. That's how it works.*

*I am silent at this. I am afraid to ask the next question—Will I be able to play again?—because I despise what it reveals about me. We are all the centres of our individual worlds, but most of us are capable of seeing others who exist within our singular boundaries. But I have never been capable of that. I have seen only myself from the very first time I became conscious that I had a self to see. To ask about my music now seems monstrous to me. That question would act as a repudiation of my innocent sister's entire existence. And I've done enough*

423

*repudiating of Sonia to last me the rest of my life.*

*Do you believe your father? you ask me. What he said about Sonia's death and the part he himself played in her death . . . Do you believe him, Gideon?*

*I'll believe nothing till I talk to my mother.*


## 13 NOVEMBER

*I begin to see my life in a perspective that makes much clear to me, Dr Rose. I begin to see how the relationships I've attempted to form or have formed successfully were actually ruled by that which I didn't want to face: my sister's death. The people who didn't know how I was involved in the circumstances of her death were the people I was able to be with, and those were the people most concerned with my own prime concern, which was my professional life: Sherrill and my other fellow musicians, recording artists, conductors, producers, concert organisers round the globe. But the people who might have wanted more from me than a performance on my instrument . . . those were the people with whom I failed.*

*Beth is the best example of this. Of course I couldn't be the partner in life that she wanted me to be. Partnership of that sort suggested to me a level of intimacy, trust, and revelation in which I could not afford to participate. My only hope for survival was to effect an escape from her.*

*And so it is with Libby now. That prime symbol of intimacy between us—the Act, if you will—is beyond my power. We lie in each other's arms, and feeling desire is so far removed from what I'm experiencing that Libby may as well be a sack of potatoes.*

*At least I know why. And until I speak to my mother and learn the full truth of what happened that night, I can have nothing with any woman, no matter who she is, no matter how little she expects of me.*

### 16 NOVEMBER
*I was returning from Primose Hill when I saw Libby again. I'd taken one of the kites out, a new one that I'd worked on for several weeks and was eager to try. I'd employed what I thought was an intriguingly aerodynamic design, crafted to ensure that the height reached would be a record-breaking one.*

*On the top of Primrose Hill, there is nothing to impede the flight of a kite. The trees are distant, and the only structures that could get in the way of anything airborne are the buildings that stand far beyond the hill's crest, on the other side of the roads that border the park. As it was a day of good wind, I assumed that I'd have the kite aloft within moments of releasing it.*

*That wasn't the case. Every time I released it, began to jog forward, and played out the twine, the kite shuddered, tossed and turned on the wind, and plummeted to the ground like a missile. Time and again, I made the attempt, after adjusting the leading edge, the stand offs, even the bridle. Nothing helped. Eventually, one of the bottom spreaders fractured, and I had to give up the whole enterprise.*

*I was trudging along Chalcot Crescent when I encountered Libby. She was heading in the direction I had just come from, a Boots bag dangling from one hand and a can of diet Coke in the other. Picnic lunch, I assumed. I could see the top of a baguette rising out of the bag like a crusty appendage.*

*'The wind'll be a nuisance if you're planning to eat your lunch out there,' I said with a nod in the*

direction I'd just walked.

'Hi to you, too,' was her reply.

She said it politely, but her smile was brief. We hadn't seen each other since our unhappy encounter in her flat, and although I'd heard her come in and go out and had admittedly anticipated her ringing my bell, she hadn't done so. I'd missed her, but once I'd remembered what I needed to remember about Sonia, about Katja, and about my part in the death of one and the imprisonment of the other, I realised it was just as well. I wasn't fit to be any woman's companion, be that her friend, her lover, or her husband. So whether she realised it or not, Libby was wise to steer clear.

'I've been trying to get this one up,' I said lifting the broken kite by way of explaining my statement about the wind. 'If you stay off the hill and eat down below, you might be all right.'

'Ducks,' she said.

For a moment I thought the word was another strange, California term I'd never heard before. She went on.

'I'm going to feed them. In Regent's Park.'

'Ah. I see. I thought . . . Well, seeing the bread—'

'And associating me with food. Yeah. It makes good sense.'

'I don't associate you with food, Libby.'

'Okay,' she said. 'You don't.'

I shifted the kite from my left hand to my right. I didn't like the feeling of being at odds with her, but I had no clear idea how to bridge the chasm between us. We are, at heart, such different people, I thought. Perhaps, just as Dad had seen it from the first, it was always a ridiculous affiliation: Libby Neale and Gideon Davies. What had they in common after all?

'I haven't seen Rafe in a couple of days,' Libby said, indicating the direction of Chalcot Square with a toss of her head. 'I was wondering if something happened to him.'

The fact that she'd given me an opening prompted me to realise that she always had been the person to provide the openings in our conversations. And that realisation was what prompted me to say, 'Something has happened. But not to him.'

She looked at me earnestly. 'Your dad's okay, right?'

'He's fine.'

'His girlfriend?'

'Jill's fine. Everyone's fine.'

'Oh. Good.'

I took a deep breath. 'Libby, I'm going to see my mother. After all this time, I'm actually going to see her. Dad told me she's been phoning him about me, so we're going to meet. Just the two of us. And when we do, there's a chance that I'll get to the bottom of the violin problem.'

She put her can of diet Coke into the Boots bag and rubbed her hand down her hip. 'I guess that's cool, Gid. If you want it to be. It's, like, what you want in life, right?'

'It is my life.'

'Sure. It's your life. That's what you've made it.'

I could tell by her tone that we were back to the uneven ground we'd walked over before, and I felt a surge of frustration run through me. 'Libby I'm a musician. If nothing else, it's how I support myself. It's where the money to live comes from. You can understand that.'

'I understand,' she said.

'Then—'

'Look, Gid. Like I said, I'm heading out to feed the ducks.'

'Why don't you come up afterwards? We could have a meal.'

'I've got plans for tapping.'

'Tapping?'

She looked away. For a moment her face expressed a reaction I couldn't quite grasp. When she turned her head back to me, her eyes appeared sorrowful. But when she spoke, her voice was resigned. 'Tap dancing,' she said. 'It's what I like to do.'

'Sorry. I'd forgotten.'

'Yeah,' she said. 'I know.'

'What about later, then? I should be home. I'm just hanging about waiting to hear from Dad. Come up after your dancing. If you've a mind to, that is.'

'Sure,' she said. 'I'll see you around.'

At that, I knew she wouldn't come up. The fact that I'd forgotten her dancing was, apparently, the last straw for her. I said, 'Libby, I've had a lot on my mind. You know that. You must see—'

'Jesus,' she interrupted me. 'You don't get anything.'

'I "get" that you're angry.'

'I'm not angry. I'm not anything. I'm going to the park to feed the ducks. Because I've got the time and I like ducks. I've always liked ducks. And after that, I'm going to a tap dancing lesson. Because I like tap dancing.'

'You're avoiding me, aren't you?'

'This isn't about you. I'm not about you. The rest of the world isn't about you. If you, like, stop playing the violin tomorrow, the rest of the world will just go on being the rest of the world. But how can you go on being you if there's no you in the first place, Gid?'

'That's what I'm trying to recapture.'

428

*'You can't recapture what's never been there. You can create it if you want to. But you can't just go out with a net and bag it.'*

*'Why won't you see—'*

*'I want to feed the ducks,' she cut in. And with that, she swung past me and headed down to Regent's Park Road.*

*I watched her go. I wanted to run after her and argue my point. How easy it was for her to talk about one's simply being oneself when she didn't have a past that was littered with accomplishments, all of which served as guideposts to a future that had long been determined. It was easy for her simply to exist in a given moment of a given day because moments were all she had ever had. But my life had never been like that, and I wanted her to acknowledge that fact.*

*She must have read my mind. She turned when she came to the corner and shouted something back at me.*

*'What?' I called to her, as her words were taken by the wind.*

*She cupped hands round her mouth and tried again. 'Good luck with your mother,' she shouted.*

## 17 NOVEMBER

*I'd been able to put my mother from my mind for years because of my work. Preparing for this concert or that recording session, practising my instrument with Raphael, filming a documentary, rehearsing with this or that orchestra, touring Europe or the US, meeting my agent, negotiating contracts, working with the East London Conservatory . . . My days and my hours had been filled with music for two decades. There had been no place in them for speculation*

429

*about the parent who'd deserted me.*

*But now there was time, and she dominated my thoughts. And I knew even as I thought about it, even as I wondered, imagined, and pondered, that keeping my mind fixed on my mother was a way to keep it at a distance from Sonia.*

*I wasn't altogether successful. For my sister still came to me in unguarded moments.*

*'She doesn't look right, Mummy,' I remember saying, hovering over the bed on which my sister lay, swaddled in blankets, wearing a cap, in possession of a face that didn't look as it should.*

*'Don't say that, Gideon,' Mother replied. 'Don't ever say that about your sister.'*

*'But her eyes are squishy. She's got a funny mouth.'*

*'I said don't talk like that about your sister!'*

*We began in that way, making the subject of Sonia's disabilities* verboten *among us. When they began to dominate our lives, we made no mention of them. Sonia was fretful, Sonia cried through the night, Sonia went into hospital for two or three weeks. But still we pretended that life was normal, that this was the way things always happened in families when a baby was born. We went about life in that way till Granddad fractured the glass wall of our denial.*

*'What good are either of them?' he raged. 'What good is any one of you, Dick?'*

*Is that when it began in my head? Is that when I first saw the necessity to prove myself different from my sister? Granddad had lumped me together with Sonia, but I would show him the truth.*

*Yet how could I do that when everything revolved round her? Her health, her growth, her disabilities, her development. A cry in the night and the household was rallied to see to her needs. A change in*

430

*her temperature and life was halted till a doctor could explain what had brought it about. An alteration in the manner of her feeding and specialists were consulted for an explanation. She was the topic of every conversation but at the same time the cause of her ailments could never be directly mentioned.*

*And I remembered this, Dr Rose. I remembered because when I thought of my mother, my sister was clinging to the shirttails of any memory I was able to evoke. She was there in my mind as persistently as she'd been there in my life. And as I waited for the time when I would see my mother, I sought to shake her from me with as much determination as I'd sought to shake her from me when she was alive.*

*Yes, I do see what that means. She is in my way now. She was in my way then. Because of her, life was altered. Because of her, it was going to alter still more.*

*'You'll be going to school, Gideon.'*

*That must be when the seed was planted: the seed of disappointment, anger, and thwarted dreams that grew into a forest of blame. Dad was the one who broke the news to me.*

*He comes into my bedroom. I'm sitting at the table by the window, where Sarah-Jane Beckett and I do our lessons. I'm doing maths. Dad pulls out the chair in which Sarah-Jane generally sits, and he watches me with his arms crossed.*

*He says, 'We've had a good run of it, Gideon. You've thrived, haven't you, son?'*

*I don't know what he's talking about, and what I hear in his words makes me wary immediately. I know now what I heard must have been resignation, but at the moment I cannot put a name to what he's apprently feeling.*

*That is when he tells me that I will be going out to*

431

school, to a C of E school that he's managed to locate, a day school not too far away. I say what first comes into my mind.

'What about my playing? When will I practise?'

'We'll have to work that out.'

'But what will happen to Sarah-Jane? She won't like it if she can't teach me.'

'She'll have to cope. We're getting rid of her, son. We can't afford her any longer, Gideon.' He doesn't add the rest, but I do, in my head. We can't afford her because of Sonia. 'We have to cut back somewhere,' Dad informs me. 'We don't want to let Raphael go, and we can't let Katja go. So it's come down to Sarah-Jane.'

'But when will I play if I'm at school? They won't let me come to school only when I want to, will they, Dad? And there'll be rules. So how will I have my lessons?'

'We've spoken to them, Gideon. They're willing to make allowances. They know the situation.'

'But I don't want to go! I want Sarah-Jane to keep teaching me.'

'So do I,' Dad said. 'So do we all. But it's not possible, Gideon. We haven't the money.'

We haven't the money. Hasn't this been the leitmotif of all of our lives? So should I be the least surprised when the Juilliard offer comes and must be rejected? Isn't it logical that I would attach my inability to attend Juilliard to money?

But I am surprised. I am outraged. I am maddened. And the seed that was planted sends shoots upward, sends roots downward, and begins to multiply in the soil.

I learn to hate. I acquire a need for revenge. A target for my vengeance becomes essential. I hear it at *first, in her ceaseless crying and the inhuman demands she places upon everyone. And then I see it, in her, in my sister.*

*Thinking of my mother, I dwelled upon these other thoughts as well. In considering them, I had to conclude that even if Dad had not acted to save Sonia as he might have done, what did it matter? I had begun the process of killing her. He had only allowed that process to run its course.*

*You say to me: Gideon, you were just a little boy. This was a sibling situation. You weren't the first person who has attempted to harm a younger sibling and you won't be the last.*

*But she died, Dr Rose.*

*Yes. She died. But not at your hands.*

*I don't know that for certain.*

*You don't know—and you can't know—what's true right now. But you will. Soon.*

*You're right, Dr Rose, as you usually are. Mother will tell me what actually happened. If there's salvation for me anywhere in the world, it will come to me from my mother.*

## CHAPTER TWENTY-SIX

'He wouldn't even take a wheelchair,' the nurse in charge of casualty told them. Her name badge said she was Sister Darla Magnana and she was in high dudgeon over the manner in which Richard Davies had departed the hospital. Patients were to leave in *wheelchairs,* accompanied by an appropriate staff member who would see them to their vehicles. They were *not* meant to decline this service and if they *did* decline it, they were not to be discharged. *This* gentleman had actually walked off on his own without being discharged at all. So the hospital could not be held responsible if his injuries intensified or caused him further grief. Sister Darla Magnana hoped that was clear. 'When we wish to keep someone overnight for observation, we have a very good reason for doing so,' she declared.

Lynley asked to speak to the doctor who'd seen Richard Davies, and from that gentleman—a harassed looking resident physician with several days' growth of stubble on his face—he and Havers learned the extent of Davies' injuries: a compound fracture of the right ulna, a single break of the right lateral malleolus. 'Right arm and right ankle,' the doctor translated for Havers when she said, 'Fractures of the whats?' He went on to say, 'Cuts and abrasions on the hands. A possible concussion. He needed some stitches on the face. Overall, he was very lucky, however. It could have been fatal.'

Lynley thought about this as he and Havers left the hospital, having been told that Richard had departed in the company of a heavily pregnant woman. They went to the Bentley, phoned in to Leach, and learned from him that Winston Nkata had given the incident room Noreen McKay's name to be put through the DVLA. Leach had the results: Noreen McKay owned a late model Toyota RAV4. That was her only vehicle.

'If we get no joy from those prison records, we're back to the Humber,' Leach said. 'Bring that car in for a once over.'

Lynley said, 'Right. And as to Eugenie Davies' computer, sir?'

'Deal with that later. After we get our hands on

that car. And talk to Foster. I want to know where *she* was this afternoon.'

'Surely not pushing her fiancé under a bus,' Lynley said, despite his better judgement which told him not to do or say anything that might remind Leach of Lynley's own transgressions. 'In her condition, she'd be rather conspicuous to witnesses.'

'Just deal with her, Inspector. And get that car.' Leach recited Jill Foster's address. It was a flat in Shepherd's Bush. Directory enquiries gave Lynley a phone number to go along with the address, and within a minute he knew what he'd already assumed when Leach gave him the assignment: Jill wasn't at home. She'd have taken Davies to his own flat in South Kensington.

As they were spinning down Park Lane in preparation for the last leg of the trip from Gower Street, Havers said, 'You know, Inspector, we're down to Gideon or Robson shoving Davies into the street this evening. But if either one of them did the job, the basic question remains, doesn't it? Why?'

'*If*'s the operative word,' Lynley said.

She obviously heard his doubts because she said, 'You don't think either of them pushed him, do you?'

'Killers nearly always choose the same means,' Lynley pointed out.

'But a bus is a vehicle,' Havers said.

'But it's not a car and driver. And it's not *that* car, the Humber. Or any vintage car for that matter. Nor was the hit as serious as the others, considering what it could have been.'

'And no one saw the shove,' Havers said

thoughtfully. 'At least so far.'

'I'm betting no one saw it at all, Havers.'

'Okay. So we're back to Davies again. Davies tracking down Kathleen Waddington before going after Eugenie. Davies setting his sights on Webberly to guide our suspicion onto Katja Wolff when we don't get there fast enough. Davies then throwing himself into the traffic because he's got the sense we're not taking Wolff seriously as a suspect. All right. I see. But *why's* the question.'

'Because of Gideon. It has to be. Because she was threatening Gideon in some way and he lives for Gideon. If, as you suggested, Barbara, she actually meant to stop him playing—'

'I like the idea, but what was it to her? I mean, if anything, it seems that she'd want to keep him playing, not stop him, right? She had a history of his whole career up in her attic. She obviously cared that he played. Why cock it up?'

'Perhaps cocking it up wasn't her intention,' Lynley said. 'But perhaps cocking it up was what would have happened—without her knowing it—if she met Gideon again.'

'So Davies killed her? Why not just tell her the truth? Why not just say, "Hang on, old girl. 'F you see Gideon, he's done for, professionally speaking."'

'Perhaps he did say that,' Lynley pointed out. 'And perhaps she said, "I've no choice, Richard. It's been years and it's time . . ."'

'For what?' Havers asked. 'A family reunion? An explanation of why she ran off in the first place? An announcement that she was going to hook up with Major Wiley? What?'

'Something,' Lynley said. 'Something that we

may never find out.'

'Which toasts our muffins good and proper,' Havers noted. 'And doesn't go very far towards putting Richard Davies in the nick. *If* he's our man. And we've got sod all evidence of that. He has an alibi, Inspector. Hasn't he?'

'Asleep. With Jill Foster. Who was, herself, most likely asleep. So he could have gone and returned without her knowledge, Havers, using her car and then bringing it back.'

'We're at the car again.'

'It's the only thing we have.'

'Right. Well. The CPS aren't likely to do back flips over that, Inspector. Access to the car's not exactly hard evidence.'

'Access isn't,' Lynley agreed. 'But it's not access alone that I'm depending on.'


### Gideon

**20 NOVEMBER**

*I saw Dad before he looked up and saw me. He was coming along the pavement in Chalcot Square, and I could tell from his posture that he was brooding. I felt some concern but no alarm.*

*Then something odd happened. Raphael appeared at the far end of the garden in the centre of the square. He must have called out to Dad, because Dad hesitated on the pavement, turned, and then waited for him a few doors away from my own house. As I watched from the music room window, they exchanged a few words, Dad doing the talking. As he spoke, Raphael staggered back two steps, his face*

437

crumpling the way a man's face crumples when he's received a punch to the gut. Dad continued to talk. Raphael turned back towards the garden. Dad watched as Raphael walked back through the gates to where two wooden benches face each other. He sat. No, he dropped, all of his weight falling in a mass that was merely bones and flesh, reaction incarnate.

I should have known then. But I did not.

Dad walked on, at which point he looked up and saw me watching from the window. He raised a hand but didn't wait for me to respond. In a moment, he disappeared beneath me and I heard the sound of his key in the lock of my front door. When he came into the music room, he removed his coat and laid it deliberately along the back of a chair.

'What's Raphael doing?' I asked him. 'Has something happened?'

He looked at me, and I could see that his face was awash with sorrow. 'I've some news,' he told me, 'some very bad news.'

'What?' I felt fear lap against my skin.

'There's no easy way to tell you,' he said.

'Then tell me.'

'Your mother's dead, son.'

'But you said she's been phoning you. About what happened at Wigmore Hall. She can't be—'

'She was killed last night, Gideon. She was hit by a car in West Hampstead. The police rang me this morning.' He cleared his throat and squeezed his temples as if to contain an emotion there. 'They asked if I would try to identify her body. I looked. I couldn't tell for certain . . . It's been years since I saw her . . .' He made an aimless gesture. 'I'm so sorry, son.'

'But she can't be . . . If you didn't recognise her,

438

*perhaps it's not—'*

*'The woman was carrying your mother's identification. Driving licence, credit cards, cheque book. What are the possibilities that someone else would have had all of Eugenie's identification?'*

*'So you said it was her? You said it was my mother?'*

*'I said I didn't know, that I couldn't be sure. I gave them the name of her dentist . . . the man she used to see when we were still together. They'll be able to check that way. And there are fingerprints, I suppose.'*

*'Did you ring her?' I asked. 'Did she know I wanted to . . . Was she willing . . . ?' But what was the point of asking, the point of knowing? What did it matter, if she was dead?*

*'I left a message for her, son. She hadn't got back to me yet.'*

*'That's it, then.'*

*His head had been dropped forward, but he raised it, then. 'That's what?' he asked.*

*'There's no one to tell me.'*

*'I've told you.'*

*'No.'*

*'Gideon, for God's sake . . .'*

*'You've told me what you think will make me believe that I'm not at fault. But you'd say anything to get me back on the violin.'*

*'Gideon, please.'*

*'No.' Everything was becoming so much clearer. It was as if the shock of learning of her death suddenly blew the fog from my mind. I said, 'It doesn't make sense that Katja Wolff would have agreed to your plan. That she would give up twenty years of her life . . . for what, Dad? For me? For you? I wasn't anything to her and neither were you. Isn't that true?*

439

*You weren't her lover. You weren't the father of her child. Raphael was, wasn't he? So it makes no sense that she agreed. You must have tricked her. You must have . . . what? Planted evidence? Twisted the facts?'*

*'How the hell can you accuse me of that?'*

*'Because I see it. Because I understand. Because how would Granddad have reacted, Dad, to the news that his freak of a granddaughter had just been drowned by her freak of a brother? And that's what it must have come down to in the end: Keep the truth from Granddad no matter what.'*

*'She was a willing participant because of the money. Twenty thousand pounds for admitting to a negligent act that led to Sonia's death. I explained all that. I told you that we didn't expect the press's reaction to the case or the Crown Prosecution's passion to put her in prison. We had no idea—'*

*'You did it to protect me. And all your talk about leaving Sonia in the bath to die—of holding her down yourself—is just that: talk. It serves the same purpose as letting Katja Wolff take the blame twenty years ago. It keeps me playing the violin. Or at least it's supposed to.'*

*'What are you saying?'*

*'You know what I'm saying. It's over. Or it will be once I collect the money to pay Katja Wolff her four hundred thousand pounds.'*

*'No! You don't owe her . . . For God's sake, think. She may well have been the person who ran over your mother!'*

*I stared at him. My mouth said the word, 'What?' but my voice did not. And my brain could not take in what he was saying.*

*He continued to talk, saying words that I heard but did not assimilate. Hit and run, I heard. No accident,*

440

*Gideon. A car ploughing over her twice. Three times. A deliberate death. Indeed, a murder.*

*'I didn't have the money to pay her,' he said. 'You didn't know who she was. So she would have tracked down your mother next. And when Eugenie hadn't the money to pay her . . . You see what happened, don't you? You do see what happened?'*

*They were words falling against my ears, but they meant nothing to me. I heard them, but I didn't comprehend. All I knew was that my hope for deliverance from my crime was gone. For if I had been unable to believe anything else, I did believe in her. I did believe in my mother.*

*Why? you ask.*

*Because she left us, Dr Rose. And while she might indeed have left us because she couldn't come to terms with her grief over my sister's death, I believe that she left us because she couldn't come to terms with the lie she'd have had to live should she have stayed.*

*20 NOVEMBER 2:00 P.M.*

*Dad departed when it became apparent that I had finished talking. But I was alone ten minutes only— perhaps even less—when Raphael took his place.*

*He looked like hell. Blood red traced a curve along his lower eye lashes. That and flesh in a shade like ashes were the only colours in his face.*

*He came to me and put his hand on my shoulder. We faced each other and I watched his features begin to dissolve, as if he had no skull beneath his skin to hold him together but rather a substance that had always been soluble, vulnerable to the right element that could melt it.*

*He said, 'She wouldn't stop punishing herself.' His hand tightened and tightened on my shoulder. I wanted to cry out or jerk back from the pain, but I couldn't move because I couldn't risk even a gesture that might make him stop talking. 'She couldn't forgive herself, Gideon, but she never—she never, I swear it,—stopped thinking of you.'*

*'Thinking of me?' I repeated numbly as I tried to absorb what he was saying. 'How do you know? How do you know she never stopped thinking . . . ?'*

*His face gave me the answer before he spoke it. He'd not lost contact with my mother in all the years that she'd been gone from our lives. He'd never stopped talking to her on the phone. He'd never stopped seeing her: in pubs, restaurants, hotel lounges, parks, and museums. She would say, 'Tell me how Gideon is getting on, Raphael,' and he would supply her with the information that newspapers, critical reviews of my playing, magazine articles, and gossip within the community of classical musicians couldn't give her.*

*'You've seen her,' I said. 'You've seen her. Why?'*

*'Because she loved you.'*

*'No. I mean, why did you do it?'*

*'She wouldn't let me tell you,' he said brokenly. 'Gideon, she swore she would stop our meetings if she ever learned that I'd told you I'd seen her.'*

*'And you couldn't bear that, could you?' I said bitterly because finally I understood it all. I'd seen the answers in those long ago flowers he'd brought to her and I read it in his reaction now, when she was gone and he could no longer entertain the fantasy that there might be something of significance that would bloom one day between them. 'Because if she stopped seeing you, then what would happen to your little*

442

*dream?'*

He said nothing.

'You were in love with her. Isn't that right, Raphael? You've always been in love with her. And seeing her once a month, once a week, once a day, or once a year had nothing to do with anything but what you wanted and hoped to get. So you wouldn't tell me. You just let me believe she walked out on us and never looked back, and never cared to look back. When all the time you knew—' I couldn't go on.

'It's the way she wanted it,' he said. 'I had to honour her choice.'

'You had to nothing.'

'I'm sorry,' he said. 'Gideon, if I'd known . . . How was I to know?'

'Tell me what happened that night.'

'That night?'

'You know what night. Don't let's play the happy idiot now. What happened the night my sister drowned? And don't try to tell me that Katja Wolff did it, all right? You were with her. You were arguing with her. I got into the bathroom. I held Sonia down. And then what happened?'

'I don't know.'

'I don't believe you.'

'It's the truth. We came upon you in the bathroom. Katja began screaming. Your father came running. I took Katja downstairs. That's all I know. I didn't go back up when the paramedics arrived. I didn't leave the kitchen till the police turned up.'

'Was Sonia moving in the bathtub?'

'I don't know. I don't think so. But that doesn't mean you harmed her. It never meant that.'

'For Christ's sake, Raphael, I held her down!'

'You can't remember that. It's impossible. You were

443

*far too young. Gideon, Katja had left her alone for five or six minutes. I'd gone to talk to her and we began to argue. We stepped out of the room and into the nursery because I wanted to know what she intended to do about . . .' He faltered. He couldn't say it, even now.*

*I said it for him. 'Why the hell did you make her pregnant when you were in love with my mother?'*

*'Blonde,' was his miserable, pathetic reply. It came after a long fifteen seconds in which he did nothing but breathe erratically. 'They both were blonde.'*

*'God,' I whispered. 'And did she let you call her Eugenie?'*

*'Don't,' he said. 'It happened only once.'*

*'And you couldn't afford to let anyone know, could you? Neither of you could afford that. She couldn't afford to let anyone know she'd left Sonia alone as long as five minutes and you couldn't afford to let anyone know you'd got her pregnant while pretending you were fucking my mother.'*

*'She could have got rid of it. It would have been easy.'*

*'Nothing,' I said, 'is that easy, Raphael. Except lying. And that was easy for all of us, wasn't it?'*

*'Not for your mother,' Raphael said. 'That's why she left.'*

*He reached for me again, then. He put his hand on my shoulder, tightly as he had done before. He said, 'She would have told you the truth, Gideon. You must believe your father in this. Your mother would have told you the truth.'*

444

*So that is what I'm left with, Dr Rose: an assurance only. Had she lived, had we had the opportunity to meet, she would have told me everything.*

*She would have taken me back through my own history and corrected where my impressions were false and my memory incomplete.*

*She would have explained the details I recall. She would have filled in the gaps.*

*But she is dead, so she can do nothing.*

*And what I'm left with is only what I can remember.*

## CHAPTER TWENTY-SEVEN

Richard said to his son, 'Gideon. What are you doing here?'

Gideon said, 'What's happened to you?'

'Someone tried to kill him,' Jill said. 'He thinks it's Katja Wolff. He's afraid she'll come after you next.'

Gideon looked at her, then he looked at his father. He seemed, if anything, inordinately puzzled. Not shocked, Jill concluded, not horrified that Richard had nearly died, but merely puzzled. He said, 'Why would Katja want to do that? It would hardly get her what she's after.'

'Gideon . . .' Richard said heavily.

'Richard thinks she's after you as well,' Jill said. 'He thinks she's the one who pushed him into the traffic. He might have been killed.'

'Is that what he's telling you?'

'My God. That's what happened,' Richard

445

countered. 'What are you doing here? How long have you been here?'

Gideon didn't answer at first. Instead he appeared to make a mental catalogue of his father's injuries, his gaze going first to Richard's leg, then to his arm, then coming back to rest on his face.

'Gideon,' Richard said. 'I asked you how long—'

'Long enough to find this.' Gideon gestured with the card he held.

Jill looked at Richard. She saw his eyes narrow.

'You lied to me about this as well,' Gideon said.

Richard's attention was fixed on the card. He said, 'Lied about what?''

'About my sister. She didn't die. Not as a baby and not as a child.' His hand crumpled the envelope. It dropped to the floor.

Jill looked down at the photograph she was holding. She said, 'But, Gideon, you know that your sister—'

'You've been going through my belongings,' Richard cut in.

'I wanted to find her address, which I expect you have squirrelled away somewhere, haven't you? But what I found instead—'

'Gideon!' Jill held out the picture Richard intended for his son. 'You're not making sense. Your sister was—'

'What I found,' Gideon went doggedly on, shaking the card at his father, 'was this, and now I know exactly who you are: a liar who couldn't stop if he had to, Dad, if his life depended on telling the truth, if everyone's life depended upon it.'

'Gideon!' Jill was aghast not at the words but at the glacial tone in which Gideon spoke them. Her

446

horror momentarily drove from her thoughts her own affront at Richard's behaviour. She pushed from her mind that Gideon was speaking the truth at least as it applied to her own life if not to his: In never mentioning Sonia's condition, Richard had indeed lied to her, if only by omission. Instead, she dwelt on the intemperance of what the son was saying to the father. 'Richard was nearly killed less than three hours ago.'

'Are you sure of that?' Gideon asked her. 'If he lied to me about Virginia, who's to know what else he's willing to lie about?'

'Virginia?' Jill asked. 'Who—'

Richard said to his son, 'We'll talk about this later.'

'No,' Gideon said. 'We're going to talk about Virginia now.'

Jill said, 'Who is Virginia?'

'Then you don't know either.'

Jill said, 'Richard?' and turned to her fiancé. 'Richard, what's this all about?'

'Here's what it's all about,' Gideon said, and he read the inside of the card aloud. His voice carried the strength of indignation although it trembled twice: once when he read out the words *our daughter* and a second time when he came to *lived thirty-two years.*

For her part, Jill heard the echo of a different two phrases reverberating round the room: *She defied medical probability* was one and the other comprised the first three words of the final sentence: *Despite her problems.* She felt a wave of sickness rise up in her, and a terrible cold worked its way into her bones. 'Who is she?' she cried. 'Richard, who is she?'

447

'A freak,' Gideon said. 'Isn't that right, Dad? Virginia Davies was another freak.'

'What does he mean?' Jill asked, although she knew, already knew and couldn't bear the knowing. She willed Richard to answer her question, but he stood like granite, bent-shouldered, crooked-backed, with his eyes fixed steadily on his son. 'Say something!' Jill cried.

'He's thinking how to shape an answer for you,' Gideon told her. 'He's wondering what excuse he can make for letting me think my older sister died as a baby. There was something badly wrong with her, you see. And I expect it was easier to pretend she was dead than to have to accept that she wasn't perfect.'

Richard finally spoke. 'You don't know what you're talking about,' he said as Jill's thoughts began to spin wildly out of control: another Down's Syndrome, the voices shouted inside her skull, a second Down's Syndrome, a second Down's Syndrome or something else something worse something he couldn't bring himself even to mention and all the while her precious Catherine was at risk for something God only knew what that the antenatal tests had not identified and he stood there just stood there and stood there and stood there and looked at his son and refused to discuss . . . Jill was aware that that picture she was holding was becoming slick in her hands, was becoming heavy, was becoming a burden she could hardly manage. It slipped from her fingers as she cried out, 'Talk to me, Richard!'

Richard and his son moved simultaneously as the picture clattered on the bare wood floor and Jill stepped past it, stepped around it, feeling she

448

couldn't bear her own impossible weight a moment longer. So she stumbled to the sofa where she became a mute onlooker to what then followed.

Hastily, Richard bent for the picture, but his actions were hampered by the plaster on his leg. Gideon got there first. He snatched it up, crying, 'Something else, Dad?' and then he stared down at it with his fingers whitening to the colour of bone upon the wooden frame. He said hoarsely, 'Where did this come from?' He raised his eyes to his father.

Richard said, 'You must calm down, Gideon,' and he sounded desperate and Jill watched both of them and saw their tension, Richard's held like a whip in his hand, Gideon's coiled and ready to spring.

Gideon said, 'You told me she'd taken every picture of Sonia with her. Mother left us and she took all the pictures, you said. She took all of the pictures except that one you kept in your desk.'

'I had a very good reason—'

'Have you had this all along?'

'I have.' Richard's eyes bored into his son's.

'I don't believe you,' Gideon said. 'You said she took them and she took them. You wanted her to take them. Or you sent them to her. But you didn't have this because if you'd had it, on that day when I wanted it, when I needed to see her, when I asked you, begged you—'

'Rubbish. This is bollocks. I didn't give it to you then because I thought you might—'

'What? Throw myself onto the railway tracks? I didn't know then. I didn't even suspect. I was panicked about my music and so were you. So if you'd had this then, on that day, Dad, you'd have

449

handed it over straightaway. If you thought for a moment it would get me back to the violin, you would have done anything.'

'Listen to me.' Richard spoke rapidly. 'I had that picture. I'd forgotten about it. I'd merely misplaced it among your grandfather's papers. When I saw it yesterday, I intended at once to give to you. I remembered you wanted a picture of Sonia . . . that you'd asked about one . . .'

'It wouldn't be in a frame,' Gideon said. 'Not if it was yours. Not if you'd misplaced it among his papers.'

'You're twisting my words.'

'It would have been like the other. It would have been in an envelope or stuffed into a book or placed in a bag or lying somewhere loose but it wouldn't—it wouldn't—have been in a frame.'

'You're getting hysterical. This is what comes of psychoanalysis. I hope you see that.'

'What I see,' Gideon cried, 'is a self-involved hypocrite who'd say anything at all, who'd do anything at all if that's what it took—' Gideon stopped himself.

On the sofa, Jill felt the atmosphere between the two men suddenly become electric and hot. Her own thoughts were charging round madly in her head, so at first when Gideon spoke again, she didn't comprehend his meaning.

'It was you,' he said. 'Oh my God. You killed her. You had spoken to her. You had asked her to support your lies about Sonia but she wouldn't do that, would she? So she had to die.'

'For the love of God, Gideon. You don't know what you're saying.'

'I do. For the first time in my life, I do. She was

going to tell me the truth, wasn't she? You didn't think she would, you were so certain she'd go along with anything you planned because she did at first, all those years ago. But that's not who she was and why the hell did you think it might be? She'd left us, Dad. She couldn't live a lie and live with us, so she walked out. It was too much for her, knowing that we'd sent Katja to prison.'

'She agreed to go. She was party to it all.'

'But not to twenty years,' Gideon said. 'Katja Wolff wouldn't have been party to that. To five years, perhaps. Five years and one hundred thousand pounds, all right. But twenty years? No one expected it. And Mother couldn't live with it, could she? So she left us and she would have stayed away forever had I not lost my music at Wigmore Hall.'

'You've got to stop thinking that Wigmore Hall is connected to anything but Wigmore Hall. I've told you that from the first.'

'Because you wanted to believe it,' Gideon said. 'But the truth is that Mother was going to tell me that my memory wasn't lying to me, wasn't she, Dad? She knew I killed Sonia. She knew I did it alone.'

'You didn't. I've told you. I explained what happened.'

'Tell me again, then. In front of Jill.'

Richard said nothing although he cast a look at Jill. She wanted to see it as a look that begged for her help and her understanding. But she saw instead the calculation behind it.

Richard said, 'Gideon. Let's talk about this later.'

'We'll talk about it now. One of us will. Shall I be

451

the one? I killed my sister, Jill. I drowned her in her bath. She was a millstone round everyone's neck—'

'Gideon. Stop it.'

'—but especially round mine. She stood in the way of my music. I saw the world revolving round her and I couldn't cope with that so I killed her.'

'No!' Richard said.

'Dad wants me to think—'

'No!' Richard shouted.

'—that he was the one, that when he came into the bathroom that evening and saw her under water in the tub, he held her there and finished the job. But he's lying about that because he knows that if I continue to believe I killed her, there's a very good chance I'll never pick up the violin again.'

'That's not what happened,' Richard said.

'Which part of it?'

Richard said nothing for a moment, then, 'Please,' and Jill saw that he was caught between the two choices that Gideon's words had brought him to facing. And no matter which way he chose to go, both choices amounted to a single one in the end. Either he killed his child. Or he killed his child.

Gideon apparently saw the answer he wanted within his father's silence. He said, 'Yes. Right, then,' and dropped the picture of his sister onto the floor.

He strode to the door. He drew it open.

'For God's sake, I did it,' Richard cried out. 'Gideon! Stop! Listen to me. Believe what I say. She was still alive when you left her. I held her down in the bath. I was the one who drowned

Sonia.'

Jill caught herself in a wail of horror. It was all too logical. She knew. She saw. He was talking to his son but he was doing more: He was finally explaining to Jill what was keeping him from marriage.

Gideon said, 'Those are lies,' and he began to leave.

Richard started to go after him, hampered by his injuries. Jill struggled to her feet. She said, 'They're all daughters. That's it, isn't it? Virginia. Sonia. And now Catherine.'

Richard stumbled to the door, leaned against the jamb. He roared, 'Gideon! God damn it! Listen!' He shoved himself out into the corridor.

Jill staggered after him. She cried, 'You didn't want to marry because it's a daughter.' She grabbed onto his arm. He was still hobbling towards the staircase, and heavy as she was, he dragged her with him. She could hear Gideon clattering downwards. His footsteps pounded across the tiled entry.

'Gideon!' Richard shouted. 'Wait!'

'You're afraid she'll be like the other two, aren't you?' Jill cried, clinging to Richard's arm. 'You created Virginia. You created Sonia and you think our baby's going to be damaged as well. That's why you haven't wanted to marry me, isn't it?'

The front door opened. Richard and Jill reached the top of the stairs. Richard shouted, 'Gideon! Listen to me.'

'I've listened long enough,' came the reply. Then the front door banged closed. Richard bellowed as if struck in the chest. He started to descend.

Jill dragged down on his arm. 'That's why. Isn't

it? You've been waiting to see if the baby's normal before you're willing to—'

He shook her off. She grabbed at him again. 'Get away!' he cried. 'Get off me. Go! Don't you see I've got to stop him?'

'Answer me. Tell me. You've thought there was something wrong because she's a daughter and if we married, then you'd be stuck. With me. With her. Just like before.'

'You don't know what you're saying.'

'Then tell me I'm wrong.'

'Gideon!' he shouted. 'God damn it, Jill. I'm his father. He needs me. You don't know . . . Let me go.'

'I won't! Not until you—'

'I. Said. Let. Me . . .' His teeth were clenched. His face was rigid. Jill felt his hand—his good hand—climb up her chest and push at her savagely.

She clung to him harder, crying, 'No! What are you doing? Talk to me!'

She pulled him towards her, but he swung away. He jerked free and as he did so, their positions shifted precariously. He was now above her. She was below. And so she blocked him, blocked his passage to Gideon and his reentry into a life she could not afford to understand.

Both of them were panting. The smell of their sweat was rank in the air. 'That's why, isn't it?' Jill demanded. 'I want to hear it from you, Richard.'

But instead of replying, he gave an inarticulate cry. Before she could move to safety, he was trying to get past her. He used his good arm against her breasts. She backed away in reflex. She lost her footing. In an instant she was tumbling down the stairs.

# CHAPTER TWENTY-EIGHT

Richard heard only the breath in his ears. She fell and he watched her and he heard banisters cracking when she hit them. And the sheer weight of her body increased her velocity so even at the meagre excuse for a landing—that single inadequate slightly wider step that Jill so hated— she continued to hurtle towards the ground floor.

It didn't happen in a second. It happened in an arc of time so wide and so long that forever seemed inadequate for it. And every second that passed was a second in which Gideon, a Gideon able-bodied and unhampered by a plaster cast enclosing his leg from foot to knee, gained more distance from his father. But even more than distance, he gained certainty as well. And that could not be allowed.

Richard descended the stairs as quickly as he could. At the bottom, Jill lay sprawled and motionless. When he reached her, her eyelids— looking blue in the faint light from the entry windows—fluttered, and her lips parted in a moan.

'Mummy?' she whispered.

Her clothing rucked up, her great huge stomach was obscenely exposed. Her coat spread above her head like a monstrous fan.

'Mummy?' she whispered again. Then she groaned. And then cried out and arched her back.

Richard moved to her head. Furiously, he searched through the pockets of the coat. He'd seen her put her keys in the coat, hadn't he? God damn it, he'd *seen* her. He had to find those keys. If he didn't, Gideon would be gone and he had to find him, had to speak to him, had to make him know . . .

There were no keys. Richard cursed. He shoved himself to his feet. He went back to the stairs and began to haul himself furiously upwards. Below him, Jill cried out, 'Catherine,' and Richard pulled on the stair rail and breathed like a runner and thought about how he could stop his son.

Inside the flat, he looked for Jill's bag. It was by the sofa, lying on the floor. He scooped it up. He wrestled with its maddening clasp. His hands were shaking. His fingers were clumsy. He couldn't manage to—

A buzzer went off. He raised his head, looked round the room. But there was nothing. He went back to the bag. He managed to unfasten the clasp, and he jerked the bag open. He dumped its contents onto the sofa.

A buzzer went off. He ignored it. He pawed through lipsticks, powder, chequebook, purse, crumpled tissues, pens, a small notebook, and there they were. Hooked together by the familiar chrome ring: five keys, two brass, three silver. One for her flat, one for his, one for the family home in Wiltshire, and two for the Humber, ignition and boot. He grabbed them.

A buzzer went off. Long, loud, insistent this time. Demanding immediate acknowledgement.

He cursed, located the buzzing at its source. The front bell on the street. Gideon? God, Gideon? But he had his own key. He wouldn't ring.

The buzzing continued. Richard ignored it. He made for the door.

The buzzing faded. The buzzing stopped. In his

456

ears, Richard heard only his breathing. It sounded like the shriek of lost souls, and pain began to accompany it, searing up his right leg and, simultaneously, burning and throbbing from right hand to shoulder. His side began to ache with the exertion. He didn't seem able to catch his breath.

At the top of the stairs, he paused, looked down. His heart was pounding. His chest was heaving. He drew in air, stale and damp.

He began to descend. He clutched onto the rail. Jill hadn't moved. Could she? Would she? It hardly mattered. Not with Gideon on the run.

'Mummy? Will you help?' Her voice was faint. But Mummy was not here. Mummy could not help.

But Daddy was. Daddy could. He would always be there. Not as in the past, that figure cloaked by an artful madness that came and went and stood between Daddy and yes my son you are my son. But Daddy in the present who could not did not would not fail because yes my son you are my son. You, what you do, what you're capable of doing. All of it you. You are my son.

Richard reached the landing.

Below him, he heard the entry door open.

He called out, 'Gideon?'

'Bloody sodding hell!' came a woman's reply.

A squat creature in a navy donkey-jacket seemed to fling herself at Jill. Behind her came a raincoated figure whom Richard Davies recognised only too well. He held a credit card in his hand, the means by which he'd gained access through the warped old door to Braemar Mansions.

'Good God,' Lynley said, dashing over to kneel by Jill as well. 'Phone an ambulance, Havers.' He handed her a mobile. Then he raised his head.

At once his eyes came to rest on Richard, midway down the stairs, Jill's car keys in his hand.

\*　　\*　　\*

Havers rode with Jill Foster to hospital. Lynley took Richard Davies to the nearest police station. This turned out to be in the Earl's Court Road, the same station from which Malcolm Webberly had departed more than twenty years ago on the evening he was assigned to investigate the suspicious drowning of Sonia Davies.

If Richard Davies was aware of the irony involved therein, he didn't mention it. Indeed, he said nothing, as was his right, when Lynley gave him the official caution. The duty solicitor was brought in to advise him but the only advice Davies asked for was how he could get a message to his son.

'I must speak to Gideon,' he said to the solicitor. 'Gideon Davies. You've heard of him. The violinist . . . ?'

Other than that, he had nothing to say. He would stand by his original story, given to Lynley during earlier interviews. He knew his rights and the police had nothing on which to build a case against the father of Gideon Davies.

What they had, however, was the Humber, and Lynley went back to Cornwall Gardens with the official team to oversee the acquisition of that vehicle. As Winston Nkata had predicted, what damage the car had sustained in striking two—and probably three—individuals was centred round its front chrome bumper which was fairly mangled. But this was something that any adroit defence

458

lawyer would be able to argue away and consequently Lynley was not depending upon it to build a case against Richard Davies. What he was depending upon and what that same adroit barrister would find difficult to discount was trace evidence both beneath the bumper and upon the undercarriage of the Humber. For it was hardly possible that Davies could strike Kathleen Waddington and Malcolm Webberly and run over his former wife three times and leave not a deposit of blood, a fragment of clothing, a sliver of skin, or the kind of hair they desperately needed—hair with human scalp attached to it—on the underside of the car. To get rid of that sort of evidence, Davies would have had to think of that possibility. And Lynley was betting that he hadn't done so. No killer, he knew from long experience, ever thought of everything.

He phoned the news to DCI Leach and asked him to pass the message along to AC Hillier. He would wait in Cornwall Gardens to see the Humber safely off the street, he said, after which he'd fetch Eugenie Davies' computer as had been his original destination. Did DCI Leach still wish him to fetch that computer?

He did, Leach told him. Despite the arrest, Lynley was still out of order for having taken it and it needed to be logged among the belongings of the victim. 'Anything else you lifted, while we're at it?' Leach asked shrewdly.

Lynley said there was nothing else belonging to Eugenie Davies that he had taken, nothing at all. And he was content with the truth of this answer. For he had come to understand for better or worse that the words born of passion which a man puts on paper and sends to a woman—indeed, even those words that he speaks—are on loan to her only, for whatever length of time serves their purpose. The words themselves always belong to the man.

\*      \*      \*

'He didn't push me,' was what Jill Foster said to Barbara Havers in the ambulance. 'You mustn't think that he pushed me.' Her voice was faint, a weak murmur only, and her lower body was soiled from the pool of urine, water, and blood that had been spreading out beneath her when Barbara knelt by her side at the foot of the stairs. But that was all she was able to say because pain was taking her or at least that was how it seemed to Barbara as she heard Jill cry out and she watched the ambulance man monitor the woman's vital signs and listened to him say to the driver, 'Hit the sirens, Cliff,' which was explanation enough of Jill Foster's condition.

'The baby?' Barbara asked the medic in a low voice.

He cast her a look, said nothing, and moved his gaze to the IV bag he'd fixed to a pole above his patient.

Even with the siren, the ride to the nearest hospital with a casualty ward seemed endless to Barbara. But once they arrived, the response was immediate and gratifying. The paramedics trundled their charge inside the building at a run. There, she was met by a swarm of personnel, who whisked her away calling out for equipment, for phone calls to be made to obstetrics, for obscure drugs and arcane procedures with names that camouflaged their purposes.

'Is she going to make it?' Barbara asked anyone who would listen. 'She's in labour, right? She's okay? The baby?'

'This is not how babies are intended to get born,' was the only reply that Barbara was able to obtain.

She remained in casualty, pacing the waiting area, till Jill Foster was taken in a rush to an operating theatre. 'She's been through enough trauma,' was the explanation she was given and 'Are you family?' was the reason that nothing else was revealed. Barbara couldn't have said why she felt it was important for her to know that the woman was going to be all right. She put it down to an unusual sisterhood she found herself feeling for Jill Foster. It had not, after all, been so many months since Barbara herself had been whisked away by an ambulance after her own encounter with a killer.

She didn't believe that Richard Davies had not pushed Jill Foster down the stairs. But that was something to be sorted out later, once a recovery period gave the other woman time to learn what else her fiancé had been up to. And she *would* recover, Barbara learned within the hour. She'd been delivered of a daughter: healthy despite her precipitate entry into the world.

Barbara felt she could leave at that point, and she was doing so—indeed she was out in front of the hospital and sussing out what buses, if any, served Fulham Palace Road—when she saw that she was standing in front of Charing Cross Hospital, where Superintendent Webberly was a patient. She ducked back inside.

On the eleventh floor, she waylaid a nurse just

461

outside the intensive care ward. *Critical* and *unchanged* were the words the nurse used to describe the superintendent's condition, from which Barbara inferred that he was still in a coma, still on life support, and still in so much danger of so many further complications that praying for his recovery seemed as risky a business as thinking about the possibility of his death. When people were struck by cars, when they sustained injuries to the brain, more often than not they emerged from the crisis radically altered. Barbara didn't know if she wished such a change upon her superior officer. She didn't want him to die. She dreaded the thought of it. But she couldn't imagine him caught up in months or years of torturous convalescence.

She said to the nurse, 'Is his family with him? I'm one of the officers investigating what happened. I've news for them. If they'd like to hear it, that is.'

The nurse eyed Barbara doubtfully. Barbara sighed and fished out her warrant card. The nurse squinted at it and said, 'Wait here, then,' leaving Barbara waiting to see what would happen next.

Barbara expected AC Hillier to emerge from the ward, but instead it was Webberly's daughter who came to greet her. Miranda looked just about done in, but she smiled and said, 'Barbara! Hello! How very good of you to come. You can't still be on duty at this hour.'

Barbara said, 'We've made an arrest. Will you tell your dad? I mean, I know he can't hear you or anything . . . Still, you know . . .'

'Oh, but he can hear,' Miranda said.

Barbara's hopes rose. 'He's come out of it?'

'No. Not that. But the doctors say that people in

462

comas can hear what's being said round them. And he'll certainly want to know that you've caught who hit him, won't he?'

'How is he?' Barbara asked. 'I talked to a nurse, but I couldn't get much. Just that there wasn't any change yet.'

Miranda smiled, but it seemed a response that was generated to soothe Barbara's worries more than a reflection of what the girl herself was feeling. 'There isn't, really. But he hasn't had another heart attack, which everyone considers a very good sign. So far he's been stable, and we're . . . well, we're very hopeful. Yes. We're quite hopeful.'

Her eyes were too bright, too frightened. Barbara wanted to tell Miranda that she had no need to play the part for her sake, but she understood that the girl's attempt at optimism was more for herself than anyone else. She said, 'Then I'll be hopeful as well. We all will. D'you need anything?'

'Oh gosh, no. At least, I don't think so. I did come from Cambridge in a terrible rush and I've left a paper behind that I have due for a supervision. But that's not till next week and perhaps by then . . . Well, perhaps.'

'Yeah. Perhaps.'

Footsteps coming along the corridor diverted their attention. They turned to see AC Hillier and his wife approaching. Between them, they were supporting Frances Webberly.

Miranda cried out, 'Mum!'

'Randie,' Frances said. 'Randie, darling . . .'

Miranda said again, 'Mum! I'm so glad. Oh, *Mum*.' She went to her and hugged her long and hard. And then, perhaps feeling a weight lifting off her that she should never have had to bear in the first place, she began to cry. She said, 'The doctors said if he has another heart attack, he might . . . He really might—'

'Hush. Yes,' Frances Webberly said, her cheek pressed against her daughter's hair. 'Take me in to see Daddy, won't you, dear? We'll sit with him together.'

When Miranda and her mother had gone through the door, AC Hillier said to his wife, 'Stay with them, Laura. Please. Make sure . . .' and nodded meaningfully. Laura Hillier followed them.

The AC eyed Barbara with a mere degree less than his usual level of disapproval. She became acutely aware of her clothing. She'd been doing her best to stay out of his way for months now, and when she'd known she'd be running into him, she'd always managed to dress with that expectation in mind. But now . . . She felt her high top red trainers take on neon proportions and the green stirrup trousers she'd donned that morning seemed only marginally less inappropriate.

She said, 'We've made the arrest, sir. I thought I'd come to tell—'

'Leach phoned me.' Hillier walked to a door across the corridor and inclined his head at it. She was meant to follow. When they were inside what turned out to be a waiting room, he went to a sofa and sank into it. For the first time, Barbara noted how tired he looked and she realised he'd been on family duty since the middle of the previous night. Her guard slipped a notch upon this thought. Hillier had always seemed superhuman.

He said, 'Good work, Barbara. Both of you.'

She said cautiously, 'Thank you, sir,' and waited for what would happen next.

He said, 'Sit.'

She said, 'Sir,' and although she'd have preferred to be off on her way home, she went to a chair of limited comfort and perched on its edge. In a better world, she thought, AC Hillier would at this moment of emotional *in extremis* see the error of his ways. He'd look at her, recognise her finer qualities—one of which was decidedly not her fashion sense—and he'd summarily acknowledge them. He'd elevate her on the spot to her previous professional position and that would be the end of the punishment he'd inflicted upon her at the end of the summer.

But this was not a better world, and AC Hillier did none of that. He merely said, 'He might not make it. We're pretending otherwise—especially round Frances, for what little good it's doing—but it's got to be faced.'

Barbara didn't know what to say, so she murmured, 'Bloody hell,' because that's what she felt: bloody, bowed, and consigned to helplessness. And sentenced, with the rest of mankind, to interminable waiting.

'I've known him ages,' Hillier said. 'There've been times when I haven't much liked him and God knows I've never understood him, but he's been there for years, a presence that I could somehow depend upon, just to . . . to *be* there. And I find I don't like the thought of his going.'

'Perhaps he won't go,' Barbara said. 'Perhaps he'll recover.'

Hillier shot her a look. 'You don't recover from something like this. He may live. But recover? No.

465

He'll not be the same. He'll not recover.' He crossed one leg over the other, which was the first time Barbara noticed *his* clothes, which were what he'd thrown on the night before and had never got round to changing during the day. And she saw him for once not as superior but as human being: in hound's-tooth and Tattersall, with a pullover that had a hole in the cuff. He said, 'Leach tells me it was all done to divert suspicion.'

'Yes. That's what DI Lynley and I think.'

'What a waste.' And then he peered at her. 'There's nothing else?'

'What do you mean?'

'No other reason behind Malcolm's being hit?'

She met his gaze steadily and read the question behind it, the one that asked if what AC Hillier assumed, believed, or wanted to believe about the Webberly marriage and its partners therein was really true. And Barbara didn't intend to give the assistant commissioner any part of that piece of information. She said, 'No other reason. Turns out the superintendent was just easy for Davies to track down.'

'That's what you *think*,' Hillier said. 'Leach told me Davies himself isn't talking.'

'I expect he'll talk eventually,' Barbara said. 'He knows better than most where keeping mum can get you.'

'I've made Lynley acting superintendent till this is sorted out,' Hillier said. 'You know that, don't you?'

'Dee Harriman passed along the word.' Barbara drew in a breath and held it, hoping, wishing, and dreaming for what did not then come.

Instead he said, 'Winston Nkata does good work,

466

doesn't he, all things considered.'

What things? she wondered. But she said, 'Yes, sir. He does good work.'

'He'll be looking at a promotion soon.'

'He'll be glad of that, sir.'

'Yes. I expect he will.' Hillier looked at her long, then he looked away. His eyes closed. His head rested back against the chair.

Barbara sat there in silence, wondering what she was meant to do. She finally settled on saying, 'You ought to go home and get some sleep, sir.'

'I intend to,' Hillier replied. 'We all should, Constable Havers.'

\*     \*     \*

It was half past ten when Lynley parked in Lawrence Street and walked back round the corner to the St James house. He hadn't phoned ahead to let them know he was coming, and on the way down from the Earl's Court Road, he'd determined that if the ground floor lights in the house were off, he wouldn't disturb its occupants. This was, he knew, in large part cowardice. The time was fast approaching when he was going to have to deal with harvesting the crop he'd long ago sown, and he didn't particularly want to do that. But he'd seen how his past was seeping insidiously into his present, and he knew that he owed the future he wanted an exorcism that could only be managed if he spoke. Still, he would have liked to put it off and as he rounded the corner, he hoped for darkness in the house's windows as a sign that further procrastination was acceptable.

He had no such luck. Not only was the light

467

above the front door blazing, but the windows of St James's study cast yellow shafts onto the wrought-iron fence that edged the property.

He mounted the steps and rang the bell. Inside the house, the dog barked in response. She was still barking when Deborah St James opened the door.

She said, 'Tommy! Good Lord, you're *soaked*. What a night. Have you forgotten your umbrella? Peach, here. Stop it at once.' She scooped the barking little dachshund from the floor and tucked her under her arm. 'Simon's not in,' she confided, 'and Dad's watching a documentary about dormice, don't ask me why. So she's taking guard duty more seriously than usual. Peach, none of your growling, now.'

Lynley stepped inside and removed his wet coat. He hung it on the rack to the right of the door. He extended his hand to the dog for purposes of olfactory identification, and Peach ceased both barking and growling and indicated her willingness to accept his obeisance in the form of a few scratches behind her ears.

'She's impossibly spoiled,' Deborah said.

'She's doing her job. You shouldn't just open the door like that at night anyway, Deb. It's not very wise.'

'I always assume that if a burglar's calling, Peach will go for his ankles before he can get into the first room. Not that we have much worth taking, although I wouldn't mind seeing the last of that hideous thing with peacock feathers that sits on the sideboard in the dining room.' She smiled. 'How *are* you, Tommy? I'm in here. Working.'

She led him into the study where, he saw, she was in the process of wrapping the pictures she'd

468

selected for her December show. The floor was spread with framed photographs yet to be protected by plastic, along with a bottle of window cleaner that she'd been using to see to the glass that covered them, a roll of kitchen towel, myriad sheets of bubble-wrap, tape, and scissors. She'd lit the gas fire in the room, and Peach repaired to her ramshackle basket that stood before it.

'It's an obstacle course,' Deborah said, 'but if you can find your way to the trolley, have some more of Simon's whisky.'

'Where is he?' Lynley asked. He worked his way round her photographs and went to the drinks trolley.

'He went to a lecture at the Royal Geographic Society: somebody's journey somewhere and a book signing to follow. I think there are polar bears involved. In the lecture, that is.'

Lynley smiled. He tossed down a hefty gulp of the whisky. It would do for courage. To give himself time for the spirits to work in his bloodstream, he said, 'We've made an arrest in the case I've been working on.'

'It didn't take you long. You know, you're completely suited to police work, Tommy. Who would ever have thought it, the way you grew up?'

She rarely mentioned his upbringing. A child of privilege born to another child of privilege, he'd long chafed beneath the burdens of blood, family history, and his duties to both. The thought of it now—family, useless titles that were every year rendered more meaningless, velvet capes trimmed in ermine, and more than two hundred and fifty years of lineage always determining what his next move should be—served as a stark reminder of

469

what he had come to tell her and why. Still, he stalled, saying, 'Yes. Well. One always has to move quickly in a homicide. If the trail begins to cool, you stand less chance of making an arrest. I've come for that computer, by the way. The one I left with Simon. Is it still up in the lab? May I fetch it, Deb?'

'Of course,' she said although she gave him a curious glance, either at his choice of subject— considering her husband's line of work, she was more than aware of the need for speed in a murder investigation—or the tone with which he spoke about it, which was too hardy to be at all believable. She said, 'Go on up. You don't mind my carrying on down here, do you?'

He said, 'Not at all,' and made his escape, taking his time to trudge up the stairs to the top floor of the house. There, he flipped on the lights in the lab and found the computer exactly where St James had left it. He unplugged it, cradled it in his arms, and went back down the stairs. He placed it by the front door and considered calling out a cheerful goodnight and going on his way. It was late, after all, and the conversation that he needed to have with Deborah St James could wait.

Just as he was thinking of another postponement, though, Deborah came to the study door and observed him. She said, 'All's not right with your world. There's nothing wrong with Helen, is there?'

And Lynley found at last that he couldn't avoid no matter how much he wanted to. He said, 'No. There's nothing wrong with Helen.'

'I'm glad,' she said. 'The first months of pregnancy can be awful.'

He opened his mouth to reply but lost the words. Then he found them again. 'So you know.'

She smiled. 'I couldn't help knowing. After . . . what is it, now? seven pregnancies? . . . I've become pretty well-attuned to the signs. I never got far in them—the pregnancies, I mean . . . well, you know that—but far enough to feel that I'd *never* get over being sick.'

Lynley swallowed. Deborah went back into the study. He followed her, found the glass of whisky where he'd left it, and took a momentary refuge in its depths. He said when he could, 'We know how you want . . . And how you've tried . . . You and Simon . . .'

'Tommy,' she said firmly, 'I'm pleased for you. You mustn't ever think that my situation—Simon's and mine . . . well, no . . . mine, really—would ever keep me from feeling happiness for yours. I know what this means to you both, and the fact that I'm not able to carry a baby . . . Well, it's painful, yes. Of *course* it's painful. But I don't want the rest of the world to wallow round in my grief. And I surely don't want to put anyone else in my situation just for the company.'

She knelt among her photographs. She seemed to have dismissed the subject, but Lynley could not because, as far as he was concerned, they had not yet come to the real topic. He went to sit opposite her, in the leather chair St James used when he was in the room. He said, 'Deb,' and when she looked up, 'There's something else.'

Her green eyes darkened. 'What else?'

'Santa Barbara.'

'Santa Barbara?'

'That summer when you were eighteen, when

471

you were at school at the institute. That year when I made those four trips to see you: October, January, May, and July. July, especially, when we drove the coastal road into Oregon.'

She said nothing, but her face blanched, so he knew that she understood where he was heading. Even as he headed there, he wished that something would happen to stop him so he wouldn't have to admit to her what he could hardly bear to face himself.

'You said it was the car on that trip,' he told her. 'You weren't used to so much driving. Or perhaps it was the food, you said. Or the change in climate. Or the heat when it was hot outside or the cool when it was cold indoors. You weren't used to being in and out of air conditioning so much, and aren't Americans addicted to their air conditioners? I listened to every excuse you made, and I chose to believe you. But all the time . . .' He didn't wish to say it, would have given anything to avoid it. But at the last moment, he forced himself to admit what he'd long pushed from his mind. 'I knew.'

She lowered her gaze. Her saw her reach out for the scissors and bubble wrap, pulling one of her pictures towards her. She did nothing with it.

'After that trip, I waited for you to tell me,' he said. 'What I thought was that when you told me, we'd decide together what we wanted to do. We're in love, so we'll marry, I told myself. As soon as Deb admits that she's pregnant.'

'Tommy . . .'

'Let me go on. This has been years in the making and now we're here, I have to see it through.'

'Tommy, you can't—'

'I always knew. I think I knew the night that it happened. That night in Montecito.'

She said nothing.

He said, 'Deborah. Please tell me.'

'It's no longer important.'

'It *is* important to me.'

'Not after all this time.'

'Yes. After all this time. Because I did nothing. Don't you see? I knew, but I did nothing. I just left you to face it alone, whatever "it" was going to be. You were the woman I loved, the woman I wanted, and I ignored what was happening because . . .' He became aware that still she wasn't looking at him, her face fully hidden by the angle of her head and the way her hair fell round her shoulders. But he didn't stop speaking because he finally understood what had motivated him then, what was indeed the source of his shame. 'Because I couldn't sort out how to work it,' he said. 'Because I hadn't planned it to happen like that and God help anything that stood in the way of how I planned my life to work out. And as long as you said nothing about it, I could let the entire situation slide, let everything slide, let my whole damned life slide right on by without the least inconvenience to me. Ultimately, I could even pretend that there was no baby. I could tell myself that, surely if there was, you'd have said something. And when you didn't, I allowed myself to believe I'd been mistaken. When all the time I knew at heart that I hadn't. So I said nothing throughout July. In August. September. And whatever you faced when you finally made your decision to act, you faced alone.'

'It was my responsibility.'

'It was ours. Our child. Our responsibility. But I

473

left you there. And I'm sorry.'

'There's no need to be.'

'There is. Because when you and Simon married, when you lost all those babies, what I had to think was that if you'd had that first child, ours—'

'Tommy, no!' She raised her head.

'—then none of this would have happened to you.'

'That's not how it was,' she said. 'Believe me. That's *not* how it is. You've no need to punish yourself over this. You've no obligation to me.'

'Now, perhaps not. But then I did.'

'No. And it wouldn't have mattered, anyway. You could have spoken about it, yes. You could have phoned. You could have returned on the very next plane, and confronted me with what you believed was going on. But nothing would have changed with all that. Oh, we might have married in a rush or something. You might even have stayed with me in Santa Barbara so that I could finish at the institute. But at the end of it all, there still wouldn't have been a baby. Not mine and yours. Not mine and Simon's. Not mine and anyone's as it turns out.'

'What do you mean?'

She leaned back on her heels, setting the scissors and the tape to one side. She said, 'Just what I say. There wouldn't have been a baby no matter what I did. I just didn't wait long enough to find that out.' She blinked rapidly and turned her head to look hard at the bookshelves. After a moment, she returned her gaze to him. 'I would have lost our baby as well, Tommy. It's something called balanced translocation.'

'What is?'

474

'My . . . what do I call it? My problem? Condition? Situation?' She offered him a shaky smile.

'Deborah, what are you telling me?'

'That I can't have a baby. I'll never be able to have one. It's incredible to think that a single chromosome could hold such power, but there you have it.' She pressed her fingers to her chest, saying, 'Phenotype: normal in every way. Genotype . . . Well, when one has "excessive foetal wastage"—that's what they call it . . . all the miscarriages . . . isn't that obscene?—there's got to be a medical reason. In my case, it's genetics: One arm of the twenty-first chromosome is upside down.'

'My God,' he said. 'Deb, I'm—'

'Simon doesn't know yet,' she said quickly, as if to stop him from going on. 'And I'd rather he not just now. I did promise him that I'd let a full year go by before having any more tests and I'd like him to think I've kept that promise. I intended to. But last June . . . that case you were working on when the little girl died . . . ? I just had to know after that, Tommy. I don't know why except that I was . . . well, I was so struck by her death. Its uselessness. The terrible shame and waste of it, this sweet little life gone . . . So I went back to the doctor then. But Simon doesn't know.'

'Deborah,' Lynley said quietly. 'I am so terribly sorry.'

Her eyes filled at that. She blinked the tears back furiously, then shook her head just as furiously when he reached out to her. 'No. It's fine. I'm fine. I mean, I'm all *right*. Most of the time I don't think about it. And we're going through the

475

process of adoption. We've filled out so many applications . . . all this paperwork . . . that we're *bound* to . . . at some time. And we're trying in other countries as well. I just wish it could be different for Simon's sake. It's selfish and I know it, it's all sorts of ego, but I wanted us to create a child together. I think he wanted . . . would have liked that as well, but he's too good to say so directly.' And then she smiled, despite one large tear that she couldn't contain. 'You're not to think I'm not all right, Tommy. I *am*. I've learned that things work out the way they're meant to work out, no matter what we want so it's best to keep our wants to a minimum and to thank our stars, our luck, or our gods that we've been given as much as we have.'

'But this doesn't absolve me from my part in what happened,' he told her. 'Back then. In Santa Barbara. My going off and never saying a word. This doesn't absolve me of that, Deb.'

'No, this doesn't,' she agreed. 'It doesn't at all. But, Tommy, you must believe me. I do.'

\*       \*       \*

Helen was waiting for him when he got home. She was already in bed with a book lying open in her lap. But she'd dozed off while she was reading, and her head rested back against the pillows she'd piled behind her, her hair a dark blur against white cotton.

Quietly, Lynley crossed to his wife and stood gazing down at her. She was light and shadow, perfectly omnipotent and achingly vulnerable. He sat on the edge of the bed.

476

She didn't start as some might have done, roused suddenly from sleep by another's presence. Instead, her eyes opened and were immediately focussed on him with preternatural comprehension. 'Frances finally went to him,' she said as if they'd been talking all along. 'Laura Hillier phoned with the news.'

'I'm glad,' he said. 'It's what she needed to do. How is he?'

'There's no change. But he's holding on.'

Lynley sighed and nodded. 'Anyway, it's over. We've made an arrest.'

'I know. Barbara phoned me as well. She said I should tell you all's right with the world at her end of things. She would have rung you on the mobile, but she wanted to check in with me.'

'That was good of her.'

'She's a very good person. She says Hillier's planning to give Winston a promotion, by the way. Did you know that, Tommy?'

'Is he really?'

'She says Hillier wanted to make sure she knew. Although, she says, he complimented her first. On the case. He complimented both of you.'

'Yes. Well, that sounds like Hillier. Never say "well done" without pulling the rug out just in case you're feeling cocky.'

'She'd like to be reinstated in her rank. But of course, you know that.'

'And I'd like the power to do that for her.' He picked up the book she'd been reading. He turned it over and examined its title. *A Lesson Before Dying*. How apt, he thought.

She said, 'I found it among your novels in the library. I've not got far, I'm afraid. I dropped off to sleep. Lord. Why have I become so exhausted? If this goes on all nine months, by the end of the pregnancy I'll be sleeping twenty hours a day. And the rest of the time I'll spend being sick. It's supposed to be more romantic than this. At least, that's what I was always led to believe.'

'I've told Deborah.' He explained why he'd gone to Chelsea in the first place, adding, 'She already knew as things turned out.'

'Did she really?'

'Yes. Well, obviously, she knows the signs. She's very pleased, Helen. You were right to want to share the news with her. She was only waiting for you to tell her.'

Helen searched his face then, perhaps hearing something in his tone that seemed misplaced, given the situation. And something was there. He could hear it himself. But what it was had nothing to do with Helen and even less to do with the future that Lynley intended to share with her.

She said, 'And you, Tommy? Are *you* pleased? Oh, you've said that you are but what else *can* you say? Husband, gentleman, and a party to the process, you can hardly go tearing from the room with your head in your hands. But I've had the feeling that something's gone badly wrong between us lately. I didn't have that feeling before we made the baby, so it's seemed to me that perhaps you aren't as ready as you thought you were.'

'No,' he said. 'Everything's right, Helen. And I *am* pleased. More than I can say.'

'I suppose we could have done with a longer period of adjustment together all the same,' she said.

Lynley thought of what Deborah had said to

him, about the source of happiness coming from what's given. 'We have the rest of our lives to adjust,' he told his wife. 'If we don't seize the moment, the moment's gone.'

He set the novel on her bedside table, then. He bent and kissed her forehead. He said, 'I love you, darling,' and she pulled him down to her mouth and parted her lips against his. She murmured, 'Talking of seizing the moment . . .' and she returned his kiss in a way, he realised, that connected them as they hadn't been connected since she'd first told him she was pregnant.

He felt a stirring for her, then, that mixture of lust and love that always left him at once both weak and resolute, determined to be her master and at the same time completely within her power. He laid a trail of kisses down her neck to her shoulders, and he felt her shiver as he eased the straps of her nightgown gently down her arms. As he cupped her bare breasts and bent to them, her fingers went to his tie and unknotted it and began to work on the buttons of his shirt.

He looked up at her then, suddenly tempered by concern. 'What about the baby?' he asked. 'Is it safe?'

She smiled and drew him into her arms. 'The baby, darling Tommy, will survive.'

## CHAPTER TWENTY-NINE

Winston Nkata came out of the bathroom and found his mother seated beneath a standard lamp whose shade had been removed to give her better light in which to work. What she was working on was her tatting: she'd taken a class in this form of lace-making with a group of ladies from her church, and she was determined to perfect the art. Nkata didn't know why. When he'd asked her the reason she'd begun messing about with cotton reels, shuttles, and knots, she said, 'Keeps my hands busy, Jewel. And just 'cause something's not done much any longer, doesn't make it worth chucking out.'

Nkata thought it actually had to do with his father. Benjamin Nkata snored so ferociously that it was impossible for anyone to sleep in a room with him unless they managed to drop off first and lie like the dead once they got there. If Alice Nkata was up past her usual retiring time of ten forty-five, it stood to reason that she was practising her lacework in lieu of suffocating her snorting and bellowing husband in sheer insomniac frustration.

Nkata could tell that was the case tonight. The moment he stepped from the bathroom, he was greeted not only with the sight of his mother at her lace but also with the sound of his father at his dreams. It sounded as if bears were being baited inside his parents' bedroom.

Alice Nkata looked up from her work, over the top of her half-moon glasses. She was wearing her ancient yellow chenille dressing gown, and her son frowned with displeasure when he saw this.

He said, 'Where's that one I got you for Mothering Sunday?'

'Where's what one?' his mother asked.

'You know what one. That new dressing gown.'

'Too nice to sit around in, Jewel,' she said. And before he could protest that dressing gowns weren't intended to be saved just in case one was invited to tea with the Queen so why wasn't she *using* the one he'd paid two weeks' wages to buy her at Liberty's, she said, 'Where you going this hour?'

'Thought I'd go round to see what's up with the super,' he told her. 'Case got resolved—th' inspector nabbed the bloke who made the hits—but the super's still out and . . .' He shrugged. 'I don't know. Seemed like it's the right thing to do.'

'At this hour?' Alice Nkata asked, casting a look at the tiny Wedgwood clock on the table beside her, a gift presented by her son at Christmas. 'Don't know of any hospital round here that likes having visitors in the middle of the night.'

'Not the middle of the night, Mum.'

'You know what I mean.'

'Can't sleep anyway. Too wired up. If I c'n give a hand to the family . . . Like I said, it seems the right thing to do.'

She eyed him. 'Dressed nice enough to be going to his wedding,' she noted acerbically.

Or his funeral, for that matter, Nkata thought. But he didn't like even getting *close* to that idea with regard to Webberly, so he made himself think of something else: like the reasons he'd set his sights on Katja Wolff as the killer of Eugenie Davies as well as the driver who'd injured the superintendent so grievously, like what it actually *meant* that Katja Wolff was not guilty of either offence.

He said, 'Nice to show respect where respect's due, Mum. You brought up a boy knows what's called for.'

His mother said, 'Hmph,' but he could tell she was pleased. She said, 'Mind how you go, then. You

481

see any no-hair white boys in Army boots hanging 'bout on the corner, you give them a wide berth. You walk th' other way. I mean what I say.'

'Right, Mum.'

'No "Right, Mum" like I don't know what I'm talking about.'

'Don't worry,' he said. 'I know that you do.'

He kissed her on the top of the head and left the flat. He felt a twinge of guilt at having fibbed—he hadn't done that since adolescence—but he told himself it was all in a good cause. It was late; there would have been too much explaining to do; he needed to be on his way.

Outside, the rain was making its usual mess of the estate where the Nkatas lived. Pools of water had collected along the outdoor passages between the flats, deposited on the unprotected uppermost level by the wind and seeping down to the other levels through cracks between the floor of the passages and the building itself that had long existed and not been repaired. The staircase was consequently slick and dangerous, also as usual, because the rubber treads on the individual steps had been worn away—or sometimes had been cut away by kids with too much time on their hands and too little to do to fill it—leaving bare the concrete. And down below at what passed for the garden, the grass and flower beds of ancient times were now an expanse of mud across which lager cans, take away food wrappers, disposable nappies and other assorted human detritus made an eloquent statement about the level of frustration and despair that people sank to when they believed —or their experience taught them—that their options were limited by the colour of their skin.

482

Nkata had suggested to his parents more than once that they move house, indeed that he would *help* them move house. But they had refused his every offer. If people set about digging up their roots first chance they had, Alice Nkata explained to her son, the whole plant could die. Besides, by staying right where they were and by having one son who'd managed to escape what could indeed have ruined him forever, they were setting an example for everyone else. No need to think their own lives had limits when among them lived someone who showed them that it wasn't so.

'Besides,' Alice Nkata said, 'we got Brixton Station close. And Loughborough Junction as well. That suits me fine, Jewel. Suits your dad as well.'

So they stayed, his parents. And he stayed with them. Living on his own was as yet too expensive and even if it weren't, he wanted to remain in his parents' flat. He afforded them a source of pride that they needed, and he himself needed to give that to them.

His car was gleaming under a street lamp, washed clean by the rain. He climbed inside and belted himself in.

The drive was a short one. A few twists and turns put him on the Brixton Road where he headed north, cruising in the direction of Kennington. He parked in front of the agricultural centre where he sat for a moment looking across the street through the sheets of rain that the wind was waving between his car and Yasmin Edwards' flat.

He'd been propelled to Kennington in part by the knowledge that he'd done wrong. He'd told himself earlier he'd done this wrong for all the right reasons, and he believed that there was a lot of truth to the assurance. He was fairly certain that Inspector Lynley might have used the same ploys with Yasmin Edwards and her lover, and he was absolutely positive that Barbara Havers would have done the same or more. But of course, they'd have had intentions a good sight nobler than his own had been, and beneath their behaviour would not have run the strong current of an aggression that was inconsistent with their invasion into the women's lives.

Nkata wasn't sure where the aggression came from or what it indicated about him as a police officer. He only knew that he felt it and that he needed to lose it before he could move with absolute comfort again.

He shoved open the car door, carefully locked it behind him, and dashed across the street to the block of flats. The lift door was closed. He began to ring the buzzer for Yasmin Edwards' flat, but he stopped with his finger suspended above the appropriate button. Instead, he rang the flat beneath it and when a man's voice asked who it was, he gave his name, said he'd been phoned about some vandalism in the car park, and would Mr—he looked at the list of names quickly—Mr Houghton be willing to look at some pictures to see if he recognised any faces among a group of youths arrested in the vicinity? Mr Houghton agreed to do so and buzzed the lift open. Nkata rode to Yasmin Edwards' floor with a pang of guilt for the manner in which he'd gained access, but he told himself he'd stop below afterwards and apologise to Mr Houghton for the ruse.

Her curtains were shut, but a thread of light

licked at the bottom of them and behind the door, the sound of television voices spoke. When he knocked, she wisely asked who it was and when he gave his name, he was forced to wait thirty eternal seconds while she made up her mind whether to admit him.

When she had done, she merely opened the door six inches, enough for him to see her in her leggings and her oversized sweater. Red this was, the colour of poppies. She said nothing. She looked at him squarely, her face without the slightest expression, which reminded him inadvertently again of who she was and what she always would be.

He said, 'C'n I come in?'

'Why?'

'Talk.'

'About?'

'Is she here?'

'What d'you think?'

He heard the door open on the floor beneath them, knew it was Mr Houghton wondering what had happened to the cop who'd come to show him pictures. He said, 'Raining. Cold and damp're getting inside. You let me in and I stay a minute. Five at the most. I swear.'

She said, 'Dan's asleep. I don't want him waked. He's got school—'

'Yeah. I'll keep my voice low.'

She took another moment to make up her mind, but at last she stepped back. She turned from the door and walked to where she'd been before he'd knocked, leaving him to open the door wider and then to close it quietly behind him.

He saw that she was watching a film. In it, Peter

485

Sellers began to walk across water. It was an illusion, of course, the stuff of make believe but suggestive of possibility, nonetheless.

She took up the remote control but did not turn the television off. She merely muted the sound and continued to watch the picture.

He got the message and did not blame her for it. He would be even less welcome when he'd said what he'd come to say.

'We got the hit-and-run driver,' he told her. 'It wasn't . . . Not Katja Wolff. She had a square alibi, 's things turned out.'

'I know her alibi,' Yasmin said. 'Number Fifty-five.'

'Ah.' He looked at the television, then at her. She sat straight-backed. She looked like a model. She had a model's fine body, and she would have been perfect wearing trendy clothes for pictures except for her face, the scar on her mouth that made her look fierce and used and angry. He said, 'Following leads 's part of the job, Missus Edwards. She had a connection with who got hit, and I couldn't ignore that.'

'I 'xpect you did what you had to do.'

'You did 's well,' he said to her. 'That's what I came to say.'

'Sure I did,' she said. 'Grassing's always the thing to do, isn't it?'

'She didn't give you a choice once she lied to me 'bout where she was when that woman was hit. You either went along for the ride and put yourself in danger—'long with your boy—or you told the truth. If she wasn't here, then she was somewhere and f'r all anyone knew about it, that somewhere could've been up in West Hampstead. You couldn't

486

stand by that, keep your mug shut, and take another fall.'

'Yeah. Well, Katja wasn't up in West Hampstead, was she? And now we know where she was and why, we c'n both rest easy. I won't be getting into trouble with the cops, I won't be losing Dan into care, and you won't be tossing round in your bed nights, wond'ring how the hell you're goin' t' stick something onto Katja Wolff when she never thought once of doing it.'

Nkata found it hard to digest that Yasmin would still defend Katja, despite Katja's betrayal. But he made himself think before he replied, and he saw that there was sense in what the woman was doing. He was still the enemy in Yasmin Edwards' eyes. Not only was he a copper, which would always put them at odds with each other, he was also the person who'd forced her to see that she was living within a charade, one party to a relationship that existed only in lieu of another, one that was longer standing to Katja, more desired, and just out of reach.

He said, 'No. I wouldn't be tossing in bed 'cause of that.'

'Like I say,' was her contemptuous reply.

'What I mean,' he said, 'is I'd still be tossing. But not over that.'

'Whatever,' she said. She held the remote at the television again. 'That all you come to say? That I did the right thing and be happy, madam, 'cause you're safe from being called an accessory to something someone never did?'

'No,' he said. 'That's not all I come to say.'

'Yeah? Then what else?'

He didn't really know. He wanted to tell her that

487

he'd had to come because his motives in forcing her hand had been mixed from the first. But in saying that, he'd be stating the obvious and telling her what she already knew. And he was more than acutely aware that she'd long ago realised that the motives of every man who looked at her, spoke to her, asked something of her—lithe and warm and decidedly alive—would always be mixed. And he was also more than acutely aware that he didn't want to be counted among those other men.

So he said, 'Your boy's on my mind, Missus Edwards.'

'Then take him off your mind.'

'Can't,' he said and when she would have made a retort, he went on with, 'It's like this. He's got the look of a winner, you know, if he follows a course. But lots out there c'n get in his way.'

'You think I don't know it?'

'Didn't say that,' he said. 'But whether you like me or hate me, I c'n be his friend. I'd like to do that.'

'Do what?'

'Be somebody to your boy. He likes me. You c'n see that yourself. I take him out and about now and then, he gets a chance to mix it up with someone who's playing it straight. With a man who's playing it straight, Missus Edwards,' he hastened to add. 'A boy his age? He needs that pretty bad.'

'Why? You had it yourself, you saying?'

'I had it, yeah. Like to pass it along.'

She snorted. 'Save it for your own kids, man.'

'When I have them, sure. I'll pass it to them. In the meanwhile . . .' He sighed. 'It's this: I like him, Missus Edwards. When I got the free time, I'd like to spend it with him.'

'Doing what?'

'Don't know.'

'He doesn't need you.'

'Not saying he needs me,' Nkata told her. 'But he needs someone. A man. You c'n see it. And the way I'm thinking—'

'I don't care what you're thinking.' She pressed the button and the sound came on. She raised it a notch lest he miss the message.

He looked in the direction of the bedrooms, wondering if the boy would wake up, would walk into the sitting room, would show by his smile of welcome that everything Winston Nkata was saying was true. But the increase in volume didn't penetrate the closed door, or if it did, to Daniel Edwards it was just another sound in the night.

Nkata said, 'You got my card still?'

Yasmin didn't reply, her eyes fastened on the television screen.

Nkata took out another and set it on the coffee table in front of her. 'You ring me if you change your mind,' he said. 'Or you c'n page me. Any time. It's okay.'

She made no reply, so he left the flat. He closed the door quietly, gently, behind him.

He was below in the car park, crossing its puddle-strewn expanse to reach the street, before he realised that he'd forgotten his promise to himself to stop at Mr Houghton's flat, show his warrant card, and apologise for the ruse that had gained him admittance. He turned back to do so and looked up at the building.

Yasmin Edwards, he saw, was standing at her window. She was watching him. And she was holding in her hands something he very much

489

wanted to believe was the card he'd given her.

## CHAPTER THIRTY

Gideon walked. At first he'd run: up the leafy confines of Cornwall Gardens and across the wet, narrow strip of traffic that was Gloucester Road. He hurtled into Queen's Gate Gardens then up past the old hotels in the direction of the park. And then mindlessly he ducked to the right and dashed past the Royal College of Music. He hadn't actually known where he was till he'd veered up a little incline and burst out into the well-lit surroundings of the Royal Albert Hall, where an audience was just pouring out of the auditorium's circumference of doors.

There, the irony of the location had hit him and he'd stopped running. Indeed, he'd stumbled to a complete halt, chest heaving, with the rain pelting him, and not even noticing that his jacket was hanging heavy with the damp upon his shoulders and his trousers were slapping wetly against his shins. Here was the greatest venue for public performance in the land: the most sought after showplace for anyone's talent. Here, Gideon Davies had first performed as a nine-year-old prodigy with his father and Raphael Robson in attendance, all three of them eager for the opportunity to establish the name Davies in the classical firmament. How appropriate was it, then, that his final flight from Braemar Mansions—from his father, from his father's words and what they did and did not mean—should bring him to the very *raison d'être* of everything that had happened: to Sonia, to Katja Wolff, to his mother, to all of them. And how even more appropriate was it that the very *raison d'être* behind the other *raison d'être*—the audience—did not even know that he was there.

Across the street from the Albert Hall, Gideon watched the crowd raise their umbrellas to the weeping sky. Although he could see their lips moving, he did not hear their excited chatter, that all too familiar sound of ravenous culture vultures who were sated for the moment, the happy noise of just the sort of people whose approbation he'd sought. Instead what he heard were his father's words, like an incantation within his brain: *For God's sake I did it I did it I did it* Believe *what I say I say I say She was* alive *when you left her you left her I held her* down *in the bath the bath I was the one who* drowned *her who drowned her. It wasn't you Gideon my son my* son.

Over and over the words repeated, but they called forth a vision that made a different claim. What he saw was his hands on his sister's small shoulders. What he felt was the water closing over his arms. And above the repetition of his father's declaration, what he heard was the cries of the woman and the man, then the sound of running, the *blam* of doors closing, and the other hoarse cries, then the wail of sirens and the guttural orders of rescue workers going about their business where rescue was futile. And everyone knew that save the workers themselves because they were trained to one job only: maintaining and resuscitating life in the face of anything that stood in life's way.

But *For God's sake I did it I did it I did it Believe*

491

*what I say I say I say.*

Gideon struggled for the memory that would allow this belief, but what he came up with was the same image as before: his hands on her shoulders and added to that now the sight of her face, her mouth opening and closing and opening and closing and her head turning slowly back and forth.

His father argued that this was a dream because *She was alive when you left her when you left her.* And even more importantly because *I held her down in the bath in the bath.*

Yet the only person who might have confirmed that story was dead herself, Gideon thought. And what did that mean? What did that tell him?

That she didn't know the truth herself, his father told him insistently as if he walked at Gideon's side in the wind and the rain. She didn't know because I *never* admitted it, not then when it counted, not when I saw another far easier way to resolve the situation. And when I finally told her—

She didn't believe you. She knew that I'd done it. And you killed her to keep her from telling me that. She dead, Dad. She's dead, she's dead.

Yes. All right. Your mother is dead. But she's dead because of me, not because of you. She's dead because of what I'd led her to believe and what I'd forced her into accepting.

Which was what, Dad? *What?* Gideon demanded.

You *know* the answer, his father replied. I let her believe you'd killed your sister. I said *Gideon was in here in here in the bathroom he was holding her down I pulled him off her but my God my God Eugenie she was gone.* And she believed me. And that's why she agreed to the arrangement with

492

Katja: because she thought she was saving you. From an investigation. From a juvenile trial. From reams of publicity. From a hideous burden that would weigh you down for the rest of your life. You were Gideon Davies, for the love of God. She wanted to keep you safe from scandal, and I used that, Gideon, to keep everyone safe.

Except Katja Wolff.

She *agreed.* For the money.

So she thought that I—

Yes she thought. She thought, she *thought.* But she did not know. Any more than you know right now. You were not in the room. You were dragged away, and she was taken downstairs. Your mother went to phone for help. And that left me alone with your sister. Don't you see what that means?

But I remember—

You remember what you remember because that's what happened: You held her down. But holding her down and keeping her down are not the same. And you know that, Gideon. By God, you *know* it.

But I remember—

You remember what you did as far as you did it. I did the rest. I stand guilty of *all* the crimes that were committed. I am the man, after all, who could not bear to have my own daughter Virginia in my life.

No. It was Granddad.

Granddad was simply the excuse I used. I dismissed her, Gideon. I pretended she was dead because I wanted her dead. Don't forget that. Never forget that. You know what it means. You *know* it, Gideon.

But Mother . . . Mother was going to tell me—

Eugenie was going to perpetuate the lie. She was going to tell you what I'd let her *believe* was the truth for years. She was going to explain why she'd left us without a word of goodbye, why she'd taken every picture of your sister with her, why she'd stayed away for nearly twenty years . . . Yes. She was going to tell you what she thought was the truth—that you drowned your sister—and I refused to let that happen. So I killed her, Gideon. I murdered your mother. I did it for you.

So now there's no one left who can tell me—

*I* am telling you. You can believe me and you must believe me. Am I not a man who killed the mother of his own children? Am I not a man who hit her in the street, who drove a car over her, who removed the picture she'd brought to town with her to sustain your guilt? Am I not a man who drove off quietly and felt *nothing* afterwards? Am I not a man who went happily home to his young lover and got on with his life? So am I not thus also a man who is fully capable of killing a sickly worthless cretin of a child, a burden to us all, a living illustration of my own failure? Am I not that man, Gideon? Am I not that man?

The question echoed through the years. It forced upon Gideon a hundred memories. He saw them flicker, unspooling before him. Each asked the same question: Am I not that man?

And he was. He was. Of course. He was. Richard Davies had *always* been that man.

But an admission of that fact—a final embracing of it—did not produce one gram of absolution.

So Gideon walked. His face was streaked with rain, and his hair was painted onto his skull. Rivulets ran like veins down his neck, but he felt

494

nothing of the cold or the damp. The path he followed felt aimless to him but it was not so despite the fact that he barely recognised when Park Lane gave way to Oxford Street and when Orchard Street turned into Baker.

From the morass of what he remembered, what he had been told, and what he had learned emerged a single point that he clung to at the last: Acceptance was the only option available because only acceptance allowed reparation finally to be made. And he was the one who had to make that reparation because he was the only one left who could do so.

He could not bring his sister back to life, he could not save his mother from destruction, he could not give Katja Wolff back the twenty years she'd sacrificed in the service of his father's plans. But he could pay the debt of those twenty years and at least in that one way he could make amends for the unholy deal his father had struck with her.

And there was indeed a way to pay her back that would also close the circle of everything else that had happened: from his mother's death to the loss of his music, from Sonia's death to the public exposure of everyone associated with Kensington Square. It was embodied in the long and elegant inner bouts, the perfect scrolls, and the lovely perpendicular f-holes crafted two hundred and fifty years ago by Bartolomeo Giuseppe Guarneri.

He would sell the violin. Whatever price it fetched at auction, no matter how high and it *would* be astronomical, he would give that money to Katja Wolff. And in taking those two specific actions, he would in effect be making a statement of apology and sorrow that no other effort on his part would permit him to make.

He would allow those two actions to serve to close the circle of crime, lies, guilt, and punishment. His life would not be the same thereafter, but it would be his own life at last. He wanted that.

Gideon had no idea what the time was when he finally arrived in Chalcot Square. He was soaked to the skin and drained of energy from the long walk. But at last, secure in the knowledge of the plan he would follow, he felt possessed by a modicum of peace. Still, the last yards to his house seemed endless. When he finally arrived, he had to pull himself up the front steps by the handrail, and he sagged against the door and fumbled in his trouser pockets for his keys.

He didn't have them. He frowned at this. He relived the day. He'd started out with the keys. He'd started out with the car. He'd driven to see Bertram Cresswell-White and after that he'd gone to his father's flat where—

Libby, he recalled. She'd done the driving. She'd been with him. He'd asked her to leave him all those hours ago and she had obliged. She'd taken his car on his own instructions. She would have the keys.

He was turning to go down the stairs to her flat when the front door swung open, however.

Libby cried out, 'Gideon! What the *hell*? Couldn't you get a taxi? Why didn't you call me? I would've come . . . Hey, that cop rang, the one who was here the other day to talk to you, remember? I didn't pick up but he left a message for you to call him. Is everything . . . ? Geez, why didn't you *call* me?'

496

She held the door wide as she was speaking, and she drew him inside and slammed it behind him. They headed for the stairs. Gideon said nothing. She continued as if he'd made a reply.

'Here, Gid. Put your arm around me. There. Where've you been? Did you talk to your Dad? Is everything okay?'

They climbed to the first floor. Gideon headed towards the music room. Libby guided him towards the kitchen instead.

'You need tea,' she said. 'Or soup. Or something. Sit. Let me get it . . .'

He obliged.

She chatted on. Her voice was quick. Her colour was high. She said, 'I figured I should wait up here since I had the keys. I could've waited in my own place, I guess. I did go down a while ago. But Rock called, and I made the mistake of answering because I thought it was you. God, he is *so* not who I thought he was when I hooked up with him. He actually wanted to come over. Let's talk things out, was how he put it. Unbelievable.'

Gideon heard her and did not hear her. At the kitchen table, he was restless and wet.

Libby said, even more rapidly now as he stirred on his seat, 'Rock wants us to get back together. Course, it's all totally dog in the hay stack stuff, or whatever you call it but he actually said "I'm good for you, Lib" if you can believe that. Like he never spent our whole frigging marriage screwing everything with the right body parts that he ran into. He said, "You know we're good for each other," and I said back, "Gid's good for me, Rocco. You are, like, so totally bad." And that's what I believe, you know. You're good for me, Gideon.

497

And I'm good for you.'

She was moving about the kitchen. She'd settled on soup, evidently, because she rooted through the fridge, found a carton of tomato and basil, and produced it triumphantly, saying, 'Not even past its sell-by date. I'll heat it in a flash.' She rustled out a pan and dumped the soup inside it. She set it on the cooker and took a bowl from the cupboard. She continued to talk. 'How I figured it is this. We could blow London off for a while. You need a rest. And I need a vacation. So we could travel. We could go over to Spain for some decent weather. Or we could go to Italy. We could go to California, even, and you could meet my family. I told them about you. They know I know you. I mean, I told them we live together and everything. I mean, well, sort of. Not I sort of told them but we sort of live . . . you know.'

She put the bowl on the table along with a spoon. She folded a paper napkin into a triangle. She said, 'There,' and reached for one of the straps of her dungarees, which was held together by a safety pin. She clutched at this as he looked at her. She used her thumb against it, opening and closing the pin spasmodically.

This display of nerves wasn't like her. It gave Gideon pause. He studied her, puzzled.

She said, 'What?'

He rose. 'I need to change my clothes.'

She said, 'I'll get them,' and headed towards the music room and his bedroom which lay beyond it. 'What d'you want? Levis? A sweater? You're right. You need to get out of those clothes.' And as he moved, 'I'll get them. I mean, wait. Gideon. We need to talk first. I mean, I need to explain . . .' She stopped. She swallowed, and he heard the sound of it from five feet away. It was the noise a fish makes when it flops on the deck of a boat, breathing its last.

Gideon looked beyond her then and saw that the lights in the music room were off, which served to warn him although he could not have said what the warning was. He took in the fact that Libby was blocking his way to the room, though. He took a step towards it.

Libby said quickly, 'Here's what you've got to understand, Gideon. You are number one with me. And here's what I thought. I thought How can I help him—how can I help us to really be a real us? Because it's not normal that we'd be together but not really *be* together, is it. And it would be totally good for both of us if we . . . you know . . . it's what you need. It's what I need. Each other, being who we really are. And who we are is who we *are*. It's not what we do. And the only way I knew to make you, like, see that and understand it—because talking myself blue in the face sure as hell wasn't doing it and you know that—was to—'

'Oh God. No.' Gideon pushed past her, shoving her to one side with an inarticulate cry.

He fumbled to the nearest lamp in the music room. He grabbed it. He switched it on.

He saw.

The Guarneri—what was left of it—lay next to the radiator. Its neck was fractured, its top was shattered, its sides were broken into pieces. Its bridge was snapped in half and its strings were wrapped round what remained of its tailpiece. The only part of the violin that wasn't destroyed was its perfect scroll, elegantly curving as if it still could bend forward to reach towards the player's fingers.

Libby was speaking behind him. High and rapid. Gideon heard the words but not their meaning. 'You'll thank me,' she said. 'Maybe not now. But you will. I swear it. I did it for you. And now that it's finally gone from your life, you can—'

'Never,' he said to himself. 'Never.'

'Never what?' she said and as he approached the violin, as he knelt before it, as he touched the chin rest and felt the cool of it mix with the heat that was coming into his hands, 'Gideon?' Her voice was insistent, ringing. 'Listen to me. It's going to be okay. I know you're upset, but you've got to see it was the only way. You're free of it now. Free to be who you are, which is more than just a guy who plays the fiddle. You were always more than that guy, Gideon. And now you can know it, just like I do.'

The words beat against him but he registered only the sound of her voice. And past that sound was the roar of the future as it rushed upon him, rising like a tidal wave, black and profound. He was rendered powerless as it overcame him. He was caught within it and all he knew was reduced in that instant to a single thought: what he wanted and what he planned to do had been denied him. Again. *Again.*

He cried out, 'No!' And 'No!' And 'No!' He surged to his feet.

He did not hear Libby cry out in turn as he leapt towards her. His weight fell against her, fell hard upon her. Both of them toppled to the floor.

She screamed, 'Gideon! Gideon! No! Stop!'

But the words were nothing, less than sound and fury. His hands went for her shoulders as they'd done in the past.

   And he held her down.

501

# Acknowledgments

I couldn't have completed a project of this size in the time I allowed myself without the contributions and assistance of various individuals both in the United States and in England.

In England, I would like to express my appreciation to Louise Davis, Principal of Norland College, for allowing me to watch nannies in training and for giving me background information on the professional lives of child care givers; to Godfrey Carey, Q.C., Joanna Kerner, Q.C., and Charlotte Bircher of the Inner Temple, all of whom were instrumental in assisting me in my understanding of British jurisprudence; to Sister Mary O'Gorman of the Convent of the Assumption in Kensington Square for giving me access to the convent and the chapel and for providing me with two decades of information about the square itself; to Chief Superintendent Paul Scotney of the Metropolitan Police (Belgravia Police Station) for assisting me with police procedures and for proving once again that the most forgiving audience among my readers exists within the ranks of the British police; to Chief Inspector Pip Lane who always and generously acts as liaison between the local police and me; to John Oliver and Maggie Newton of HM Prison Holloway for information about the penal system in England; to Swati Gamble for everything from bus schedules to the locations of hospitals with casualty wards; to Jo-Ann Goodwin of the *Daily Mail* for assistance with the laws that deal with press coverage of murder investigations and trials; to Sue Fletcher for generously lending me the services of the resourceful Swati Gamble; and to my agent Stephanie Cabot of William Morris Agency to whom no obstacle is too much of a challenge.

In the United States, I'm deeply grateful to Amy Sims of the Orange County Philharmonic, who took the time to make certain I was able to write about the violin with a fair degree of accuracy; to Cynthia Faisst, who allowed me to sit in on some violin instruction; to Dr Gordon Globus, who added to my understanding of psychogenic amnesia and therapeutic protocols; to Dr Tom Ruben and Dr Robert Greenburg, who weighed in with medical information whenever I needed it; and to my writing students, who listened to early sections of the novel and gave helpful feedback.

I am particularly indebted to my wonderful assistant Dannielle Azoulay without whom I could not possibly have written the rough draft of this rather lengthy novel in ten months. Dannielle's assistance in every area—from doing necessary research to running errands—was absolutely crucial to my well-being and my sanity, and I extend to her my deepest thanks.

Finally, I'm grateful, as always, to my longtime editor at Bantam—Kate Miciak—who always asked the best questions about the most convoluted turns of plot; to my literary agent in the U.S.— Robert Gottlieb of Trident Media—who represents me with energy and creativity; to my fellow writer Don McQuinn who gallantly stood on the receiving end of my doubts and fears; and to Tom McCabe who graciously stepped out of the way of the creative locomotive whenever it was necessary.